Academic Tales

Elliott M. Abramson

iUniverse, Inc.
Bloomington

Academic Tales

iUniverse books may be ordered through booksellers or by contacting:

iUniverse
1663 Liberty Drive
Bloomington, IN 47403
www.iuniverse.com
1-800-Authors (1-800-288-4677)

ISBN: 978-1-4697-9406-8 (sc)
ISBN: 978-1-4697-9405-1 (hc)
ISBN: 978-1-4697-9404-4 (e)

Library of Congress Control Number: 2012904511

Printed in the United States of America

iUniverse rev. date: 3/12/2012

Contents

STOPPING (BUT NOT BY THE WOODS) ON A SNOWY EVENING

AH, IT WAS STARTING TO snow substantially. A graduate student in English Literature like Martin Levin might even be tempted to think that the snow was general throughout Harvard Yard, maybe all of Cambridge, as he tromped on the entire winter's packed accumulation, striding through the newly descending flakes, in evening's rapidly accelerating darkness.

What a time for a make—up c lass in "The Imagery of James Joyce." Two hours, beginning at 5:00, on a late February afternoon, so that already much beleagured students would have to make their way home, by various bicycles, busses, slippery paths, when they should have already been there.

But Martin supposed that Professor Lever, one of the top Joyce experts in the world, if not, indeed, THE Joyce expert, was frighteningly busy and could find no other reasonable time to schedule the class. After all, the make—up itself was necessitated because Lever had to miss the regular session since he'd been at an international Joyce conference at which he had been the keynote speaker.

Martin couldn't speak for all his Ph. D. aspirant classmates, but he certainly wanted to be home with Jane and the baby, enjoying a very satisfying warm meal led off, perhaps, by piping hot, almost burning, tomato soup, his favorite. He hoped that when he arrived there would be, at least, some sort of soup to slake his need for something really warm and soothing.

But first he had to get to the bus, wait the indeterminate time until it showed up and then ride it for the fifteen—twenty minutes it took to get to Arlington,modest suburban location of the one bedroom apartment. Martin still hadn't decided whether it was cramped or cozy, but he was sure it was small. He'd probably have to stand all the way too, because although it was late it was still early enough to catch the residue of the rush hour hordes.

He stepped up his pace with a quick glance at his watch, which now showed almost 7:10. He thought he remembered, from the bus schedule, (he was pretty good at memorizing that sort of thing once he'd glanced at it once or twice,) that there was a 7:12. He figured that if he really hustled, like one of his favorite ballplayers, and the bus was even a minute or two late, a *definite* possibility, especially at this time and in the snow,that he could just catch it.

After about a minute of highly accelerated walking, with the stop just another minute or so away, he spotted ahead, and soon came abreast of, a figure very slowly, haltingly in fact, making his way in the same direction. He took a quick, more or less furtive, sideways glance, still committed to passing and plowing on, full speed . It was a middle—aged appearing African—American man proceeding gingerly and tappingly with a blind man's cane. Martin pushed on a bit, but, then, slowed, stopped and waited for the man to come up even with him.

Although they were now on a cleared surface, the old snow having been shoveled to add to the mounds abutting the path, the aveugle, (the French word for a blind person, somehow immediately sprang to Martin's mind,) seemed to be flailing, more than tapping, with his cane. As he came forward Martin judged him, with the help of a rare nearby street lamp, to be on the youngish side of middle—age.

"Are you o.k?"

'Oh, yeah, sure, I'm o.k. Just didn't expect this new snow. Wasn't doing it when I went into class. But no problem, not to worry, I'm definitely o.k. Maybe a little slowed down for now, but A—o.k, sure enough"

"What class were you in? Where are you coming from?"

"Oh, this semester I'm taking a Nineteenth Century European History course in the Adult Education Program that Harvard runs over in Memorial Church back there. You know, for we poor schnooks who didn't get enough education, or at least not all we wanted when we were younger, but now have to work all day to support ourselves."

"Right. Gotcha. Do you work in Boston?"

"Yes, yes I do. Live in Cambridge, just a few more blocks from here, actually, but work in the Hancock Tower. In The Hub itself."

'Oh sure, the ever famous Hancock Tower...."

'Yeah, and I even work for them , themselves. I'm an actuarial assistant and such. Always was pretty good with numbers, but I just didn't read enough. You know what I mean—history, literature, Poly Sci, material like that. Just never got to them."

"Well, I can understand.... I mean.... But never too late,and that's the spirit, as they say."

Martin shuffled onward a bit and the man started moving beside him.

Martin noticed that, stupidly, he was speaking more loudly than he would have normally to someone so close by. He's blind, moron, not deaf, Martin admonished himself.

"Just how many blocks, actually, do you live from here?"

"Oh, once we get to Harvard Square, just two , three blocks along Mass Avenue. Not far at all. But first I'm going to stop off at the Brigham's in the Square and get me a double scoop of their double chocolate in a sugar cone. And topped with chocolate jimmies, of course."

"You like chocolate, I detect."

"That's right," he shot back with mock belligerence. "Is that a problem for you?" he staccatoed.

"No, no," Martin laughed. "Not at all. I admire a man who goes all the way with his enthusiasms."

"So do I!"

"I was just wondering if you'd mind if I joined you. Haven't had a Brigham's with jimmies for quite a while now."

"Well now, that would be just fine. Very welcome. If I'm not holding you up from anything, or anything like that. We could visit a little.

"Nah, don't worry about it. I was just heading home to Arlington. Dinner's probably not even ready yet. I'd just have to give Jason his bath."

"I see, a family man. Are you sure I wouldn't be delaying you or anything?"

"Nope, not at all. Just a quick Brigham's. Wow, there it is right across the avenue, straight ahead. It's been so long I'd practically forgotten where it is."

Martin thought about taking the older man by his elbow, both to give him better balance and to speed things along. But he decided against it as maybe condescending, too paternalistic. He was making his way, only slightly pokily, and did it all the time since he lived right in the area. His deliberateness came only from his being very cautious about not slipping on the newly falling snow.

They talked about negotiating the broad avenue, with its considerable traffic, stretching from the edge of Harvard Yard to the entrance to Brigham's, as they zig and zagged across, and, soon enough, they were in the bright, colorful warmth of the ice cream parlor.

There were only three or four other customers, so almost all of the small tables for four at the most,were unoccupied. Martin gently guided the blind man toward one near the back and said, "Why don't you sit here while I get your double scoop of double chocolate, in a sugar cone with chocolate jimmies, if I recall correctly, and my own dish of one scoop of cherry vanilla. Can't let the waistline get too out of hand. But I'll splurge with multi—colored jimmies."

"You've got a good memory for ice cream flavors. Sounds good to me. Very good."

Martin paused , unsure, but then he said, "You're a real chocolate man, aren't you?"

The man was absolutely silent for a few seconds, but then came explosive, almost raucous, laughter.

"That's a good one! That's a *very* good one!! You're definitely one of those clever Harvard types."

"I'll be right back with the goodies," Martin assured, pleased his sally had succeeded.

He went to the counter, ordered, waited, paid and brought the confections back to the table. The man was sitting erect and motionless, his hands folded in front of him. As Martin sat down he reached into his coat pocket, took out several dollar bills and held them out to Martin.

"No, no, my treat; hardly worth figuring out how much yours was and how much mine was."

"But I know how much it is. Two dollars, seventy nine. With the tax." He pushed the bills further forward.

"Nevertheless, forget it. My treat."

"O. K., most kind of you. I can tell, you're a kind person."

" I don't know that everyone would agree, but thank you. Thank you."

The man laughed slightly, much more subduedly this time, and they started discussing the taste delights provided by their respective selections. Also how a Brigham's was always good for a lift. But, then, conversation began to peter out as the regular aficionado licked methodically, but with obvious contentedness, at the bulbous double scoop. His progress was very gradual. He took no outright bites, seeming to cultivate the melting mound as long as possible. He was definitely a deferred gratification man. Something Martin understood well.

Martin tried to nudge the conversation along and they came to exchange some personal information. Martin mentioned Jane and Jason, again, and also that he was in his fourth year of working towards his Ph.D. His dissertation topic, he revealed, was the poetry of Robert Frost. The older man offered that he'd once been married, in his early twenties, but that she'd left him after the accident that had blinded him. At first she'd tried to help, but then.... Martin commiserated, as best he could, but the man emphasized resolutely thanking the Lord that there hadn't been any children.

Once he'd gotten going, the African—American also told about his brother who had a family. So he had a nephew and a niece in California. And a sister—in—law who was very kind to him. His brother hadn't made a hash of *his* marriage. They all tried to get together at least once every year or two. But it was expensive; even if he were the only one to fly and much more, of course, if they came this way. His job wasn't completely monotonous, just largely so, and, in any event, it paid the rent and allowed him to save a little toward the trips to California and presents for his niece and nephew.

Martin's single scoop was devoured before the double scoop of double chocolate vanished, but not too many minutes before.

" Do you need some help getting home?"

"No, thanks, but not at all. Do it all the time from here. Often come in after class."

Martin thought about the wet snow but took this as dispensation from insisting. A quick glance at the wall clock and he was already calculating, with the aid of his memorized schedule, which bus he could make.

Coats were re—buttoned, scarves pulled tight again and they headed out the door. A cutting wind was now conspiring with the swirling snow, driving them to huddling mode once just outside. There were muffled good—byes and multiple nice-to-have—met- yous before Martin started across the avenue to wait at the bus stop, while the other man turned left down one of the several streets coming into Harvard Square on the diagonal. He disappeared into the snowflakes and enveloping darkness as Martin took one more look, just as he boarded the 7: 40 to Arlington.

~

When he closed the apartment door behind him, not many minutes after eight, the first thing Martin heard was Jason's squeal of delight at seeing him. The as yet unbathed Jason, Jane quickly informed him. By the time Martin had accomplished the bath, the putting on of pajamas, read the bed—time story and tucked in the by then utterly soporific boy, it was almost 9:00.

But his fondest dreams were realized. There was soup, indeed, and it was tomato bisque. Hot and soothing, just as hopefully anticipated all the way home. While slurping he told Jane, by general acclamation a dark—eyed,, brunette, beautiful woman, about his encounter with the Brigham's devotee.

"Well," she responded, "It's one of those fortuities that can make you feel good. Or, at least, a little better."

"But, actually, I don't really feel good about it. In the end, I mean. Do you know what I mean?"

"No, I guess not. I don't know what you mean. What are you trying to say? Why are you saying that?"

"Because I didn't follow through."

"Follow through?"

"Yeah, I just treated him to an ice cream cone, we chatted a little, and that was it. A dollop of noblesse oblige and 'I'm outta here.'"

"What else should there have been?"

"Well, can't you see? I mean I even thought about exchanging names and addresses, phone numbers and so forth. But on the spot a 'responsibility" alert flashed by me."

"Responsibility?"

"Yeah, you know, calling, trying to arrange a time to get together, deciding where we could go, what we should do.... The whole friendship bit."

"Why would you think that that's your responsibility?"

" I got the sense that he's pretty lonely."

"He has some family, he has colleagues where he works. You don't know that for sure."

"No, not for sure. But I bet he is."

"Well, it looks like we're going to be here for another year or two, at least. Maybe you'll run into him again. Maybe you could try to contrive same time, same place. Or you might even try to run him down through the course which he told you he's taking."

"Yeah, I suppose so."

But Martin didn't—in either case.

THE ADMINISTRATOR

EDWARD INGERSOLL HAD WORKED FOR the New York office of the Federal Trade Commission for almost three weeks, in the '60s, before he met Ernest Lambrusco. But before he met him he knew that everyone called the chief of Administrative Services "Ernie," without more, ever. And, sure enough, when Lambrusco briskly strode into Ingersoll's office, suitably modest for a neophyte attorney, just out of Yale Law School, he advanced, hand outstretched, as Ed looked up from his desk, with "Lambrusco, I'm Admistrative Services, call me' Ernie'."

Ed stuck his hand out. "Nice to meet you, Mr. Lambrusco, Edward Ingersoll."

"I thought we agreed on Ernie, Ed" Lambrusco smiled, pumping Ed's hand vigorously.

Conscious of the vise—like strength of Lambrusco's grip, Ed was about to wave at the chair at the side of his desk and offer a seat but the chief dropped into it heavily before Ed could be formally polite. He gave a perfunctory gaze around the office as Ed noticed the rich blue serge material of his suit, the sparklingly crisp white shirt with the faint vertical blue stripes and the less than bright red tie with the small white perimetered circles dotting it throughout. Lambrusco's face, good enough looking, as well as his middle, visible through the unbuttoned suit jacket, announced well fed, contented doing fine.

"Well, this isn't too bad for someone who's only been here for three weeks. You know, even though you went to Yale, and Columbia for college, it's still the guvmint. They're not going to plump it up like the Taj Mahal or anything. But," his eyes roamed around the small room again, a little more dartingly this time, "there are still some things you can do in here, to make it look a little better, more like home, whatever. Maybe next time I'll bring in some paintings we have in the tenth floor storeroom. If you're ever up there, on the way to the big cheese's office, whatever, take a look and see whether there's anything catches your fancy. Some of them ain't too bad. Or, I'll bring some with me next time I stop by. But I don't know if you'd like my taste." A smile that somehow seemed imploring wandered across his beefy features.

Ed was still wondering how he knew that he'd been working there exactly three weeks to the day and where he'd gone to school but realized that he should fumble toward some assurance that Lambrusco's artistic taste was very likely just fine, totally agreeable.

"Oh, Im sure that…."

Lambrusco waited only for the barest beginning of the hemming and hawing before he burst in with, "Let me tell you why I'm here. Besides that I heard you're an alright guy from various people here, some of my sources. One of my many duties here is being in charge of the U.S. Savings Bond program. You'll wanna sign up for the weekly deduction plan. A painless little withdrawl from your paycheck every week applied to the current ten year bonds at 3.2% or 4.1% for the twenty year really adds up after a while. You can have five bucks, ten, fifteen, whatever, deducted every week and apply it toward a fifty or hundred dollar bond. You put in thrirty—seven fifty on the ten year and get fifty bucks after year ten. On the twenty you put in fifty and get back eighty plus,almost double your money, after twenty years. And safe as rain. The guvmint ain't gonna grab your dough and take off with it. They go under and there's no more world, anyway, if you catch my drift. A swell deal to build a little nest egg. You just got married more or less." He winked, knowingly. "Any kids coming down the pike? This is a good deal, take it from Ernie. So what should I put you down for? Wanna start with a deduction of ten a week, see how that goes, and then maybe up it to twenty or twenty—five?"

Ed calculated quickly, and frantically, that his $6,500 annual salary meant a gross take home pay of $125 per week and that he couldn't afford to have anything at all taken out of his paycheck since Marsha still hadn't landed a teaching job. But he sensed that saying an outright "No" wouldn't be wise.

Lambrusco detected the hesitation in Ed's eyes. "Listen, don't worry, if the constant deduction every week is something you can't handle yet we can go with the lump sum $18.75 of a five year every three months. Or, even, every six, if that's all you can do. But, take it from me, kid, you're hurting yourself by doing too little. This is money in the bank, buddy, money in the bank. Better—it's the guvmint's bank, held in trust for you."

"You're probably right Mr. Lambrusco… I mean Ernie.. But let me think about what's the best way to go for a day or two. Ed felt that one of the most valuable things he learned in law school was that you didn't have to make every decision that everyone wanted you to make at exactly the time someone wanted you to make it. "I'll think anout it" were poserful words of social solvent. But whenever Ed employed this gambit there also flashed into his mind that a Political Science professor at Columbia had mentioned that Sam Rayburn, a long—time Speaker of the House of Representatives, was fond of intoning "You've got to go along to get along."

"It's's up to you kid. You're smart, you wouldn't be here if you weren't. You're an attorney, you went to those schools , I didn't. But let me tell you—there ain't that much to think about. This is one good deal. And backed up by the word of Ernie Lambrusco and the U.S. of A. guvmint.>" His whole fleshy face participated in the wide swath of grin, but Ed wasn't sure that no insidious malign lurked in the overtly benign.

After Lambrusco departed with a "See ya, kid," and a cheerful wave of his right arm Ed felt that he needed some counsel himself. He ambled two offices down and saw, through her open office door, that his Branch Chief, Kathy Roberts, a young to middle—aged career attorney with the FTC, honors grad NYU Law School, mom of two, was in and alone. She was bent over her desk studying an imposingly thick looking sheaf of papers. Perhaps a brief or Commission "Complaint" almost ready to be filed. After Ed had loomed outside for a few moments she looked up and smiled. But just barely.

"I was wondering if you had a few minutes?"

She flicked a penciled check mark at the place on the page where she'd been reading and gently slid the page aside. "Sure, you look like you need some advice. And what's a Branch Chief for. We certainly don't do much real work."

Ed grinned, went into her office and wound up standing right across from her, a foot or two from the desk. She pointed to the chair beside the desk and Ed occupied it. It was a typical government issue chair—a little small, straight—backed, a little too metallic and not at all inviting the user to settle in.

"So how, and as to what, can I advise?" Kathy remarked. "I thought you were still more or less still getting acquainted with people and how things work around here and hadn't really dug into anything yet."

"No, you're right, I'm still more or less getting the feel.... It's not about work... as such, I mean."

"Sounds a bit mysterious. Mysterious and serious?"

"No, no," Ed smiled and made a negative motion with his hand. "It's just that.... Well, Mr. Lambrusco just came into my office, and...."

"Oh, Ernie paid you his visit?" Kathy inserted. The inflection in her voice was draped in knowingness.

Ed's face must have registered confusion. Kathy laughed gently and continued.

"He came calling for his country, did he?" pealing a subdued chuckle to accentuate her words.

She must have thought that Ed was still looking considerably unfocused because, almost immediately, she continued, "I mean he pitched the bonds, right? He does to every new employee. Did he convince you to commit your earnings for life?"

Ed opened a smile, his hands, too, palms upward and shrugged. "Well no, not yet at least. But I guess that's why I'm here. Should I have?"

"Only if you wanted to. Ernie's an FTC career operative. He's been here fifteen—twenty years, even longer than me.,and he's acquired a little clout here, a little clout there. He's in charge of a lot of procurement for the office. You know clerical supplies and major items like furniture and such. And it's been said, for more than a few years now, that those lucky enough to get supply contracts are those who've treated Ernie the sweetest, not necessarily those who offer the best deal to the FTC. But nobody's ever proved anything. "

"Well, would it be inadvisable, I mean not the way to go, to not buy the bonds. Or not buy them in the quantities he suggests?"

"Oh, I don't think so. His affected bark is a lot more aggressive than his effective bite. Why don't you just buy one every few months, or twice a year or something. Just to ensure that the lion stays at bay. He probably gets a small commission. But they're a decent investment anyway. A little better than keeping it in a savings account."

"Who's got anything to put in a savings account! But I gotcha. I'll go up there in a few days and buy one."

"That's the spirit and that should take care of it. Oh, and did I just hear a tad of complaining about the munificent salaries they lavish on us here?"

"No, no, nothing as dramatic as a complaint. It's just that I haven't paid off my law school debts yet, and with a child on the way…."

" I remember what you mean. Just tweaking a bit."

"In any event, I see that you still have that impressive looking document there to peruse, so I'll let you get to it."

" Right, thanks, I can hardly wait, but…. Anyway, good luck with Ernie and with things in general around here, too."

Ed returned to his office and began reviewing some files with which he'd been told to familiarize himself.

A few days later he went up to Lambrusco's office. Someone had just emerged, shutting the door as he left. Ed knocked.

"Come in," the voice boomed, almost in public address announcer style. He was seated behind his massive desk, hands interlocked behind his head, supporting it, as he leaned well back in the large, leather, generously upholstered swivel chair. There was hardly anything on the desk except for two isolated sheets of paper.

"Eddie, my boy, good of you to drop by. How can I serve you? Or, putting it in lingo I'm more comfortable with, and maybe you, being a lawyer, are too, what can I do you for?" He waited for effect, but then, shot out "Just joshing."

"Well, Ernie I decided that you're a good investment advisor and that I need to add a bond to my portfolio."

"You've made a good decision, kid. You want to go on the weekly withholding plan? Maybe the monthly?"

"No, Ernie, all I want right now is one fifty dollar bond. You know, I'm a young man starting out with a new family. That's all I can afford now."

"That's just why you want to look ahead, Ed, and provide for the future. For your kids, whatever."

"Sorry, Ernie, the thirty—seven fifty is all I can spring for right now. Maybe another one in a while. But don't hold your breath for the duration. And don't push me. I can only do what I can do. Why, Ernie, if it weren't for your persuasive powers….."

"Gotcha, my boy. Fork me the thirty-seven fifty and I'll put it through and have them start processing the papers and issuing the bond. Who's the owner? You and your wife? Whatever you want."

"Edward and Marsha Ingersoll. And you mean I give you the dough, but I don't get the bond yet? Can you be trusted Ernie?" As soon as he'd said it Ed thought that maybe he'd dripped too much sarcasm on the last sentence.

But Lambrusco showed no reaction, saying merely, "You can trust me just like you can trust the bond. My word is my bond and the bond is solid."

"O.K., Ernie, I hope so," Ed remarked as he handed the cash to the older man.

"But I'll give you a receipt anyway," Lambrusco replied at the same time he started writing one and handed a form to Ed to fill out.

Each did his paper work and as Lambrusco held out the receipt he remarked, "A pleasure doing business with you, Ed; I hope we'll do a lot more."

"Not for a while, Ernie, remember?" Ed commented as he started sidling from the office.

"You should do it sooner than you think, kiddo. It's a real good investment in the future---yours and your country's."

"O.K., Ernie, we'll see about the future," Ed dismissed as he turned to depart.

It didn't seem to Ed that it was more than ten days later, perhaps two weeks, that Lambrusco came charging through Ed's office door with a supremely hearty—voiced, "Ed, my boy. Long time no see."

"What d'ya mean,I bought something only a week or two ago and, in any event, we saw each other in the elevator just a few days ago."

"Just a figure of speech, kiddo. I'm here to look after your financial well being. Not that I just don't like to chat in general, shoot the breeze about the world, with a Yale Law School man."

"Yeah, I'm sure you're very impressed with that. Almost as much as you're concerned with my well being."

"I am Eddie, boy, I am. How're they treatin' ya around here? Catching on to some of the ropes and stuff? Roberts ain't bad to work for, is she? She's got her bad moments during the month, if you get my drift," Lambrusco delivered a broad wink, "but she's pretty much an o,k, egg. No slave driver or anything, right?"

"Yes, she seems fine," Ed interpolated quickly. He wasn't about to share any feelings or reactions, whatever they were,with Lambrusco. "But Ernie, stop diverting me. I'm not buying another bond so soon after the other one."

"Did I say anything about you having to buy a bond or anything? I'm just here to chat a little with one of my favorite young attorneys. I also happen to help you keep track of the time as far as your financial well being and future goes. "

"Right, Ernie. Yeah, thanks."

"As long as you appreciate it kiddo," Lambrusco rejoindered as he crinkled a medium bright hale—fellow—well—met smile. "Well, I'll be running along now, let you get back to the serious work of helping out Kathy. But I'll be dropping in again, soon, Eddie boy. I'm always thinking of your well being even if you're not."

"Right, thanks. You must ponder it non—stop. I'll be looking forward."

A few months went by during which Ed didn't encounter Lambrusco other than in passing in the halls or the elevators. Limited to "Hi"s and "How are you?"s Although he didn't always find it very stimulating, Ed got more and more involved in the work of his branch and he could sense that Kathy Roberts thought he was doing a good job—especially for a neophyte. He was feeling more confident, as though he had some authority flowing from knowledge and a little practical experience he'd acquired, and that things were going well in general. In his expansiveness it struck him that he should buy another bond and a few days later he headed for Lambrusco's office. When he got there the door was open but two other Commission employees were standing inside. All three occupants had grins on their faces, as though they'd just reveled in a hearty laugh. Ed went off to accomplish a chore in the Commission library, a floor above, returning fifteen minutes later.

"Eddie, old pal," Lambrusco intoned, looking up from the newspaper on his otherwise virtually clear desk.

"Ernie, I'm going to subject myself to another fleecing from you. I have another thirty—seven fifty here in my hot little hand."

"You know who to bring it to, kid.You know what that other thirty—seven fifty is worth already? I think it's probably at least almost thirty eight bucks."

"Yeah, that's what I mean, Ernie, I'd probably do better investing in subway tokens," Ed retorted, looking at the cleared surface of the desk, now that Lambrusco had folded the newspaper and lowered it to the floor at the side of his chair.

Lambrusco's features clouded momentarily, tinged by hurt, but he, as though by sheer willpower, mustered a smile and muttered, "No,no,no. This is the real deal. Safe and conservative, but productive, too."

"Whatever you say Ernie," Ed said as he held out the money.

In the next year Lambrusco came into Ed's office about a half—dozen times, sometimes on a pretense, sometimes not, and solicited a bond purchase. Ed refused to buy and, as he became more and more confident in his job , received more accolades and got more friends in the one hundred person office,he became more sarcastic and short, verging on brusque, in his repartee with Lambrusco. Almost dismissive, if not palpably hostile. However, once or twice in that period he wen t to Lambrusco's office and offered up his thirty—seven fifty. On these occasiuons too, though, Ed's general demeanor suggested that he was doing Lambrusco a favor, indulging him, since he certainly wasn't obligated.

During one of those visits, consistentwith his growing sense of self—esteem and growing authority, Ed was wearing a new suit as well as a new tie purchased especially to go with it. Lambrusco, himself attired in a rich woolen suit and soft, obviously expensive,shirt with a silk tie of tasteful design pointed to Ed's tie and observed, "That's a nice tie, Eddie boy. But those bright regimental stripes clash with the vertical stripes of your shirt. You can't do stripes against stripes."

Ed, reduced to some fluster, was the one to register disturbance on his features this time. He could only say," Oh, right. O.K., Ernie, if you say so."

"I do, kid. I do."

Into his second year at the office Ed was just schmoozing, generally, one day, with Kathy Roberts when she suddenly said," I don't really know why, maybe somebody found something out, but Ernie Lambrusco isn't Chief of Administrative Services any more."

"Really?" Ed inquired, genuinely surprised.

"Yes, he's now called something like Special Assistant to the Regional Administrator, or some such euphemism, and he's been demoted a few pay grades and put into a much smaller office than the one he had. In fact it's little more than a broom closet."

"I didn't hear a word."

"No, it's not the kind of thing which anyone makes a big announcement about. Least of all Ernie, of course. And, by the way, you don't have to worry about the bonds any more. That's been taken away from him

"We know that you don't like applause…or clapping at the end of the course….But the ten of us all wanted to thank you….For how much you've given us in here…. this semester. We all got together and got you this. A gift certificate…to the bookstore."

He held out his hand to accept it while saying words like, "I appreciate it," "It's so nice of you.," "Thank you very much," which he'd mastered to perfunctoriness since this kind of thing had happened occasionally over the years. Nothing new under the sun. But, then, as everyone stood awkwardly around waiting for someone else to be first to leave, he strode to the door and was gone before he felt the tears seep and finally flow.

It was no longer astonishing just how good some of the classes at the great university were. After all, he'd been there over two years now. Of course, saying that a class was good really meant that the professor who taught it was stimulating—either by means of virtually encyclopedic knowledge of the subject matter or provocativeness, incisiveness, dash in presenting it. But J.B. seemed particularly impressive. This was the second course Schwartz had taken from him.

It had taken a lot of hard work to get there. Studying away at the kitchen table, unto one and two in the morning, in the three room apartment, during high school. Conceiving imaginative papers, writing them, typing them up, not to mention preparing assiduously for all those relentless tests on which he got all those excellent grades. But it must have been worth it, to get to such a remarkable place of intellect. It had opened so much to him and now he was the beneficiary of another round of peerless teaching from J.B.

He'd first had J.B. for an introductory philosophy course, one of those "general education" courses which helped fulfill some graduation "distribution" requirement. There J.B. had been even more aloof and distant than he was in the current, more specialized, class. Schwartz was taking it, "Recent Themes in American Philosophy," because, although he was a Political Science Major, he was "minoring," (another graduation requirement) in Philosophy. As would be expected, there were fewer students in the advanced course and, although J.B. did nothing, specifically, to foster the feeling, Schwartz sensed more connection between professor and at least several students in there. There was less lecturing "down" to them and more conversing with them, engaging one student and another in Socratic dialogue more than infrequently. J.B. even introduced a glint of humor now and then in his always deadly serious intellectual excursions and expositions. Sometimes there was even an extra—curricular recommendation of a non—academic book to read or play or film to see. But the highly sober, formal mien seemed never to leave him. The erudite, patrician, Protestant professor mold never cracked.

Schwartz may have been enrolled in one of the great universities of the world, but he still commuted there, each day, from the three room apartment in which he lived with his mother and rapidly aging father. He had been a later- in-marriage "surprise" for his immigrant parents. And that same kitchen table, after the three of them would finish "supper," and the dishes had been hand washed and wiped, was still the site at which Schwartz did the work of his demanding courses at the university he was growing to love. His car for going between here and there was a subway car.

Schwartz not only liked hearing J.B. speak perfectly formed sentences running into trenchant paragraphs, about the assigned readings, or in responding to an invariably sounding simplistic student question. He particularly loved hearing him read what he deemed an especially important or revealing passage written by one of the philosophers covered in the course.His nasal voice conveyed a sense of distance, just as the man himself did, and the perfectly placed nuances and inflections of his reading voice seemed to draw every last bit of meaning, connotation, intention from the words.

Schwartz's favorite philosopher for these J.B. intoning purposes was John Dewey. Dewey's formulations, even individual sentences, seemed so awkward and cumbersome, packed as they were with suggestion and exactly qualified assertion. He was "difficult" reading on the page and Schwartz often found himself reading over, and then over again, especially thorny Dewey material. Yet, when J.B. read from Dewey the message seemed to leap into the listener's mind with direct force and utter limpidity. Schwartz, and he thought this must be true for almost every student in the class, was in no doubt as to what Dewey "meant," or meant to say, even before J.B. expatiated on what he had just read—if he chose to do that, too.

Of course, even without the teacher's nurturing and cultivation of the power of Dewey's thought, this dean of Ameican philosophy was one of Schwartz's intellectual heroes. In addition to his clandestine appreciation of Dewey's rambling, ramshackle and "grand" writing, (a style which came somewhat naturally to Schwartz, himself—sometimes his papers were graded down a bit by impatient faculty irritated by it,) Schwartz was enamored of Dewey's insistence that social problems could be solved, social conditions improved, by the application of human intelligence to questions of value. Putting it acutely shortly, Dewey had a rational and tenaciously purposeful approach toward creating a brighter world and did not believe that man's fate was eternally, irretrievably lost. With late teen—age fervor, Schwartz wanted to help the downtrodden, heal the sick, relieve the oppressed. He found inspiration in Dewey's confidence. He hoped and felt that philosophy could play an activist role; that highminded intellect could be applied to concrete, day to day, advance and improvement. After all, hadn't Dewey written, "Of all things theory is the most practical."

"Applied" suggested law school. Schwartz's grades made it almost certain that he would be accepted by one of the elite ones. Yet, from friends a few years older, Schwartz had heard things about law school which he didn't like. He picked up that there seemed to be much reveling in totally precise clinical detail, exultation in picking a nit. Schwartz craved the sweep, the drive, the passion of large hearted social policy. Whatever else might be said of the body of work of that most insistent of social revolutionaries, Karl Marx, his apercu that "Until now philosophers have interpreted the world; the point, however, is to change it," continued to glow and resonate.

Yet there was the aromantic, but necessary, matter of earning a living.A lawyer had options which a Ph.D in Political Science or Philosophy simply did not. Most Ph. D.s entailed, (as a philosopher might say,)academia's ivory tower for a regular pay check. A peripheral issue, although Schwartz didn't know how marginally it might actually turn out, was that Schwarz's parents, who had nurtured him so conscientiously to this launching point, would surely understand, and approve of, his becoming an attorney, but might not at all comprehend, from their "immigrant mentality," the Ph.D.—college professor route. The first was practical, the second.... There was only practical—except maybe for Albert Einstein, 1879—1955. From memory Schwartz knew the dates of that great scientist—humanist, as he did with many of his intellectual heroes. Dewey was 1859—1952.

The academy meant J.B.; the erudite, urbane,supremely articulate J.B. How could Schwartz aspire to that level? No matter how hard he studied, how much deeply intellectual material he absorbed and mastered, he could never be like that. So would he be satisfied to be a lesser version? Just to be able to profess in the academy. Or, then, would he only feel like an unsatisfactory part of what he wanted to be. It certainly wasn't clear that to take the less travelled road would make him happiest. He didn't mind sacrificing material gain for more transcendent values, but what if there was only sacrifice and inadequate payoff.

As Schwartz's junior year proceeded and J.B. became more and more riveting, brilliant, provocative, inspiring, his lectures seeming to ascend higher each week,Schwartz found out about a university fellowship for which high ranking juniors were encouraged to apply. It provided a generous annual stipend to be paid for the five academic years succeeding a recipient's college graduation. The purpose was to support the fellow in attending graduate school in a program leading to a Ph.D.

The university would award three of these fellowships designed to entice a high achieving student to make a commitment to graduate study by settling the question of financial security more than a year before the student would even be entering graduate school. It could be thought of as "bribing" excellent students to go the Ph.D. route rather than head for a professional career in, e.g., medicine or law. Schwartz thought he was definitely in the range of students who would be competitive. Discussions with other students with high averages confirmed this.

He felt himself drawn more and more to the academy, as a profession and life, by the example of J.B. And, in any event, what harm would there be in applying. If he succeeded then he could make a final choice between teaching Philosphy or Poly Sci at a university and law and its various sequale, (a J.B. taught word.) And he didn't need to tell his folks of his choice until he actually made one. They'd make occasional stabs at finding out what his post—college plans were and he'd gently repulse these with a response in the vein of, "I've been thinking about law school." Such an answer seemed to satisfy, if not exult, them. Medical school might have been even better but they would have known it was a bogus answer. They kept sufficient track of the courses he took, and those he was planning to take, to know that that road was really not open.

Schwartz was also motivated to apply because selection was done "completely on the papers." You filled out the multifarious forms, answered the endless questions, wrote your essay on why you wanted the fellowship, provided financial details, submitted your transcripts and then—waited. "They" didn't even give you an idea of when their selections would be made or applicants informed.

So Schwartz submitted and Schwartz waited. Since no time frame had been given, Schwartz didn't even keep track of weeks elapsed. But it didn't take that long—maybe a month, six weeks. The letter was on the usual letterhead of the university but there was a modestly lettered "Committee on Fellowships" above that. The body of the letter was straightforward:

"The Committee, after carefully reviewing and discussing all applications submitted for the Ruskin Fellowships, is pleased to advise that you have been selected as one of the three successful candidates.

"Your academic achievements thus far suggest a bright future in an intellectual discipline of your choosing leading to a career in university teaching and scholarship.

"In due course you will be receiving papers and forms by which to indicate acceptance of the fellowship which will begin providing support toward a Ph.D. program in which you enroll in the September subsequent to your graduation from college. If you believe that, for any reason, you will decline the fellowship, please advise this office as soon as possible.

"Our heartiest congratulations on your having been chosen as a Ruskin fellow and all best wishes for continued success in your future endeavors."

Schwartz was so elated by the news, if, even, just for the honor, alone, that he almost didn't notice the signatory of the letter. But, an instant before his eyes swept from the page, he did. He was shocked to see that it was none other than "J_____ B-------, Chair." He was brought up short. He'd had no idea.

He wondered whether J.B. even knew whom he was, whether, as he went over Schwartz's application , he realized that Schwartz was in his course, that he had taken a previous course from him, that he had done very well in that course. Naturally, all this information was available to J.B. from Schwartz's transcripts, but that didn't mean that J.B. had actually noted it, or taken it all in. Perhaps, even, the committee members divided up the applications and Schwartz's had not been one of those J.B. was chiefly responsible for processing.

As the days went by he kept on wondering. And the more he wondered the more he convinced himself that J.B. must have been instrumental in his receiving the fellowship. It couldn't be that it was a mere coincidence that J.B. was not only on the committee but, also, chaired it. He resolved to communicate with J.B. The least he could do was thank the man. The intellectual treasure he'd conferred in class was incalculable, but ethereal, intangible, beyond thanks in a way. But for this practical, concrete benefit, which J.B. had participated in arranging, if, indeed, he wasn't primarily behind it, the least Schwartz could do would be say "Thank you."

But that might be a little trickier than it seemed. Schwartz thought about just going up to J.B. after a class and quickly, casually mentioning how happy he'd been to get the fellowship and how grateful he was to J.B. for whatever role he'd played. But, simple as that approach seemed, it could turn out to be awkward, basically unwieldy. You never knew who else would be hanging around the front of the room, after class, schmoozing with, waiting to say something clever to, ask a purportedly intelligent question of, J.B. The more Schwartz thought about it, the more difficulties seemed to loom that way the more he knew he'd simply have to muster the courage to formally, directly express his thanks. The only suitable way to do it, with the appropriate sincerity, would be to tell him in his office. Beard the lion in his den, as it were.

This would be far from easy for Schwartz. He was particularly diffident when he had to speak to people he didn't really already know. He was made edgy, uncomfortable by even simple business calls, about trivial details, to "strangers." He had even become anxious about calling the Philosophy Department secretary to try to set up an appointment to see J.B. He was only finally able to do it after swearing to himself, one day, that he would surely make the call the next day. He always kept his word to himself. That was his methodology for doing what had to be done, but which he greatly feared doing.

The appointment he got was for a week off. Plenty of time for him to muse upon and agonize over exactly what he'd say to J.B. once he was actually in the man's office. He sifted many scenarios in his mind, day after day, night after night. If he said this, and J.B. responded with that, and he.... Or, if J.B. greeted him that way, and he said, and J.B. answered.... Finally he realized that he would not be able to decide upon, or know what he would say, until he was saying it.

As it always does, the day came. But to add to his torment, the appointment was not until 2:00. So Schwartz had to attend two classes in the morning, study in the library a while, have lunch amidst a bull session with some fellow students and wait. He'd told no one that he was scheduled to see J.B.

He waited and waited and, naturally, showed up at the Philosophy Department ten minutes early. The secretary was cordial enough. She told him to have a seat, gesturing to two spare chairs along the wall, said he might want to riffle through some of the magazines scattered on a small nearby table and assured that she would " buzz the professor in a few minutes." She did at just about precisely 2:00 and suddenly he was just behind her as she opened the door to J.B.'s office and said, "Here is Mr. Schwartz, professor."

J.B. was sitting at his desk, not far from ramrod—straight. His tie and jacket were crisp and impeccable, every thick grey hair firmly in place. Just as things always were when he was at the head of the classroom. A book was open on the otherwise uncluttered desk his eyes on it. He only lifted his gaze slightly, just enough to clear his glasses, as he, gestured to a straight—backed chair, just a foot or so from his desk, and said, "Have a seat Mr. Schwartz; please sit down."

Schwartz did as he was told, fumbling some of his text books, as he lowered himself into the chair. One got away, thudding to the floor and he scrambled to retrieve it, half sitting, half standing, before looking up at J.B. again. The professor appeared to be simultaneously continuing to read his book while partially observing Schwartz. Gradually J.B. shifted his eyes directly to Schwartz, but said nothing. He continued to wait.

There were to be, apparently, no J.B. facilitated preliminaries or pleasantries. The essentially forbidding patrician mien was not yielding. It clearly was up to Schwartz.

"I just wanted to thank you," Schwartz's voice cracked and croaked. Despite all the versions of this encounter he'd played out in his mind, he hardly knew where to go after that. J.B., just more or less staring at him, wasn't giving Schwartz much, anything actually, to work with.

Schwartz bum bled ahead. "I wanted to thank you for all that you've taught me in the two classes. You know, I was in the "Philosophy As A System" one, too, back a few semesters...." J.B. nodded, almost imperceptibly, it seemed to Schwartz. Maybe he hadn't even nodded.He certainly wasn't going to pick up the ball.

"As I say, I've learned a lot, a tremendous amount, actually....but I suppose I wouldn't be here just for that. I wanted to thank you very much, I can't express how much, for the fellowship. I was so happy to get it. It means so much to me....Especially coming from you."

"Others selected you, too," J.B said, hardly achieving enough animation, it seemed, to get the words out. Hands still folded on the desk in front of him he continued to stare at Schwartz.

Schwartz felt futility. Mission not accomplished. He'd said the words he meant to say, ones he'd practiced,but, somehow he had not really gotten his message across. He hadn't made J.B. understand, feel, just how appreciative he was.

"I mean, I had been thinking of going to graduate school, but I didn't know if I could, or whether it was the best idea. I mean the money and not having a regular job for that long… my folks might not understand. They're working people, they didn't have the advantages they gave me…. I mean, I just didn't know….This gives me some breathing room," he trailed off again. "It's extremely meaningful to me and I wanted you to know how thankful I am to you, just how much I appreciate it, how much I admire you, your example….."

He petered off into blankness despite all the mental rehearsing. J.B. was still looking at Schwartz, quite impassively, showing no more inclination than he had previously to enrich the conversation or even move. Schwartz felt profoundly that he had failed, but, simply, didn't know what else he could do. He clutched his books and started to get up. As he was nodding at J.B., with a hesitant, constricted smile, about to mutter "Good—bye," turn and leave, J.B. pulled himself up even straighter in his chair, leaned his right arm on the desk, using it to support his head, and suddenly began talking, although his voice remained measured, deliberate even.

"Mr. Schwartz," J.B. started, as though it were necessary to gain Schwartz's attention,"I rather think that some day, you'll be sitting behind a desk like this one." Schwartz started to protest, but J.B. cut him off instantly with a curt wave of his hand. "When you do, there are two things I'd like you to remember. The first is that you always help the poorest and the least; the poorest and the least. The second is something that Henry Adams wrote quite a while ago: "A teacher affects eternity. He can never tell where his influence stops." J.B. continued staring at Schwartz, whose own eyes were riveted on the professor, for a few seconds after that. Then he shifted his eyes back to the book on his desk and Schwartz, knowing the encounter was over, went out.

THE POWER OF POETRY

Peter Vittorino's affection for poetry had started in high school. Mostly the Americans—William Cullen Bryant, Edwin Arlington Robinson, Edgar Lee Maters;(did they all have three names?)---but there was also Robinson Jeffers--- and all that. He liked the way the words rolled and rolled and, finally, left you with an imperishable sensation. But he really didn't know much about it, or very much of it.

Once in college, even though he would major in a social science, like History or Government, with law school probably his ultimate destination, poetry seemed like something to pursue in elective courses. It took a few years. About to register for the first semester of his Junior year, looking through the English courses section of the catalogue, he came across "Literature 19-20: Modern British and American Poetry." All the great names were mentioned: Emily Dickinson, Wilfred Owen, Randall Jarrell, Robert Frost, Alan Seeger, Theodore Roethke, W.B. Yeats, etc., etc. And the instructor was the eminent Professor D.W. Frederickson, David Wardell Frederickson, to be exact, a world—class expert on the novels of Thomas Hardy, but doubtless, with much to say and impart about many poets who were, more or less, contemporaries of Hardy's. An elective with allure for sure. Peter enrolled and looked forward.

He liked the course, very much, from day one. Frederickson was a ruddy, verging on beefy, energetic, good looking man in his mid—fifties with an understated, yet unmistakably authoritative manner about him. He was clearly there for business—but the business was art, the art of the poem. He spoke on the softer rather than the louder side of lecturing and proceeded moderately rapidly, sometimes swallowing a word or two. So a student had to listen attentively, lest one of the humorous, sardonic gems, which Frederickson could bite off at any time, slip by.

He also tried to run the course so that in addition to giving his own insights and comments the twenty—five or so students had a chance to express their feelings and reactions . He definitely attempted to generate discussions about most of the poems covered in class. Peter liked the way Frederickson pronounced it "poym" also. It seemed like an affectation, but he mumbled it quickly and unobtrusively enough so that he got away with it. At least as far as Peter was concerned.

Usually, however, the discussants were the same four or five students, with Peter almost always not amongst them. Yet, occasionally, when he felt strongly enough about something in a poem or about a comment that Frederickson had made, Peter would volunteer a comment. In the middle of the semester he offered an observation about which he felt pretty deeply, putting it intensely, almost as a cri de Coeur . When he'd concluded Frerickson just looked at him without speaking. But then he nodded, almost imperceptibly.

What Peter liked best about going to class was hearing Frederickson read the poetry. He'd often do that when he began discussing a particular poem, or a poet's oeuvre in general. For example, some of Yeats' magnificent lines, such as "The best lack all conviction/While the worst are full of passionate intensity," or "Death and life were not until man made up the whole/ lock, stock and barrel out of his bitter soul," "That is no country for old men. The young/in one another's arms, birds in the tree." Or T.S. Eliot's "April is the cruelest month, breeding/lilacs out of the dead land, mixing/Memory and desire, stirring dull roots with spring rain." And one of his real favorites, the first two lines from Hardy's "Weathers:" "This is the weather the cuckoo likes,/And so do I;/ When showers betumble the chestnut spikes/ And nestlings fly."

Some Hardy selections were included in the basic text they used, but, unsurprisingly, considering his expertise on Hardy's novels, Frederickson also handed out unanthologized Hardy poems in class. He read in a quite nasal voice, cultured, but distinctive. Like a piece of music that you got to like a lot he embedded his tones in your ear so that Peter heard his voice reading the compelling lines long after first hearing. Any one of the lines he especially appreciated could re—assert itself in Peter's memory, at almost any time. Suddenly, out of the blue, he'd remember a line long after Frederickson had read it, long after the course had concluded. For years and years, actually.

The mid—term exam was during a normal class session so it was less than an hour long. Peter was a good exam—taker and almost always did well. On limited mid—terms particularly, because he prepared thoroughly, often extensively, and usually had much more to say than he could possibly write in the allotted time. However, on Frederickson's test, while Peter understood the essay question, as such, there was a tinge of ambiguity, almost mystery about it which made him doubt himself and linger over "interpreting it," trying to comprehend just what it was that Frederickson wanted. He suddenly realized that almost half the exam time had elapsed and he'd yet to write a single sentence. He panicked and waded in, deciding on an approach that seemed feasible and sticking with it, as best he could, by being consistent and educing illustrative support from the poems themselves whenever he could. Once finished he felt that he hadn't said much at all and that what he had tried to say hadn't been expressed very deftly.By the time he handed in the blue book he was certain that he'd performed poorly , raggedly, especially in comparison with his generally excellent academic record. He wondered if it had been such a good idea to take the course.

A day later Peter got the flu and was in bed, at home, when Frederickson handed back the exams later in the week.. He got back for the next class session and asked the sophomore whom he usually sat next to what had happened in the class he'd missed. He told him that Frederickson had spoken a bit about the exams as he'd returned them. Mostly about how unsatisfactory and unresponsive to the question he'd actually asked they had been. The fellow student said that Frederickson had claimed that very few papers had even approached addressing what he wanted and, also, did a bit of lamenting about how he'd apparently not been getting through to them. The fellow poetry lover also said that Frederickson had read one paper aloud which he allowed had at least been passable and which he felt at least represented a good faith effort to come to grips with the issue he thought he'd posed. The student also mentioned a few other things about this paper, emphasizing particularly how relatively brief it had been.

From this description , Peter flirted with the thought that the exam in question might have been his. He never actually confirmed this, but his suspicion grew when he went to Frederickson's secretary to pick up his blue book and saw that he'd received an "A-" on it. This was a signal grade from Frederickson, a man known to be exceedingly parsimonious with "A"s. As a former student had remarked: 'Dante would have a fighting chance to get an 'A,' but only if he sharpened up the sloppy parts of 'The Divine

Comedy.'" Frederickson was the kind of legendary academic figure about whom students liked to concoct and tell such vignettes.

One of them, true it turned out, was that he had married late and to a considerably younger woman. They lived in a suburb almost eighty miles from the university. So Frederickson would stay in an apartment, in town, for the first three days of the week, when he taught classes, and then return to the idyllic, pastoral suburb and the beautiful, passionate young wife. The core elements about his schedule and the house in a far suburb were factual; the younger wife was too. The embellishments, about the idyll and the wife's unflagging ardor for him, were likely accretive fancies of student imaginations. Although, perhaps, for all any student really knew, they too could be true. There seemed an air of surreptitious, yet dashing "romance" about the man. "This is the weather the cuckoo likes/And so do I…." "That is no country for old men…."

There was also the one about Frederickson being an aficionado of the then new, all the rage rock star, Chubby Checker. (A "response" to Fats Domino.) It was rumored that on the nights Frederickson stayed in his city pied a terre he'd go to the a la mode place for that type of music, The Peppermint Lounge, where Checker often warbled and gyrated. More unverified assertions—but they seemed to be plausible about Frederickson as his students saw him. They sensed restlessness, an urge for adventure, a perpetual questing for fresh experiences.

It was also bruited about the university that as a very young man, shortly after graduating from Yale, he'd worked on the docks in New York City and, a bit later, had actually been a candidate for the United States Senate from New York on the Socialist Party ticket. That particular scenario seemed consistent with the air of compassion and sensitivity he projected.

The choicest of all anecdotes about the esteemed professor happened to be entirely on the mark. Its veracity doubtless contributed to just how prominent it became in the student repertoire of Frederickson tales. It had to be true because reported, widely, by the student who was there, the other protagonist. Ted Lester, an acquaintance of Peter's, had had Frederickson for a Shakespeare seminar, (the teacher's range was wide.) He'd even become the slightest bit friendly with D.W. since he'd gone to his office, several times, to further discuss a subtle point which Frederickson had made in that course. The summer afterwards Lester had worked on a cruise ship and had lost his virginity and more. He was a good looking young man and very popular with both married and unmarried women who were also cruising. He was delighted to oblige and fulfill their various needs. He had a more or less continual orgy during the ten days the cruise lasted.

When Lester returned to college in the Fall he was happy to regale just about everyone with whom he spoke, friends, classmates, bare acquaintances, with plentiful details of his conquests and their various intricacies and intimacies. Soon he ran into Frederickson, in passing on campus, and did not except the professor from this recounting of his sexual adventures and exploits. By Lester's own account he went on and on, while Frederickson, shifting from leg to leg, patiently listened. When he had finally spent every cent's worth of the narrative and paused,Frederickson, in that wry nasal voice remarked,"Ah yes, Mr. Lester....uh fucking... I remember that."

Was smug, omnisicient, condescending youth ever brought up more shortly! To Lester's credit he told the story on himself with great relish and understanding. All the more reason to credit its authenticity.

Two thirds through the semester a ten page term paper was due. Frederickson said it could be on any aspect of the course, or any assigned material that had been "interesting" to the student writer. Peter was completely at a loss for a topic. He thought of going to Frederickson's office, during the posted office hours, but he couldn't screw up his courage. He was sure he'd make a complete fool of himself and very probably compromise any paper he was thinking of writing, in Frederickson's eyes, before he'd put down a word. He mulled and mulled, struggled and struggled and finally hit upon "T. S. Eliot's Conception of Action." He didn't really know what he meant by that. But he'd found a few places in Eliot poems where acting, as opposed to inaction, seemed to be on the great poet's mind.

As with his previous experience with term papers, once Peter started jotting just a few ideas one thing led to another, this became associated with that and pretty soon he had an outline that promised to yield a good deal more than ten pages, unless he selected, pruned, chopped and edited. But abbreviating, concision, was difficult for Peter .Instead his style tended to qualify, expand, roll out ornate phrases and revel in polysyllabic words almost for their own sake. He loved language almost as music, at least music that he heard, but too often blunted its precision and communicative gracefulness. By the time he finished the paper he found that he had a lot more to say than he thought he would. He was rather pleased with many of the rolling and rumbling sentences in which he had eventually wrapped his ideas and reactions.

Frederickson handed back these papers, graded by him personally he was sure to point out, (no graduate student "readers" for him,) at the end of a class period. Peter was hoping for an "A-" but thought, given Frederickson's stringent standards that, he might have to accept his floor on a grade; viz., "B+." So he was shocked when he saw the penciled "B-" at the top of the first page of his essay. Also, scrawled beneath the grade itself, it said, "You have some good ideas and some invigorating observations. However, your 'style' is such that this sounds like a first translation from a heavy academic article in German." That was all. That was enough. Peter, the virtually always successful student, was devastated.

He remained depressed about such an undistinguished grade for a few days. Not customary for a typical nineteen year old—certainly not Peter. His way of throwing off the shadows of low esteem was to begin intensely preparing, more so than usual even, for the final exam. The final, his final chance. He went over every word of his copious class notes and every word of every poem they'd studied—multiple times. Whether that was what did it or not, he found the questions on the exam congenial to him, right down the alleys paved by his fervid studying. He got "A-" and a "B+" in the course.

Peter didn't have such troubles in many, if any, other courses and finished with a very impressive academic transcript. He was admitted to some of the elite law schools, including Harvard.

In the Fall he went to Cambridge. As expected, a highly stimulating place intellectually.But Peter didn't find law school that way. The manner in which human situations, the stuff of life, were analyzed into abstract dispositive categories first frustrated, then irritated, finally disenchanted him.

In truth, Peter basically hated Harvard Law School. A flagrant difference from college. The reading load was enormous and there seemed no time to do anything else but feverishly accomplish that and go to not overly exciting classes. In revenge he tried to set aside at least an hour or two each week when he would read some "non—legal," humanistic material. For example, Herman Hesse's novel "Siddartha" or J. D. Salinger's short stories,(of which he especially loved "Laughing Man.") And, as Fall sidled away into the relentless, unremitting gray of a Cambridge winter, Peter thought more and more of Thomas Hardy's poem "Weathers." The line that kept playing in his mind, as he'd trudge to and from class, back and forth from his sparsely furnished dormitory room, was "This is the weather the shepherd shuns/ And so do I."Each time he recited it to himself he tried to emulate the nasality of Frederickson's voice with greater and greater fidelity. Also the resignation in it.

He began feeling a need to express his affection for the humanities and how discouraged he was about law school as a place in which to learn how to change the world. The previous summer he'd read Irwin Shaw's novel about World War II, "The Young Lions." He'd enjoyed it immensely both on the story level line and because he thought Shaw had drawn a superb portrait of an intriguing and subtly nuanced character, the German officer, Christian Diestel. He wrote to Shaw saying how much he admired the book, good writing in general and how little he admired most of what went on at Harvard Law School. He mentioned that, from time to time, he'd tried a little writing himself.

He felt better once he'd mailed the note—but not for long. The law school routine was utterly grim and grinding for him. Tedious case after irritating case and class after class where professors reviled students who responded less than incisively to their complex questions. A few weeks afterward Peter grew excited when he saw a return address, in his dorm mail box, which indicated that Shaw had actually replied. The novelist thanked him generously for his complimentary words and then, in the next and final paragraph, wrote, simply, "If you want to be a writer but are at law school instead I pity you." Peter didn't know whether that sentence had been kind of Shaw or cruel. Or whether he'd been cruel only to be kind.

As the first semester wound to conclusion, Peter did often think about leaving law school behind. Not necessarily for writing, because he strongly doubted that he had the talent to live, for example, as a working novelist,, but for something less soul searing, less suffocating. But he simply didn't know what else to do, what other career was a feasible possibility. He'd talk about this tangentially with his friends but, in that tentative, unfocused context, no one came up with any spectacularly appealing options. And there was certainly no one in the Law School administration to whom he could turn to about such a problem.

So Peter kept plugging along in the law library as he continued trying to perfect his simulation of Frederickson enunciating Hardy's aching line. He so often thought of "Weathers" and other "poyms" whose rhythms, stresses, cadences, inflections were deeply etched in his mind, because of Frederickson's imperishable readings, that it finally struck him that it was Frederickson with whom he was really yearning to communicate. Also, that it was Frederickson with whom he should communicate.

He promised himself that on the coming Saturday afternoon, between his customary post morning classes pick up basketball game, (still Saturday classes then,) and resuming poring over text book cases, he would actually write a letter to D.W. himself. He thought about just what he would say for the remainder of the week and was more or less ready to write when Saturday came.

"Dear Professor Frederickson:

" In a way this has been a summer and Fall of paying debts and there is a large one I owe you which I want to try to discharge.

"There's no reason you should remember, but about two years ago I was in your 'Literature 19-20: Modern British and American Poetry' course; (its title must now be disguised by all sorts of intricate numbers, letters and notations.) It was a scintillating and revelatory experience. That despite the fact that on my paper, on the poetry of Eliot, you wrote, ' This sounds like a first translation of a heavy academic article in German.'

"I hope that my writing learned something from that observation and, in any event, as winter clamps down on Cambridge and perpetually wintry Harvard Law School, I can still hear you reading many lines, from many poems. But, perhaps, particularly 'This is the weather the shepherd shuns/And so do I.' For that and so much else that you left with me, forever, I thank you deeply.

"I hope and trust that you are well and revealing much, to many more, in 'Literature 19—20' and elsewhere, as well.

"Sincerely,

"Peter Vittorino, first year student, Harvard Law School"

He'd deliberately concluded as though it were a routine thank—you note requiring no response. Although he surely hoped for one, he was highly dubious and didn't want to be "expecting" something that would never come. After all, thank you was thank you. A thank you for a thank you? Not a reasonable hope.

Nevertheless, in less than two weeks, there was an envelope bearing the return address of Columbia's English Department with "D.W. Frederickson" penned above it.Peter purposely postponed opening it until he'd dealt with his other mail He wanted to savor anticipating Frederickson's message—whatever it might be. Finally he'd earned disclosure and he carefully slit the flap of the envelope with his thumbnail. The stationery was the university's but the professor had written in his own hand. His penmanship took a bit of deciphering, but it wasn't the worst Peter had ever seen. He puzzled over a word here, scrutinized one there. Soon he had it all.

"My dear Vittorino,

"Your charming note was a ray penetrating some bad weather here, too—gloomy and sour.

"Yes, your intuition was unerring: the course is now coded as LIT23XPO—24YPO and I'm still up to my illicit mischief of duplicating, sans permission, all sorts of material which I try not to think is probably still under copyright. When they finally catch up with me I'm counting on you to be fully steeped and armored, (better than mired,) in the arcane ways of the law so that you'll be eager to conduct a vigorous, and, more crucial, a successful defense.

"Incidentally, if your writing style ever came across as a first translation from turgid German academese it certainly doesn't any more.

"I hope the weathers in Cambridge will not conspire to make the going too heavy up there. I also hope that when you are back in these environs you'll drop into 320 Harding Hall so that we can, sunnily, catch up a bit.

"All the best luck in law school,
D.W. Frederickson"

In subsequent years, even after leaving Cambridge with his J.D., Peter thought about "Weathers." And, also from the course, Stephen Spender's famous tribute, "I Think Continually Of Those Who Were Truly Great." He also thought about what Frederickson had said about dropping in to his office sometime. Peter knew that he didn't *really* mean it, in the sense that Frederickson actively hoped for it. Yet he'd said it and Peter did, from time to time, think about doing it. But circumstances and courage never coalesced to galvanize him into actually trying.He would had to have called first to set up an appointment, wait for the return call from the departmental secretary, etc., etc.

Peter was ten years along in his career as a lawyer with the Anti—Trust division of the Justice Department when the ubiquitous grapevine of former classmates revealed that Frederickson had retired and moved to the Northern California area with the now middle—aged, but still considerably younger, (and presumably still ravishing,) wife. Her father had bought them a condominium out there.

Ted Lester, surprisingly, had become an English professor and, at that time, was teaching in a large public university in the same Northern California area. One day Peter got an excited call from Ted who ecstatically reported that he'd gotten in touch with Frederickson and persuaded him to come to the university to deliver a guest lecture on Hardy.

Unfortunately, Lester's subsequent call telling about the event itself was not nearly as enthusiastic. It seemed that Frederickson had lost a good deal of acuity. He spoke rather haltingly and, at times, even seemed distracted, if not outrightly confused. Ted lamented that he had caused the great man to be embarrassed that way. And he hadn't remembered much of the old stories and memories, from college days, which Ted had been so keen to revisit. Peter tried to re—assure Ted that he'd only meant well but his former classmate was inconsolable.

About seven years after that discouraging news, Peter was scanning through the "Milestones" column in one of the weekly newsmagazines when his eyes suddenly caught the name: "Died: D.W. Frederickson, 78, former Professor of Literature and leading authority on nineteenth century novelist and poet, Thomas Hardy,in Fresno, California, August 17th, of a drug overdose. He is survived by his wife, Marina."

Peter told this saddening news to his wife to whom he'd spoken about Frederickson and Hardy many times. He also clipped out the item and sent it by intra—office mail to a colleague with whom he'd been friendly for a number of years. He attached a note.

" He was one of my very favorite professors in college. He taught a wonderful poetry course which I still remember glowingly. And there was something about him that made kids want to emulate him. An exemplar, so to speak."

But the colleague never answered or even said a word about this note.

SISTERS

It was Sister Doris's Golden Jubilee. Fifty years since she had entered the order, The Immaculate Heart of Mary. Sandy Myerson had known her for only ten of those years, but naturally, she and her husband, Jacob, would be at the mass and the subsequent celebratory lunch. "Two celebrations, so to speak," Jacob remarked, as they were driving to the church. Sandra, the jewess, "The gift of the God of the Hebrews," Sister Irene, the principal of St. Bernadette's School called her, and Doris, the nun, who through the tumultuous sixties and seventies had remained true to her vows,had had a very rich decade together.They had striven and struggled to provide specially challenged, (as they were now called,) elementary school kids with the coping mechanisms and skills that would give them a chance. Not, to be sure, as rocket scientists, but as teachers' aides, auto mechanics, chefs, beauticians. Livelihoods where they could function with and compensate for the disabilities which God had made their burden.

The first time that Sandy had come on the grounds of St, Bernadette's, for her interview with Sister Irene, she had witnessed Doris in action. As she crossed the street just outside the schoolyard she saw that two girls, seventh or eighth graders they seemed, were physically swiping and clawing at each other. Doris had run over and inserted herself between them. She strenuously pulled and pushed them apart. By the time Sandy had approached the combatants were standing shamefacedly, heads down, while Doris, in the middle, a restraining hand still on each, admonished and lectured. Softly, almost gently, yet, nevertheless, firmly.

Doris was still teaching a regular fifth grade class at that time. And she continued for a year after Irene had hired Sandy to initiate and administrate St. Bernadette's maiden voyage in specific services for special education kids. Most were merely dyslexic and, therefore, having trouble learning to read. That could be remedied fairly straightforwardly with easy to master techniques. However, some had attention deficit and/or hyperactivity disorders which made absorbing any academic material more or less a battle if remedial strategies were not learned, re—learned and rehearsed.

During her first year at St. Bernadette's , (or" Bernie's" as she came to refer to it to herself,) Sandy had her own battle in orienting many of the classroom teachers toward identifying and accepting such problems. Too many of them, perhaps in the Catholic educational tradition of strictness and regimen, tended to attribute any student problems or failures to "laziness" or inadequate effort. It had been a very hectic first year-- proselytizing teachers, administering screening tests to possibly needy students, and, then, finally, trying to teach remedial skills and techniques to those who needed them. Sandy realized that she would have to have help the next school year if all the school's children who could, in fact, benefit were to be served.

She went to Sister Irene.

"Sister, I think I'll need someone to help me next September if we want to reach all the kids who could get something out of the remedial program."

"Oh, I see," ruminated the principal, tapping her fingers softly, but regularly, on her desk, in just about the only surface space not slathered over with loose papers and bulky books. "Well, getting someone for you would mean that we'd have to charge enough for the special education services to cover not only your salary but also the assistant's."

"I guess so Sister…."

"Oh, not your concern, Sandra. That's my problem."

"Yes, frankly, I'm not very good at that sort of thing."

"Don't worry. I am. Actually, from the rate at which you've been identifying problem kids this year, it pretty well seems that next year there'll be sufficient clients for your program so that if we charge even only a modest amount and, only to those parents who can afford it of course, we'll be able to cover your salary as well as an assistant's. Or, going at it another way, the salary of someone I'd have to hire to replace someone who's already here who could become your helper."

"If it works out for you I would really appreciate the back—up."

"Just do a little investigation and then give me some ideas on someone here who could possibly, maybe probably is a better way to put it, effectively assist you and support you with the program next year."

"Oh, I'll be more than glad to do that. As soon as I can. And thank you so much sister."

Sandy did as was agreed and, as had also been agreed, when September came she was assigned an aide. It was Sister Doris.

In her first year at Bernie's Sandy had gotten to know Doris a bit.They talked occasionally, mostly in passing. In the corridors, the lunchroom, the teachers' lounge.She'd actually been one of the teachers most receptive to the special ed program Sandy was trying to implement and had periodically and promptly identified students in her class whom she thought Sandy should screen for problems. Doris had almost always been right. When she suggested that a boy or girl seemed to be in academic deep water, they almost always surely were. They would have drowned without a lifeline.

Late in her first year Sandy had pointed out this accuracy to Sister Doris and she seemed glad that Sandy had noticed. They started having more interchange.One time Sandy had taken Doris to lunch and they'd enjoyed a hearty Italian meal over shop talk.

In fact, Mama Rosita's happened to be an old style Italian neighborhood restaurant. There were red and white checkered table cloths and huge sizzling pizzas which reminded Sandy of the Brooklyn of the fifties in which both she and Jacob had been born and raised. Once Doris had shown it to her Sandy had sometimes brought Jacob there for dinner because she thought he'd really enjoy it too. So he did. They started going there almost regularly. And almost each and any time it would stir some nostalgic memories which they would review.

For Jacob, many of these related to his beloved Brooklyn Dodgers, long since removed to Los Angeles, and their core pillar, the great and redoubtable Jackie Robinson. The hero supreme, who had integrated Major League baseball in 1947. He liked to remind Sandy that Robinson, too, had been a needy child, at loose ends, who'd been guided toward more productive paths by a discerning and wise minister. And one of the anecdotes he repeated most often revolved around the tragic death, in a car accident of Robinson's oldest son when Jackie himself was already a revered world wide figure and symbol. A famous sports reporter had written a note of sympathy to the great athlete and subsequently dedicated social activist in which he had consoled Robinson that he had "thousands of sons and daughters, now adults of a certain age, who remember the bravery and the searing truths, as much as we remember the flashing spikes and the headlong dive to save a game." Jacob had memorized the enkindling words. So many, all over the world, (one always heard of a new, "incredible" place, never to be expected,) had responded to the inspiration and the example Number 42 had provided.

Sandy had been happy when told by Sister Irene that Sister Doris would be her new assistant. So pleased that she'd changed the stationery. When she had first established the program Sandy had designed stationery for it on the computer. The last line of the letterhead had been "Sandra Myerson, M.Ed., Director." During the second week of working with Sister Doris Sandy had changed that line to "Sandra Myerson and Sister Doris Ann McGilvary, Directors." When Doris saw the new stationery she approached Sandy with a sheet, pointing to the revised line, and embraced her in a silent hug. They started going to a lot more lunches at Mama Rosita's together.

Sister Doris loved the new job and the children loved her. She was the good cop. Only very rarely would she bridle at a child's negligence or passivity. Sandy would develop a learning program for a child and Doris would teach it. When a child was casual about doing homework Sandy would come down on the malefactor as the disciplinarian. Doris would reap the learning successes—and the emotional ones.

After some time Sandy showed her colleague the various kinds of tests she administered and how she used their results to analyze what remediation a child needed. Doris became more and more knowledgeable as things went along, but she never wanted to directly participate in much besides tutoring the children. When it was necessary to call a parent in she attended the conference but there, too, it was Sandy who played bad cop. She admonished the father who wanted to have little to do at home with ensuring that his son completed assignments. She broached sharp reality to the mom who persisted in believing that a severely learning disabled daughter would one day go to Harvard.

Harvard had come into Doris's life that year at Christmas time. Before she had been assigned to St. Bernadette's by her order, Doris, herself, had been the principal of a smaller school in a suburb of Birmingham, Alabama. One of her second—graders had been the only child of a family which had just immigrated from Somalia. Africans, not African—Americans yet. The little girl had been pretty devastated by the move to a country so different from Somalia. The need to adjust to the school in Alabama almost delivered a knockout blow. Each day when she came into the building she started crying.Sister Doris had personally shepherded her, even sitting in her classroom seat with her, each day, until the crying stopped. Sometimes they'd eat lunch together in Doris's office. After a while Chisl stopped crying when she came to school and even smiled and laughed sometimes. In a few more months she had many friends and was excelling in every subject.

The family and Sister Doris had stayed in touch, even if only sporadically, over the years. In early December of Doris's first year working with Sandy they had sent Doris a letter saying that Chisl had been accepted into a Ph. D. program in Molecular Biology at Harvard and that they would love Sister Doris to come and celebrate that achievement as well as Christmas with them. She'd gone to Alabama for a week and had been high as a kite on exhiliration-- both before and after.

As Sandy and Doris became more and more friendly there were occasions when the Myersons had taken the nun out to dinner on a week—end, or a concert, (she loved classical music,) or, perhaps, to a suitable movie. During these encounters the good cop—bad cop routine of Sandy and Doris was often a topic of amusement. Sandy almost, but never actually, reached envious chagrin at how nearly all the children Doris taught adored her. The ones in the lower grades would frequently throw their arms around her ample waist in a fierce hug. Quite a few loved Sandy too. But she didn't get vritual unanimity the way Doris did.

They complemented each other. Sandy diagnosed each of the youngsters sent to them , more and more over time, and formulated the appropriate individual learning program. Doris, in addition to her peerless tutoring, was a whiz at entering all of Sandy"s written work into the computer and crafting the necessary mailing lists and notices to parents. When Sandy lost an important paper, (she couldn't handle too many of them on her desk at one time,) Sister knew where it was, or should have been---almost always.

There was the day that Sandy had an appointment to be at a meeting in Sister Irene's office with some officials from Washington who were evaluating. St. Bernadette's for a "School of Excellence" award. The time for the meeting came and went but Sandy, oblivious to the notation in her calendar book, was still diagnosing, formulating, planning at her desk. Doris, while tutoring a third-grader across the room she and Sandy shared, finally asked, "Sandy, do you know where Sister Irene might be around now?"

In complete bafflement Sandy responded," No, I don't.... I haven't seen her yet today. No, no, I just don't know."

Doris, as though in sudden revelation, remarked, "Oh, I remember. I bet she's closeted in her office with those muckety—mucks from D.C."

Sandy, in true revelation, abruptly jumped up, exclaiming, "Oh, my God, I forgot all about that…." and bolted toward the principal's office.

Sandy told Jacob that was the nuns' way. There were no judgments of deficiency. Failings were simply guided toward correction.

Doris was greeting her friends, hardly any of her relatives were left, just inside the St. Bernadette church. Both Myersons got huge, sloppy kisses . Doris seemed only slightly tinged by nervousness.

By this time Jacob and Sandy had been to more than a few masses, so they knew pretty well what to expect today.They participated in just about all the risings and re—seatings, but they deferred on eating the wafer and drinking the wine. Although they extravagantly respected what the nuns did and how beautifully they conducted themselves day to day, their jewish background made the concept of transubstantiation difficult for them.

The parish priest who officiated, a good friend of Doris, was a charming Irishman toward the end of his career. He had a huge curiosity about all things human, an utterly captivating gift of the gab and a very lively wit. One evening when Jacob had come to pick up Sandy and was waiting for her, after a presentation to St. Bernadette parents, Father Heaney had come up to him and whispered, "Are you that woman Sandra's husband?" When Jacob acknowledged his status , the priest whispered again: "It must be sheer hell for you at home; she's VERY clever."

In his homily, Heaney told of how, as a bible reading lad in Ireland , he had loved Frankie Laine's recording of "Jezebel." A different form of the biblical story. He went on to speak not only specifically and glowingly of Doris's long career, but mentioned how women who served the church , especially nuns, had too often not received, and perhaps were still not receiving, the credit and recognition they merited. Jacob, who always found it hard to turn off his skeptical lawyer's mind, wondered if Father would have been as bold if the Archbishop were present. He dismissed the doubt, deciding that Heaney was so authentic a person that he might well have spoken just the same.

After the mass Doris was once again positioned to give and receive enthusiastic hugs and kisses. Yet, there seemed to be a holding back too. Perhaps she was just being nunly—maybe even a nun celebrating her Jubilee should be reserved, restrained, undemonstrative. She seemed more thoughtful than exuberant.

Most of those who'd been at the mass proceeded to the St. Bernadette gym. A modest, yet abundant, buffet had been set up. The tables at which the guests were to sit, while consuming and quaffing, had place cards. Jacob and "Sandra" had been put with some of the St. Bernadette teachers with whom Sandy had worked and their husbands, (and their children, too, if they were younger teachers.) But everyone was free to stroll about before, after, or, even , while, eating and could speak to anyone and everyone. Many did.

And there were photographs, all along the walls, at eye level, of Sister Doris at various points in her life and career. As a very small girl. A grade—schooler. With her parents when she had entered the order. With other novitiates. With her first second grade class. With a whole crowd of children who were gazing at, and reaching for, her admiringly and with the pure love of innocence. As principal of the school in Alabama. With the Archbishop of this diocese.With former nun colleagues. With the bright—eyed ninety—three year old woman who had been her mother's friend and whom Doris still looked after.

There was music too. An eighth grade St. Bernadette boy had set up all sorts of electronic "mixing" equipment at one end of the gym and was enthusiastically booming out every type of sound---from the soulful ballads of the thirties and forties to the very latest in heavy and heavier metal vibes. People had just about succeeded in accommodating this constant din into the background of conversation and joyous exclamations when a new surprise materialized. Suddenly a few of the nuns took to the floor and started dancing to the vigorous beat. A few with each other and some just alone, soloing. Another minute or two and two youngish priests joined in. Then Doris went in too. Some of the nuns extended hands beseeching onlookers to participate also. And some, who weren't too busybeing slack jawed and gaping in amazement, did.A young Hispanic man, Hispanics were an increasing part of the parish, cut a very stylish, impressive rug. Jacob was specifically urged to join but demurred. They already knew he was an uptight stick—in—the—mud lawyer, but they forgave him. Sandy's husband was Jake, as it were, by them.

The dancing was the undeniable high spot. After it was over the well-wishers gradually, quite slowly, began to thin out. The Myersons, whispering as discreetly as possible to each other, agreed that after a few more people left it would be acceptable for them to head out too. Soon it was, indeed, time. More kissing of Doris and more words of affection, as well as affection itself, expressed. Both ways. Three ways actually.

Back in the car, heading homeward, Jacob, driving with one hand, briefly caressed Sandy's left hand. That didn't rouse her from staring straight ahead, seemingly in thought or reverie. Jacob needed his caressing hand to steer into another lane, but he said, "Doris was her more or less her usual, genial, self, I suppose. But maybe some of it was show rather than really felt. I don't know, I thought she seemed… well, a little sad. Something underlying. Second thoughts about it all? Maybe I'm just standing in her shoes with other feet. Not a life I could imagine living."

"Well, I don't know that she would take a different path. But I'm sure that she regrets that she never had children."

Jacob mulled for about fifteen seconds. "Yes, I suppose so. But, then, 'Jackie Robinson .'"

"'Jackie Robinson'"?

"Yes, she had many children."

"Oh, yes. I guess so. More than most."

Having successfully changed lanes Jacob put his right hand back on Sandy's left and resumed caressing.

STUDENT AND TEACHER

Donald Hirschorn was unremarkable as a professor at a highly prestigious law school. Naturally he was extremely intelligent, intellectually aggressive, aggressive otherwise as well and didn't suffer fools at all gladly. His classroom manner could, at its most benign, be called "edgy" and he more darted than paced as he formulated comments to make to the class after some unlucky soul had been severely peppered by his rat-a-tat questions and had responded less than shiningly. He was a paragon of "tough—mindedness" and panther quick to seize on any soft analysis or imprecise observation a student might desperately blurt when under the pressure of his fierce interrogation.

The courses he taught, "Business Planning" and "Corporate Taxation" befit his style and manner. He was, indeed, all business—and highly practical. Vague mush was sacrilege and absolutel y prohibited. Excoriated if proffered. His students doted on the gems and nuggets he'd throw out and although they feared him almost as much as they respected him his courses were always overflowing with SRO attendees because what one learned was thought so utterly valuable in shaping neophyte legal minds to their ultimate vocation.

If he was tough minded he was going to make his students the same. Or, maybe, just tough. Once he asked the class how a certain case could have been decided the way it was when the line of cases they'd been studying for several weeks suggested evolution toward a decidedly contrary disposition. He called upon student after student to "reconcile" the present case with the similar ones which all pointed exactly the other way. And student after hapless student, in the manner of peons being "Socraticized," spun rationalization after rationalization, some mightily elaborate, of why the case in question really meshed consistently with the former ones which seemed so contradictory. After each attempt,however extravagant or feeble, Hirschorn would skewer the inept reasoning of the victim and irrefutably demonstrate how there remained a flagrant and irreconcilable conflict.

"How can this be? How can this case have been decided as it was in the face of the clear line that had developed precisely au contraire? How can they be reconciled? What is the key? Who has the key?" After about the sixth student he called on had shown himself to be bereft of the key, Hirschorn modulated his voice and finally remarked in his unmistakably New England accent, which some thought a trifle affected, notwithstanding he'd been born in Boston and lived there all his life, "It's easy."

He stopped and paused pregnantly, as though ensuring that every other breath in the classroom was bated in anticipation of the great revelation. "Thah feex waaas een" he boomed with triumphalism flooding his voice. "Judge Manton, who, as you know, wrote the opiniuon, those of you who read that tripe, was convicted of accepting a $10,000 bribe , nice money in those days, for deciding the inconceivable way he did." After the silence of assimilation, the class roared. Hirschorn had brough the house down, just as he'd designed.

Another of Bob Mendel's favorite Hirschorn moments came in a discussion of whether a Federal statute was a legitimate exercise of Congressional power under the so—called "Commerce Clause" of the Constitution. An aggressive sounding student had the temerity to assert that the law was too distant in its alleged relation to inter-state commerce to be a valid expression of Congressional will under that constitutional authorization. He argued, vociferously, that not EVERYthing could be said to be related to interstate commerce—that, too often, an over—the—shoulder association was found, after the fact, as a means to justify legislation that Congress wanted to enact as a matter of what it felt was sound social policy.

Hirschorn parried with some formal legal analysis embedded in prior and historical decisions. However, the callow skeptic persisted and continued his passionate assault, essentially undismayed. Hirschorn then allowed these fulminations to peter into gradual silence and, finally, looking directly at his audacious adversary, said in, for him, subdued, even tones: "Why Mr.Jorgensen—that jacket you're wearing, that pen you're using to take notes, the cereal you ate for breakfast this morning---why you're nothing but interstate commerce." The metaphorical house of the lecture hall fell again, with Bob Mendel amongst the heartiest of laughers. Students seemed to be especially enthusiastic in such a response when it was at the expense of one of their fellows. Probably somewhat out of deep relief that someone else was the butt this time. Although, but for the grace of Hirschorn….

Mendel respected, perhaps liked, Hirschorn's toughness—verging on brusque viciousness. He defended him to detractors, of which there were many. One was Mendel's roommate, Barry Sansome. He didn't even take Hirschorn's course, since he tended toward the less nitty—gritty subjects, like English Legal History and Jurisprudence, whenever possible. The fewer numbers the better. But he'd heard plenty about Hirschorn "the legend," as in the sort of classroom episodes where a student was skewered, roasted and spit out. Sansome contended that Hirschorn was basically denigratory, indeed insulting, to young fellow professionals, i.e. his students.

"What's the use of keeping everyone on edge that way all the time? Hoping they won't be the next sacrificial lamb on the altar of his cruel sense of what he thinks humor is. It just impedes learning. Instead of concentrating on the material, trying to understand it fully, you sit there hoping he won't call on you as his next victim."

"Oh, come on," Mendel replied." He's just preparing us for the kind of give and take we're actually going to have to give and take out there in the, you know, real world. No one is going to take it easy on you on Wall Street or in the Beltway because you're a good—hearted humanist."

Sansome was in to it now. "Well, part of the reason Wall Street and the Beltway are as rough and tumble, as jungle—like as they are, is because people like Hirschorn keep perpetuating those kinds of attitudes as acceptable. Desirable, even. I'm inclined to believe that he really likes that stuff, that he's a bit of the thug himself. In other words he may not just be teaching you self—defense, so to speak, but he may actually be delighted to show you the glories of a take—no—prisoners offense. The harder you hit, the harder they fall, the more you get."

This caused Mendel to reflect for a moment, but he wasn't daunted for long. "Chicken or egg, who knows. But the fork in the road has been closed. Hirschorn's way is the way it is, the way it's going to be. The jungle won't be cleared and smoothed to a picturesque scene by letting the animals of human nature run all over you. Not all the good will and best intentions in the world is going to tame those beasts. So, frankly, if you're not prepared to live in that jungle, prepared by people like Hirschhorn who've actually lived and struggled in it, you're going to get the short end. Maybe a very short end. He, at least, tries to give you a fighting chance."

"Yup, he sure gives you fighting," Sansome retorted, just the slightest bit heatedly. (They'd had this discussion too many times to get freshly worked up.) "But if someone doesn't stop fighting, or try to stop the fighting, it will persist. By inertia. Newton's first law. A body traveling in a straight line will continue to do so unless acted on by some outside force. Or something like that. There'll always be fighting and brutality unless there's intervention. Ethics completely out the window, devil take not only the hindmost, but just about anyone, and everyone, who isn't right at, or really damn close to, the front, the top, whatever."

"Maybe so, but I don't want to be the one who is the sacrificial lamb on the altar of someone else's skullduggery, or triumphant success by stealth or deception. And even if there were others who romantically sacrificed themselves—you know what, that wouldn't calm the jungle creatures. Those innocent, oh so well—meaning idealists, would just be disdainfully exploited by the ruthless, avaricious ivory hunters. In short, they'd be looked upon, and played for, abject fools. 'You want to be a schmuck and make it easy for us. O.K., thanks sucker. We'll take all you give and then we'll go on and do the same with some other starry—eyed sucker/loser.' You think they'd be impressed by such idealism as some sort of *transformative* example. Don't make me laugh more uproariously than they would.They'd just thank the devil in heaven for throwing down this kind of manna."

"The continual endorsement of brutality just breeds more brutality. No question there.Wouldn't you aggressivetypes just like to relax a tad from the need to always be brutally vigilant or vigilantly brutal. Just once in a while? Aren't you tired yet? I don't know, maybe brutality could be eased off gradually;small incremental degrees, so everyone could keep on being pretty hard--nosed–just a little less so,a little more less so, as time goes by. Isn't that the way things always progress,more or less? More or less, but forward. And,yes, I do believein progress.Social Security,Unemployment Insurance, Workmen's Compensation,Medicare, and all the rest of it.That's progress.Big time! It seems lkie a lot of folks oppose such things until they,themselves, need them."

"Not everyone caves in on logical abstractions out of personal, selfish needs. There are plenty of people who are willing to die by the sword, if they've lived by it."

"Why would anyone want to die, or why should they, if they didn't have to? If help helps why not accept it? I think the kind of progress I mentioned has happened because in the brutishness of the real world, as

Hobbes might have had it, it turns out that most people do need help, from time to time, of one sort or another and that they truly welcome it when the time comes. Anyway, Gandhi, once wrote that 'To argue that what has not occurred in history shall not occur at all is to argue disbelief in the dignity of man.' I guess I believe in the essential, or, at least, the eventual, dignity of man."

"Well, you keep on believing that. You're a sweet guy," Mendel decelerated resignedly, or was it self—satisfiedly. But keep your eyes open to make sure that you don't get gouged, taken and ripped off, by one of those jungle animals who doesn't know how dignified and cooperatively he's supposed to act."

As Hirschorn's course proceeded Mendel seemed to appreciate him, lionize the man, more and more. The teacher's logic and analytical sharpness grew finer and finer.Many a bumbling student was intellectually shaved, if not completely sliced and diced by it. Mendel, almost involuntarily, like a reflex, would periodically express his growing admiration and respect for Hirschorn to Sansome, often instigating one of their debates about pedagogy, the safety net and human nature in general. Sometimes the battle was chiefly confined to one of these pivots, other times it involved another, or all of them. But the sparring almost invariably was along familiar, repetitious lines. They were almost like a married couple. The same argument, the same points, over and over again. Yet the passion each had for his own position did not wane. No convincing of the other was occurring, but each seemed to harden and become more enthusiastic about where he had started from. Each was a whet for the other and each became increasingly self—righteous.

One day when Hirschorn called on a student to analyze a particular aspect of a case, the young man started out in ringing, what in times past might have been called stentorian, tones. Unfortunately what he actually said was painfully obvious, very simplistic and highly redundant of what Hirschorn had said in just introducing the case for discussion. After the booming voice had stopped reciting what was apparent to all Hirschorn commented "And the sun rises in the East" and instantly called upon another student to proceed. The stentorian orator stared down with great intensity at his book, without seeing anything, as the crimson spread completely over his face.

Sansome heard about this incident from another friend who was taking Hirschorn's course. He attacked Mendel about it: "Why does he have to do that?" he spiritedly queried. "Why not just lead him into coming to grips with the real problems of the case better than he had. Just show him, by the much lauded, supposedly ubiquitous, Socratic method, a more fruitful line of analysis. "

"Because," Mendel replied, "as Hirschorn said, rebuking another asinine student comment, a few days ago, 'Is that the kind of stupid thing you're going to tell the senior partner when he asks you a question?' What's the point in stringing along obtuseness and pretending it's not. In the real life world of big—time lawyering there'll be no suffering of fools gladly. So why tolerate and indulge outright foolishness." And they were off.

In the last weeks of the course, Hirschorn asked one of the acolytes how she would have argued the plaintiff's position in a certain case. She advanced a rather imaginative approach which seemed plausible to many of her classmates. But the guru was quick to point out how her suggestion, while seemingly meeting technical requirements, actually endorsed a sham transaction and , therefore, was not likely to pass IRS muster. Rather than ruefully or resignedly seeing the light, she tried again with another way of going at the problem. She projected this idea very articulately with a good deal of vitality and again had a good part of the class believing that she had come up with something. Hirschorn peered at her, but not too piercingly. He seemed to be grounded in a previous era of classroom mores so that he usually "took it easier" on the women in the class than he did on the males. After he was through peering, he said, almost deferentially, "Well, Ms. Vitti, you know, you can wrap it up in cellophane and it looks prettier, but you can still see right through it." Despite his seeming gentility the class roared pretty loudly—yet again. And Ms. Vitti, although she did it much more prettily, certainly blushed no less extensively than Mr. Stentorian Voice.

Sansome was told about this incident as well by his in—class informant. Another illustration of Hirschorn's gratuitous slaughtering of egos—even if, this time, modified a bit out of "courtliness." Further evidence by which to prove to roomie Bob M. how counter—productively brusque Hirschhorn was. But Sansome had also heard something else through the Hirschorn grapevine. "Stories" circulate amongst students about their teachers, some true, many not, and Hirschorn seemed the subject of a considerable share of them.

"Maybe Hirschorn seems to take it easier on women because of his past," Sansome said to Mendel.

"His past?"

"They say that he loved a young woman when he, himself, was in law school, but that he wasn't successful in his pursuit."

"I have a feeling that that nugget doesn't surprise you."

"Well, that just might be.Although he might have been different then. Or different then and now, personally, as opposed to professionally. Anyway, she broke his heart and he lost interest in women. Other women that is.He decided he would wait for her. It took fourteen years, but she divorced her husband and Hirschorn tried again. Bingo! This time he made it. He's been married to her for twelve years now ."

"Maybe, maybe not," Mendel replied. "You know how we students like to make up apochrypha about these mentors on whom we fixate so much."

"In this case," Sansome retorted,"on whom you fixate so much."

"Well, I'll tell you—fixate or not,the stuff in that course is getting really hairy as we come down the stretch here. There's less than two weeks to go and I don't have a really comfortable feel about the material. It is a truth universally acknowledged, as Jane Austenwrote, that it would not be good to fail to graduate in a few weeks because I failed Hirschorn's course."

'Oh, come on. You're not going to go anywhere near failing the class. It can't be *that* hard. And, anyway, you're good at that sort of stuff."

"I may be o.k. at it, but his standards are impossible and the material is very, very involved and complex. I'd better start putting it, and myself, together here. Maybe we can curtail our debating society about Hirshchorn, and all the other ills of the world, so I can spend more time on studying."

"Far be it from me to stand in the way of a serious student of the law," Sansome acquiesced.

In point of fact, Mendel did step up his studying of that course and found himself putting in three and four hours a night on reviewing it alone. He knew he was sacrificing to some extent in his four other courses but he thought that he could compensate in them in ways he wouldn't be able to in Hirschorn's course. No cutting, none, of corners there. He followed every single thread that Hirschorn had raised, at least according to his class notes, until he felt he knew, reasonably, where each ultimately led. He outlined, summarized and synthesized until his command of the material became greater and greater, sharper and sharper. By a few days before the exam he had satisfied himself that he was in control. Solid control. Just as Hirschorn would want.

As with almost all of the exams, it was three hours, four essay questions. A lot of thinking and writing in forty—five minutes. Four times. Mendel liked to proceed question by question—answering the first before going on to the second, and so on, unlike many students who preferred to look over the entire test, first, and start writing on the question with which they felt most comfortable, then go to the one they thought they knew next best, etc. Mendel, early in law school, had determined that for him this second method might be unduly anxiety—producing. Since if you were to feel insecure with all, or even three of the questions you could become instantly demoralized , not to mention panicky.

So, he read the first question and started to mentally organize his approach. It was a knottier problem than he might have expected, even from Hirschorn, but he spotted some areas on which he thought he could get some purchase and write something intelligible, if not overly incisive by Hirschorn's standards. With only about thirty—five minutes, or less, to actually write each essay, after reading and trying to analyze a question, there wasn't all that much a student could get down about any one question anyway. He grappled and wrote, deleted and revised, reconsidered and concluded. He indicated what seemed like some, at least, of the major issues embedded in the problem and tried to suggest some tolerable resolution of the conundrums they intimated. It hadn't gone as smoothly as he would have liked, but he thought he'd done creditably enough to keep Hirschorn from getting irritated and grouchy. He went a bit over the time he should have taken on that initial question, but that usually happened on these exams. It took a while to get fully warmed—up.Just as in athletics, many times.

He read the second question, but realized he didn't really understand it. The fact pattern presented seemed vaguely reminiscent of some of the scenarios they'd discussed in class, but he couldn't get a grasp on what the "issues" involved were. Where were the "problems" that Hirschorn would want discussed in the characteristic on-the-one-hand, on-the-other-hand, on- the- third- hand fashion? Mendel urged himself to remain steady and calm. This kind of block had happened in the past and he'd recovered by going on to the next question(s) and leaving the thorny one for last. By that time, inevitably, it seemed to have resolved itself into something he could deal with adequately, or better.

So, telling himself not to worry, he moved to the third question. But here it was as though he were being addressed in a foreign language in which he just barely recognized, quite dimly, some words and phrases. Buzz words which should have instigated at least the beginning of a response from him only produced an increasingly desperate blackness. Blankness and bleakness too. He started to sweat and image a scene where he was informing his parents that he would not be graduating with his class. Admonishing himself to concentrate, he decided that what sometimes happened once could happen on two questions and he decided he would answer the fourth question and, after dispatching that, would return to the two miscreants .

But his confidence had seeped away and as he tried to read the last one he couldn't come close to comprehending what was actually there, much less what Hirschorn might be searching for in response. The sweating increased to a general dampness. He felt he was practically, literally, drowning in ignominy. He tried to clear his head and come at the second question anew. But whatever he did he couldn't allay the panic and as he read the question again he felt he was mentally striking out wildly for something, *anything*,regardless of pertinence, to write down.

Hirschorn had drubbed him. He would fail the course. He would not graduate. His parents would be flabbergasted. There was nothing to be done. At least nothing he could do.

He could only think of confessing. While the exams were proctored by graduate students, young instructors in the college, anyone who knew his way around academic exams and needed a few extra bucks, Mendel suddenly remembered that he'd once read, in one of the law school's publications, that the prof whose test was being administered was supposed to be in his offices during the exam should any "questions" arise which the proctor felt at a loss to answer. Well he had some questions—e.g. what the hell are the questions you asked about? What do they have to do with the course? What do they mean? What are they questioning? He was in extremis. He needed to talk to someone. Why not the man himself, the source of his peril.

He left the room, as if in need of the Men's Room, and headed for the third floor where the faculty offices were. Looking for Hirschorn's office he passed some open doors and espied some other teachers whose courses he'd had. Some were behind desks, some pacing, hands behind backs, some peering out windows in reflective poses. Some doors were closed and when he came to Hirschorn's office that one was too. His despair deepened. Maybe Hirschorn wasn't there, notwithstanding the school "rule" mandating he should be. But three quick, urgent raps on the door were answered with an impatient sounding "Come in."

Mendel thankfully opened the door to find the professor in a multi—colored, short sleeved sport shirt, behind his desk. Strewn on its broad surface were many open case report volumes and various scribbled/doodled upon legal pads. Hirschorn looked up, took Mendel in, registered a surprised expression but, finally, curiosity.

Mendel blurted, "Sir, I'm in your Business Planning course….."

"Yes, I know. I've seen you there and, if I'm not mistaken, we've even had a bit of chit—chat about the cases there."

"Yes. But I was taking the exam…."

"Correct, and that's where you should be now. So, may I ask, why are you here instead? Is there something unclear about the exam?"

Of course the question was asked with a sharpness which left Mendel under no doubt, whatsoever, that Hirschorn couldn't conceive that anyone could possibly think there was any lack of clarity in the exam he'd constructed.

"Well, uh…. No sir, there wasn't anything unclear. As such , I mean."

"Then if not as such, was there anything unclear in any other way?"

"No, no sir," Mendel quickly answered, feeling the clammy sweat re-forming on his back and in his armpits. "It wasn't that it was unclear… More that I just didn't understand what you wanted, what you were looking for. I don't know, I guess that could be called unclear to me. I don't know what to call it. I'm confused. I just don't know…."

Hirschorn peered at Mendel over eyeglasses which had slid halfway down his nose. It wasn't a bellicose look, but neither was it overtly friendly or inviting. "I only wanted you to write answers to the questions propounded. Isn't that what an exam is supposed to be? Have I become unorthodox or defied conventionality in any way?"

"No sir, I don't think…. I'm sure you haven't." Mendel felt himself utterly floundering in desperation. "The truth of it is, sir, that I studied and prepared, really hard, for this test and I thought I knew the material really well. At least that's how it felt to me, and friends that I studied with saw it the same way. But I got in there today, and after the first question, which I think I did o.k. on, I started having difficulty. I sort of drew a blank with the second question and then I read the other two, and I….well, I got blanker and blanker….If you know what I mean." Mendel shrugged resignedly.

"I think I do know what you mean, even if you don't have a question as such, as you might say."

"The thing of it is, sir, that I would just accept that I screwed up and take my medicine. You know, flunk the course and have my GPA lowered, whatever….. But I need this course to graduate. Without it I won't have the 108 credit hours. I know that that doesn't really make a difference…. That it doesn't have anything to do with the fact that as far as this exam goes I can't produce; just can't cut it."

Hirschorn barely changed the level or intensity of his stare. "I think you may not be as blank as you seem to think you are."

"What do you mean, sir?"

"Well, for example, think of the second question and tell me some of the things that come to mind."

"But that's the trouble, professor; not very many things that are relevant came to mind."

"That's o.k. Just tell me whatever it is that might be relevant that comes to mind."

Mendel dredged up and mumbled some phrases such as "Sub Chapter S Corporation," "goodwill" and "amortized" expenses and dribbled off into silence.

"That's not bad. I bet that if you think about it a little you can link up those concepts to a discussion of the fact situation of question two."

Almost simultaneously with Hirschorn's remark Mendel felt a little more spirited and something did click in about about how referring to Sub Chapter S Corporations might help in analyzing the overall situation described by that question.

Hirschorn glanced at his watch and said, "Time is moving, but let's talk a bit about the last two questions. " He then prodded Mendel similarly and evoked the mention, at least, of some concepts and principles of plausible application.

By the time their colloquy had finished, Mendel had stopped perspiring and felt armed with quite a few points he could write about on the last three questions.

"Sir, I just don't know how to thank you enough. You don't know what this means to me….To my folks…."

"Oh, I think I do have some idea. Why not avoid aovidable disappointments. But," looking at his watch again, "Mr. Mendel, we've consumed about fifteen--twenty minutes . You're going to be very pressed to get through the exam in the time remaining. Let me walk you back and tell the proctor that you confessed to me that you had an abnormally difficult call of nature, which took much more time than you could have imagined it would, and that you should be allowed to write for twenty minutes after 'Time' is called." He, then, briskly rose from his desk chair, in his characteristically energetic and feisty manner, and moved to his office door, while he motioned Mendel to follow him.

Mendel started spewing profuse thanks again, but Hirschorn gave a curt wave of his hand to signal that he should cease and again motioned Mendel to the door. They did not speak as they walked rapidly back to the exam room . When they got there Mendel , with a smile to Hirschorn, hurried to the seat he'd abandoned twenty minutes previously.

As Mendel started writing, Hirschorn instructed the proctor that the student who had just returned was to be given an additional twenty minutes, beyond the four o'clock conclusion of the exam, due to extenuating circumstances to which the professor very briefly alluded.

Mendel wrote furiously, not looking up until the proctor did yell "Time" at exactly four P.M. He kept on writing furiously for the additional twenty minutes until the proctor tapped him on the shoulder and collected his paper.

Once he had resumed answering the questions many ideas came to him in addition to the ones Hirschorn had helped him summon from the place he'd buried them beyond his own retrieval. Ultimately, , he had much more to say and could have written for many more minutes but for the proctor's tapping.

When he thought back upon the test that night he did not know how "smart" or "clever" his answers had come out, particularly from a Hirschornian perspective, but he was confident that he'd thrown down enough material, demonstrated sufficient "proficiency," to have passed. He told Sansome that his graduation was not in doubt. His roommate agreed and commiserated about the ordeal Mendel had been through.

And he was right. He did pass the course. He was officially informed so, a few days prior to graduation, by a communication from the Registrar which contained his final semester's grades as well as all the grades he'd received in the three years. The grade in "Business Planning" was a "D." The only grade that low on the entire transcript. The envelope also contained a handwritten note from Hirschorn.

> "Mr. Mendel,
>
> " Your exam had some decent ideas and approaches, but you did not present them in a well organized, incisively analytical fashion, or with the requisite clarity and cogency.
>
> "I believe that with some reflection you should be able to gain a surer grasp of the materials and principles of the course."
>
> D. Hirschorn"

THE MOTHER

WE KNEW LISA DIDN'T HAVE a husband but not quite why.We kids, whether on our own or through parents' gossip, surreptitiously overheard by us, figured that since it was only a few years after the end of World War II he must have been killed in Europe, or the Pacific, not very long ago. It didn't matter to us. Her sons, the Meadows brothers, Steven, ten--eleven and Freddy eight or nine. were our ball-playing friends. Freddy was the youngest in our group. Because he was smaller than anyone else, Davey, my pal, spontaneously labeled him "Worm."

I, a year or two older than Steve, was a pretty good stickball player in those salad days, (could hit the pink rubber ball over two sewers with the thin broomstick,) and usually wound up being one of the team captains. I loved having Worm on my side because he was such an enthusiastic and, therefore, determined player. He seemed to feel privileged that we bigger, verging on puberty, guys let him play in our games and he sought to show appreciation by always hustling and trying very hard. But he wasn't just all effort. He was fast and hit with a good deal of power for his size. He was also very alert and intelligent with a good "diamond" sense; seemed to know to go to the right places at the right times as a fielder. Steven was a solid player, too; a pesky hitter who often moved runners along, kept a rally going, a la Pee Wee Reese of our beloved Dodgers, and very competent, with a good arm, in the field. But it was Worm I really valued on my team. He was always doing something that helped us win, or come close to it, at least. Almost as much as I liked Bones (Martin) Cohen, another kid who was just a year or so younger than most of us. A slashing batter who seemed to come up with the key hit, at the crucial time,when you really needed it.

In addition to Lisa in her mid—late thirties, the Meadows boys lived with an uncle, Lisa's brother Harvey, also in that age range, who tried to replace their dad, as best he could and their granddad, father of Lisa and Harvey. Mom Lisa and uncle Harvey worked regularly, but granddad was at home with the boys, most of the time These were the years Jackie Robinson was leading the Brooklyn Dodgers to glory in the National league, season after season, aided by other great Negro players like Roy Campanella and Don Newcombe, for whom he'd blazed opportunities. Steven and Worm were as rabid Dodger fans as the rest of us. A group of us would often go to a Sunday doubleheader at the shrine, Ebbets Field. We'd bring our lunches in paper bags, get there in mid-morning, watch every minute of batting practice before the first game started at one and stay until the last out of the second game, often not until the early evening.

Unfortunately, granddad,while also a nominal Dodger fan,was a bigot. He still referred to the black Dodger players as "niggers." This embarrassed Steve and Worm in front of the rest of us raging liberals. (Jackie, from second base, had solved the race relations problem for most Booklynites.) But they wouldn't denounce or criticize him. He was good to them and they loved him. As they loved Uncle Harvey who, on evenings and week-ends,would play catch with them in front of the medium sized apartment house in which they lived. It fronted on the street on which we played our stickball games, but just around the corner, on the commercial avenue, there were stores. Such as a laundry, dry cleaner and tailor, a baby carriage shop, a small grocery store. If we got up a stickball game while they were playing catch with a real baseball, with Uncle Harvey, they wouldn't leave him to join our game. We'd either have to wait until Uncle Harvey went back upstairs or play without them. But sometimes darkness descended before we could get the game going. I could be irritated at their loyalty to Uncle Harvey and their relegation of we other guys to players-in-waiting. We surely couldn't complain to them while Uncle Harvey was there. He beamed a smile frequently and had a very amiable, easygoing manner. But it was mostly for them. He didn't really exchange much with the rest of us An occasional nod, perhaps a lazy, casual toss of the ball, every now and then..

We didn't see Lisa much, but she did appear from time to time.. She would come along, home from work, carrying some groceries while we were in the middle of one of our hotly contested games.Steve and Freddy would waive brightly to her, as she trudged past, but they wouldn't have to leave the game until she called, from the window of their second storey apartment, that dinner was ready. She would waive back to them but rather more weakly than strongly. She was a pretty woman, wholesome girl-next-door open features, with light brown hair that often wasn't completely combed.She walked deliberately, with a slow motion affect, even when she was purposefully heading somewhere. But most of all, she had a resignedly sad look on her face, as though she would never be able to smile with full waatage again. When she did smile it seemed half-hearted, perfunctory, an effortful afterthought. None of us ever articulated it to the others, but, intuitively, I think ,some of us must have felt that she missed the husband she would not see again, forever.

Despite her comeliness, she didn't dress to show it off. Fairly loose fitting blouses of muted colors, wide, rather than anything close to tight, skirts and flat shoes a la loafers or such. But one time I saw her in something else. On the way to an errand for my mom, I just happened to be passing the apartment house in which the Meadows clan lived. It was a school day, but the shroud of a Fall evening had come and a stickball game was no longer a possibility. Nevertheless, in passing the building, I thought of Steve and Worm. I was walking on the side of the street opposite from their building, next to the blank brick back of a catering hall which fronted on the next street , and impulsively looked up at the windows of their apartment. Lisa was visible in profile, through carelessly semi- parted curtains, in a small window which must have been in a bathroom. She seemed to be looking at herself in a mirror. But her hair was all combed, in a style which I'd never seen her wear before. I also took in her bare right shoulder and the fact that she had nothing on top but a white brassiere. I still remember the sight as one of the most stirring of my early pubescent boyhood. She was beautiful, with full breasts challenging the brassiere's restraints. Her right hand was even gently cupping the right breast. I was ashamed at the instant rising of my penis and turned my head away and hurried past. After that, whenever I saw her in the street, in one of her dowdy get ups, I saw right through her clothes to the woman I'd seen by the bathroom window. I occasionally dreamed of that woman, too.Guiltily.

Life had yet another hit in store for her. Through the network of neighborhood gossip, (Lisa must have spoken to somebody,) it eventually filtered down to we inconsequential pre-adolescents that Steve had been diagnosed with some sort of heart ailment. It didn't seem to impair his activities, at least not as far as our ball games, but his face was much too often wan, while Freddy's was ruddy with good health. Lisa drooped even more after this. But she maintained the sometimes angelic half smile.

Although, from time to time, I had nocturnal visions of the woman in the white brassiere, framed by the bathroom window, there were only two occasions on which Lisa and I actually spoke, as differentiated from nodding at each other, smilingly or not, whenever we might pass in the street. The first time may have even been before I responded to her beauty. I think, actually, I was still pre-pubescent.

I had found, just lying in the gutter of the street, outside Steve and Freddy's building, one of the pink rubber balls,("spaldeens" because manufactured by the A.G. Spalding company, which also made the baseballs used in the major leagues,) with which we played our intense stickball games. No one else was around and I just picked it up and began pitching it into one of the chalked boxes, representing the strike zone, on the armory wall, about a hundred yards down from the apartment house. I had been doing this for a few minutes when, with the good peripheral vision I had then, I noticed Lisa emerge from her building and start heading in my direction. She was more or less trudging in her characteristically unanimated fashion. Maybe a little faster than usual. When she had neared close to the box into which I was throwing she crossed the street diagonally, clearly headed toward me. I stopped pitching and waited for her.

Once within speaking distance she quietly said, "I was wondering where you got that ball you are using."

Somewhat unnerved, I responded, "I just found it. It's mine."

"Well, I think it's really Steve's. He lost one just before right outside the house," she explained patiently. "He just couldn't find where it had rolled."

Our guys' credo, in the neighborhood, had always essentially been "Finders-keepers." In my pre-adolescent conception of sovereignty and property ownership the ball was mine.

"But I found this. Isn't it finders-keepers?"

"Well it probably is in a lot of things at a lot of times."

"But not this time,?" I started yielding.

"I was hoping you would give it to me," she said as she held her hand out.. "We're not rich and it does cost a quarter....Steve had just bought it today with this week's allowance...."

She broke off, as though in mid thought and with the very slight, enigmatic smile looked down. But her hand was still outstretched in my direction.

I handed her the ball. She smiled more fully, said "I knew you were a nice boy," and turned to head back to the house. She was still, basically, shuffling.

The other time we spoke was post—brassiere vision. We fellows were all involved in one of our stickball games, Steve and Worm included, when she came down the block, after work, on her defeated way home. Our team was at bat and I was just waiting to hit, due to be the third or fourth one up that inning,so she felt free to beckon to me to come over to the sidewalk once she had drawn abreast. This time as I approached I pubescently assessed her attractiveness. But it was still dicey to do so because she was dressed, as usual, not to allure. The plain white loose fitting blouse, with some sort of brown jacket over it, since Fall was in the air, and a spaciously floating skirt. And the inevitable sliding loafers as well. When I got within speaking distance, taking furtive glances at her chest, she had a kindly, smiling expression. That enigmatic half—smile, as habitual, it seemed, as the shuffle.

"I was just wondering. I hear, as I pass, that you call Fred 'Worm,' sometimes. Why do you do that since his name is Fred?"

"Oh, no reason. Someone just started calling him that. I guess because he's the shortest amongst us. You know he's a few years younger than anyone else….." We don't mean anything by it."

"I know you don't ," she said, broadening her smile."But I did name him Fred and that's what we all call him upstairs. I guess I'd appreciate if you and the others would do the same."

"Oh, yeah, I guess, sure. We didn't mean anything, but … Yeah, sure, I guess so…. We didn't mean anything…." I continued to insist, trying to keep my eyes looking at hers rather than her chest area.

She took no cognizance, that I could tell, of my straying sight lines.

"I know, I know. Don't worry about it. But I would just appreciate it if you would remember, 'Fred.'"

"Yeah, why not. I'll sure try. I think we can." I was trying to modulate how flustered I was but I don't think I succeeded very much.

"I think I can count on you.," she said with one of her most quintessentially Mona Lisa smiles, as she started continuing on her way, now eager to end the conversation.

I told the other guys, except Steve and Freddy, of course, what she'd said about Worm's real name. And we definitely started calling him "Freddy" a lot, with only an occasional "Worm," soon after she spoke to me. I don't know whether Steve and Freddy were aware or thought anything was strange. They certainly didn't remark on it. But gradually the "Worm"s increased again and the "Freddy"s diminished and before too long things were back to normal, with "Worm" this and " Worm" that. "Nice play, worm," "Great hustle worm."

I think it was the last "conversation" I ever had with her . But it wasn't the last time I saw her in an atypical encounter; something other than passing her on the street, coming and going, here and there.

One of the small shops in the neighborhood was owned by a distinctly grim and dour middle-aged, verging on older, man. People called him Morris. He actually lived in the same building, a block up from Steve and Freddy's, in which my family's apartment was located . He rented one of the small studio units, just a living room and kitchen. He kept to himself, as they say, and no one seemed to know much about him. He came and went according to approximately normal 9-5 business hours Monday through Saturday, when the store was open. But he usually closed it from about noon until one, when he would come back to his apartment for lunch.There was a rumor that he was a refugee from the not so long before concluded World War II. Someone said a concentration camp number was seen on his right arm. But he seemed to always be in the same blue gabardine suit, with a long-sleeved white shirt and a tie, too. So the camp number "sighting" was dubious. He was the only one in the store, too. There were no clerks. He didn't seem to have enough business for his dry goods and sewing supplies to justify him being there, either. People gossiped that they hardly ever saw a customer in there. His personality wasn't the inviting type.

Nevertheless, one Saturday, and not because, at least as much as anyone had noticed, business had picked up, I saw Lisa at the cash register as I walked by and reflexively looked in.. It appeared like she'd been hired to ring up sales—maybe it was optimism on Morris's part. More likely just wishful thinking or believing that Lisa would be a customer lure. But whenever I walked by on Saturday's after that Lisa would be sitting on a stool at the register. Morris was often just leaning on one of the counters staring off. But, sometimes he was staring at her, as she read or held a pencil poised over a newspaper. Probably doing the crossword puzzle.

On one Saturday afternoon, maybe just a month or two after Lisa had been hired by Morris, I was heading out of our apartment, bouncing my basketball, on the way to the schoolyard to congregate and compete with my friends Basketball was second only to stickball in our religion.. Walking toward the front entrance to our building I happened to turn my head left to glance down the corridor of ground floor apartments. Just at that moment Lisa and Morris emerged from his apartment. He was turning the key in the door to close it. I looked at my watch and saw that it was just after one, time to re-open Morris's dry goods shop. Lisa was dressed as I'd never seen her before. High heels and stockings, sheath like black skirt and a very tight pale blue sweater which shouted attention to those beautiful breasts. They didn't seem aware of me.Nor did they seem to be saying anything to each other. But after replacing the key in his jacket pocket Morris applied his hand in a soft carress to Lisa's thigh and buttock. I hastened out the door, basketball to chest, before they could turn and see me. They must have heard the front door closing or my running steps, but I didn't look back.

Quite soon after this incident the Dodgers won the World Series, of 1955, the only one the team ever won while in Brooklyn. It was the first time a team had lost the first two games of the Series and gone on to win. The Dodger announcer, Vin Scully, said after the last out, merely, "Ladies and gentlemen, the Brooklyn Dodgers are champions of the world." He later admitted that had he tried to say more his emotions would have seized him into tears. My stickball playing pals and I were exultant and Steve and Fred were amongst the most triumphant. There was many a re-enactment, of key Series moments, in the stickball field streets.

At that time,I was already a senior in high school and soon after, when I went away to college, I lost complete contact with Steve and Freddy who were still at the high school stage. But I did have one more encounter with a Meadows family member.. A year after I graduated law school I was to be married. Just about a week before the ceremony, when I was heading down the stairs to the subway, in the same neighborhood I'd been raised in, having just visited my mom, I spot, coming up the stairs, none other than Fred "Worm" Meadows. We greeted each other and stopped to talk, right in the middle of the stairway, (to some annoyance by other coming and going passengers.) I told Freddy about my impending nuptials and he told me that Steve had gotten an accounting degree and that he, himself, was doing well at Brooklyn College and looking forward to law school, probably Columbia. He also quickly mentioned that his grandfather had died. Probably because of the awkwardness of the stairs situation we didn't talk very long and I didn't have a chance to inquire about how his mom was.

LEADING THE BLIND

I RETIRED FROM PROFESSING LAW, a few years before schedule, when it became unmistakably clear that Anna's illness could no longer be denied, even by her. That didn't help. She died, on that schedule, as we all knew she would. Then I was alone with the depression. But it didn't gradually, or at any other pace, lift. Dr. Olsen suggested that volunteering to do some useful work might help. That was how I started working at the local Lighthouse For The Blind, an hour or two a day, twice a week.

I began by helping people to learn to type on the computer keyboard. That session went for about forty—five minutes and was one of six to eight classes which Lighthouse "clients" would attend in a normal day. They would have a multi—month training period, mostly in living skills, such as how to get around a kitchen or bathroom, designed to prepare an unsighted person, or one with substantially im-paired, or inexorably failing, vision, to function successfully in the "real," outside world.

The typing class didn't seem like a favorite of the students. I didn't sense much enthusiasm or even commitment. It was run by a middle—aged, rather heavy—set, distinctly un—prepossessing woman who, frankly, ignored too much facial hair and didn't seem to notice the stringy, streaked straw on her head, either. She was a paid employee, although not extravagantly so, I'm sure, and didn't seem to have any vision problems herself. Nevertheless, she exuded a sustainedly dour, verging on depressed, affect. She would assign me which client to help on which day. When I couldn't make it on one of my regular days I would call and let her know. But each time she seemed surprised that I would bother to call and she surely didn't respond in any way which suggested that she cared in the slightest if I showed up or not. She would work with clients, too, sometimes going from one to another and leaving some, usually there were only three or four in the room at one time, to "practice on their own."

Maybe it was just defensiveness, stemming from the fact that it became clear, early, that this experience wouldn't be very stimulating for me, myself, but before too long it seemed to me that she very often had me working with the least motivated, most intractable and very likely the most depressed folks. The thought crossed my mind that she may have felt that I was after her job. But I didn't know how to effectively allay such a fear.

Clients would start by learning the keyboard, where various letters were in relation to central placement of the fingers on home keys. So they had to learn to find the central keys, which fingers on which hand corresponded to which letters and, then, how the rest of the alphabet could be reached from that position. After gaining some mastery of this technique a student would be read to and would try to transcribe that material.

The job of "trainers," such as myself, was to read to the "learner" the letters to be struck or the text to be typed. So, in working with a novice, I might call for an entire line of "A"s to be typed—then, perhaps "V"s or "M"s--- whatever the manual I was given suggested. With a student who supposedly had learned how to find the various letters on the keyboard I'd read textual material, (often "Life in These United States" vignettes from that "Reader's Digest" department,) at a pace suitable to the typing speed of that client. Naturally, in both cases, I would "correct" errors made; e.g. "No, you just typed 'I,'" instead of 'g,'" or, "You made a mistake when you typed 'different.' Try it again."

Some of the people, whether out of lack of interest, sheer inability, or considerable, unyielding depression, were pretty much hopeless—at least as typists. A few never even got the location of the letters straightened out and in some cases where the person could actually transcribe from what I read the pace was absolutely glacial, but the errors rife. After I read a sentence, eons would seem to pass before the typist was ready for me to read the next one. And all too often the eons were elongated further, even more unbearably, when I had to point out errors and then wait until they were laboriously corrected.

In the glacial/laborious category I recall, particularly, a very dignified, elegant and elderly African—American man who, was unremittingly lethargic, uninterested and completely lackadaisical. I'd usually try to enage him in a bit of chat, even banter, but no matter how brightly I chirped his responses were almost always taciturnity incarnate, pervasively monosyllabic. Nevertheless, despite his profoundly gloomy mien he was unfailingly courteous to me.

I don't know quite how it happened, but one day, as I persisted in trying to get him to talk a bit, he suddenly, unprompted, launched into the story of how he'd lost his sight. He'd been in the army, he'd left it at "When I was in the army," and had developed cataracts. Or, at least, what a U.S. Army doctor said were cataracts. I decided that the army must have been his career, since a young person, just serving two or three years of required military service, would be unlikely to already have cataracts, an older person's disease. He told me that that they'd operated but that the surgeon, who he said he didn't doubt was trying his best, had botched the job. No claim of racial prejudice, which certainly came to my mind, or anything like that. But that was it—he was blinded. So, the story of a life. One which, it seemed had evolved into a non—life. Or, at the very best, a deeply ravaged one.

This revelation of how his life had been shattered did not suddenly, or ever, change our relationship. Rather immediately he went back to being just as laconic and withdrawn with me as always. He had told me, as it's said in Yiddish, "the Emmus," the very gist of the truth. That was it. That was what was the matter. That's all there was.

I must admit, I also had a very excellent and determined typing student. She was extremely unusual. However, in a way, just because she was so competent and lively she was very short—lived as my student.

She was Venezuelan, had been in this country only a few years, and had developed vision problems quite early in middle age. There was some accent in her English but she was articulate, elegant and dressed flatteringly, although in a businesslike and dignified manner. I would not only read the substance of what she was to type to her, but several times we discussed its substance. No "Life In These United States" extracts for her. I didn't have to tread lightly on calling her on any mistakes she made and I delighted in sometimes instructing her beyond the typing. We had some good discussions and she told me that she wanted to get herself into position to apply for a responsible job in the outside, the real, world.

I no longer remember if I told her, or she otherwise found out, about my professional background. But during one session she spontaneously turned to me and said "You are a very good teacher." That was all. No embellishement after I thanked her. But she had stroked my vanity considerably, perhaps where it's greatest. I don't know that she could have pleased me more had she said, "You know, you are a most attractive man."

I think she was smart and sensitive enough to know that conferring the innocent compliment was, in a way, tantamount to lavishing the more provocative one.

As for such matters, she gave the impression of being rather nice—looking, but I couldn't clearly verify that sense because she wore dark glasses, with way over—sized circular frames, so that too much of her face was covered for beauty evaluation purposes. But I did notice that she was trim, yet unmistakably shapely as well.

She made me look forward to my days at the Lighthouse and to helping her. She awakened me enough so that I wanted to sparkle for her, wanted her to actively like me. By no means just another low response client who had to be endured for the prescribed time and through futile resignation that nothing was being accomplished. However, as suddenly as she'd appeared she was not there on a day she was supposed to be. Without trying to tip too much interest I asked the every-day-is-a-bad-hair-day supervisor whether the South Anerican was ill. No, no she assured, she'd merely transferred to another program which she felt could give her more pertinent training for the type of job she eventually wanted to get. I missed her instantly.

In the room directly across from the one in which I "taught" typing lessons in Braille were given by an unsighted instructor. Justitifiably or not, I grew increasingly bored with the grind of going through the motions with the putative typists and I finally asked the typing lady whether I could spend some of my time learning and, then, teaching Braille. I had cleared it previously with the Braille teacher. She'd assured me that she'd be willing to teach me as she would any other client/student.

I had to be indulged a bit because I made some modest, yet more than inconsiderable, monetary contributions to the Lighthouse. For example, I'd purchased a new blood—sugar measuring device since many of the clients' problems were diabetes related. Also, on a vacation, I'd sought out a hard to find, even for the cab—driver, address in Paris and spoke intense Franglish with a simpatico young woman for many minutes in order to buy a set of Braille learning materials in French, to be shipped back to the Lighthouses's Braille instructor. These would be very useful in teaching the increasing Haitian population she worked with.

I gradually increased the time I spent in the Braille room, correspondingly decreasing my typing involvement. Eventually, even after once evincing pique at being assigned to help a student who had made it abundantly clear to the supervisor that he simply wasn't going to, or couldn't,learn how to type individual letters at the most rudimentary level I diminished my typing efforts to zero. I thought I saw a flicker of hurt in the typing boss's face when I conclusively told her that all my time would be spent in the Braille room. But I justified the decision to myself on grounds of her deviousness in increasingly trying to stick me with the most intractable typing students.

Once I started in the Braille room I felt more obliged than ever to learn it, even though that wasn't necessary as far as heping a client. I could just check in the teacher's manual as to the student's accuracy in decoding first the letters, then the phrases, finally the simple sentences in the text book. But, of course, if you really knew Braille yourself, or even just a bit of it, you could guide the student out of mistakes more intelligently and effectively. For example, "No, you remember, it's the 'B' that has two bumps on the left and one on the right, not the 'D.'" It must be that the more a teacher knows about any subject, the better a teacher of it she or he will be. Also, it just seemed "right" to know Braille if I were to teach it. And, admittedly, learning Braille involved being with the youngish, middle—aged instructor who just happened to fill out snug sweaters very appealingly and who had very softly radiant auburn hair. All that was added to the fact that she was an excellent instructor. Crisp, but also patient. Not to mention that she, herself, could read Braille at a truly awe inspiring pace.

However, even with Braille there were still the student problems. An elderly, diabetic man I taught for several weeks, good—natured and pleasant, seemed to have no aptitude or memory whatsoever for learning Braille. We never got past the first five or six letters of the alphabet and each time I thought he was finally progressing by consolidating some knowledge he dashed my hopes at the very next sessions. If on Tuesday he finally seemed to have some fluency in decoding "A," "B" and "C," inspiring me to start getting "D," "E" and "F," under his belt, by Thursday he'd be back to jumbling almost incoherently with the first three letters, as though he'd just been introduced to them seconds before.

He'd mention problems with neuropathy in his fingers, a loss of feeling and sensation, fairly common amongst diabetics, and this could certainly have contributed to his Braille difficulties. He was easy and pleasant to talk to and we would converse about news events from many years before which we both remembered. But I certainly didn't think that any learning was being accomplished. Whatever bumps he did feel on the Braille letters he surely did not "remember" enough from day to day to enable him to decode. An "A" yesterday became an "F" today. Maybe he even "recalled" configurations, but what felt like two bumps on Tuesday felt like three, or only one, on Thursday. Whatever the cause the result was clear: he was making absolutely no progress in mastering Braille reading.

Finally, after some weeks of going nowhere, I pointed this out to Vicki, the sweater enhancing instructor. I asked whether the situation ought not be reported to an administrator so that he, me too, could be more fruitfully re—assigned. She urged persistence for a while and I complied. But when it became clear that things remained the same, and I told her again, she just shrugged her attractive shoulders and left it at that. So did I.

Some of the students, of course, were better, much better, and there was satisfaction in helping them advance. But, frankly, the best thing about my adventures in Braille was Vicki. She was not only a good teacher but a charming and congenial one. We could talk about things like her husband and two kids, what there was to do on the week—ends and, most of all, about what a "slow" Braille student I was.

Still, as I've mentioned, patience was one of her many virtues so she would good—naturedly sit with me, for at least fifteen—twenty minutes, each day I was there, as I struggled first to decipher all the letters of the alphabet and, then, to read extremely simple sentences constructed from them. Sometimes Vicki would have on the blue sweater which initially attracted me, sometimes a red one in which she looked equally spectacular, occasionally a jumper with a brilliantly white blouse underneath, perhaps slacks with a colorful jersey top. It didn't matter much: she glorified whatever she was wearing. Rather no clothing could detract from her natural, youthful bounce and prettiness. Not overwhelmingly beautiful—just softly, very appealingly, pretty. I deduced, from evidence here and there, that her background was Hispanic, although I don't think I ever found out exactly which nationality. Her English was virtually completely accentless, as well as lively, clear and bantering.

We started enjoying our tutoring sessions, at which we'd sit side by side chatting, between my efforts to decipher Braille sentences, more and more. She had an intensely clean, fresh smell too. After a few weeks I actually developed some fluency. I started being able to decode one simple sentence after another, to the point of being able to read very simple paragraphs. Nothing, naturally, like Vicki, who could read the most varied Braille material, technical, literary, humorous, at a pace which an average to good normal, sighted, reader would maintain with non—Braille text. She told me that once she'd stopped denying her increasing vision loss, and had faced the fact that she was steadily going blind, she had tackled Brail,le with utter determination and had made very rapid progress.

At just about the time that Vicki revealed this about her Braille evolution a new client, for both typing and Braille, showed up. She was a late teen—age, early twentyish woman. She brimmed with elan and joie de vivre but knew that she was gradually, irreversibly, losing her sight.

Sometimes at night, before falling asleep, or when not able to get back to sleep after awakening, I would think of this buoyant young person and, also, of the Vicki of fifteen, twenty years ago, who also finally realized that her youth and part of her life were being purloined. I would think of their courage and indomitability, how they insisted on sucking from life's nectar all that they could still taste. I would cry for them. And, perhaps, I surmised,with them. Each in his own bed, weeping.

One day Vicki was tutoring me. We were alone in the room, she at my left, I to her right as we bent over the text. Almost imperceptibly she shifted right in her chair, coming, bit by bit, closer and closer to me. Soon I sensed her right breast against my upper left arm and shoulder. Pleasant as the sensation was it acutely disconcerted me.However, since I was certain that the insistent pressure, was mere insouciant absent—mindedness, emblematic of how conscientiously and intensely she taught, I sidled slightly to the right in my own chair,putting some space between my arm and her breast.

There flashed into memory a scene of my tutoring a girl in geometry, in the high school library, after the final period, when much the same thing had happened. We both had the same Math teacher and she asked that I help my fellow student. This tutee had very prominent breasts and had repeated such pressure on several separate occasions. But each time I withdrew. She gradually lost enthusiasm for the endeavor and started concentrating on geometry. She then learned rapidly, said I taught it much better than our teacher and that she wouldn't have needed tutoring at all if I were the teacher.

Belying my innocent, absent—minded, totally involved theory, Vicki moved correspondingly rightward in her seat, a minute or two after I had. Then sure enough, I again felt the pressure of her full breast against my left arm. Now I was surely old enough to realize that another effort to act as though nothing had happened would not mean it hadn't. A gesture, now unequivocal in import, had been made. This time I kept my arm where it was, deciding to enjoy the treat it was being given. Things stayed this way for the few minutes of the Braille lesson which remained prior to the period ending bell ringing. We said our normal good—byes and "See 'ya on Thursday"s and I left. Deep in thought, walking on air and also reverie and hope.

Two days later we resumed the decoding, from exactly where we'd left off, as though nothing but the study of rudimentary Braille had occurred at the previous tutoring session. But, only a few minutes after we'd begun, Vicki shifted rightward in her chair and, as we both leaned over the text book, pushed her firm, yet pliable breast directly against my upper arm. Trying to feign as much nonchalance as possible, I nudged back with my arm and she pushed a little harder still. We were again alone in the room although its door was open and the typing room, its door open as well, and with some students in there, was directly across the hall. I was pretty excited, especially for a mature man, though through all the mutual pressure, as though nothing else was going on, Vicki and I persisted, as teacher and student, in advancing through the Braille book.

But after some minutes of this I impulsively turned in my chair and moderately pecked her right cheek. It was so sweet. She offered her mouth and we kissed, almost chastely, not quite, and I very lightly fondled those so shapely, appealing breasts. She, gently, fumblingly, brushed my left hand away from her right breast and mumbled, barely audibly, "Back to the lesson, the Braille one I mean."

That was it for that day. Again we said our usual good—byes. But this time I, like the most callow school boy, could hardly think of anything but Vicki's allure and how she might try to project it at our next meeting. How "far" it might take us.

I was eager, putting it mildly, to show up at the next session and arrived fifteen minutes early. But Vicki was talking to a young client, mid—twenties or so, who had a pronounced Hispanic accent. I busied myself a bit in the typing room and by just walking the corridors until the period ending bell rang. Once I saw the client coming out of Vicki's room I entered, moving by him.

After I identified myself, Vicki gave me a very warm smile and said, "Let's see who shows up today; I don't think there'll be many. Maybe no one—when I was downstairs before, near the office, I heard that the flu is going around and there are quite a few absences."

"Oh, is that so," I softly replied.

We waited for about five or ten minutes chatting about Vicki's family. She and her husband were in a debate about whether to buy a new house. They were looking at possibilities while the debate flourished. The younger child was in one corner about moving, the older one in the other. Vicki was conflicted. She didn't want to move for the obvious reason of how difficult it would be for her to adjust to a new physical set—up. Yet she sort of agreed with her husband that the family could use more room and a school district with better opportunities for the kids. Her husband appreciated how hard it would be for Vicki, but....

When it became clear that no Braille students would be coming into the room for instruction during that period Vicki and I pulled up our chairs and I started the usual decoding under her monitoring. We went like this for five or ten minutes, but them Vicki turned at forty—five degrees to me and placed her right hand flat on my left thigh. She started to curl a grip on it, slightly yet firmly. I brushed her arm with my fingers and lightly ran the fingers of my other hand over her left breast. She took that hand away and we sought each other's lips, my closed eyes equally blind, and kissed gently, briefly and supremely tenderly.

Vicki gradually withdrew, saying, "Let's try the next paragraph."

We did do more Braille for a few more minutes until I put my left hand on her right thigh and she brought her lips to mine for a longer, harder, almost rough kiss. Then it was Braille again, until, ten minutes before the period would end, the young man with the heavy accent came in, feeling his way through the door frame, and asked Vicki whether she'd be going to the cafeteria for lunch soon. She told him to wait for her and she and I proceeded to finish up the page we'd been working on until the bell rang. Then, as usual, I headed for home, feeling virtuous about having served but, also, exhilarated.

The next few times I went to the Lighthouse I arrived early, usually to find Vicki teaching clients or just chatting with someone like the young man with the decided accent. But whenever we were alone we would engage in the kissing, squeezing, fondling behavior we'd already dared. But each time there was at least a slight extension over the previous episode: an extra pressure or probing to a kiss, a deeper squeeze of a thigh, my hands hefting her perfect breasts a little longer. When we worked together but others were in the room, we were limited to seemingly fortuitous touching of arms and shoulders with hands,or light brushings of thighs, knees, etc.

I didn't really know what was happening in any ultimate, meaningful sense and was too enthralled, as well as too confused, to try to rationally sort much out. I did think a lot about what MIGHT happen at each succeeding session and started mentally toying with ideas of meeting Vicki somewhere outside the Lighthouse. But then I'd think of her family, which

I felt like I'd gotten to know, and felt sharp guilt. I would try to rationalize and convince myself that our minimal "frolicking" was the proverbial "nothing" and wouldn't have lasting, or even any, impact on Vicki's life with her family. But then I'd fantasize about proceeding beyond mild petting with her….

In the meantime, I looked forward to the next Braille session as soon as one had ended. I continued about my normal and regular activities, but they became more or less perfunctory events which I mechanically walked through until it was time to see Vicki again.

This went on for a few weeks, at least. But, finally, I decided not to see Vicki any more.

I was so anxious to be with Vicki one day that I came very early . Intending to surprise her, I silently entered her room.She was pinned to the wall by the young man with the accent. His body was pressed against hers at just about every conceivable surface and their mouths mutually, almost rapaciously explored, with all the usual accompanying sighs and moans.

I withdrew just as silently as I'd entered. I never saw Vicki again. I never even went to the Lighthouse again.

But I kept on making donations and, so, continued to receive the Lighthouse's quarterly newsletter. About a year later, I noticed, in the small section headed "Employee Doings," that Vicki had gotten married to "former Lighthouse client Emilio Jimenez." I had no way of knowing conclusively, but I was pretty certain it had to be the young stud with the thick accent. But it didn't really matter who, specifically. Presumably Vicki had divorced from the husband she had when I met her. I wondered whether she would have divorced him for me. I thought, and think, not.

FRIENDS AND COUPLES

CAROL AND MIRIAM HAD BEEN friends since high school. They met on the cheerleaders squad, the crème of Jackson High School female society. But Miriam was only cheerleader pretty. Carol was drop—dead beautiful. That was always the word people couldn't help using when talking about her. Girls maybe even more than guys. Yet that adjective wasn't really adequate. Exquisite, absolutely perfect features set off by wavy, auburn hair. Throw in a curvaceous, yet elegant figure, certainly broad enough where a broad should be broad, and plenty of sex appeal was generated. But that was too crude and simplistic. It was more "allure." Clean, wholesome, yet irresistibly siren—like. Breathtaking, as they say. As a teen-ager she had inflamed even high school teachers and college professors. Some would ask that she come to their offices, presumably to discuss a paper or exam. Some, whether consciously or not, even hoped against hope. Such aspirations were always in vain. And, of course, just about every boy, not only those on teams Miriam and Carol cheered on, but in the whole school of three thousand students, fantasized about going out--and more (even though there was none)-- with Carol. No one would have turned down a date with Miriam either, and some did ask for one, but the level of motivation kindled by adolescent desire wasn't the same. Nowhere near it.

Both Carol and Miriam were aware of this state of affairs, but neither was overly impressed. Carol appreciated her great popularity, but she was iconoclastic in ways and knew that she was not a goddess, the role so many of the boys seemed to confer on her. No one could have fulfilled the fantasies they wove about her. Miriam appreciated Carol for the person she was. Someone , in spite of it all, rather unassuming, with good decent values , who was a supportive, non—competitive, simpatico friend. The only qualm Miriam had about their relationship was that when she went places with Carol, for example the beach, where boys might approach, or try to "pick them up," most of the focus was on Carol and Miriam, despite her own considerable attractiveness, had to be mostly content with the after-thought category. But she had learned to live with that especially since Carol was not at all snobbish or obnoxious about the situation. Also, if Miriam went some weeks without a date Carol would often try to set her up with an attractive boy. Perhaps one of her own "rejects."

In fact, Carol would have to give Miriam pep talks about dating. Carol was normally anxious, sometimes skittish, for a teen-ager, but Miriam was unusually, flagrantly, nervous. On more than one occasion when Carol had "fixed—up" Miriam, as the parlance then went, Miriam would call Carol the day before, or even with just a few hours to go, and complain that she was on the verge of throwing up and much too nervous to actually go through with the date. Carol would then, with a maturity somewhat greater than her mere years had earned, talk Miriam down from the high—anxiety precipice and into enough confidence to be able to function.

More surprisingly, much more, Miriam would actually get Carol a date occasionally. For example, there was the time, when about to be seniors in college, Miriam and Carol had taken a summer week—end drive to a picturesque area in the Adirondack Mountains . Carol had slept in, a bit, on Saturday morning while Miriam, the seemingly more energetic because the more anxious, swam first and sunbathed afterward around the motel pool. Two young men, also in their very early twenties, were lounging at the pool as well and one started talking to Miriam who was sufficiently comely in a bathing suit despite a meager bust line. It turned out that boy, as well as girl, was from Manhattan and he asked her for her telephone number. During the following week he called Miriam and asked whether she wanted to go out. She accepted and said that she had a friend who was gorgeous, if he had a friend who would be interested. They double dated, twice actually, before both Carol and Miriam tired of the attentions of such callow fellows. Miriam was majoring in Art History at Barnard and aspired to a "relationship" with someone "sophisticated." Or, at least, a doctor, the standard objective of an attractive Jewish girl. She was the daughter of older parents who had cherished her and doted on her as no one but an only child, especially a daughter, can experience those phenomena.

Early in her senior year, Carol had broken up with a boy friend of a month or two and was in a dry spell. She didn't even seem to care much about meeting new people or having conventional dates. She was almost twenty-one and rather fatigued by the tedium of date after date, with a succession of immature males who had little , if anything, stimulating to say, (Carol was an English Literature major, at NYU, particularly interest in both twentieth century American literature and Shakespeare,) but were most intent on perfecting their groping "technique." It all got so tiresome—fighting off a person with whom, to start with, she really didn't want to spend time. Miriam had gone out a few times with a pre—med student at Columbia, Bob Schwartz. She wasn't crazy about him but he did keep asking her out and he had applied to medical schools at places like Harvard, Bellevue --- NYU, Columbia's Pysicians and Surgeons and Cornell Medical College ,on Manhattan's upper East side. On their third or fourth date she revealed that she had a very beautiful, very smart friend who had been moping around for a few weeks. Might he have a friend who would want to go out with her? Well, it just happened that during this summer he had worked with a classmate, Stan Dambrodt, a Chemistry major, at a packaging/shipping company. They had been on the midnight, the so--called graveyard, shift together. A lot of loading of trucks.They cut up a great deal but they still got their assigned work done and, then, at 8:00 A.M., each went home and slept a good part of the day so that he could work the graveyard shift, again, that night. But that was only Monday through Friday. On the week—ends, toward the end of the summer, Bob had started going out with Miriam: to movies, art galleries, restaurants—the cornucopia of New York dating sites for the young and educated..

So it eventually transpired that Bob and Miriam and Stan and Carol double—dated. Stan, a serious type, who had not had a rousing social life to that point thought Carol, just as Bob, by way of Miriam's assurances, had described her, superlatively beautiful. And he thought it wonderful, decidedly against all odds with a girl who was that much of an absolute knock—out, far beyond his fantasies even, that she had serious thoughts in her head, not merely frivolous sallies, and could, and seemed to want to,converse intelligently about a variety of subjects.

The double date was a Sunday expedition to Central Park, Manhattan's heart, with a row on the lake the focus of activity. After that , (actually quite a bit before,)and some animal viewing in the zoo, Stan knew that he very much wanted to extend the date and asked Carol if she would like to get an early dinner. She agreed with alacrity and Stan happily asked Bob and Miriam to join them. But Bob, with great seriousness, demurred saying he had some studying to do and Miriam quickly chimed in that she too couldn't make it because she had promised her parents that she would go to dinner with them. Carol didn't know whether that was true or was just the extravagantly punctilious Miriam getting out of the way, making sure that she wouldn't be "interfering." Who knows, Stan thought, maybe Bob and Miriam wanted to go off by themselves. Carol and Stan had a fine time at dinner in the modest Italian restaurant into which they just casually meandered. They hit upon books which they both liked and had fun and laughter in trying to stump each other with trivia questions about such common favorites. A good part of their discussion centered on their mutual admiration for J.D. Salinger, every adolescent and college student's A-list novelist and short story writer at that time.

When Stan dropped Carol off at the apartment she still shared with her parents and younger, junior high school age brother, he didn't want to be in suspense about whether she would go out with him again. He proposed, since they'd had such a good time in Central Park, that they return in four days when there would be a production of "King Lear" in Joseph Papp's "Shakespeare In The Park" series. People lined up for the free tickets for several hours prior to curtain time, but, according to all accounts, of the various and venerable Drama critics of the then multiple New York papers, it was well worth the effort. To Stan's delight, and relief, Carol reacted with enthusiasm. Subdued, lady-like enthusiasm, but with what surely seemed like authentic enthusiasm. She said that she'd heard so much about this series, from friends and friends of friends and would look forward to going. Stan said that maybe they could get another early dinner to fortify themselves for the vigil for tickets and she liked that idea too. Stan was exultant.

On the agreed evening, at the risk of seeming plodding and unimaginative, Stan suggested the same Italian trattoria in which they'd eaten on their first date. Carol approved saying it would be comfortable and allow them to talk quietly. Not long after dinner started Stan presented Carol with a paperback copy of J.D. Salinger's "Nine Short Stories."

"I'm sure you've read this and probably even have your own copy, but I was browsing in a bookstore the other day and came across it and just couldn't resist. If you already have it just give it to a friend who doesn't."

"I actually don't have a copy of this, although I did read some of the stories when they were in the 'New Yorker.' Even if I did I'd want to keep this one."

That comment, oblique as it might have been, made Stan's heart jump pleasantly. More exultation. There was a story in the book, "Laughing Man," which Stan particularly cherished. It was about a young man who was in charge of a group of pre-adolescent boys after school each week—day. He drove a bus by which he transported them to Central Park for about two hours of ice—skating, softball, or lake activities, depending on season. One of his ways of entertaining them, on a continuing basis, was to regale them with a saga he called "Laughing Man" and episodes of which he added, each day, as necessary. In the course of his time in this job,this young man, whom his charges called "Chief," was dating and falling in love with a sparkling young woman. (The now adult narrator of the story refers to her, Mary Hudson, as one of the three unclassifiably great beauties he's[1] seen in his life.) One day the Chief decides to take the boys to Central Park to play softball and asks his beauteous girl friend to join them. He divides the boys into two teams but Mary demands to play as well. Finally the Chief reluctantly finally relents and assigns her to one of the squads. When she comes to bat, after demonstrable impatience, so eager she could hardly wait, she smacks the first pitch solidly and fetchingly legs the hit all the way into a triple. The Chief gazes with delight at her as she stands on third base waiting for play to continue. She notices him looking at her and waves to him. Salinger writes, "Her stickwork aside, she happened to be a girl who knew how to wave to somebody from third base." Stan, an avid Brooklyn Dodger fan, just loved this line. He would even say it to himself occasionally, at various times. It was virtually emblematic of his ideal woman and it always brought him pleasure to marvel at how pitch perfectly Salinger had caught the protagonist's love for the young beauty.

Stan had marked the page on which that line appeared and asked Carol to turn to it. "If you read page 88, there's one line that's particularly great. Or at least I think so. I was wondering if you find something there that you feel is that well written. Or, at least, that you think I think is so good," he finished with a nervous laugh.

"I'll give it a try," Carol remarked as she started reading the page, brow just the slightest bit furrowed. She certainly looked like Mary Hudson to Stan. She stopped after going through only about a third of the page. "I don't know, I mean I can't be sure, of course, but as for me it's got to be

'Her stickwork aside, she happened to be a girl who knew how to wave to somebody from third base.'"

"That's it, exactly!!" Stan exulted again. "You know, you also prefaced it with, 'as for me.' I have a story about that. "

"I'd love to hear it."

"Are you sure? It might be boring."

"I said I would . And I don't think too many things you would say would be boring."

"Well, in that case…." Stan exclaimed, gaining confidence with this terrific young woman.

He told her an anecdote about a French Literature course he'd taken as a sophomore at Columbia. The class had been studying the poems of the nineteenth century master, Charles Baudelaire, and the professor told them of an incident which had occurred in Paris, when he'd been in the army, just after the end of World War II. In uniform he'd gone into a bar and one conversation led to another and the patrons soon discovered that the young American private was a serious student of French literature. Some, both the skeptical and the believers, started quizzing him about French writers and poets throughout the centuries. He told the class that he had been doing quite well until a certain poem was quoted and the interlocutor demanded that he identify the poet. The professor said he had not been able to recall having heard or read the excerpt before. However, it was about the doings of a cat. He did know that Baudelaire was an aficionado of cats. Therefore he answered, "Je ne sais pas, mais, quant a moi, c'est Baudelaire." ("I don't really know, but, as for me, it must be Baudelaire.")This deft deduction occasioned the cultured, and even less cultured, Parisian bar flies to erupt in cheers and "Vive l'Americain!"s. Additonally, the professor told the students, that he was plied with free drinks for the remainder of the afternoon.

"So, you see, 'As for me' has always stuck in my head," Stan finished the anecdote.

"Oh yes, I can see. Although it's not that long that it's been lodged there. Only a year or two."

The production of "King Lear" which they saw that night was brilliantly acted and very stimulating. They had plenty to talk about on the subway ride back to Carol's home. So, it turned out that after just two dates Carol liked Stan quite a bit. More than she had liked any boy, or young man, for a long time. In addition to being nice enough looking, in a dignified, unflashy way, he treated her like a serious person, not just a good—looking toy.He seemed to really want to know just what she thought about this, that and the other. Especially regarding books she particularly liked and respected. It wasn't just Salinger. He was a voracious general reader, history, biography, other fiction, despite having to do that mound of technical reading in the sciences. Stan couldn't believe that a young woman as blazingly attractive as Carol could also be so sensitive, sensible and just plain pleasant. They got to like each other, quite a bit, then very much, very soon. They kept going out and they started going out frequently , almost at every opportunity. They liked touching, feeling and holding each other— also at every opportunity.

Bob and Miriam were not doing nearly as well. Each seemed intent on keeping some distance from the other, rather than trying to get to know the other as well as possible, the way Stan and Carol had. Actually , their date on the double—date on which Stan and Carol first met was their next—to—last. So they were finis just as Stan and Carol started to see each other repeatedly. Bob just found that he didn't want to call Miriam again. She was very nervous, even by the third date, and authentic "communication," much less some affection , seemed long off. Miriam felt basically the same way, but she was disappointed and discouraged. She felt that if Bob had called again she probably would have continued going out with him. Perhaps as long as he continued calling. He was a potential doctor.

As Carol's relationship with Stan matured and ripened into verging on ubiquitous contact Carol was sure to keep Miriam as a close friend. First of all, she tried to get Miriam another boy friend by asking Stan to provide friends who would take Miriam out—whether on double dates or otherwise. Stan did prevail on three or four of his friends to date Miriam , at least once, one twice, but none of those fix—ups really clicked. The common complaint was that Miriam just came across as too "distant," "stand—offish," or, even, in the word of one disappointed swain, "cold." But Carol also would sometimes ask Miriam along when she and Stan were just going out on a casual "date." For example, if they were taking a picnic to the park Carol would ask Miriam to join them. Or even on just an outing to the Metropolitan Museum of Art. Actually, especially on museum outings because of Miriam's art history expertise. Sometimes Miriam would come with them. But many other times when she was asked she felt "burdensome"and didn't want to play the "three's a crowd" role.

But one time the three of them were sitting around the kitchen table in Carol's home playing Scrabble. About half—way through the first game

Stan could have sworn that Miriam, who was looking especially pretty, that night, just very lightly brushed his leg with her own, under the table. It couldn't have been Carol because she was sitting opposite him ,while Miriam was essentially sitting next to him, at a forty—five degree angle, as the three of them were at a rectangular, almost square table. It seemed to Stan that Miriam was also being especially bright and bubbly and directing most of her patter and repartee toward him. And sure enough, just at the conclusion of the second of the two Scrabble games, he was pretty certain that he again felt Miriam's left leg brush his right one, in the most fleeting way. Miriam also kept speaking principally to Stan with just minimal comments and interpolations to Carol. In fact, when Miriam was ready to leave, after the second game, she enthusiastically told Stan how she looked forward to seeing him soon, again, and said "bye" to Carol almost perfunctorily, as an after thought.

After she was gone Stan had a pre—occupied look on his face.

"A penny, maybe even more, for your thoughts, " Miriam commented.

"Oh, it's nothing much, I was just trying to sort something out."

"And what would that be? Can I help?"

"Maybe. But probably not. I mean...."

"Is it a mystery for me to discover. Shall I begin guessing or do you want to give me some clues at least?"

" I don't quite know how to put this. I mean, you know, just how to describe the problem."

"How about just starting."

"O.K., not too long after we started playing tonight I felt Miriam's leg sort of nuzzle mine. It wasn't just like a touching for a mili—second, the way people's legs sometimes accidentally collide under a table. It was more sustained and there was a little back and forth. But, still, I thought maybe it was just an accident. You know , she might have been lost in thought and she was just moving her leg more or less unconsciously."

" That's exactly what it almost certainly was," Carol said brightly and confidently.

"Yeah, well, I might be able to convince myself to go along with that , except that it happened again, later on in the evening, not too long before she was ready to go. And did you notice how she was talking and chirping so much to me and not too much, really hardly at all, to you."

"Oh, Stan, I just can't really believe that Miriam would try to play footsie with my fiancé, in my own house, under a table, where I'm also sitting." Carol had again spoken confidently, but perhaps a shade more ambivalently than previously.

"I'd like to believe that, too, Carol. But I just don't know.... It just doesn't seem like it was an accident or 'innocent'."

"Well, we're not going to definitively know, will we? Best to just forget it, n'est-ce pas?" Carol finally said, trying to sound conclusive.

"I guess we have no choice."

Stan and Carol were married within a year. (Not before a few of Carol's old boy friends, from high school and early college, had written her letters telling her how much she'd meant to them and how they still loved, longed for, her.) Within the same year, not too long before the Carol and Stan wedding, Miriam had been fixed up, by another friend, with Neil a young, rather good—looking doctor. Only out of medical school several years, he was still a Chief Resident in Psychiatry at New York's Mount Sinai Hospital. He was Miriam's dream, a handsome doctor and she was, therefore, willing to more or less overlook his sometimes pompous air, especially when talking about his specialty. There was also his all too often condescending manner to the hoi polloi, those ignorant , totally benighted souls who did not have an M.D. degree, or, at the very least, a Ph D. in a "hard" science such as Physics or Chemistry. Neil found Miriam pretty enough and he liked the cultural veneer she provided to a young doctor aspiring to significant things in a burgeoning field. He was the science, she the art. He, even, pedantically, instructed Miriam in sexual practices.

After Neil and Miriam had been going out for about two months, Miriam set up a double date with the recently wed Carol and Stan. A movie and dinner afterward. Things went smoothly enough. Neil and Stan had a little baseball and other sports talk. Miriam and Carol caught up. They always had plenty to talk about. They drew on a reservoir of some years, now. Afterwards, Stan and Carol naturally discussed Neil. Stan thought he was o.k., pleasant enough to go out with, but he did mention that Neil gave off some sense of being rather pleased with himself and knowing it all, or, at least, a great deal of it. Carol did not want to say, or even think, negatively because she definitely wanted to retain Miriam as a friend and Miriam seemed to be getting pretty serious about Neil-- thus the double date with Carol and Stan. but she was dubious about Neil being "right" for Miriam. She voiced concern to her husband over whether Miriam was someone meaningful, as a person, to Neil or whether she was more a convenient trophy to him, an attractive appendage. And she had doubts about whether Miriam really liked Neil a great deal or was just mesmerized by the "concept" of an appealing young psychiatrist on the move.

Nevertheless, when Miriam called, pretty early the next day, to anxiously inquire what Carol "thought," Carol was glowing about Neil's attributes. She mentioned his looks, how suave he was, how enthusiastic he was about his profession. She bubbled delight for Miriam and asked Miriam whether she was happy.

"Yes, I'm happy. Happy enough. We'll see what happens."

What happened was that about a year after that Miriam and Neil married. Carol was the bridesmaid, the best man was Neil's mentor in Psychiatry, a man of whom he spoke in virtual reverence, at one of the most prestigious New York hospitals. It so happened that on the very same night, after the wedding reception was over, the first child of Carol and Stan was conceived. Their second child was born a little more than three years after that, several months after the birth of Miriam's first child. A year and a half after their wedding Neil and Miriam moved to an "old" house in Connecticut , where Neil set up a private practice in Greenwich. It started off with only a few patients and it grew just moderately. Also rather slowly. Neil seemed to specialize in middle—aged women with grown children, bored, quasi—alcoholic, empty --nesters. Carol and Stan were still living in an apartment in a middle—class section of Queens.

Once Miriam and Neil had moved from the city, the number of times the couples socialized diminished. Even the phone conversations between Carol and Miriam decreased. First to one a week, then once every two weeks, to monthly,at the most. But the couples still made the effort, (or at least Carol and Miriam did,) to at least have dinner every three or four months. Most of the time at a restaurant in Manhattan. However, every third or fourth time, Carol and Stan would drive out to Connecticut to a restaurant, usually French, selected by Neil as the hot spot du jour. Carol and Miriam found they no longer had that much to say to each other, since whatever they did have to report, for example about the progress of children, had been gone over in a recent phone conversation. Neil and Stan grappled for common ground and kept up some continuing sports talk. Much of the general conversation was initiated by Neil in the form of stories about psychiatric patients, his own and some, involving more prominent people, of other practitioners. On one occasion, Carol in seeking to generate something to say mentioned that she was happy her recent physical had gone so well, but that the internist had mentioned that she had a cyst on her cocyx bone and that that must have been what was causing her some discomfort in her lower back. At the end of the evening Neil, in physicianly manner, patted her on the coccyx, perhaps even a bit lower, and said, "Take care of that cyst."

Not long after that evening, one February week day, when Stan and Carol's oldest was about five and a half, Carol was just undressing the children, getting their snowsuits off, from an early afternoon outing in the neighborhood park. Suddenly the phone jangled insistently. Rather annoyedly Carol picked up. To her complete surprise it was Neil.

After identifying himself he asked Carol what she was doing.

"Nothing much, for the moment. I just brought the kids back from the park and I'm getting their parkas off. I'm sure you're doing something a lot more interesting than that."

"Well, not really. I attended the morning session of a conference on schizophrenia being held at Queens College, in Jamaica. It's only about fifteen minutes from you, I checked. Then I had lunch with some interesting and influential colleagues and now I'm getting ready to head back to Greenwich. "

"Yes, you must have patients to see this afternoon."

"Well, no; not really."

"Oh."

"Yeah, I didn't know exactly when I'd be getting out of the conference so I cancelled the whole day."

"Well, a mental health day off from the usual always helps, right, doctor?"

"Yup, sometimes."

Carol was groping for something to say in the silence which followed. She never had found it "easy" to talk to Neil. Fortunately, he resumed.

"Well, since I'm really close by, I thought maybe you could use a little male company. I could check out the kids or something. It's on my way."

Carol was initially surprised, then silent, again, trying to guage what to say. "Well, I'm just, as I mentioned, getting them undressed and then the little one takes his nap and maybe Brian, too, since it was a bit brisk and enervating out there today."

"Do you undress after you get them undressed?"

"No, Neil, I don't actually."

"Well, it doesn't matter, you look great with your clothes on, too."

"Thanks, but what's that got to do with anything?"

"Oh, nothing. Just like I said, I am very nearby and thought you might like a little male company."

"No, actually I wouldn't like any company right now. As soon as I get the kids down I have about a thousand menial chores around the house to do."

"Yeah, but we could chat or something while you do them."

"No, I don't think so. That would just slow me down. Why don't you hop right in your car and head for Connecticut. You might be able to still re—schedule some patients for later this afternoon."

"O.K., Carol, you've got it. I was just kidding around, you know; I thought we might lighten it up for each other."

"No, it's light enough here. Maybe when you hit Connecticut the gloom will lift and it will be lighter there."

"Yeah, maybe. Well, thanks for listening.... You know, to my comedy routine. I thought you might get a kick out of it."

"Yeah. Right. 'Bye."

"Goodbye Carol."

Carol realized that beads of sweat had broken through her forehead and that her underarms were suddenly very clammy. Her back, too. She did finish the parka and glove removal process and put each child in his bed with soothing words. The clock read 2:30. She felt the need to lie down in her own bed.

After she reviewed the conversation in her mind and thought about it for a few minutes she had an impulse to immediately call Miriam. But then, she mused, what if Neil had really been "joking." Or, at least, "sort of" joking. And, in any event, he could easily deny and revise her report, or interpretation, of the conversation. She really couldn't say anything to Miriam. But what about Stan? She was sure he wouldn't think it was a josh. No, he wouldn't find it funny, at all. If she told Stan that might well be the end of the couples' seeing each other, even in the rather cursory way that they now did. It could lead to the end of her long friendship with Miriam.

FULL

As always, Professor Sebastian Fuller had started the class exactly on time. And, unless a universe ending cataclysm were to occur, he would end it precisely on time. But right now there were still ten minutes to go and Fuller, (the students liked to call him "Professor Full—of—himself," sometimes) "Professor Bastard Full—of—himself," sometimes "Professor Full—of—it") was casting around for his next victim of ruthless interrogation techniques. It wasn't a Trial Practice course, but cross-examination it surely was. Ed Sherman, sitting only moderately back in the large classroom, well within Fuller's preferred range, not that the ogre wouldn't reach further when he felt like it, basically prayed that it wouldn't be him. It might take a lot of piety to get wish fulfillment. Fuller hadn't called on him for some weeks, now. He was "due." The class was big, but not that big. About a hundred students.or, rather, subjects for flagellation by Fuller der Fuehrer, another favorite student appellation amongst the poetically inclined.

Prayers answered. Fuller's laser beam eyes lit upon Mary Turpin, a petitie, attractive first year student of Contracts, but not one, who by conventional classmate wisdom, had overly distinguished herself in classroom jousting with the august law school faculty. When Fuller unloaded "Ms. Turpin," like a rumbling explosive, Ed sighed relief simultaneously with feeling sympathy for the delicately affecting Mary.

"Well, now, Ms. Turpin, did you read the March case, the one now at hand?"

"Yes, professor, I did read it." Virtually sub silentio she added, "I'm almost sorry to say."

Not quite "sub." Fuller pacing briskly, behind the lectern, seemed to spring a bit taller than his already towering lean frame. "Never be sorry for reading, ms. Turpin. It's potentially educational. You are here for an education, Ms. Turpin, are you not?"

To himself Ed thought, the game is on. It's not as though he's going to coast or ease up to the final bell.

"Yes, professor, I expect so."

"Well, Ms. Turpin, I expect you'll be getting one." A very rigorous and solid one. Certainly in this course. Wouldn't you agree?"

"Yes, professor. I've already learned quite a lot."

"Thank you, Ms. Turpin. Perhaps after I've queried you about Marsh the kudos shall be mutual. So, since you read the case and since it's fairly straightforward, perhaps less there than meets the eye, and since tempus fugit, did you ever take Latin, Ms. Turpin, all good lawyers used to, I don't think we need the usual laborious statement of the all too often tedious facts of the case. As though a statement about ANYTHING could be confined to just 'facts.' Be that as it all may, Ms Turpin, in this case did the offeror succeed in revoking the offer to the offeree, before the latter accepted, so that there is no contract? Or, au contraire, were you a French student Ms. Turpin, did acceptance transpire prior to revocation so that there is, indeed, a contract as per the originally offered terms and conditions. But before you answer, Ms. Turpin, are you aware that your namesake, Randy Turpin,an Englishman of color, was Middleweight Champion of the World in the '50s, having most unexpectedly defeated, in London, the GREAT Sugar Ray Robinson, who is still considered to be, pound for pound, as they say in sporting circles and parlance, the greatest sheer boxer who ever lived?"

"No, professor I did not know about Mr. Turpin. I do not know if we're related....but I doubt it. Oh, and no to Latin, yes to French."

"It is lamentable that you don't know that bit of recent history. It's always lamentable when anyone doesn't know anything, especially Latin, I might add, but I, too, would wager against there being an ancestral relationship. Is that and any Latin some of the few things you do not know Ms. Turpin, or be there a myriad of others?"

"Well, I'm not sure, professor.... I hope there are not TOO many things of which I know absolutely nothing....if I should know...."

"I'd warrant there is quite a good deal of knowledge that is, shall we say, not within your ken. I won't say 'no matter,' as the great Samuel Beckett, Nobel Prize winner Literature, did when he wrote. 'Ever failed.

No matter. Try again. Fail again. Fail better.'—but, in any event, let's advance to the question at hand: contract or not; offer accepted or revoked prior to attempted acceptance?"

"I think it was revoked, professor. The offeror did say 'I revoke' before the offeree voiced acceptance."

"How do you know?"

"He said so."

"Did the offeree say anything?"

"Yes, he said he accepted; I think his exact words were, 'No, you're too late, I accept.'"

"And the offeror was too late?"

'No, to the contrary, I would say, professor. The offeree sort of admits that he, the offeree, is too late in accepting when he says 'You're," meaning the offeror, 'too late, I accept.' That statement sort of admits that the withdrawl of the offer came before his acceptance." Mary Turpin sat back from the edge of her hardbacked chair for a moment and allowed herself a tinge of a self—satisfied little smile.

"So it would seem, wouldn't it Ms. Turpin" Fuller said calmly, almost casually.

This remark, in conjunction with the clock having advanced to just a minute or so before the hour initiated the rustling of student papers and text books starting to be gathered.

Suddenly Fuller thundered out , "However, things are not always what they seem!"

Mary propelled herself to the very edge of her chair again.

"Wouldn't you agree Ms. Turpin?"

"Well, yes, abstractly.... I mean there are times...."

"Abstractly?" Fuller boomed again. "Are there not non—verbal ways of communicating, Ms. Turpin?"

"Well, sometimes...."

"In view of the lateness of the hour, rather than my extracting from you, excruciatingly slowly, what you should have discerned by yourself, unguided, from a scrupulous reading of the case, I will advise you, and the rest of you out there as well, as follows. The original offer suggested that if offeree was well disposed to the offer he should meet offeror on the designated train station at a given hour. Which is exactly where and when the colloquy we've been considering occurred. Therefore, "Donc" en francais Ms. Turpin, is it not manifestly clear that when the offeree dis—embarked from the train and waved in greeting to the offeror, who was down the platform , that the offeree had in effect already accepted the offer and wouldn't have been there at all if not for the purpose of communicating that very thing to the offeror. I'm disappointed that you weren't able to make that analysis just as incisively as I just did, even in the short time that remained in the period when I called on you. Hopefully your mental apparatus will become sharper and more vigorous as you proceed through law school."

Immediately after Fuller's last word the period ending bell rang. Ed Sherman allowed himself a tremor of sympathy for Mary Turpin as he finished collecting his own text book and notebook.

~

As Ed exited the cavernous classroom, the horde bottlenecking a bit, notwithstanding the double doors, he came face to face with Mike Jarvis, with whom he'd been at a student cafeteria table several times and who had been in pick—up basketball games, at the university gym, that Ed had also played in. Jarvis was a Texan, one of only a very few in the class. He was big—boned, fairly tall, but not gigantic, fairly jovial natured and by no means amongst the absolute brightest or most intense of Ed's fellow students.He lavished a bon—homie greeting on Ed and they started walking down the corridor together.

"How y'll been doing Sherman? Haven't seen you on the hardwoods lately."

"Nope. That's one thing you're definitely right about Jarvis. I've been pretty well busting my ass on the books and haven't even thought about taking my patented jump shot lately."

"You haven't missed much. Except the shots you would have missed. A lot, as I recall. Just like me," Jarvis laughed easily. "So, what did you think of the end of class today? Even Turpin's cute little ass didn't save her pretty little head from the analytical carnage of the Full man's fusillade."

"Good alliteration, Mike. I like it. I didn't know you were such a fan of Samuel Taylor Coleridge."

"Is he 'The Ancient Mariner" guy?"

"Bingo, again."

"Well, whatever. Turpin was skewered alive in merely seconds."

"Seems to have been."

"The iceman cometh again. By the way, did you know that his wife is an invalid. Confined to a wheelchair."

"Eugene O'Neill play, right? Mike you're absolutely stunning me with this display of literary omniscience. No, I hadn't heard anything about Full man's wife. A sad story, apparently."

'Sure is. I wonder what he does for sex. Maybe not much—maybe that's why he's so mean. Yeah, I'm really somethin', ain't I? It's not for nothing that I went to a good liberal arts school—even if I did spend most of my time playing football for them. Somebody had to do it."

"They knew their man. You came through. AND got into this place."

"'We Have Come Through,'—an early D.H. Lawrence novel, poem maybe, I forget. Anyway, ain't Fuller just the iceman's iceman? TOTALLY frigid, clinical, cerebral analysis. Just the intellectual analysis ma'am; leave the humanity out of it. By the way, 'Just the facts ma'am' is Jack Webb, as Sergeant Friday in 'Dragnet,' early t.v. show of the fifties."

"Yup, I guess you could say that Mike. The man tries to be all intellectual rigor. Resulted in Ms. Mary's Waterloo today, unfortunately."

"Napoleon, but that's all he wrote."

"You're good to the last drop, Mike. Touche again. But, at the expense of further literary and historical enlightenment, I've got to duck down here to the bulletin board outside the Dean's office. Have to check out the summer job posts. If I don't get gainful employment I might not be able to come back to this cornucopia of learning in the fall."

"Yeah, I know what you mean. I should do that too. I think dad's getting fatigued writing checks. But not now. I'm off to the gym. I have many shots to miss, many shots to miss before I sleep."

Ed called "Frost" after Jarvis who raised an arm in affirmation as he strodeaway.

Ed scanned the job board without much expectation or hope. However, as he was perfunctorily getting to the last corner, after cursorily reading all the jobs and notices that didn't apply to him, a short post, it was all on a single index card, jumped out at him. "First year student desired for summer internship as research assistant. See Professor S. Fuller."

His initial reaction was to be somewhat flabbergasted. But then Ed got a bit excited and thought why not try. He went back to his dorm room and phoned Fuller's all—business sounding secretary. He was told to appear at 4:00 the next day.

When he was escorted into Fuller's room, by the taciturn secretary, the professor was head down over what looked like, from Ed's inverted perspective, a law review article. He grasped a pencil, red at one end, blue at the other, as though poised to strike any peccadillo of style, not to mention a wayward or insufficiently precise formulation.

Without raising his head Fuller intoned, "Sit Sherman, sit. I'll be with you, or at least I'll talk to you, shortly."

"Thak you, sir," Ed mumbled as he settled into a big armchair, mostly leather covered, in front of Fuller's desk—and exactly between its left and right sides. Ed waited expectantly, but the esteemed professor turned a page, peered more closely at the periodical and wielded his scalpel ever closer to the textual target. This went on for at least thirty seconds and Ed started to wonder whether he was in for indefinite silence. Just as he'd decided that that was entirely possible Fuller remarked, "I expect it's now four o'clock, at least, so let us begin."

Ed looked at his watch. "Yes, sir."

"Why do you say 'yes'? I haven't asked you anything."

"Yes…er. Sir…. I just meant I was ready."

"Oh, so you think so?

Ed just smiled, very weakly, starting to feel as uncomfortable as in class.

"Well, in any event, Sherman, you are presumably here because you want to work this summer. More precisely you want to work for me."

"Yes…. Yes, sir. It would be an honor."

"I think that that is not your primary motivation. Rather the need to earn, as you youthful people say, 'some bread.'"Fuller held up both hands, two fingers extended on each, like quotation marks, when he said "bread." Just in case that Ed might think that he, Fuller, could possibly utter such terminology unsatirically.

"It's not an honor that's apposite Sherman. It's solid, totally precise, eminently usable research that's required. Are you up to that?

"Yes, sir. I mean I hope so."

'I hope so too. And think you are. I was glad to see that your name was in my appointment book today vis a vis this little job. I've liked some of your comments in class. That's why I haven't called on you lately. I think you've been pretty well sharpened up.Unlike some others I might mention. One of whom I had to subject to a bit of intellectual badgering yesterday."

"Yes, sir…. You did," Ed remarked, as non-commitally as possible. He still felt sorry for Mary Turpin.

"Don't be reticent Sherman. I know that most students think I am enormously heartless and ruthless---and I hope I am! It's my job—and it's life. No room for sloppy wool—headed let's hope for the best approaches out there. Not if you want to be effective. Get it Sherman?—It IS a jungle. But for now, that's really neither here nor there. Although it does suggest just how rigorous my demands on your research abilities will be."

"I would try to meet whatever you needed of me sir."

"Good; let's get on with it. I will assign you a topic to research for something I'm writing in the first week, let's say on the Tuesday, after the conclusion of the examination period. You'll bring your report to me on the Tuesday after that, I'll point out the many things you did in a slipshod, infelicitous manner and give you your next assignment. You'll return a week from then and so on and so forth. Is that a schedule you can faithfully adhere to, throughout the summer, Sherman? Pretty much until classes resume in the fall?"

"Yes, sir, should be no problem," Ed answered with alacrity, although he mentally rued that there wouldn't even be a full week off between the end of upcoming finals and the beginning of this job.

"Then good, Sherman. Come and see me on the appropriate date, according to what I just mentioned, at 10:00 A.M. On your way out tell Greta to put it down in my book."

"Thank you, sir," Ed mumbled as he rose. But it didn't matter any more. Fuller had picked up the multi--colored pencil once again and had resumed poring over the thick periodical volume laid out on his desk.

Perhaps, even, despite himself, Ed felt exhilarated as he left the building. It wasn't everyone, not even every law student at an elite school, who got a job with Sebastian Fuller, B.A., M.A., J.D., SJD. He felt like doing something celebratory. However, with exams but several weeks away there was an extravagant amount of studying to do. It would be nice to have someone to share this with beyond a brief phone call to his folks. They might actually be disappointed that he would not be coming home for the summer so that they could continue coddling their only child as though he were still pre—adolescent. For some reason, at that moment, he thought of Fuller's patsy yesterday, Mary Turpin, and how pretty, trim, pert and neat she always looked and acted. It would be great to hold her hand while walking to a good restaurant where wine and a succulent dinner waited. Why not? Because he was scared absolutely motionless by the thought of calling her and actually asking for a date.

But, by the time he'd gotten back to his room, he'd almost swaggeringly determined "Why not?" His social life was empty anyway. If she turned him down and it remained the null set, so what? Nothing lost. Still, his more cautious, self-protective antennae argued against for a few minutes more. But an atypical boldness took over. He looked her up in the student directory and dialed the number—being pretty confident, of course, that she wouldn't answer. Probably a roommate or some machine would. And likely no call back.

A female voice did answer. He asked for Mary. "This is Mary," was the, to Ed, frightening response. He gulped and coped, explaining whom he was. She made it easy.

"Oh sure, I know who you are.You sit about two or three rows behind me, off to my left, in Contracts. You make good comments. Fuller seems to like you quite a bit. Unlike myself, especially yesterday."

And they were off. Even for Ed it was easy to talk about classes and cases glibly. She was very outgoing in her conversation and repartee, he detected "southerness," and made it easy on his characteristic reticence. She was also highly congratulatory and effusive when he disclosed the job with Fuller and when he got to croaking out the date proposal she didn't hesitate. No hemming and hawing at all. His exhilaration heightened. What a day!!

The date went well. The conversation continued to flow, even when they went past the ubiquitous law school chat. Each was a Democrat and moderately interested in national politics.And they both thought the greatest short story ever written was the final one in James Joyce's collection, "The Dubliners;" viz., "The Dead." A story about ineffable loss. Each also loved Joyce's youthful novel, "A Portrait of the Artist as a Young Man," although Mary glowed about it even more than Ed. They discussed why her enthusiasm was greater than his and continued discussing a whole variety of things. Dinner lasted almost three hours. When Ed took Mary back to her dorm room they agreed that there really wasn't much time for formal dating at this exams imminent point , but that in the few weeks remaining in the semester they would occasionally study together. They did: they studied, they stared, the fondled, they kissed. But no more. It was an earlier time.

Each did pretty well on the tests, Ed a little, but not much, better than Mary. Her grade from Fuller pulled her down. Ed's margin there, his Contracts grade was very good, was almost the whole distance between them. Even better news, at least Ed thought so, was that a week into the two week exam period Mary had been notified that she'd been selected for a summer internship at a local, prestigious law firm.They exulted together and looked forward to this development allowing them to continue their "formal" socializing; i.e. non—study dates. Ed was really delighted. Having Mary there might make working for Fuller for the whole summer bearable, maybe even palatable. He so enjoyed talking to her. And certainly not only about the law. She was quiet, serene seeming, yet incisive in her observations and analysis of just about any subject they'd talk about. He liked her avery much. The classic formulation applied., each time: he couldn't wait to see her. And talk to her. And be with her. And touch her.

~

When Greta took Ed into Fuller's inner office, on the appointed Tuesday, the professor was already in what Ed had come to think of as his characteristic posture: head bowed over some text, right hand half raised, multi—colored pencil gripped, almost ferociously. Or, maybe, Ed was imputing the"ferocity." This time Fuller looked up immediately when Greta announced: "Mr. Sherman, sir."

"Ah, yes, right on time. Good start Sherman. Of course no other sort would be tolerated."

"I don't doubt it, sir."

"Quite accurate, Sherman."

As Ed, this time without waiting for direction, seated himself in the leather covered arm chair, Fuller put the pencil down on his desk.

"So, Sherman, I assume you're all set to go."

"Yes, by all means, sir."

"Whether or not—let us begin. My, isn't that, I mean 'Let us begin,' the final line of Philip Roth's comic tour de force, namely 'Portnoy's Complaint'?"

"I read it a while ago, but, yes, I think it is."

'Shouldn't matter how long ago you read it. That's a memorable concluding line. Finishing by beginning. A good lawyer should be steeped in good literature."

"Because it informs us about human nature?"

'Yes, of course. About human nature, human affairs and life in general. I recommend 'By Love Possessed,' by James Gould Cozzens. Much overlooked these days. But it shouldn't be. Some of the characters are even lawyers. The species itself. Cozzens was a very skilled novelist."

"Well thank you for the reference, sir. I'll look into it."

"Don't just look into the book; read it thoroughly. Thoroughness in everything actually. In a way, our byword here. But to turn to other matters. I want you to do some research on the so—called 'Parol Evidence Rule.' You'll remember that from our just completed course together, won't you Sherman? I've no doubt that you will since you did creditably enough on your final exam and there was a part of a question that dealt with it."

"Thank you sir."

"No thanks pertinent. You put in the work, you have the ability you got good, if not brilliant, results. Brilliant, of course, is exceedingly rare."

"Yes, sir. I mean thank you again, sir. Or, just yes sir."

"Stop dithering inanely, Sherman. Let us return to the matter at hand: can you have for me, by next week, about three to five pages on the rationale of the rule in a context of analyzing its efficacy and fairness?"

"Oh,sure, sir.That should be no problem. I can get started on it right away."

"Of course you can get started on it right away. You're working for me for the entire summer. Why wouldn't you get started right away. Or not, as you wish. All I care about is results, Sherman. High quality, usable material. Intelligent background for my own theories and formulations. I don't care if you do the work itself at 3:30 in the morning, after a booze—filled orgy, while you're soaking in the bathtub trying to get sober."

Ed allowed himself a smattering of a laugh, but Fuller didn't return the smile or indulge frivolity in any other way.

Ed quickly sought to return to a serious mien. "I can assure you that the work won't be done under those conditions, sir. I like libraries and, in any event, I will start in right away."

"Fine Sherman.That seems like a solid business-like approach. I'll see you here next week, same time."

With that Fuller gave a half—wave toward the door to the outer office and Ed quickly rose and briskly walked out. He nodded and smiled at Greta who with extravagant ebullience for her, said, "See you next week, Mr. Sherman."

"Yes, next week."

For the entire intervening week Ed worked extremely diligently on the project. Outside of three dates with Mary he spent practically all his waking time on it. Eight hours a day was a mere beginning. The basic research went smoothly enough and he soon determined the crux of what he wanted to say;what he thought Fuller would most value. So, he actually spent most of his time revising draft after draft of the memorandum, trying to get concision and cogency, a la the way Fuller habitually expressed himself. Part of Ed's preparatory efforts had involved reading two law review articles that Fuller himself had written. Ed found them just brilliant. Almost every sentence was an exquisite, seemingly repeatedly polished, gem. To the highest possible gleam. Ed did his best, worked and worked, but, apparently, for some reason, known only to the muses, only Fuller could sound like Fuller.

Tuesday approached and Ed made his final revisions. Until very late into the night before. He couldn't sleep much anyway.

By the time Greta led him into Fuller's office Ed was just short of quaking with fear. This time Fuller, in his characteristic pose, kept peering at some papers in front of him for thirty, forty—five seconds before looking up.

"Ah, Sherman, you're on time again." Ed held out the five page memo, the umpteenth version, to Fuller.

"Thank you Sherman. And I have something for you. Your check." Fuller took Ed's work with his left hand, reached into his inner jacket pocket with his right hand, extracted a very crisp looking white business envelope and extended it to Ed.

"Oh… oh, why thank you, professor."

"Again, Sherman, thanks not pertinent. Fair value for fair value. At leastI hope that I find what you've just given to me to be of some value.. Let' see about that."

Fuller leaned back in his swivel chair and started reading. Scanning was more like it.Ten seconds on the first page, about the same on pages two and three and even less on the last two pages.He looked up and fixed Ed with a stare from under his bushy eyebrows, themselves resident under a very broad and high forehead.

"This is fine, Sherman. Quite competent." Ed hoped Fuller didn't hear him expelling breath. "But, frankly, I don't think you wrote it yourself.I do not suggest plagiarism. No, by no means. The great mass of men could not produce nearly anything as good. .But, it doesn't sound like YOURself; more like MYself. For next week's assignment why don't you write as you would normally. You did that well enough on your exam. And, as I've noticed, on your other exams, too. Don't mimic me. You can't really do it effectively anyway.You should have your own style. Do you know that the great Russian emigre novelist, Vladimir Nabokov, perhaps unfairly most remembered for 'Lolita,' once observed, 'What do I have but my style'? No matter how great a pianist is, when he has a very talented student he must insist, as integral to the pedagogy, that the student play the great works the student's way, not necessarily as the master would play them. Incidentally, speaking of masters, do you know who wrote the words, 'The great mass of men lead lives of quiet desperation'?"

"Well, yes; yes and no, sir. I mean I think I understand what you're saying about writing in my own voice rather than as I think you would write it. At least I think I do. But no, I do not know who wrote the words you quoted."

"That's too bad, Sherman. I'm a bit dsiappointed. Those words are from one of the greatest American writers, none other than Henry David Thoreau, in 'Walden.' You've read it? I hope so and that you merely forgot that sentence."

"I think I've read some of it, sir."

"Not good enough. Not good enough at all. You have to get the precision of is writing, on the one hand, and the magnificent sweep of its ideas on the other. Brilliant work. I think I shall ask you to read it for next week's assignment. Yes, indeed. Read the entire work and write a précis of up to five pages for me. But in YOUR style, Sherman, YOUR style. Incidentally, the great mass of men do lead lives of quiet, or not so quiet, desperation. Are you aware of that, Sherman?"

"Yes and no again sir. I will read the book and write the report and no, not really. I wasn't aware that most men lead such embattled lives."

"Oh, yes, Sherman, most fight a great battle. Indeed, a medieval Jewish philosopher, acute folks those semites, once commented, 'Be kind to everyone you meet. For each is fighting a great battle.' I'm confident that you do not know who wrote that nor that it was ever written."

"Yes, sir. I can't say that I do, nor that it was."

"Well, Sherman, it's useful to have such aphorisms to guide one through life. Gives one something to hang on to. Grounds one in the essential. The great Beethoven conductor, Josef Krips, you might look into some of his recordings, was known by the Nazis to be unfriendly to their regime. So they stuck him in a pickle factory, to work on the assembly line, during World War II. After the war an interviewer asked him whether he'd felt terribly demeaned having to do that for a couple of years rather than conduct Beethoven, Brahms and Mozart. He answered that it was quite to the contrary—he had gained experience of life, of the very stuff of human affairs, as most people know life,that he never would have gotten in the rarefied classical music circles in which he customarily travelled. He valued it, overall, as some revelatory years. But I suppose I digress, Sherman. And, in any event, I must turn to other things now. I'll expect you back here next Tuesday, same time of course, loaded for bear as far as discussing Thoreau's two years at Walden Pond."

"O.K., sir, definitely.I'll be here and ready."

As Ed left the building he was worried. What stratagem or "trick" was Fuller up to. Ed seemed to recall from whatever he'd read of, mostly short excerpts, or heard about,"Walden," that there was nothing, as such, about law in it. Thoreau's "Civil Disobedience," of course, was another story. Did Fuller want Ed to somehow analogize or compare and contrast "Walden" and "Civil Disobedience," as far as "law" or legal issues? Were there oblique references to legal stuff in "Walden" which Fuller wanted to see whether Ed could pick up? Even if there were, of what relevance could such material be to Fuller or to the type of article he customarily wrote and published?

These anxieties only grew in the first day or two that Ed intensively read and re—read "Walden." But finally he concluded that there simply wasn't really anything substantial in the book about the law—even if one stretched certain passages to expansive interpretations. He decided that the best he could do would be to treat the assignment as a sort of book report and write about some issues presented by the book which he, himself, found stimulating or provocative.

He genuinely felt certain passages as rather inspiring. For example, "Have you built your castles in the air? Good, now put the foundations under them." Or, the justly famous, "If a man does not keep pace with his companions perhaps it is because he hears a different drummer. Let him step to the music which he hears, however measured or far away." And the arrestingly expressed closing passages, particularly, "The light which puts out our eyes is darkness to us. There is more day to dawn. The sun is but a morning star." Ed found it easy to write about the messages delivered in these and other beautifully expressed sentences and the five blank pages were filled rapidly once he began writing.

Once Tuesday morning arrived he was, outside of his usual trepidation when a Fuller encounter loomed,fairly eager to discuss "Walden" with someone as intellectually bristling as Fuller. He just fervently hoped that Fuller didn't expect the entire discussion to be about "Walden" and the law.

He didn't and it wasn't. Immediately upon entering Fuller's inner sanctum the sallow cheeked professor proffered the crisp white business envelope to Ed simultaneously with Ed handing his essay to the teacher.

Fuller then, as last time, briefly scanned each of the five pages before leaning back in his chair.

"Good, Sherman. I see that you've raised some of the major and more interesting matters that Thoreau delves into and, also, that this time you've written it in your own, very good, voice. Good work, Sherman, good. That's solid progress. Now let's have a go at some of the brilliant recluse"s formulations."

They did, for almost a full hour. Until five to eleven.At that point Fuller abruptly broke into what Ed happened to be saying and announced that it was time to assign Ed next week's project.

" I want you to read 'By Love Possessed,' by James Gould Cozzens and also another novel of his, 'Guard of Honor.' I think I've previously mentioned that there is some depiction of the legal profession, itself, in 'By Love Possessed.' And 'Guard of Honor,' as I recall it, deals with some actual legal proceedings as part of the plot."

"So, sir, you want me to write about the legal issues, questions, considerations, what have you, implicated in these two books? Perhaps put together some synthesis on how Cozzens sees the law?"

"That's a possibility, Sherman, but it's not, necessarily, what I want. I want what you think worthy of writing about and want to write about after you've carefully read the books. In other and plain words—more of what you did today. That's what, and all, I want."

Ed pressed on the broad arms of his chair and started pushing off. But this time Fuller didn't bury his head back into the material he'd been squinting at when Ed came in.

'Oh, say, Sherman, I was passing through the student cafeteria the other night, actually I'd had dinner there myself, and I thought I saw you sitting at a table. With Mary Turpin, wasn't it?"

"Yes, sir. We ate there last Thursday night."

"Yes, that was it, Thursday. You know, she's an attractive girl without being at all brassy or obvious."

"Yes, sir. I think she is. Very definitely."

"And she showed some lawyerly spunk, on her feet,as it were, in class from time to time. Didn't collapse when I probed. And, I must admit, her exam was more lucid and cogent than I might have, off—hand, predicted."

"Oh, yes sir. She's got some good ideas and analyzes things very sensibly."

"Good, Sherman, good. That sounds fine."

Then he glanced at his watch and quickly said, almost stutteringly, "O.k., o.k., Sherman, until next week and James Gould Cozzens, a serious man's novelist."

It was an easy "work week." Ed found plenty to comment about in Cozzens's two novels and was greatly stimulated by both his reading and subsequent writing. He was anxious to get to Fuller's office the next Tuesday morning.

Same routine. Ed gives the essay to Fuller, Fuller gives the crisp white business envelope containing the pay check to Ed. Ed loved the discussion and felt the hour had been thirty minutes, at most, when Fuller interrupted and pronounced it time for next week's assignment. This time it was another novel which Fuller had mentioned a few weeks ago., Philip Roth's "Portnoy's Complaint." He also threw in Roth's classic short story, "Goodbye Columbus." As Ed was leaving the professor asked whether Mary Turpin knew that Ed was working for Fuller throughout the summer.

"Yes, she does, professor, she does. Sometimes, professor, I even tell her a bit of what we've discussed in here, get her opinion on it."

"That's good Sherman. That's fine. I expect she's helpful."

~

"I just don't get it," Ed complained. "I can't figure out what he's up to."

"What do you mean," Mary asked, gently spearing a shrimp. It was the two month anniversary of their first date and they were enjoying a dinner at an upscale neighborhood restaurant. It had opened only recently but had rapidly gained considerable popularity. Its prices were beyond their normal means or inclinations. But this was a special occasion.

"Well. He started out with an assignment on the Parol Evidence Rule and I got the impression I'd be helping him write THE definitive article on the subject. You know, one of those exhaustive, and exhausting, 'Harvard Law Review' jobs that starts out with a case in 1400 that sort of hatches the rule and then traces its evolution all the way to the present and, then, finally, conducts a ruthless analysis of whether there's any conceivable contemporary validity for it as an operative legal doctrine. You know, I mean one of those things that goes on and on for a hundred and thirty pages or so. And you start to fall asleep at page ten or twelve, if not sooner. But no, then he started assigning me to, in effect, write book reports. On books that he'd mentioned in his various, what should I call them…in his intellectual digressions, and we don't seem to be getting anywhere in particular, certainly not regarding the Parol Evidence Rule."

Ed shook his head, side to side, a truly puzzled expression creasing his face. "As I say, I just don't get it. What's he up to?" He paused for a bite of the perfectly prepared pasta.

"You don't?" Mary asked, sipping just a bit of wine.

"No, I don't. Why? Do you? The one constant is our little exchange of papers at the beginning of each session. I go into his room, we nod at each other, I give him the pages I've written, he gives me the check. By the way, did I tell you that yesterday, when I got back and opened the envelope, there was a note in there saying the check was twenty—five dollars more than what it had been, what he told me, at the start, my salary would be, and that it would continue being the increased amount for the rest of the summer. And then he wrote, in his usual acerbic manner, 'Don't foolishly waste the increase all at once.' I really just do not get what it's all about."

Mary scrunched her features into her "thinking cap" affect and said quietly, "Is it a university check or his personal one?"

"What's the difference?Anyway, it's a personal check."

"I think that's what it's all about. The check."

"Whattaya mean the check? What about the research?"

"It seems to me," Mary continued, using one of the linguistic stratagems they'd learned in their first year at the law school, to soften a controversial, disagreeable or problematical statement, "that for some reason he decided that he doesn't need or want the research he originally had in mind, but that he was determined to keep you' employed,'" she mimicked the quotations signs with two fingers on each elevated hand, just as Fuller would sometimes do, "all summer. Just as he'd promised. Wouldn't you think he'd take promises seriously. Contracts, promises? She sat back a little, as she tended to do when she thought she'd made a well thought out point.Then, resuming , she moved slightly forward. "You thought you had a summer job and he wasn't going to disappoint or frustrate you. It was too late to get another job. It would have been unfair to make you scramble then."

"So you think he's giving me charity?" Ed asked, with almost emphatic disbelief, maybe wonder.

Mary's features contracted again. "Sort of. Somebody could call it that. But he doesn't want you to feel its charity. That's why he keeps the assignments coming and why he insists on discussing your 'work,'" the two extended fingers again, "and your' findings' with you."

" I don't know. It's hard to believe. Very hard. That the crusty old bastard...."

"Maybe not so crusty as he likes to lead the first year novices to believe. But maybe, also, there's some crust left."

"What do you mean by that?" Ed responded, getting more and more puzzled.

"I don't think it's just the paycheck. The charity as you call it."

"Well, wouldn't that be what it is under those conditions?"

"Not exactly, no. He's getting something out of it too."

"What could he be getting out of it? You agree that he doesn't need the research he's assigning me."

"Right, but he needs to teach. Particularly someone he's identified as promising. Teaching is his essence, however he might do it. With whatever little barbs, even outright nastiness."

"What's he teaching? Literature?"

" Not as such. More what literature has to teach about life. Maybe about why the great mass of men lead lives of quiet desperation. Remember? You told me that he quoted that sentence from Thoreau. And he said something like, 'Yes, there's much desperation out there.'"

"Yeah, that's right. But this whole thing is very confusing. I just can't get a clear shot at what it's all about."

"I think I told you. Maybe you need to be more willing to receive what's right in front of you and being given to you."

THE OUTSIDER

UNLIKE MANY OF MY CLASSMATES, I didn't mind seeing Leo coming. (I thought sometimes he lay in wait for me.) I got something out of it. But, no question, Leo was different. At least that's the way the other teen—agers who came into contact with him felt. Certainly most of them.

He was ebullient and enthusiastic about his interests. Mostly intellectual. In our high school he was known as "a brain." He was passionate about philosophy and classical music. Not too many of the other freshmen related to that. Leo was so focused on explaining what Georg Friedrich Hegel or Jeremy Bentham "really" meant that he tended to include some saliva spray along with his crisply articulated insights. Not too many people, of any kind, were comfortable with that.

Believe it or not, Leo was actually crazy about basketball too. He loved to play. But he was clumsy and awkward and if he didn't throw the ball away ineptly trying to get it to a pick—up game teammate he tended to foul the opponent he was defending against with his abrupt, clumsy movements. He didn't play baseball, but he knew and reveled in the Major League game. He commanded the stats of all the leading players and everything about everyone on our local big—league team. He rooted for them avidly. A loss was a personal defeat for Leo, searingly frustrating.

He wasn't a bad looking guy. Rather broad and masculine, maybe a trifle too beefy, but with bright, kind eyes, underneath the pretty thick lenses. He had robust, sandy colored hair, but it never seemed to have been available to a comb or urged into any design. Most of the time when speaking to someone he was warm and smiling. Intent on what he was saying, usually pretty serious, but not oblivious or unresponsive to what you were saying. Even some humor; mostly of the intellectual bantering type, but not exclusively.

As I say, there was something in it for me.. I liked some intellectual discussion myself. He wasn't my supremely favorite kind of pal, but I guess I more than tolerated him. I didn't mind running into him. We had things to talk about. Some of the discussions were stimulating. But one of our favorite and repetitive conversations was more "personal," about a very impressive Philosophy professor we both had—but for different courses. Leo would tell me what J.B. said in the "World Views" course he had with him and I would tell him what J.B. said and did in the"Language, Truth and Logic" course I took.

"Do you know what he said today?" Leo asked eagerly, almost as soon as he saw me.

" No, Leo, I don't. I wasn't in'World Views', you were."

"Yes, right. Of course. Touche. But, anyway, he made some statement or other about Aristotle and some guy raised his hand and said, 'But Professor Colbert, (I was actually thinking of taking his course next semester, Leo also blurted,) says that we may not make statements of such sweeping philosophical judgments.' J.B. just stared at him impassively for a few seconds. Then, very staccato—like he said, 'Who is to stop us.?'"

By the time Leo enunciated the punch line he was grinning with vast satisfaction at J.B.'s comeback. His admiration for J.B. as a teacher and model, as well as deliverer of intellectual one—liners, was unbounded. Mine was not at all far behind. (J.B. often began a rejoinder with "Not at all.")

In between our freshman and sophomore years Leo and I each had summer jobs but we stayed in telephone touch and occasionally agreed to go to an evening event, like a baseball game or outdoor concert. He wanted to go more times than I did and I had to give him "excuses" several times.It took energy, which I didn't always have, to be with Leo. I started getting the sense that I may have been his only friend. Or what, for him, passed as a friend.

One night we went to a concert at Lewisohn Stadium, the summer home of what was essentially the New York Philharmonic. An all—Beethoven program, much to the delight of both of us. We were still in the nascent throes of discovering the ringing glories of classical music. A Beethoven symphony, almost any Beethoven symphony, was the quintessence for us. This program hit the jackpot--- the Fifth Symphony and the "Emperor"

Piano Concerto, Beethoven's last, with that imperial, yet passionate, artist, Rudolf Serkin, as the soloist. Very stirring, enormously inspiring.

But such music emboldens young men—even those as retiring as Leo and myself. During Serkin's sublime performance of the "Emperor" there was a young woman, just about our age, maybe a few years older, in the row only one ahead of us. She was unself—consciously distinctly swaying to the turns and runs of the music and I thought I even heard her humming, almost inaudible as it was, from time to time. She was enraptured. We were enraptured. By her, as well as the music. Not too long afterwards I read a short story by J. D. Salinger in which he wrote a line something like "She was one of the two most unqualifiedly beautiful girls I'd ever see." He must have seen this one.

During intermission Leo was beside himself with enthusiasm.

"Wow, wow!! Isn't she beautiful!" he said sotto voce, so she wouldn't hear. But not that sotto—she might have heard, but gave no indication if she had.

"Yup, no one could deny it. She's really something."

"Wouldn't it be great to get a date with her!" (Leo had not had many dates. Very few in fact. And no second ones, to my knowledge.)

"Well, Leo, right now there's only one way of finding out if you could get one."

"Whaddya mean?"

"Well you could go up to her and start talking and see what happens."

"You must be kidding. I couldn't start talking to someone who looks like that."

"Why? Impeccably gorgeous as she is, she's only human. She would like to have young guys talk to her, too. Just the way her friends, who don't look like that, are approached by young guys."

"Yeah, but…."

"You know what Leo—you're absolutely right. I feel exactly the same as you do about approaching her, despite high, and I mean really high, motivation. For guys like us she's unapproachable."

Leo nodded sagely and sadly. Which didn't stop us from whispering urgently, throughout the Beethoven symphony, in the second half of the program, about just how perfect her appearance was. Bottom line conclusion: totally unparalleled "piece of ass." We talked a big game. In the beginning was the end.

During the following Fall semester I didn't see Leo as frequently as I'd had in our freshman year. We had no common classes and I just didn't run into him on campus as much as previously. But one gray morning we found ourselves approaching from opposite directions. The sputtering began even before we were really up to each other. Again he was verging on the uncontrollable in enthusiasm.

"Can you imagine what happened yesterday!"

"Well, Leo, that's a big topic. But, no, I do not think I can imagine exactly what you're referring to."

"Touche. Too broadly phrased a question. Let me try again. Can you imagine what happened in J.B.'s class yesterday?"

"Still 'no,' Leo. You're taking that one, not me."

"Right, right. Well, I'm taking 'Phenomenology And Other Ologies and Isms' and he was talking about Edmund Husserl, a key figure, as you know, in Phenomenology and J.B. said one sentence which I just didn't get at all. I mean not at all. I just didn't know what he was talking about."

"Always upsetting, irritating, etc., etc."

"Right, I was hanging on every word, but…. So, anyway , I had never done this before, but, I got up the courage to go up to him after class and ask him about what he meant."

"That was good Leo. Not so easy to do; that I can imagine."

"Yeah, right. If I hadn't wanted to know so badly…. Well, anyway, I approached, you know, as he was gathering his stuff, and said I had a question. But he said he couldn't stop then,he had to bolt off to some Philosophy Department meeting for which he was already late.

"Well, that was that and no cigar, Leo, but you tried. Trying is good. Although you don't want others to find you trying."

"What? Oh yeah!" Leo gave me the full smile. "Touche—that was a good one. But anyway,that's what I thought immediately. He, I mean HE, has no time to talk to the likes of ingenuous sophomores like me."

"Not surprising. But you gave it the old college try, Leo, pardon the expression, and that's what counts."

With a very high—waatage smile, maximal brightness, Leo, in his inimitable blurting manner, continued: "But that's not the end of the story."

"Oh, excuse me. Well, then, I'm all ears for the conclusion."

"O.K., so I'm studying at home last night, with, as usual my mom telling me not to work so hard, to go out and have some fun once in a while. By the way, you and I haven't done anything lately. So, anyway, the phone rings.

My mom says, 'It's for you, I don't recognize the voice.' So, naturally, I get on and it's HIM!! He knew my name and had called up the registrar to get the phone number."

"WOW!! A very pleasant surprise I bet."

"Well, of course, I was flustered; you know, more than usual. But he says that he remembered I had a question at the end of class that he didn't have time to answer. So he says 'What was the question?' So I sort of stuttered it out the best I could spontaneously remember it. And, incredibly, he says 'That's a really good question.' And then he talks about what an appropriate answer might be for about five minutes straight and then asks what I think of his suggestions. I was able to say one or two things and he commented and lo and behold we had a conversation for about twenty minutes. Finally, I thanked him profusely for calling, more than profusely, and he said, 'Not at all, but it is getting late.' Then good—byes and that was it."

Leo was, as they say, bursting with pride and I energetically complimented him several times on what both of us regarded as this intellectual coup. We both reveled in it, but I must confess to just a smidgen of envy and jealousy. A twenty minute discussion with J.B. on Philosophy was certainly something to be treasured.

In a graduate class I got permission to take from J.B. there was a solidly middle—aged woman. Obviously returning to the quest for her Masters or Ph.D. after getting a family underway. Maybe, even, having already raised it. She wasn't young. One day she raised her hand and made an observation on the reading under discussion. Unfortunately it seemed utterly fatuous. At best it was completely wrong and at worst it seemed completely nonsensical, without any meaning whatsoever. J.B. paused for a bit, then forcefully said: "Oh, I see what you mean…." He then went on to attribute all sorts of nuance and subtlety to her comment which I, and everyone else in the class, knew she had not intended nor, apparently, was capable of intending. The woman's face was fraught with concentration and she reflexively nodded as though J.B.'s brilliant re-formulation had been exactly what she meant. After rescuing her dignity J.B. resumed the appropriate thread of discussion.

I think I reported that incident to Leo,but we didn't have much to do with each other until, in our last year, we found ourselves as two of the ten students in J.B.'s senior seminar in "Current Problems in Contemporary Philosophy." It met once a week for three hours and each week the discussion was of a different chapter in a work of John Dewey. The analysis guided by J.B. was intense and revelatory. Many more hours were spent by Leo and I re—hashing the class discussions and construing the "real" meaning of some comment or observation that J.B. had made.

By that time I had garnered the occasional date and was even taking someone to the Senior Prom. Not so Leo. Most of his time was still spent studying, at home, with his mom nattering at him to do something else. To venture out, to go somewhere besides class or the library.

As the seminar went into its last weeks a rumor went around that J.B. was approaching the then mandatory retirement age, that this might even be his final semester. Leo and I, and several of the other students as well, started talking about presenting him with a gift after the last meeting of the seminar. Everyone in the course was willing to chip in but our collective cogitations could produce no better idea than a gift certificate to the university book store.

That was what we got him and the group decided that Leo, as the generally acknowledged star pupil of the course, should present it to J.B. at the very end of the final class. Each of us wrote something, on the card that would accompany the certificate, attesting to, and thanking him for, his brilliant teaching.

The day came, the class passed, as per always, and, finally, Leo shuffled up to J.B., while he was still seated at the seminar table, and said "Here's something we all wanted you to have." J.B., surprised, took the envelope tentatively and began reading the card. His head remained down. Suddenly his eyes were moist and his burly upper body shuddering with emotion.

None of us callow, inept philosophes knew what to do. So, with backward glances, we filed out. A week or two later, each of us received a handwritten thank—you note from J.B. There was something personal in each one, but they all contained one line. "In teaching response is all."

As chance would have it, without any design or consultation, Leo and I found ourselves, that September, at the same university in New England. I'd been admitted to the law school and he was a graduate student in the super—duper Philosophy department, probably the best in the country.

We ran into each other fortuitously at the campus bookstore early in the academic year. He told me J.B. had written a no—holds barred, totally without qualification, "One of the very finest students I've ever encountered," letter of recommendation for him .Addresses and phone numbers were exchanged amidst promises to be in touch.It simply didn't happen. I was having a hard time adjusting to the "tough—minded" approach of legal analysis proffered by most of my teachers, and students too for that matter, and waned in my social work determination to befriend the usually friendless

Leo. I do not know why he didn't call me, but I suspect Leo almost always waited to be asked rather than very often taking the iniative of asking.

In any event, I didn't spot him him on campus again and three years later I graduated with my J.D. He would have had at least a few years to go before he would have gotten the Ph.D., but I don't know if he ever did.

About fifteen years later, married, two children, Chief of an Enforcement Division in the SEC's New York Regional Office, I spotted an obituary for J.B. in "The New York Times." He had actually taught for several more years after our senior year before retiring. I immediately thought of Leo. I wanted to communicate and commiserate with him. But I had no idea where he was in those pre—internet days. The only thing I could think of was to write to our college Alumni Association requesting his current address. They responded promptly enough but indicated that their policy was not to divulge such information. However, they suggested that I could write a letter to the party I wanted to reach and send it to them and they would endeavor to get it on to him.

"Dear Leo,
A LONG hiatus!
Nevertheless, I hope you are well and doing well.
I assume you saw the obituary of our favorite teacher; viz., J.B. ("Times," Oct. 23d.) Very sad, of course, but he had a powerful, reasonably long run and did his work. And, as we above all know, he did touch lives positively.
Let me know that you received this and how and what you are doing. Then we can start seriously catching up.

Your still friend,"

He never answered. On a different whim I tried again a few years later. Same result. Perhaps the Alumni Association did not know where he was either. Perhaps he just had nothing to say. Philosophically or otherwise. After all, Wittgenstein once wrote: "Whereof one cannot speak one must be silent."

FRIENDS

EDWARD BALTING AND NELSON DEMPTSTER were of similar, but not identical, backgrounds when they first encountered each other at an elite college of a large urban university. Demptster's father was a pharmacist, his mother an elementary school teacher, while Balting's mother was a secretary to attorneys, his father a skilled worker in the so—called "needle trades," i.e. apparel manufacturing. Each was an only child and each family was middle class—Demptster's more middle and middle upper class, Balting's more middle—middle and lower.

They had a few classes together in their first semester and then began to see each other in one place and another. The cafeteria, the library reading room, and on busses and trains as well. (Each commuted to college from an area beyond the city, but not much beyond.) They startedacknowledging and smiling at one another and that led to talking about their common classes. Eventually they got to other things of interest to seventeen year old alert, energetic and vibrant boys. Such as sports and plans for the future. Dempster had already declared himself as pre—med , while Balting thought he might well end up in law school.

They'd both been excellent high school students and the college had awarded each a helpful if not munificent scholarship. They continued as excellent students in college. But Dempster was the more intense about grades. He caught the bug of the ferocious competition amongst the pre—meds almost instantly. Balting kept getting good grades, too—but almost reflexively. There just wasn't the same fierce level of competition for places in the top law schools as there was in the premier medical schools. In the several course which they were in together in their freshman year they each got "A" in one, Balting "A-", Demptster "A" in another, while in a third Balting got an "A" but Dempster received the only "A+" in the course. (One of the merest handful that the professor had ever given.) Occasionally they'd briefly study for an exam together, but mostly their friendship was expressed in playing sports together, attending professional athletic events and talking on the phone a moderate amount.

As sophomores they found themselves in the same 'Introduction to Calculus" section. Dempster had to take it as part of the "prescribed" pre—med regimen, but Balting could have taken something less rigorous in moving toward satisfying the Math/Science requirement of the college. But he'd been pretty good in Math in high school, liked its definitiveness and appreciated the power of its applications in contemporary society. But neither was a "natural" in this course. They had some trouble conceptually—neither really grasped differentiation in its incisiveness or glorious sweep. But both were adept at manipulating the mechanical calculations necessary to work out the problem sets. On the first exam Demptster got a "B+/B" while Balting got a "B/B-." On the mid—term each climbed to "A-/B+."

In this course, as in too many others, the professor computed grades "on a curve;" i.e. after giving an absolute numerical grade to each paper, based on how many errors it had, the papers were put in rank order and the final grade assigned was somewhat a product of where the paper stood in relation to all the others in the class. (Even a paper with relatively many errors could wind up with a pretty good grade if it had less errors than most of the others, while one with relatively few errors could receive a mediocre, or even worse, grade because on that particular exam most of the other apers had even fewer errors.) Therefore, at least to some extent, Balting and Demptster were "competing" against each other. The grades they were getting were so close that there couldn't have been much difference between their absolute scores. But, if one were to come out a half grade better it would be Demptster.

That wouldn't be unusual for them. Demptster seemed always to be the leader. He was also the slightly better athlete, in the various sports they played, although Balting was competent plus. And, while both were shy and awkward with girls, Demptser, somewhat better looking, had an occasional date while Balting, pleasant enough appearing, hardly ever did.

Demptster stopped commuting to classes in their sophomore year. He moved into the dorms, but Balting continued to live at home. He justified this in his own mind on economic grounds, but, really, he wasn't eager to live amongst the hurly—burly, free—wheeling, anyone -can –come- into-your- room- at- any- time dormitory atmosphere. He had solitude at home for studying when he wanted it. He could count on it when he needed it.

As the calculuscourse went into its final few weeks, only the final exam remaining, they chatted about how they would need very good grades on that exam in order to wind up with their usual caliber final "A," "A-" range grades. They talked about which areas the professor might emphasize and hoped that there would be disproportionate concentration on the second half of the course because it was more "mechanical" and computational than the more theoretically oriented initial topics.Each felt that all of his other courses were more or less under control. (More in Dempster's case, less in Baltings.)

Suddenly it was finals time. The math exam, the only one they had in common that semester, would be the last for each that semester. During the two week final exam period they had several phone conversations, mostly about the tests they'd already taken or were about to take. Characteristically, Demptster was surer of himself, more confident as to how he'd done, than Balting. Ed often doubted himself even when he'd done well. On too many exams he thought he had turned in a mediocre, at best, paper only to receive an excellent, even sterling, mark. Very few were the times he knew he had done well.

The calculus test was on a Friday morning and when they talked on the phone Wednesday evening they ran over the topics and types of problems they surmised would be on the exam. Then they wished each other well and said they'd see each other in the exam hall at 8:00 on Friday.

Neither had a final on Thursday so each studied pretty much throughout the day. Dempster felt he was getting a grip on most of the troublesome points as they day progressed. He started to feel the surge of some of his characteristic confidence. Balting too thought he was making progess in some areas, but saw problems within the problems he thought might be given. He sensed nuances and twists that could be very vexatious in the hands, or rather the mind, of a demanding test maker.

On Thursday evening, just after dinner with his mom and dad, Balting was back in his room pondering on some of the aspects of the course which gave him the most anxiety, made his stomach tighten and twist the most. The phone rang. Surprisingly it was Nelson.

"Listen, Ed, how're you doing? This stuff's really tough, isn't it? At least some of it, anyway. No matter how much you look at it, it doesn't seem to make much more sense than when you started."

You've got that right. I feel like I'm on an intellectual treadmill. The more I struggle with it the more I feel that I'm in the same place. La plus ca change la plus la meme chose." (They both took French.) "Or, maybe even, that I might have slipped back, that I comprehend less.Too much knowledge, or studying, whatever, might be worse than too little. Ignorance limits your options and you can blissfully proceed. Know too much and you don't know whether to start with going or coming."

"I know. Exactly. This has got to be the toughest stuff we've ever battled. Makes freshman Chemistry look like a pushover. Hich it basically was. Didn't you get an "A" in that too?"

"No, I got an "A-." I had a solid "A" going into the final but I let myself get flustered by one of the problems, panicked and just immobilized myself into not doing enough with it."

"Oh, that's right. I remember now. Well, anyway, I thought maybe we could help each other here.Why don't you come up to my room here. We'll pull an all—nighter and then go to breakfast and the exam together tomorrow. After that, thank God, it's the week—end and beaucoup de sleep."

"Well, I don't know, I was just going to study for a few more hours and then hit the hay...."

"I know that we've never really studied together at any length before, but this is such a tough nut, maybe if we sit side—by—side and help each other with some of the really vicious subjects we would help each other. We could take turns napping on my bed, so we wouldn't be completely sleep deprived for the exam.I don't think it could hurt. It's not like we're doing so wonderfully by ourselves, going it alone."

Balting hesitated. He didn't really want to get on the subway now and make the almost hour long trip to the college.HYe also didn't believe in staying up all—night before an exam. He just didn't function well on too much sleep. In fact, he remembered once telling nelson that in connection with some nocturnal social activity.

But Dempster persisted. "Ah, come on. Let's try it. Can't hurt and might help. It's not like we're in otherwise such good shape here. For Christ's sake, Ed, have an adventure.

Balting usually liked to please his friends. If someone wanted something of him and he could provide it he, very often, did. "O.K., but we've got to get at least a little sleep.... What if other people on the floor want to roam around all—night?"

"Most of the fellas are already gone. Not too many people have any exams left. Almost everybody is through—except for a few lucky ones like us. Anyway,we'll just lock the door and be quiet as hell and not answer any knocks or raps. Come on. Live dangerously!"

'Alright, I'll put some things together, let my folks know I'm going and hop the subway. Should be there in about an hour and a half. Your room is 904, right?"

"That's it. I'll be waiting for you."

When Balting came out of the subway he saw that just about the hour and a half he'd predicted had elapsed since he'd spoken to Nelson. Another five minutes and he'd covered the ground between the subway and the university's gates and had taken the elevator to the ninth floor of Weldon Hall. The building did seem pretty quiet, compared to the typical boisterousness, but there were still a few unhappy souls around, with one more test to go. When Balting knocked on the door of 904 there was no answer. Surprised, Balting wandered ruminatively down the hall to see whether Nelson was in one of the rooms, with an open door, throwing the bull with someone. There was a small group in one of the rooms but Nelson was not a part of it.

Then it struck Balting---Nelson wasn' tanswering his knock because he didn't know it was Ed. He must have thought it was somebody else and, as he'd promised, he wasn't going to allow anyone to distract them. So Balting went back to 904 and this time as he knocked he also, softly, said, "Nels, it's me, Ed." Still no response whatsoever. It then struck Balting that Dempster may have gone off to the library for a few minutes, perhaps to check out some fine point, and that he'd soon return.

Balting decided to wait for him in the first floor lounge. He could even resume his own studying, for a bit, there. For twenty minutes he was able to get something done, if not much, amongst the ping-pong players,smokers and talkers relaxing there. Apparetnly there were still some guys who did have an exam tomorrow or had not yet departed for intersession break. Maybe some had had late exams today and couldn't arrange for tranmsportation until tomorrow morning.

He went to check Nelson's room once more. But the gentle knocking, designed to not attract anyone else's attention, again produced no response.

Balting went down to the lounge again and studied for a few more minutes. The he thought that maybe Nelson hadn't heard him say, "It's me, Ed" which he'd tried to keep very modulated while gently rapping. So he ripped out a sheet of his notebook paper and wrote "It's me, Ed, I'm the one knocking" on it. Then he went back up to the ninth floor, again knocked softly and immediately slipped the sheet of paper under the door, pushing it as obtrusively and as far as possible, into the small dormitory room. Then, with some confidence, he waited. Nothing.

Truly puzzled he went down to the lounge again and tried to get in a little more studying. He resolved on patience and decided he wouldn't go back to 904 foranother half—hour, forty—five minutes, at least. By this time one or two more students had come into the lounge and no one besides Balting seemed to be interested in studying. Which, Ed realized, swas totally appropriate, since they had their rooms for that. The lounge was for lounging. Balting actually stayed there for another full hour before he returned to 904 with another sheet of paper indicating that it was he knocking.Knocked discreetly, shoved the sheet of paper vigorously. Same result. It was occurring to Balting that he wasn't going to link up with Nelson that night. He hoped that nothing of an emergency nature had happened in Dempster's family, or anything like that.

It was not late enough to make it problematic to return home and then get up early enough to get back here for the 8:00 exam. He knew some other guys who lived in this dorm but, in each case, they'd had their last exam two or three days ago and it was highly unlikely that they hadn't already pulled out. Nevertheless, he tried a few rooms. No success.

Ed now realized that he hadn't much choice other than to spend the night in the dormitory lounge. Regardless of how far from ideal conditions were there. So he did, studying sporadically, dozing a bit in the easy chair, occasionally exchanging breezy, insouciant comments with his fellow students, killing time the night before departures for points elsewhere. By about two A.M. he was the only one left and he dropped off to a few fitful hours of sleep during which continuous and discontinuous functions opposed each other, as though enemy armies, and dx/dy symbols marched, sharply illuminated,through a profound blackness.

When he awoke dawn was beginning to sneak in under the drapes covering the floor-to-ceiling, half the wall wide, plate glass window with a view of the campus. He thought about how few hours sleep he'd had, how de—energized, lethargic really, sheerly un—rested, un—restored he felt and started planning to get some energy infusion via breakfast. He remembered seeing a tacked up notice or two, the night before, as he'd ambled through the building, announcing that the cafeteria was already closed for the semester. He'd have to wait until a respectable hour and then walk the length of the campus to the main avenue on its other side. By that time,there would be quite a few eateries opening over there.

He studied a little more, got semi—washed in the rest room, walked to a coffee shop and had a semblance of breakfast—inlcuding two cups of fully caffeinated coffee,which made him feel somewhat sharper---- and cursorily looked over his outline of the course for a while. Now it had become only twenty minutes to exam time.

As Ed walked toward the amphitheater, where students in all sections of the course would sit for the three hour ordeal, through his semi—alert, too lackadaisical gaze he spotted Nelson striding purposefully from the opposite direction. As soon as Dempster spotted Ed he started waving and gesticulating. Once within hearing distance he started shouting:

"Ed, Ed, where were you last night? When I woke up this morning—I got about a half—hour, forty five minutes sleep—I saw those notes from you on the floor of my room. Why didn't you also knock on the door when you slipped in those notes. I was concentrating so hard I didn't notice them coming through."

" But I did knock on the door. Didn't you hear? I just didn't want to rap really loudly because I didn't want to attract anyone else's attention—in case they wanted to barge in too. How could you not have heard, though?"

"Well, you must have knocked too softly for my hearing because I just didn't hear a thing. I thought you'd decided not to come."

"But I would have called you to let you know. Did you call my folks to see where I was?" Ed suddenly had a dart of anxiety that if Dempster had followed—up his mom and dad might have no idea of what had happened to him.

"No, no. I just thought you'd changed your mind. Because, remember, at first you seemed reluctant. I just thought you'd finally decided to stay home. Well, anyway, good luck on the exam."

"Yeah… yeah…. good luck," Ed, still confused, finally said. He just couldn't understand how Dempster had heard none of his insistent knocks.

And they each did have good luck. Dempster got an "A" in the course, Balting a "B+.

There were no further classes together but they remained friends, notwithstanding that thoughts about that exam eve crossed Balting's mind from time to time. Athletics was a typical meeting ground and sometimes they'd play touch football, softball, basketball with other college pals. After a basketball session, Balting and Dempster were still chatting as the others drifted away. They decided to head for coffee and doughnuts, as well earned post—game refreshment, so that they could catch up.

Each picked one of the richest, gooiest offerings the doughnut shop had and then they took a table by the window looking out on the avenue running past the campus.

"So, what else is up?" Balting asked.

"Oh, pretty much the same," said Demptster. "I'm taking all the science courses I'm supposed to take and doing well."

"I'm sure that you're doing more than well. In fact, I'm sure that you're doing very well."

"Well, I have to take the MCAT boards in a few months and if I can keep going likeI'm going I think I have a good chance to get into P&S, Harvard, Duke, Cornell and University of California at San Francisco medical schools. Or some of them, at least. Or, at the very least, one of them."

"I bet you'll get into all of them. That's great."

"And you're still headed for surpassing Clarence Darrow?"

"Yeah, I suppose so. I'm doing well enough to think about some of the better law schools. Besides, I don't know what else to head towards...."

"Enough shop talk. Let's talk about some sheer fun," Demptster enthused. "You know, the Junior Year Dance is coming up in a few weeks and it should be a lot of fun. I even have someone in mind to take. I've been dating a freshman, here and there, for a while and I would like to go with her."

"That sounds good."

"Yeah, and she's been receptive, or at least not rejecting, whenever I've broached the idea. But there's a funny thing about it. She's a twin and she won't go without her sister going too."

"I assume she doesn't expect, or want, you to take both of them."

Dempster let out a short chuckle. 'That might not be a bad idea! But, seriously, she wants me to get a date for her sister, who's less outgoing than she is. That's the price of admission, if you catch my drift," Dempster winked, "to the twin I like."

Now Balting smiled slightly. "Well, that shouldn't be too difficult. Getting the sister a date I mean."

'Exactly. I was hoping you'd see it that way. How about helping out your old friend—you be the sister's date.

This unexpected turn in the conversation immediately tensed Ed. He had still not cracked his intense shyness with young women and except for a few occasional "fix-up"s he'd hardly dated at all so far. Also, the notion of a "formal" large scale dance would only hone his considerable insecurities to an even keener anxiety level.

"No,,,, I don't think so…. I don't even know her. I mean I haven't even seen her."

" So what, I could introduce you and we could double date once or twice before the dance.And then we could double date for the dance too."

"But what if I didn't like her… or, she didn't like me….?" Despite all his insecurities and ineptitude with women, Balting still cherished an ideal of romantic love which he believed he'd fulfill some day.

"So what. Why are you making such a big deal of it? It's just a date. Don't you want to be at the Junior Dance? They're cute, you'll like them… Her….whatever. Why make a federal case out of it? Besides, I think we might get something from them if we play our cards right. At least the one I'm dating seems ready—if you know what I mean." Another wink.

This utilitarian approach to passion only further put off Balting. "I just couldn't… I have to be motivated….I guess I'm still waiting for the ideal woman."

"Well, it might be a long wait. And this is good practice. Ah, come on. Don't make something that's straightforward and easy into such a big, complex deal."

"I'd like to help you out, but it's just not the way I operate. I have to want to…." Balting equivocated.

For the next twenty minutes Dempster urged, implored,inveighed, intimated and generally kept the pressure on Balting. Ed would normally have quickly caved in to such an assault. He wasn't resolute in resisting others, in thwarting them, or making them unhappy. In general he also just liked trying to be helpful to a friend in any way he could. In fact, just because of his insecurities he felt obligated in many instances of this sort. But this, simply, he couldn't do. Not even to relieve heavy pressure. He didn't want to go out with someone he had no motivation to date and he certainly didn't want to go to the Junior Dance under such conditions.

Eventually Demptster sensed Ed's impregnable resistance and eased off his persistence. Soon he broke off the doughnut fest , saying that he had to go to study.

Once in a while they continued to get together for an activity, usually sports related, and each continued academically successful. During their senior years Demptster was admitted to P&S, Cornell and University of Californai, San Francisco medical schools and Balting got into law school at Columbia and Harvard.

In their senior year, when some of these results started coming in, Demptster began heavily dating a sophomore girl with whom he soon became frequently intimate. Or, at least, so Demptster boasted to his friends, including Balting. At this time that assertion made many of them envious. She wasn't a particularly attractive young woman, rather plain in fact. But the achievement of bedding her was what counted with so many of Dempster's acquaintances. Balting, too, appreciated the scoring, but certainly didn't covet the girl in question. He didn't continually wish he were in Nelson's shoes, or out of them on her bed. He was still holding out.

After a few months of parading her around as his mistress and after Dempster had been admitted to the three medical schools he started dating a junior woman, Valerie Hazeltine. She, indeed, was a universal object of envy. Angelic faced, under a halo of authentically honey golden hair and with a figure that compelled the immediate attention of highly hormonal young men, she was also known around the campus as a sweet tempered, decent person. Someone usually friendly, pleasant and forthcoming. Wanting to help where she could and not flaunting her gifts and attributes. She didn't condescend to anyone who was not so fortunately, or much less fortunately, privileged.She was not intensely intellectual but did responsibly well, if not spectacularly, in school. She also was extremely well-liked by a considerable number of her classmates. Physically beautiful, she led by, and was looked up to for, her gracefulness and humanity.

Towards the very end of the academic year, when Balting and Dempster had already decided which professional schools they'd go to, a mutual firend, Howard Gordon, who'd graduated from the college the year before and was already completing his first year of medical school, and his wife, Babette, invited Balting, Dempster and Valerie and another mutual friend in Balting and Dempster's class, Sam Jacklin, over for dinner. The stated occasion was to celebrate the attainments of the three graduates. (Dempster, in fact, would graduate as Salutatorian.) Gordon had been a bit of a big brother to the other three men and was proud how all of them had come through. (Jacklin had been admitted to the graduate History program at Yale.)

Balting still got a little nervous at the prospect of such gatherings. But in addition to not wanting to turn down Gordon whose help he appreciated immensely, he liked all the other people who'd be there. Also, he was feeling pretty good about himself these days since Harvard Law School had informed him that he'd been awarded a half— tuition scholarship in recognition of his college grades and his performance on the LSAT, Law School Admission Test. He never even thought about saying "No" and by the time the appointed evening came around he was mildly looking forward.

But he did get there about twenty minutes after the 7:00 P.M. Gordon had mentioned because he always felt a little more at ease arriving after most of the others who were supposed to be at an event were already there than when he came on the early side and nervously had to wait for things to really get under way. Everyone was already there when he came in and greeted him warmly and festively. He felt a little more uneasy with Valerie because he'd only met her once,when he'd passed her and Dempster on campus and introductions were made.

But she was quite outgoing and effusive in her greeting, acting like she'd heard some things about him, knew something about him. He noticed how before dinner, when everyone was just generally mingling, she, effortlessly, chatted with each person in the room, seeming interested in what they would be doing next academic year and so on.

Just before she served dinner, Babette called out: "We have a Yale man, Sam, and a Harvard man, Ed, here. Do you think there'll be bloodshed before the night is over.?" This drew a general round of mock sounds of admiration, such as whistles and hearty phony applause. Ed felt a slight blush welling up, but concentrated on not letting it deepen and spread. He just called out, " No, but we know that we're superior to any Columbia men." Dempster evinced only perfunctory amusement at this sally, but Valerie, with great panache, asserted, "What's indubitably true is indubitably true."

During the meal Babette sat at one end of the dining room table, Howard at the other and Ed and Valerie on one side, Nelson and Sam on the other. Valerie was directly across from Nelson, Sam from Ed. There was much formalistic and nervous complimenting of Babette on the food and some general talk on the rigors of the first year at professional schools. Howard shared the benefit of his experience on that topic. Sam was prompted to say, "What about graduate school? I suppose we're not professional." For this he was inundated in boos and general derision.

Valerie commented, "I'm not graduating, so I suppose no one has any advice for me." She contorted her face into a baleful look, a child's face just prior to bursting into tears.

Ed shot in quickly, "We care about you, Valerie. We'll just defer our solicitude for a year."

"That's alright," she responded. "As long as I'm not forgotten and there's concern for me." Then, she affected a moderate southern accent and intoned, "I've always depended on the kindness of strangers."

Everyone laughed and Ed, starting to genuinely relax, called out "Touche." He was impressed that she could so lightly, so un—selfconsciously, draw upon "A Streetcar Named desire."

During a spirited discussion on whether the Cuban ambassador to the United Stations should have been invited to speak on campus, since his announced topic was to be "Communism as Freedom," Ed noticed that Valerie herself didn't say much. She seemed neutral or mildly in favor at best.. Ed who jumped in with the rabid free speech line noticed, however, that she followed the discussion closely, her large, clearly sparkling blue eyes moving from one to another of the more involved debaters. He soon realized that in addition to feeling obliged to speak for his side because he believed in it, sincerely and strongly, he was directing a lot of his eye contact and actual remarks toward Valerie in hopes of inducing her to agree with him .Somewhat similar to when an actor or lecturer, in a large auditorium,focuses on one person amidst the multitude and performs largely as if speaking to that person only.

Balting felt he'd had some success in converting Valerie because, as the discussion petered out, she made one of her few non—fragmentary comments: "So, what harm in letting him speak? Regardless of how repugnant, or even dishonest, what he said would be? If we're so sure he's wrong then what are we afraid of. Don't I remember from Freshman English, even, that John Stuart Mill wrote something about the truth becoming all the stronger by being challenged and tested in the marketplace of ideas?"

"Exactly!" Balting encouraged.

But Dempster, looking intently at Valerie, remonstrated with "But doesn't the 'marketplace of ideas,' he held up two fingers on each hand to indicate quotation marks, "presume an authentic debate? These people are just Commie ideologues."

Ed was going to start in on some of the more esoteric formulations of Marx, Engels, even Lenin, but Babette chimed in before he could get up full steam. "It seems like we're coming back to pretty much where we started on this.I don't know that anyone has convinced anyone of anything they didn't believe to begin with," she remarked. Like a good hostess who'd kept the chat moving along while it was still lively but who also knew when a discussion had exhausted itself.

That was it for table wide conversation for the rest of the short evening. From there things went to tete a tete or three way discussions on a variety of subjects and on a rotating basis.Balting found himself more at ease than usual, enjoying most of the chit—chat, both one on one and the group sort. For a good deal of the rest of the time he spoke with Valerie. About such things as who were the really outstanding professors, as teachers, at the college,what her own grade school teaching aspirations were, whether they were consistent with the theories of education of one of Ed's favorites, John Dewey, (Valerie had just taken a course on Dewey,) what Balting's aims in going to law school were and what some of the favorite novels and poems of each were.

Closng time came relatively early. Howard had a very heavy schedule in the clinic the next day, since medical students were being given more and more responsibility sooner and sooner. But the wine, as well as the conversation, had flowed freely and everyone felt satisfied, good, hopeful and energetic. The leave takings were plump with good cheer, mutual admiration and the heartiest of best wishes for continued successes and achievements.

On the way back, to his parents' place, Balting reflected on how much more enjoyable the evening had been than he'd anticipated, how much he really liked being with everyone there. He also felt good that he'd been able to talk fairly easily, comfortably, with such a strikinjgly attractive young woman as Valerie and thought that with a new start, so to speak, at Harvard, he might be able to sufficiently rout his shyness to get at least a few dates with some Radcliffe girls.

He slept a sound, wine assisted, nine hours. When he did awake he was still full of vitality and purpose. Very positive. His parents had already left for work and he took his time in putting together an immense breakfast of three scrambled eggs, bacon, two slices of generously buttered rye toast, two cups of coffee and one and a half sweet rolls. He was gluttonously sopping up the dregs of the eggs and bacon with the last segment of toast when the phone rang. Feeling that it was most likely for one of his parents and not wanting to break his own mood of well—being, he toyed with not answering. But his conscience finally persuaded him to pick it up.

"Hello," he said, reluctantly.

"Hi, this is Valerie Hazeltine.... You remember—from last night...."

PHILOSOPHY

THE COURSE REALLY BEGAN DURING the summer, before fall classes actually met.

Hank Lattimer had wanted to take "Philosophy 510, Recent Themes in Contemporary Thought," from the time he saw, near the end of his junior year, that it was being offered with just about his favorite professor, Jurgen Havemeyer. It seemed tailored to Philosophy majors,which Hank was not, (he was an English Literature man,) because many specific Philosophy courses, none of which he'd taken, excepting one, were listed as pre—requisites. The one he had taken, "Sign, Symbolism, Language," had been with Professor Havemeyer .

That's when Hank had come under the man's formidable pedagogical spell. Havemeyer was deadly serious , hardly ever cracking even the slightest smile, from scrupulously prompt beginning of class to precisely punctual end. In the fifty minute interim he spun out penetrating apercus and sharp insights galore. Sometimes these came at the expense of a hapless student who had dared ask a mal—formed or, worse, ill thought ou,t question. Havemeyer's riposte was often a rapier. Occasioanlly he even dropped a dry witticism, an iota of sparkle in his eyes, his mouth turning up a shred. But one usually needed an impressive intellectual arsenal to "get it" and these sallies were certainly few and far between.

Lattimer would normally have given up his aspiration to take Philosophy 510, but he had leanred so much from Havemeyer in the "Symbolism" course that he took unusual steps. He had done some work as a research assistant for a young professor. Kent Ginley, who'd been Hank's instructor in his freshman year Great Books course, and had maintained a nodding acquaintanceship with Ginley. He also knew that Ginley was a "friend" of Havemeyer's because the latter's name had come up once or twice in discussions Ginly and Lattimer had had, extra—curricular so to speak, of Hank's research duties.

Hank went to Ginley and told him of his passion to take Phil. 510 and asked the young professor whether there might be any way around the forbidding pre-requisites. Ginley understood and said that he would see what he could do. He reported back that he'd asked Havemeyer about Hank taking the class without having the pre—requisites or whether there was something Hank could do to compensate for not having them under his belt. Ginley didn't say so directly, but Hank felt pretty sure that Ginley would have basically recommended him, for his seriousness and competence and as someone adept enough to probably be able to navigate the course without those formal pre—requisites. The upshot was that Havemeyer wanted to talk to Hank.The prospective student was to make an appointment.

He did, with Havemeyer's secretary, and the specified time came around. When Hank was taken in to Havemeyer's office the brilliant teacher was in short sleeves, but with his conservatively striped tie still snugly in place. Hank was sure that even taking his jacket off, in the privacy of his own office, was a substantial concession by Havemeyer to contemporary mores. In his mind's ear Hank could hear him fulminating against the deterioration of standards.

The esteemed professor, behind his large, solid desk, gazed at Hank like a judge waiting for a petitioning lawyer to start his argument.

"Well, sir, I think Professor Ginley told you about my wanting to take your contemporary philosophy course, but not having....".

" He did. About your wanting to take "Recent Themes in Contemporary Philosophy, you mean?"

"Yes, right, that's it. You probably don't remember, but about a year or so ago, I took your 'Signs, Language and Symbolism" coiuse and....."

" Actually I do recall that you were in there."

"Well, I got a pretty good...."

" Yes, you did rather well.l I looked it up."

"Well, I was just wondering whether even though I don't have the proper pre—requisites, the ones you ask for, whether I could still take...."

"Yes, as I've said, Professor Ginley mentioned that you wanted to enroll in 'Recent Themes in Contemporary Thought.' What are you doing this summer?"

"Oh, I have a job lined up in the General Post Office in Manhattan. As a mail clerk. I have to earn a little...."

"Will you have time to read a history of philosophy?"

"Oh, yes, professor. I think so. I'll be working the 4:00 P.M. to midnight shift, but then...."

"Go to the university bookstore and acquire "Philosophy In The West," by W.T. Jones. Last time I looked they had a copy. Read through that during the summer and we'll see you in the course in September."

Hank's heart gave a modest, pleasant leap. "Oh, thank you, sir. Thank you."

Havemeyer just waved his hand, casually, and quickly said "You're welcome," as he returned his eyes to the open book on his desk. Hank didn't know whether the wave signified minimizing what Havemeyer had done for him or merely expressed the professor's desire for Hank to, depart as soon as possible.

~

Hank didn't read every one of the eleven hundred plus pages in the Jones tome. He skipped, judiciously, he thought, but did read a good deal of the material. He enjoyed it, as he liked reading Philosophy in general and felt that he'd learned quite a bit in a pleasurable way. It was an excellent diversion from sorting letters according to zip codes and then jamming them into appropriate pigeon holes.

At the first class meeting of Philosophy 510 Havemeyer gave no indication, whatsoever, that he and Hank had conferred about the Jones volume and summer preparation. He was all business, from the very start, with the 25—30 students in the class. He distributed the syllabus, his mien very serious, almost doleful,l and quickly plunged into introductory comments about the first section of readings.

It continued like that, session after session, eventually settling into a pattern which might have been monotonous had not the scholar's comments, remarks, even asides, about luminaries of Philosophy such as Wilhelm Dilthey, A.H. Bradley, John Dewey and the Logical Positivists, e.g. A.J. Ayer, Rudolf Carnap, Moritz Shlick, etc.l been so insightful and provocative. He stimulated, as few teachers did, chiefly by his analyses, but by his sheer opinionatedness as well. His reactions to the thrust of each thinker were not hidden under a bushel.

Indeed, there was the time when a student, after one of Havemeyer's perfectly formulated and enunciated critiques of someone, or something or other, offered. "But, sir, you have just engaged in nothing but an emotive, rather than objective, means of expression. It was in the vein that Professor____ says is impermissible. He admonishes that we just can't, we mustn't, speak like that." Havemeyer fixing the intellectual interloper with his, at once, diffident, yet unremittingly piercing eyes, rejoindered, simply, "Who is to stop us?" The callow, aspirant philosopher folded. That was that.

But Havemeyer didn't shut off all inquiry or dissent in such blunt fashion. While he mostly lectured and told "anecdotal" stories and vignettes to make his points, (for example he once, somehow, mentioned a paperback edition of the short stories of Thomas Mann and opined that the first story. "Death in Venice," was itself enough to justify purchasing the book,) he also allowed student "questions," or even "objections" and argument as to points he had made. Hank certainly wasn't audacious enough to try any of that derring--do, himself, but he enjoyed listening to the by—play engendered when others did.

Since there was a good deal of "quiet time," when Havemeyer might simply emphasize or reiterate a point he'd already made, Hank started to focus on his fellow students and ob serve as much as possible about them. He made up "histories" and "biographies for some. At twenty libido was high and he tended to concentrate on the women in the class. Almost any woman could be "evaluated" from this perspective.

He particularly noticed two of them. The first was an "older" woman. She must have been very late thirties, even early to mid—forties, with a dowdy hair—do and, indeed, an overall dowdy, middle—aged, decidedly non—glamorous appearance. She seemed to especially favor, sartorially, a loose hanging, capacious, covering a multitude of sins, dress in a bold checkered fabric. Hank also noticed that she took notes supra—intensively. She appeared to copy down each and every word Havemeyer uttered, or, at the very least, got writer's cramp trying. She took the briefest of mini—breaks to wring out her writing hand. Her face was almost always, literally, in her notebook as her pen scrawled along furiously, (since Havemeyer tended to speak fairly crisply and briskly, a master of staccato.(In bits and pieces of conversation he heard her engage in with other students, immediately before and after class, he picked up that she was a long married woman, children close to fully grown, who was returning to the university to get her Ph. D. in her college major, Philosophy.

The other woman Hank was more or less forced to notice. She was a slender person, seemingly just a bit older than most of the other students. So, almost certainly, a graduate student rather than an undergraduate. Hank thought of her as "foreign" because her skin was tinged with a brownish hue, although she couldn't have been classified as anything other than Caucasian, and her hair wasn't unyieldingly fixed in one of the common patterns that most of the young woman around the university chose. Instead it was more amorphous and "sloppier" looking. A strand here, another there, others in yet different directions. Hank also was pretty sure that he heard accented English when she occasionally chatted with some of the other students.

He usually got to class about five minutes before it began, punctually--Havemeyer was virtually unceasingly punctual--- at, almost always, exactly ten after the hour. Starting in the third or fourth week of the course Hank noticed that this young, "exotic" woman, whom, to himself he did refer to as "the foreigner," would be waiting at the classroom door when he arrived for each session. At first he assumed that she must have been waiting for another class member to whom she particularly wanted to tell something. However, as the weeks flowed on past mid—semester he grew aware that no matter how early he got to the classroom she was there, waiting outside. He also began noticing that after he went by her to enter the room she left her post and went to her normal seat in the class. In time she began unmistakably smiling at him when he approached the room, turning to face him directly, expectantly.

Hank's basic mien was polite and deferential and when she first began doing this Hank returned her smiles so as not to offend her. Finally it dawned on the naïf that she wanted him to acknowledge her, to greet her, to talk to her. This presented difficulty for the intensely shy Hank. Even he had caught on to the fact that she liked him, but he didn't know what to do about it. He wasn't especially attracted to her purely physically, but, as a nineteen year old male,he had urgent, unfulfilled, erotic impulses and she seemed appealing enough, in a generic sort of way, as well as needful of male, or more specifically, his attention.

In whatever interstices there were between Hank's extensive studying sessions he gave a great deal of thought to "the foreigner" and her continually welcoming smile. He had boldly augmented his return smile with a nod but couldn't even conceive of going further. As she persisted in seeming to desire that he go. However, several weeks after she'd started, Hank noticed that she stopped waiting for him at the entrance to the classroom. When he'd arrive she'd already be in her seat, usually chatting to someone nearby. Or she'd come just before the class began when Hank was already in his seat—rows from hers.

He was somewhat relieved, the pressure was off---but guilty. Also disappointed. In his reveries about her he had started seeing her with less, or no, clothing on and had liked what he'd seen. Slender, but shapely where a Philosophy grad student should be shapely. "Conceptually" he'd thought about asking her if she wanted to go for a cup of coffee after class. What he couldn't imagine was how he would, in reality, have done that.

Once she had stopped waiting for him before class she never even really looked at him again. Even though he had tried to catch her eye once or twice from his seat. Then he started trying not to think about how she must feel about him. Or about how hurt she must have been.

The mature woman who favored the loud checks kept on scribbling furiously. She never flagged, throughout the course. Havemeyer spoke, she wrote. Head down, face screwed into concentration, shoulders hunched. However, when only two or three weeks remained in the course, on a day when Havemeyer was soliloquizing on some aspect of the social theory of John Rawls, she suddenly stopped writing, abruptly raised her head, and her arm shot up. She waved it determinedly, vigorously, in the time tested method for a student to get a teacher's attention.

Even the unflappable Havemeyer seemed a bit non—plussed .

"Mrs. Weston?"

"Well, yes, professor.... What you were just saying about Rawls's concern for the least well off in a society, it reminded me about something that Aristotle wrote about slavery."

"Oh, yes?"

Yes, very much so."

She then mumbled something about a passage in Aristotle's "Politics" in which he mentioned, in very brief passing, that some men "deserved" to be slaves, were fit only to serve others, their betters. It had, Hank thought, nothing at all really to do with anything that Havemeyer had been saying about Rawls, or, even, anything that Rawls had written in his book. Hank could see from the totally perplexed expressions of his classmates, as well as Havemeyer's incipiently quizzical look, that just about everyone else in the room felt the same.

But, suddenly, Havemeyer's face determinedly brightened and he animatedly broke into her aimless rambling.

"Aha! I see just what you mean, Mrs. Weston. You're suggesting...." He then converted her fragmentary, disconnected comments into what he claimed she *really* meant to say. He mentioned, providing a citation, some other Aristotelian allusion to slavery and wove it into a mini theoretical formulation that he then persuasively connected to the Rawlsian material on which he'd been lecturing. Everyone realized that he'd put brilliant words into Mrs. Weston's mouth, as he went on for a few more minutes spinning the philosophical web ever more intricately and fully.

When he finished he looked at her and said, "So that's what you were driving at. I understand now."

She gazed at him for a few seconds, confusedly, and then began nodding slowly, hesitantly. Finally she sat back, a slight smile breaking through her intense concentration on Havemeyer's every word and gesture. Then she enjoyed nodding more rhythmically.

Havemeyer smiled also, broadly for him, and quietly said, "Good, good. Now let's continue with Rawls. And all that follows."

Hank kept on thinking about this incident until the final meeting of the course. When it was clear that Havemeyer had said his final words the students broke out, enthusiastically, with the customary concluding applause of appreciation. Havemeyer waved it away, remarking, "Some of you who've had me for other courses know how intensely I dislike that "*ritual.*"

Hank continued thinking about the Mrs. Weston incident long afterwards. Indefinitely, actually. He got an "A-" from Havemeyer in the class. But that was what he had really learned.

EARLY MORNING

THE TROUBLE WITH LIVING IN the suburbs but working in Chicago's Loop was that you had to allow an hour and a half on the Freeway. Under ideal conditions it should only take about a half—hour, but having to be on time for the 9:00 A.M. Contracts class Robert Manell taught, on Monday, Wednesday and Friday, was far from ideal conditions. In rush hour the trip could easily consume over an hour, sometimes up to ninety minutes. So Robert had to leave before 7:30 to ensure that he'd be there for the start of class. Even with that precaution he sometimes missed by five or ten minutes. But there was only so much you could do.

As things worked out, for some inexplicable reason, known only to traffic engineers, if even them, he would often get there not much after 8:00 a fair amount of the time. Not bad, because it was a good time to get some real work done, pen actually put to paper, without the tyrannical intrusions of ringing phones and colleagues wanting to chat about nothing much. As far as he could tell there was hardly anyone in the twenty storey building at that time. A few maintenance people at most.

However, occasionally at that time, as he rode the elevator to his ninth floor office, he ran into a pleasant looking, rather pretty, middle—aged to older woman dressed in the light blue cotton dress and sturdy, boxy, lace-up shoes uniform of a university custodial person. Usually she had a rag and a bottle of Windex, or some such cleanser, in her hands. Her hair was a dull red and worn in an extremely neat and flattering manner to her open, clear—eyed face. She'd get on the elevator at maybe four or five and get off at seven or eight, or keep on going after Robert got off at the ninth floor. The first few times this happened they each more or less looked at the other briefly and then studied a wall of the elevator, or its floor design, until the other left. Since there was no one else around to barge in, when he arrived that early Robert usually kept the door to his office open. But he never saw her pass on the way to do any cleaning on nine. She not only had pleasing, well—defined features, but she had a certain dignified bearing as well. Robert thought, quite against his customary egalitarian instincts, that she was not your "typical" maintenance worker.

He kept encountering her, early in the morning, on the elevator, every few weeks and they progressed to greeting each other with smiles and nods. But the pattern of never getting off at the same floor persisted, just as Robert never saw her working on the ninth floor. After a month or two they started speaking to each other about banalities like the weather and how bad the traffic was that morning. Robert concluded that she was interested in traffic because he'd decided that she worked the Midnight to 9 A.M. shift and was guaging how laborious driving home was likely to be for her. But on second thought he wondered whether she even had a car, whether she could afford one on the pittance she must make as a nighttime custodian. He also wondered whether she had another job during the day to make ends meet.

Their conversations expanded as the months went by and soon they were into their second year of acquaintance. But the topics remained of the extremely small talk variety. Time slid by and it was mid—November. Going up in the elevator one morning, about 7:45, Robert was musing that he hadn't seen her for a while when the elevator stopped on the fifth floor and she got in. There were mutual greetings and broad smiles.

Robert animatedly said, "I've missed you. It seems like a while since I last saw you. I hope everything is o.k."

"Oh yes, professor, everything is fine. And what of you?"

As their conversations had lengthened Robert had realized that she had the merest hint of an Irish brogue. That's where the red hair came from, he speculated. No dyes, just heritage.

"I can tell you, without any hemmig and hawing that it's cold out there today. Winter is definitely here. I mean cold!!"

'Yes, well it's to be expected. Thanksgiving is here next week, you know."

It immediately crossed Robert's mind that logical sequence required that he should ask what her plans were, where, when and how she would spend the holiday. That's exactly what he would have done with anyone else with whom he would be having this conversation. A friend, colleague or neighbor, for example. But as those words were about to come out of his mouth he thought better of them and revised his response.

"Yes, it is, and from there it's a short hop to the end of another year. As the saying goes, they seem to fly by faster and faster."

She smiled and nodded assent. "No doubt they do, especially at my age." She paused, but then continued, "But tell me professor, what are you doing for Thanksgiving?"

He was flumoxed and the thought crossed his mind that it wasn't really his answer she wanted but the return question, so that she could tell him that she had nothing to do on the holiday,---- an appeal to be included in his. But he also felt that it would be brutally impolite if he didn't ask the normal question. Politeness won out over self—protective caution.At the same time he remained circumspectly vague about his family's day.

"Oh, it'll just be the usual with the family. Wife and kids, nothing too special. How about yourself?"

"I'm going to California to be with my daughter."

Greatly relieved Robert enthused, "Oh, that's wonderful. Terrific, just great. So your daughter lives in California?"

"Yes, in the San Francisco area. She's a law student at the University of Californai, Berkeley.You know, professor, at Boalt Hall.

He certainly did know of one of the premier law schools in the country. One far better than the one for which he and the red headed maintenance lady worked. Now he was not only relieved, but genuinely enthusiastic for the woman. "That's a magnificent school, one of the very best. You must be so proud of her," he effused.

"Yes, I am" she said as the elevator stopped at the eighth floor and she got off. "Have a nice Thanksgiving."

The door closed on Robert's "You too." He went along the corridor toward his office, mentally calculating how many maintenance lady pay checks equaled one semester's tuition. But before he got there he felt his eyes moisten.

LOSING INNOCENCE

At thirteen and fourteen we boys, in the early 1950s, didn't do too much besides talk about and root for the Brooklyn Dodgers, (the only Real McCoy ones there ever were, L.A. doesn't count) schmooze about girls, rather than dating and touching them and do enough homework to get the stellar grades our parents, who remorselessly designated us as future doctors, lawyers, accountants,expected of us.

Much of this gabbing happened while we just stood or sat around. Especially in that summer of 1951 when our beloved "Brooklyns," as the sagacious Dodger announcer, Red Barber, called them sometimes, (he referred to himself as "The Ol' Red Head,) got off to a blazing start, opening a tremendous lead over their and our hated rivals, the Manhattan dwelling New York Giants. Occasionally we threw a ball back and forth as we discussed, argued and dreamed. But whether we did that or, instead, sat on one of the benches which lined the generously tree lined parkway running past the twin six—storey apartment houses in which most of us lived, or sprawled on one of the stoops which led up to the walkway to these buildings, the bull sessions went on.

Would the Dodgers again win the pennant as they had on the last day of the '49 season, or fall just short, as when they were beaten in the last game of the '50 season. Would Jackie Robinson, as he grew older, after all he was already twenty—eight when he so brilliantly broke the Major League color line in 1947, making all of us immensely proud to be Brooklynites, still be as dominant a player as he was in 1949, when he won the Most Valuable Player Award, hitting.342, knocking in 124 runs and stealing 37 bases to boot. Who was that really built girl, she seemed about fifteen, sixteen, who sometimes strode down one of the avenues bounding our block, intersecting the parkway, at about four—thirty on weekday afternoons. She never even so much as glanced our way if we lurked nearby, but we sure more than glanced at her. Even though we were still too shy to make it obvious, or emit any appreciative sounds or whistles, her entrancing bearing, head high, beautifully shaped figure moving confidently, was inscribed on our mastubatory memories.

Dan,one of the friends I spent a lot of time with was a neighbor in the next door apartment house. One summer he told me he'd gotten a real bargain on Spaldeens, (made by the A.G. Spalding Company,) the pink rubber ball with which we played our endless games of stickball on the street behind the apartment houses. Also our frequent punch ball and stick ball games. Instead of the usual 25 cents per Spaldeen price he'd seen a sign on a local sporting goods store advertising Spaldeens for nineteen cents apiece. He thought it would be a good idea to stock up since we lost them so easily. For example, by hitting them on the gutter of the roof of the armory which ran along the street of the stickball "field." He'd bought five balls for himself and five for me. I got an advance on a week or two of allowance to pay him the ninety—five cents and was delighted.

However, a few days after this transaction, a few of the balls already swatted to irretrievability, I happened to be walking past the sporting goods store, --whose owner was a real live referee in the fledgling National Basketball Association, you could even see him on television-- and saw a large sign in the window: "SALE---- Spaldeens---12 cents." So, Dan had introduced me to capitalism to make 35 cents for himself. I felt deeply betrayed and told him so. He just shrugged in his guilt. We didn't talk too much for some time afterwards.

Both of us, as well as some of the other fellows, learned something else during one of those sweet summers. There was a quite short, early middle—aged man who lived alone in a small apartment in Dan's building. He seemed to go to and from work normally enough, but there was a prominent indentation in his lower forehead, as though something exceedingly heavy had depressed the area and it had never sprung back to its normal state. We also detected an English accent when he spoke to neighbors. All-in-all we regarded him as an hilariously abnormal figure. Since we were typically sassy, maybe even nasty, adolescents this seemed to require some demonstrativeness by us. We took to following him, even if only for short distances, when he came out of and went into his building, emitting noises intended to be catcalls and jeers and declaiming words with what to us was a hysterical, convulsive laughter inspiring, mock English accent. He endured it without visible reaction for a couple of weeks. But one day, as we trailed after him plying our malicious routine, he suddenly stopped and turned. We stopped too and got a bit apprehensive about reprisal, perhaps physical. But he just genially beckoned us to come closer to him.

When we did, gingerly, he spoke very calmy and softly. "You all seem like nice lads who generally do what you should. Mind your folks and all that. But let me ask you, do you know anything about me?"

We slowly shook our heads, almost imperceptibly.

'Well, the thing of it is, is that you can't always tell everything about a person just by looking at him. You know, the saying about a book and its cover.For example, as you see, I'm quite short in stature, yet it so happens that I can lift barbells of some considerable weight. Almost two hundred pounds actually." Our eyes widened in genuine surprise as he concluded with a smile, "So, there, now, be good lads and run along to your vices and devices and try not to judge people too quickly any more."

We immediately did as we were told. And each time we came upon him after that we would smile and wave and say hello, very courteously and amiably, As he did with us.. But not very long after he'd instructed us, it couldn't have been longer than to the next summer, one of our mothers was told, and, in turn, told one of us, who told all the other guys, that the little man had passed away. No further information—just that he had died. In my jejeune way I wondered whether the forehead indentation had anything to do with his premature death. And when I grew into full adolescence I started thinking about whether when he'd told us about the weight she'd known that he was ill and likely to soon be no more. Only a few years after that, in college, did I read Keats's line "When I have thoughts that I may cease to be." The little neighbor instantly flashed into my mind.

The Dodgers kept on streaking in the summer of '51, increasing their lead over the Giants to an almost insurmountable margin before the season was almost half over. We spent a lot of time at Ebbets Field cheering them on. We'd also get there very early before games and stay after them in hopes of getting players, on their way in and out of the park, to give us their autographs. An effective method became handing a player a blank postcard addressed to yourself so that he wouldn't have to stop right there and sign for kid after kid. Virtually always these cards were, indeed, mailed back to you with the sought after autograph on the back. At the time it didn't occur to any of us that the signatures might not be authentic. Only years later did there seep into our consciousness the possibility that players had handed their stack of cards to the clubhouse boy, or trainer for the signing of the player's name and subsequent deposit in a postal box.

An extremely difficult autograph to obtain was that of Preacher Roe, the Dodgers' outstanding pitcher, whose record was 22-3 in 1951. In the off-season he taught mathematics in a high school in his native Arkansas. As he once put it, curves interested him. It seemed that no matter how late we would wait outside the clubhouse entrance he always outlasted us and our need to be back home by supper time. He must have calculated to emerge only after we'd left in frustration.

But my pal, Hank, and I decided we just had to have his autograph so one game day, with parental approval, we determined to wait, as long as necessary, until he came out. When he finally did he was certainly surprised to see us, on the otherwise deserted street, as we thrust our autograph pads at him. We'd figured that, with no one else around, he might even sign right there, on the spot. He chuckled, saying, "You caught me you little rascals," and stopped in his tracks to sign each of our books. And instead of just writing his name, which was all the postcards usually came back with, he also wrote something like "With best wishes," or "To a real fan," over his large and flourished signature. Then, as we were about to exultantly depart , he took each of us by an elbow and started skipping. He pulled us along, inexorably, and we joined him in skipping the hundred feet or so it took him to reach his car. We waved good—bye to him from the sidewalk and he waved back as he ducked behind the wheel.

Maybe major leaguers were more congenial back then, in that seemingly simple summer of '51. On another occasion I went down to the ballpark alone, no friends along, hours before a game with the Giants who were falling further and further behind the Dodgers. By mid—seaosn the gap was almost ten games. There were a bunch of we kids loitering and wandering around the players' entrance and, sure enough, before too long, striding toward us came the very tall, lean and rawly strong looking Giants pitcher, Jim Hearn. He was having an excellent season, on track for every pitcher's dream, a twenty wins year. As the horde of boys closed in around him he started grabbing the postcards held out to him and continued, now reduced to a fast shuffle,toward the locker room door. When it seemed as if he'd grabbed every proffered card and the crowd around him was parting, he suddenly, as though in afterthought, halted and faced around. In a voice that was a surprisingly thin tenor he drawled, "Who, heah, wants a free ticket to a game?"

Met with a resounding chorus of "I do"s he announced, "O.k., evuhboduh pick a numer, take a numbuh from one to fiftuh, but keep it to yerself. O.k., does everboduh have 'un?" On being assured by the minor throng that that was the case, he started pointing at individuals and asking for their numbers.

'Eight" was shouted out,then "Twenty—Three," but Hearn just wordlessly shook his head and pointed to other boys.

"Five" failed, so did "Thirty—three." "Twenty—one" didn't work, nor "Fifty."

Suddenly Hearn's finger jabbed at me. "Nineteen" I blurted.

'Yah got it," the tall Southenrer allowed, "Mah uniform numbuh."

He plucked the ticket from his jacket pocket and held it out to me with a broad smile. I barely could muster the moxie necessary to hold my hand out to take it. But I did and then he turned quickly and headed purposefully toward the players' entrance.

When I backed away from the group of autograph seekers and looked at the ticket I saw that it was a grandstand pass. An upgrade from the sixty cents bleacher seats where I usually sat but, not, on the other hand, a more expensive reserved seat. But it was good for any game, not just for the one scheduled that day. I've thought about the incident many times since, but I've never been able to decide whether I knew, consciously or sub—consciously, Hearn's number and picked "Nineteen" for that reason or whether, instead, I just got lucky.

When I wasn't with my friends I probably was studying. Reading away toward academic success. However, sometimes you had to go along with parents to visit a relative or on a special Sunday outing to Manhattan.We went on one of those in late August, '51 as the baseball season was nearing its end. The Dodgers invincible lead over the Giants had peaked at thirteen and a half games, a week or two before, and the Giants had started gaining ground to the point that what had seemed totally certain just a short time ago, the Dodgers winning the pennant, was now in increasing doubt. I regarded myself as already too old to accompany my folks on week—end excursions and was particularly annoyed at having to do it that Sunday because the Dodgers were locked in a close game when it was time to leave our apartment. As we walked the streets of Manhattan my thoughts were in Brooklyn and I was delighted when I heard Red Barber's voice delivering the play—by—play over a portable radio that a newsstand vendor was listening to intently. Breaking away from mom and dad I walked over quickly and asked the fellow fan what the score was.

"They're down by three runs in the sixth."

"Who?" I asked. "Who's winning?"

"The Bums is losin' by three. Like I said."

The crestfallen expression must have suffused my entire face.

"Kid, what're you getting' so excited for? They're playin' for money kid. They don't know or care that you're rootin' for them."

I retreated back to my parents, totally disenchanted and subdued. I thought about what he said for quite a while afterwards. At first I resisted, but then I sensed he was probably right and accepted it. But I decided it didn't matter. I still loved them, whatever their motivations or awareness.

Interest in the Dodgers paled just a little, but a little, as our interest in girls grew. Lois was the beautiful high school girl, several years older than us, actually my next door neighbor, who we would chase after any time we saw her entering the building. We'd chase her up the steps into the lobby and up the one flight of stairs to her family's place. We hadn't the slightest idea why we were chasing her—what would we have done had we caught her? She must have known how it was all bravado and that we were innocuous, but she acted as though it was urgent to outrun us. She raced away, the soft blonde hair gently bobbing, the slim legs, bobby sox and loafers churning one step after another, until we gave up.She smiled and giggled as she fled. She must have known, on some level, that we harassed her because we loved her beauty and her gentleness. We didn't chase any of the other girls in the side—by—side buildings.

The gossip was that Lois wanted to be a nun. But we weren't the only ones who appreciated her virtues. In her senior year she'd been asked out by the captain of the Brooklyn Prep, a Catholic high school, football team. She said yes and kept on saying yes. They became engaged to be married. Eventually we got to know who he was because sometimes, as when he took her home after a date, they'd walk into the apartment building together. He, like her, would smile and wave to us. He seemed like a good guy. But we didn't chase her any more. Even when she came home alone.

Girls, women, those in—between, became a greater and greater interest. We started liking them for more than softness and angelic beauty a la Lois. Howie lived on the fourth floor of one of the apartment buildings. We didn't have much to do with him since he, like Lois, was a few years older than we. But he had a younger sister, Nancy, a few years younger than us, at the very earliest stages of presenting an outward curving torso. One evening we fellows were all sitting on a bench facing the buildings. One of us, just randomly looking upwards, saw an open fourth floor window, brightly displaying Howie's sister, Nancy, as she stepped forward, backwards, to the side. Hands on hips, then shoulders, also at her sides. Forty—five degrees in one direction, same in the other. With prurient brilliance, faces reddening, we deduced that she must have been standing on her bed and modeling for, as well as examining, herself in a mirror. After a few minutes she took off the dark red sweater she'd been wearing and more or less repeated the prancing, stepping movements, her upper body clad only in her brassiere. Because of the distance at which we were doing our viewing precise details were difficult to discern but we definitely appreciated the general contours of the show. It went on that way for a few more minutes and then she removed the brassiere. There wasn't very much under it but there didn't have to be for us to feel that we'd experienced a spectacularly eventful evening.

We argued amongst ourselves, for days afterward, whether she was aware all the time, or became aware, that we horny boys were watching. Whether she had or hadn't, we never looked at her, in the street or hallways, quite as casually as before. The same with brother Howie. We felt that in some way we probably knew his sister better than he did. We felt awkward and guilty, too, about that.

In the heat the Dodgers insurmountable lead continued to melt away. It was truly mountable, as Labor Day and the start of school loomed, since more than half was now gone and the margin was down to five or six games. But it wasn't the sheer decline in the fortunes of the Dodgers that bothered me most. Even if they held on to win, the CERTAINTY, that they would win, conferred with the buds and brightness of Spring, had been a chimera. In fact it seemed, at least in baseball, that there were no sure things. You could never be safe, never secure, unless mathematically, definitively, all contingencies eliminated. This was unforgiving knowledge. It gnawed inconsolably.

Nancy was a budding girl. Lois a budding woman. For sheer lust we evaluated women, fully grown, youngish, mature, even older. From the two buildings we identified two younger middle—aged women we deemed the most sexually provocative. Not just the most—they were, in fact, highly sexually stirring. This determination was an objective one, based solely on sex appeal, as one of the women so honored was the mom of one of our group. He concurred with the rest of us that on a purely clinical basis she was entitled to the accolade.

The other woman, Lil, was just about the same age as our pal's mom, but she had no kids. She was married to Jack, an appliance salesman.

Despite Lil's unquestionable attractiveness to us, our friend's sexy mom had told her own husband that Lil felt neglected by Jack. Our friend had overheard. Infrequency of sexual relations was mentioned. We didn't find it hard to believe the negligence. Jack seemed a rather brusque type, usually hunched forward in haste, eyes straight ahead, as he zipped past us with only the scantest greeting or acknowledgment.

~

Throughout September, although the Dodgers played fairly well, winning more than they lost, they lost too many, and the Giants hardly ever did. They won thirty—seven of their last forty—four games, an incredibly torrid, defying the laws of probablilities pace. The Dodgers won twenty six of their last forty—eight---- nowhere near the superlative level at which they'd played most of the season. They felt the pressure of the onrushing Giants and it seemed to infect their own performance.

The fates that wrote the script were audacious beyond human imagining and on the next to last day of the season, when the Dodgers lost and the Giants won, the teams were tied for first place. On the very last day of the season the Giants had already won in Boston while the Dodgers trailed by four runs, in the sixth inning, in Philadelphia. We gave up---the impossible, the inconceivable, had actually happened: the Dodgers, thirteen and a half games ahead on August 13th, had lost the pennant.

Yet, and yet. We were of too little faith. The Dodgers great hitters blasted back to tie the game and send it into extra innings. Nevertheless,in the bottom of the twelfth, bases loaded, two outs, Phillies first baseman Eddie Waitkus lined a malevolent shot over second base headed for the outfield, the game winning hit in this life and death struggle. Brooklyn hearts fell irretrievably. We'd been given one last chance only to now be crushed. But yet, and yet. The great Jackie Robinson, second baseman indomitable, threw himself headlong at the ball and somehow managed to snare it in the webbing of his glove for the final out of the inning. On we went. The legendary sportswriter, Red Smith, twenty plus years later, in his magnificent obituary of Robinson, "The Death of an Unconquerable Man" wrote of "the scene that never fades," Jackie Robinson, stretched out full length, suspended in air, "in the insubstantial twilight, the unconquerable doing the impossible."

But our imperishable hero had thudded to the ground very hard and injured his shoulder and arm. When he got back to the bench he asked

Manager Chuck Dressen to take him out of the game. Pee Wee Reese, No. 1, the long—time Captain of the Dodgers came over to see what was happening.

"Jack, why do you want to come out ?" Reese inquired.

"Because I don't think I can help the team this way," No. 42 responded.

Reese, one of those most helpful to and supportive of Robinson when Jackie broke the color line in Major League baseball, four years before, said simply, "Well, if you can't I don't know who can."

Robinson stayed in. And in the fourteenth inning he lined a home run into the left field seats giving the Dodgers victory. They had fought back to a tie for the pennant after 154 games of the regular season. It would have to be settled in a three game play—off.

In the first game, at the beloved shrine, Ebbets Field, big Jim Hearn, who'd given me that free pass, pitched an outstanding game to beat the Dodgers 3-1. He choked off any outbursts from their explosive bats. They hardly threatened at any time. In the very first inning of the next game, at the polo Grounds, Jackie Robinson sent one of his patented vicious screaming liners into the left field stands to start the Dodgers off on a 10—0 romp to tie the series at a game apiece. Clem Labine, normally an outstanding relief pitcher, had started that MUST game and No. 41, to Robinson's 42, and had more than risen to the perilous occasion with a brilliant shutout.

The immortal third game was on a school day and that was where I had to be instead of in front of the television rooting the Brooklyns on. Two magnificent pitchers, Sal, "the Barber," Maglie, for the Giants and the huge Don Newcombe, who seemed to have pitched almost every day for the Dodgers in the last week of the season, battled it out in a very low scoring game. But Jackie Robinson knocked in some runs for the Dodgers. By the time I rushed in from school and turned on the television, impatiently waiting for it to "warm up," it was already the bottom of the eighth, the Giants at bat in the Polo Grounds, with the Dodgers leading 4-1. My relief was thick. Newcombe looked a bit peaked but he continued mowing the Giants down and they went quietly in the eighth.

The Dodgers, seeming to want to just get the game over with, followed suit in the top of the ninth. However, in the Giants last gasp, in the bottom of the ninth, the first two batters got hits off the tiring Newcombe. But then he got the first out on a harmless pop—up. But, alarmingly, the next hitter, tagged him for a sharp hit also, scoring a run. With the score 4-2 the Giants had the tying runs on base with only one out.

Manager Chuck Dressen finally faced up to Newcombe's fatigue and fading powers and waved in Ralph Branca from the bullpen. Branca had pitched pretty well, even if in a losing cause, as the starting pitcher in the first game. Giants third baseman Bobby Thomson, who'd hit extremely well in the Giants stretch run, and who had homered off Branca in that first play—off game, was the batter. Branca got a quick strike on him. The next pitch Thomson immediately smashed for a no—doubt about it home run into the inviting left field stands, just 257 feet, down the line, from home plate.

Absolute frenzy broke loose. The Giants chief announcer, Russ Hodges, instantly started screaming, "The Giants win the pennant; I don't believe it, the Giants win the pennant. The Giants win the pennant. The Giants win the pennant…." And so they had. I didn't believe it either, but I had to.

My mother called from her job, as secretary to the Administrator of Brooklyn Women's Hospital, to find out how the Dodgers were doing. I described what had just happened in a blizzard of profanity which, I'm sure, she'd had not the slightest idea I could command. Then I grabbed a Spaldeen and went downstairs and started flinging it violently against the low wall adjoining the stoop. Just moments after I began Dan came along furiously and repeatedly bouncing a Spaldeen. He,too, started firing the ball against the wall. We continued, almost in unison, for a long, long time, mumbling every expletive we could muster, until, finally, we, and our rage, were spent.

Bobby Thomson's "shot heard round the world," plus puberty were not easy to handle. Sexual awakening was much more pleasurable than the home run but it was a lot of turmoil for a single summer and fall.

About a year later I happened to be strolling past a neighborhood movie theater where I and my pals had often seen Three Stooges shorts, preceding movies we weren't at all sure we wanted to see, on pre—adolescent Saturday afternoons. I was on the opposite side of the street and saw Jack standing beside the wall which was the right side of the theater as you faced it. He would not be visible to someone who came out of the theater and turned left and went up the street past him, unless the person happened, at just the right moment, to turn their head to the left as they went by. As I continued walking I saw Lil leave the theater. She moved slowly and, especially to me, at that burning time, sinuously and provocatively, in a tightish skirt and heels, up the block past where Jack was standing. He let her get pretty far up the block before he started in that direction himself.

I thought about what I'd observed many times afterward, but I recognized, even then, that Jack was spying—making sure that Lil had, indeed, gone to the movies, as she must have told him she was, and, also, that she'd gone alone, that is not with a man, and that she would head home immiediately after the movie ended. I still think about the incident and its overtones.

Many summers after the Dodgers, (immortalized in the '70s in Roger Kahn's "The Boys of Summer,") had left Brooklyn for Los Angles, a still mourning zealot established the Brooklyn Dodgers Hall of Fame. Every few years there'd be a dinner to which all of the still living Brooklyn Dodgers would be invited. Too late for the great Jackie R.. But I met and shook the hands of Duke Snider, Pee Wee Reese, Don Newcombe, Ralph Branca, Clem Labine and others of those men who had so filled our youth with joy. Also seeming tragedy.

At one of those dinners I asked reliever Labine which of his two magnificent starting performances, the second play—off game against the Giants in '51, or the 1-0 ten inning victory over the Yankess, in '56, in the sixth game of the World Series, (the day after Don Larsen had pitched his perfect game,) was his favorite. He responded affably and unhesitatingly: "The play—off, the second game of the play—off." A few years after that encounter I happened to meet some people for whom Labine had worked, as a plant manager, in the off—season, while still a Dodger. I wrote to No. 41 telling him how much we'd loved him and highly these folks had spoken of him. He responded with a very gracious, beautifully written note, reminding me that Roger Kahn had mentioned Clem's love of books in "The Boys of Summer." One sentence in the note observed: "Fame is fleeting, but good friends are forever."

These dinners continue to this day and a key one is coming up to celebrate the fiftieth anniversary of the only World Series the Dodgers ever won while still in Brooklyn.When the last Yankee out of that Series, Elston Howard grounding out to Pee Wee Reese, had cemented the victory the Dodger announcer, Vin Scully, protégé of Red Barber and still the voice of the L. A. Dodgers, said, simply, "Ladies and gentlemen, the Brooklyn Dodgers are the champions of the world." He confessed afterwards that had he embellished he would have been overcome by emotion. Preacher Roe is still living in Arkansas and has been invited to every dinner that's been held. But he's never come. I'm still hopeful that he will appear at this next one.

HEARTBREAK

ELAINE WAS, IN THEORY, SMACK between attainable and unattainable. She was older than we early adolescents but not that much older; maybe, even, just a year or two. She too lived in one of the six storey apartment houses that the families of our small group of kids occupied and she had a nodding acquaintance with a few of the girls even though they were that year or more younger. She was a very pretty brunette, trim enough but not too thin, and with a tinge of what was then called pertness, or perkiness, about her, facade for a lurking, underlying seriousness. She certainly started arousing interest in we males of nascent puberty just by her appearance and the way she sort of swung herself briskly along, yet sinuously too, when she walked. But what really instigated rising lust in me, I think, was hearing an older boy, one more her own age, probably even older,exclaiming to one of his comrades, "Boy, have you ever seen Elaine in a bathing suit? Wow!! What a piece!!"

I, fully pubescent, had already been intensely stimulated by a photograph, in the entertainment section of the newspaper, of the movie star, Yvonne De Carlo. Statuesque in a bathing suit and high heels, right knee drawn up against left thigh. There had also been occasional shots of the likes of Marilyn Monroe and Jane Russell.But it was that casual, bagatelle remark which elicited scrupulous observation of Elaine. I scrutinized her fine features, the deeply ebony hair, the curve of her generous, but not outlandish, hips and most of all, the full, enticing breasts which seemed to provocatively precede she, herself. Naturally, I imagined each of her various entrancing parts unadorned and, also, of course,the whole package totally, completely, exposed. But I didn't ignore getting a sense of her personality too. The slightest bit aloof when first encountered she acted pleasantly and benignly enough, if a little subdued. But I didn't get too much chance to comprehensively size her up, (except, as I've indicated, in my mind's eye,) because her interactions with our group were sporadic and pretty fleeting. She, also, seemed to feel that she was Miss—in—between; she didn't know whether to associate with us, perhaps even guide us, or just dismiss us as beneath her more senior status.Nevertheless,, she was captivating, however she managed it, whenever one could be with her.

On a summer evening six or seven of us were sitting around on the stoop of one of the apartment buildings which fronted on a wide, long avenue. She emerged from the front door of the building, glided over to where we were and said that she'd looked out of the window in her room and had spotted us. She mentioned that she'd seen us laughing and had gotten envious of the fun we seemed to be having so decided to join us. She lilted an absolutely irresistible, low in the throat, chuckle. She sat right down on the stoop with the rest of us and was soon fully participating in the discussion, banter and general horsing around.

Someone suggested that it would be a good idea to stroll to the drugstore, two blocks down, and get ice cream cones. She liked that idea too and we all headed for "Doc's Pharmacy" where the old—fashioned fountain still could produce malteds, egg creams, sundaes and traditional ice cream sodas and cones. Doc, himself, even made them sometimes, if he wasn't busy grinding the components of a prescription.Being a registered pharmacist took actual scientific knowledge and skill back then.

To get to Doc's we went down one of the long, well lighted blocks of the tree—lined boulevard, enveloped by full darkness now. Then a right turn down a short residential block, with only a single, inadequate flickering street lamp, to the corner on which Doc's was located. Everyone in the group was in a bright mood, anticipating the extremely rich, fat—filled, ice cream and the deliciously crisp sugar cones into which Doc stuffed and pushed the double scoops. And all were in even a better mood once Doc had provided each of these bliss anticipating customers with the flavor he or she had selected.

So, with everyone contentedly licking and chomping away, we all left Doc's oasis and headed down that very dark residential block, retracing our steps.I stopped to retrieve one of the napkins I dropped soon after leaving the store and when I got up to resume walking Elaine was standing right beside me. After I startled with surprise, she smiled and we began walking after the rest of the group.We'd only taken a few catch—up steps into the darkness when she said, in that rich mezzo—soprano voice, "It's really pitch black here. I'm a little afraid," and hooked her free left hand and arm into my right one, which wasn't free—it held the cone.

But mostly I was embarrassed; one of the others might turn and see us touching. Much too brusquely I shot out, "I can't eat my cone that way," and, almost roughly, wrested my arm from hers. I felt badly as soon as I'd done it. Both because it was gauche, as well as discourteous, and because I very much wanted her arm to still be where it had been, with her left breast, too, nudging my upper right arm. She didn't say a word and in a few more steps we blended back into the other ice cream fans.

I rued my grandstand play, custom—made from shyness, for anyone who might care to see how virtuous and above board I was. I hoped she'd give me another chance. But, of course, just the reverse happened. Whenever she did associate with our group she seemed somewhat stand—offish and wary with me. Very few broad smiles and less free and easy throaty laughs. And Elaine never even came close to brushing against me, accidentally or otherwise, again. Except in my dreams, where, possibly, I hurt more than I'd caused her to hurt in reality.

She had a brother, Freddy, about five years older. He'd regularly lope and bound past us, uncoordinatedly, almost grotesquely, down and up the stoop, in and out of the apartment house, almost daily.But, even when we were all sitting there, he never said a word, or so much as acknowledged us, in his goings and comings. He just sped and jumped past us every time.Perhaps understandable in view of the age gap, but that didn't seem to really be the reason. After all, even someone "way above us," if that was the way he felt, could have passingly smiled or waved every once in a while. Even adults we knew only by sight would do that.

Actually, we never saw Freddy relate to anyone. Least of all Elaine if she happened to be with us as he hurtled by. Even to we still very callow teen—agers there seemed to be something strange. I don't know whether we used the designation "weird" then. From what we could pick up from Elaine he had some sort of pedestrian job which, apparently, accounted for his plentiful outs and ins.

Elaine, supplementing the mien of underlying seriousness, almost solemnity, which often seemed to drape her, was also a pretty good student. When she spoke about her high school classes, at least a year ahead of most of ours, it was usually to tell us about what she was learning in this one, what in that one, and how diligent she was in doing her assignments and studying for various exams. In fact, her school work seemed to fairly dominate her existence.

Surprisingly, especially considering what the older boy had said about the sight of Elaine in a bathing suit, her social life seemed rather circumscribed. Her parents, each tending toward being heavy—set and dour, were German---Jewish immigrants who believed in rules and regulations and in enforcing them.There was certainly a date here and there, how could there not be, but she, by no means, went out three times every week—end or for very long, or "seriously" with anyone. Back then, most girls of her age, didn't do much of that anyway.

One evening, when she was with our mostly—always—without—dates bunch she was very upset. She had assiduously and lovingly constructed a model, to precise scale, of a certain molecule, for her chemistry course. However, early that morning when she'd gone to her room to gather it up with her other things for school she'd found it smashed into virtual smithereens. As she told us the details she wrestled with tears. One or two fell and moistened her blouse, where her breasts protruded.Freddy had been the culprit. Her mom, doubtless where Elaine derived some of her voluptuousness, had disciplined him in some undescribed way. At least as much as one could with a young adult. But, afterwards, she'd made it a point to explain to Elaine that Freddy had his own problems, was often upset, and that the three of them had to try to understand him and empathize with him. When she related this incident Elaine seemed to be trying, very hard, to abide by what her mother had told her. But we got the impression that it was a struggle for her.

Dutiful and responsible student that she was Elaine was not as good in math and the sciences as she was in courses like English, History and French. She indicated to us that she had considerable problems in Trigonometry in her junior year. Jason, one of the fellows in our group, a rangy, fairly nice looking person, offered to help her. He was a bit older than the rest of we boys, but not as old as Elaine, and pretty much a super star in the math/science courses. He actually "knew" some of those courses even before he took them, formally, and could ask embarrassing questions of teachers who knew little beyond the text book.

Elaine accepted enthusiastically and they made an appointment for him to tutor her at her apartment. He told us this, she never mentioned a word, and he also said that she really wasn't bad at Trig at all. Mostly apprehensive because it was so different from Algebra and Geometry. He said she tended to get bogged down in the computational mechanics of the problem solving, even though she competently grasped salient concepts. He also, excitedly, revealed to we guys that when they were poring over the material at her kitchen table, trying to crack a tough exercise, she sat very close to him and smelled wonderful, with her breast practically nudging the arm with which he was writing. He tutored her another time or two with the same general result.

Jason was completely smitten and asked Elaine to go to the movies on a Friday evening. A real date. She agreed. Especially since she had done much better on the Trig test she took after Jason started helping her than she had on previous ones. Jason merely reported to us that she said she'd go. He didn't say much in anticipation. Jason had a certain forthrightness, some might find it blunt, even if feelings got bruised. He more or less said how it was, the chips falling where they might---including, sometimes, to his own disadvantage.

None of us made a special point of asking, but a few days after his date with Elaine Jason filled the guys in on what had happened. He'd picked her up in front of her building and they'd walked the block and a half to the theater chatting amiably enough. The film, "Ivanhoe," starring Elizabeth Taylor, whom Elaine resembled, was currently popular and they both were eager to see it. He reported her demure mode of dressing: pleated skirt, loafers and crisp white blouse, stretched quite tautly across that assertive, alluring chest. Her hair was up in a bun effect, displaying her flawless features as more sparkling than ever. After a decent interval, maybe twenty minutes, of watching the movie Jason put his arm around the back of Elaine's seat and slid it gradually upward until it was on her back, his right hand just brushing her right shoulder. This was allowed for about thirty seconds, but then she reached across with her left hand, took hold of his offending hand by several fingers and casually dropped it off her shoulder, restoring it to the cold, steel back of her seat. Jason said he felt encouraged by the half—minute of touching he was permitted and after another fifteen minutes or so he tried again. This time he grasped Elaine's shoulder more securely than on his previous foray. To his surprise and great consternation the liberty he was accorded was even briefer than during the initial effort. And this time his hand was virtually thrust from her shoulder, how far down the back of the chair it might wind up Elaine seemed not to care. Jason admitted that he felt pretty defeated at this point, but, for the sake of completeness of mission, he tried once more, toward the end of the film, going back to the light touch on her shoulder he'd started with. But Elaine's rebuff was even swifter and more forceful this time. It was made unequivocally clear that his hand was not to wander to her shoulder again. When the movie was over Jason, again completing all the forms, took her for ice cream cones at Doc's and then walked her to her apartment door. That was it. He finished his narrative by saying that he wouldn't ask her out again, although he'd continue to tutor her in Trig if she wanted. Just as she'd never mentioned that she had a date with Jason, she never said a word to any of us, even just the girls, about the date itself. I just don't know whether any more tutoring occurred.

We fragmented as the college years crept up and on, going off in various directions, some to out of town schools. Elaine, however, stayed home and went to Brooklyn College, just a half—hour bus ride away. Jason got in to MIT, but, for some reason, came home after the first semester and went to Brooklyn College too. But they never more than nodded a few words of greeting to each other there.

I stayed in the city, too, going to Columbia, but living at home. Nevertheless, I never seemed to run into Elaine any more, just by happenstance, going in and out of our building, for example. But I sometimes thought of her, wondered if she were dating, or dating seriously. Whom might it be, what sort of person. I rued having missed my opportunity, a la the sufferings of the young Werther, back then, in early adolescence.

Still, on rare occasions, on the odd balmy night, academia temporarily in abeyance, summer jobs finished for the day, some or all of the old group would congregate on the parkway benches, directly across from the buildings, and resume our old bull session ways. However, Elaine never appeared.

But, finally, one night she did. On the arm of Howard.He was about seven years older than Elaine and quite handsome. He was already a full—fledged pharmacist who had started working at Doc's just a few months before. Doc was sidling towards retirement and thought he needed someone to lighten the load, right then, and who might take over the business when Doc finally did retire. Elaine had walked in to make some routine purchases one day and she and Howard had begun chatting and flirting a bit when he rang up the items. She went in again, a few days later, and they talked some more. One thing led to another and they'd been going out for almost two months. Elaine seemed pleased and happy to be with him, but not nearly as exultant as he seemed to be with her. Right there, in front of us, he told her how, the next night, he wanted to introduce her to his friends, "so that I can show you off." She smiled at full power and giggled that low, seductive sound. By this time I knew that Elaine was something beautiful on which I"d missed out on long ago. I'd come to accept my loss, clinically, as one must in life, from time to time.

Time kept drifting forward and although our little band hardly congregated together any more, some of us more or less stayed in touch by the occasional phone call or letter. In any event, the news filtered down, I think Jason told it to me, that Elaine and Howard had married. Later on, that they'd moved out to a house somewhere in the Long Island suburbs and that a child had been born. But none of the gang ever saw her again, even though she must have come in, once in a while, at least, to visit her parents and brother who still lived at the old address.

Except that one day, about five years on, when I was home from law school, for Easter break, I saw someone who looked as I remembered her coming towards me on the parkway. She was pushing a stroller ahead of her. She must have been visiting her family then. The child sitting in the stroller seemed to be about a three or four year old boy. His head, tongue protruding from his mouth, was askew, drooping at an angle off to the right and downward. His face had a twist to it and his half clenched hands were held up in front of him in a meaningless, uncoordinated gesture. Cerebral palsy, severe retardation, what not, came to my ingenuous mind. He was utterly pathetic and I was instantly, overwhelmingly saddened. Elaine was determinedly pushing the stroller, head down and genuinely seemed not to have seen me. Or, perhaps, not to have recognized me.Or, maybe she had. In any case, I did not have the courage, or the heart, to stop her to talk.

Our little band of brothers and sisters had one more" formal" gathering. Ten years after I'd graduated from law school I was still corresponding with Jason, in Chicago, and Bruce, still in New York. I proposed that we all, now with mates, or as many of us as possible, anyway, have a re—union. My correspondents thought that the idea merited wary enthusiasm. The girls were a bit hard to find but Bruce knew where Diane was and she knew Sheila's married name, etc., etc.

One of the etcs. Led to Elaine, still living on Long Island, in the house to which she'd first moved with Howard. She was contacted but said she had absolutely no interest in attending. Diane called several times and cajoled. Elaine remained unyielding and did not come.Most of us did show up and it was a very pleasant, exciting, yet gentle, last hurrah. And it really was the last.

THE DINNER

Dan arrived ten minutes early. Hank wasn't there yet. Dan looked around the lobby of the hotel where the dinner would take place. In one of the ballrooms, so—called. Appropriate terminology for a baseball focused event. The lobby proclaimed elegant and luxurious—even for Manhattan. Apparently no expense was being spared for the team's "Hall of Fame" event. Well, Dan mused, that's why a reservation to the dinner must have cost so much. The greats and lesser greats of the baseball team which Dan and Hank rooted for so many years ago were to be remembered and honored. That is those who were still living and could make it to this day, this place.

This wasn't the first of these dinners that Dan had attended. There'd been several over the last decade, but the last was about four years ago. The intervals seemed to increase as time went by. Less players, less hero—worshipping fans. After the initial dinner Dan had thought: why repeat the experience? It would be repetitive and even get boring, wouldn't it? After a hard, already tedious enough day, at the large law firm at which Dan was a partner, did he really want to come to a dinner which didn't even get started until 7:30? But each time he had come he'd been stimulated. Actually exhilarated. He was bursting with impressions to foist on his almost patient wife when he finally got home, usually near mid—night. Most of the players who showed up, including a smattering of "honored opponents" of the team, were genial enough when approached for brief conversations and reminiscences and also gracious about signing autographs. Admittedly some of them, un-related to how prominent or minor the player may have been, were a little stand—offish, edgy, perhaps verging on testy even. But in almost all of them, even in the most personable and forthcoming, Dan had sensed a certain ineffable "hardness," a resolute mettle which must have driven them to have been the intense, successful competitiors they were. As pleasant, decent, "nice" as they now were, they clearly had urgently wanted to win. And they had—often. But, of course, not always. Win a lot, lose some. Good enough.

Dan began wondering where Hank was. He was usually very punctual, but, of course, a super—busy internist could have a sudden emergency or a patient whose problems turned out to be much more extensive than anticipated. Dan paced a bit near the revolving doors at the main entrance to the hotel. He hoped Hank wouldn't be really late, since the pre—dinner cocktail hour when adoring fans could get autographs and schmooze a bit with the players was one of the most enjoyable aspects of these affairs. Afterwards there was at least one former player seated at each table of ten dining idolators, but it wasn't always a "favorite" or a particularly fluent or willing conversationalist. Dan remembered the time he was at a table with one of his all—time favorite guys, a pitcher who had been 15-4 and won the Rookie of The Year award. But the man's wife had come too. Unfortunately, however, she had seemed depressed or troubled and no matter what any of the men at the table said, in attempting to draw her out, she voiced only grudging and monosyllabic responses. It put an inevitable pall on the evening, even though the pitcher himself was voluble and indulgent.

Pre—dinner a fan could pursue whoever he wanted. A time for Dan to add to the autographs he had on the frontispiece of the book which had been written about the team that he and Hank, friends living on the same block, had rooted for with complete passion in their pre, and actual, adolescence. It had been their initial and lasting bond. By now, naturally,, since they'd always maintained some sort of contact over the succeeding years, however infrequently sometimes, they had multiple bonds. Careers, families, tennis, books, classical music. Occasionally they'd attend New York Philharmonic concerts together, sometimes they battled on the tennis court.

Dan had to pace a few more minutes, with increasing nervousness, before he saw Hank hurrying across the street. He immediately noticed that Hank also was carrying his copy of the now legendary book about the team. Their custom had been to go around individually during the cocktail period trying to talk to players whose autographs they still lacked. But they'd be at the same table during the meal since when they sent in their reservations they requested that. So, after they quickly greeted each other they hastened up to the room where the tables were set and foraged singly.

In casing the room to see what notables were present Dan recalled incidents from previous dinners. Not too long before a dinner about eight years ago Dan, in the course of his practice, had met some people who had employed an outstanding relief pitcher during the off—season. He had worked as a General Manager In one of their clothing manufacturing plants. Dan was impelled to write to the player relating how glowingly the clients had spoken of him as a valued, exemplary employee. He'd added his own memories of how many exciting and important saves , in big games, the pitcher had thrown. Almost by return mail, Dan had received a note from the pitcher. He still recalled two sentences: "I am in your debt for reporting the kind words the Baskins spoke about me. Believe me, fame is fleeting, but good friends are forever." The note also enjoined Dan, the next time he was at one of the Hall of Fame dinners to come up and say hello. So Dan did at the next dinner. The pitcher was as warm in his greeting as he had been in his note. And the pitcher's wife enthusiastically asked Dan, "Were you the one who wrote that beautiful letter? It just made our day." As her remark had more than made Dan's.

And there was the dinner at which he wound up sitting next to "an honorable opponent." Namely the third baseman who had preserved a perfect game for his squad's pitcher , in a World Series game, against Dan's boys. He had pulled off an outstanding fielding play--- corralling a very hot smash by a star hitter on Dan's team, (the man was now in the Hall of Fame at Cooperstown,) and throwing the star out at first. Dan recalled remarking to him, "Don't I remember you saving ________'s perfect game with a great play off a smash by ___________"? The opponent quickly responded: "I made two great plays; ________ hit one like that, too." Another exemplification of the fiery pride of these formidable gladiators.

A friend of Dan's had brought his twelve year old son to that particular dinner. The boy had expressed his enthusiasm about the "history" of the game, as he thought of that third baseman's era. The deft glove man asked for the child's address and said he would send him some material that would interest him. Sure enough, a week after the conversation, there arrived autographed glossy photos of some of the past greats. Only several years after this encounter this honorable opponent had fallen down a flight of stairs. He became paralyzed from the waist down. But the doctors could find no organic reason for the paralysis. It was deemed a "psychological" paralysis. The player had had a son who had gone wrong and eventually had died. He blamed himself for the tragedyof his son's life. Somehow, he thought, he should have helped him. The "paralysis" was the expiation. Fortunately, after an extended period, the "paralysis" abated.

Once Dan had approached a player who'd been involved in one of the most famous broadcasting calls of all—time. A World Series no—hitter was broken up with two outs in the ninth inning by a pinch hitter who drove in two men who had drawn walks. The distinguished and popular announcer excitedly reported the hit and then shouted"... and here comes the tying run, and here comes the WINNING run!!" Dan knew the player on whom he had autograph designs had scored one of the two runs but Dan had forgotten which one. He approached and without saying anything else to the player simply inquired, "Were you the tying run or the winning run?" The old—timer immediately straightened to his playing height and with great verve enunciated "I was the WINNING run."

Dan also remembered asking one of the utility players for his autograph. The man had said, "Well, sure, but I hardly belonged on the same field as some of these guys." "You had your moments, you had your moments," Dan had ineptly assured him.

Tonight, one of the honorable opponents had struck one of the most famous home runs in all of baseball history. In the final game of a three game play—off, for the National league pennant, Dan's team led 4-1 going into the bottom of the ninth. However, it soon became 4-2, with two runners on base also. Then, suddenly, this honorable opponent hit that thereafter world famous home run driving Dan, Hank and every other fan of the team, anywhere, into utter despair. But that was a long, long time ago. Tonight the home run hitter was seated at one of the set tables, amiably signing autographs. He seemed willing to converse with each fan, who stood on line, for as long as the person might want. When Dan's turn came he just said, "Mr. _______, would you be good enough to sign this," as he proffered his very worn, dog—earred volume. The homer hitter said, "Yeah, sure, of course," and signed with a smile. Dan who didn't like to monopolize the time of these players merely said "Thanks very much, Mr._____" and made way for the next-in-line. He always made it a point to call the players by their last names, even though to most of the dinner attendees they were "Billy," "Clem," "Gen e," "Bobby" and so forth. Most were decidedly senior citizens by now, he respected them inestimably and he didn't like pre—mature informality.

As he turned away Dan practically ran right into Hank. His friend pointed and said "There's_____ over there. Have you ever gotten his autograph?" When Dan acknowledged that he never had Hank suggested that they head that way together because there wasn't much, or any, of a crowd around _____. He had been a "platoon player," an outfielder who didn't start every game. He hit left and the manager tended to play him only when the opposing pitchers were right handers. Against them he often hit with power and consistency. He had a few years of very satisfying stats. But certainly not one of the super—stars, or even close. Four members of the core team Dan and Hank loved had been elected to the Hall of Fame. ____ wasn't one of them and would never get such a nod. (One or two other team members still had hopes.)

As Hank and Dan walked up to him he noticeably brightened and affably greeted them.

"Hi, gents. I used to be a low ball hitter, but, as you can see, now I'm a high ball drinker."

"Well, that's a good evolution," Hank remarked.

"About the only way to go. The fast ball is by me now."

"It's by just about all of us, isn't it," Dan offered. "We were just wondering if we could impose on you to sign our books."

"Of course I'll sign them. My pleasure, gents." And he did so with a flourish, in each case.

"Thanks a lot," Hank said. "We really appreciate it."

"You know fellas, can I tell you something.That guys like you…." His throat caught for a moment. "That guys like you, you know very successful, I can tell that, that guys like you would remember guys like us…. Well, it really means something. To me, at least."

There was silence for a few seconds, but, finally, Dan blurted out, "Believe me, we do a lot more than just remember you. You gave all of us so many moments, so many terrific thrills…."

"Well thanks fellas, thanks a lot. It's appreciated," the outfielder said as he looked down. "The other guys, too. They appreciate also, I'm sure."

"Thanks, again," Hank said as they moved aside to let the next autograph--seeker get to this player.

The dinner itself went along smoothly, if uneventfully. The player seated at Dan and Hank's table was at the very beginning of his career during the last of the team's glory years in the Dan and Hank period of worship. He was friendly, charming even and certainly willing to reminisce. But just not part of their favorite team memories.

As they were leaving the hotel, chatting about the dinner, before hailing cabs to their respective trains, Dan suddenly turned to Hank and asked, " Do you think anyone will remember guys like us?" Hank could only shake his head.

CHEMISTRY

DORIS EDMONDS STILL LIKED CHEMISTRY. Maybe she didn't love it as much as she did when she first discovered it, about ten years ago, as a high school sophomore. Now her first love, aside from her husband of a year, was teaching. And that's what she was doing with Chemistry—teaching it at Walker High School, big and urban, almost 4000 students, in an effort to ignite teen-agers with its seductiveness as she had been swept up by its orderliness, logic and explanatory power.

Doris was first exposed to ions, molecules and bonds in the very same Walker classroom/lab in which she was now the boss. Then she went to the local college, just two leafy blocks in the middle-class residential neighborhood away, majored in the subject there and took a Masters in it at another branch of the City University. She had been one of the very prettiest girls in her Walker class. Same with college. She was always one of the prettiest, if not, indeed, THE most beautiful woman in any group of which she was a part. She had perfect features, with a particularly perfect, irresistible nose, topped by thick, luscious very dark chocolaty curls. Her hair softened her already angelic face even more. And when it was all set off against a sparkling white blouse, pushed and pulled significantly, but not excessively, by her perfectly proportioned chest, and tight, but not too tight, skirt she was, as they say, breathtaking. Breathtakingly beautiful, to be exact.

Hal Lembo certainly thought so. He was one of her over-hormoned students. Naturally good at science and math and more than smart enough in everything else too. One of the better students in the entire junior class. But not so adept at social matters. Walker had a football team, although not a frequently victorious one, and Saturday afternoon games, in the pleasantly crisp, sun dappled Fall weather, at the adjoining field, were occasions for many Walker students, especially juniors and seniors, to date—or try to find prospective dates. But Hal characteristically didn't go to the games. He might, once in a very great while, attend an especially "big" game with some male pals, but certainly not with a girl, a date. Walker didn't have too many big games, since the team was perennially weak. They did better in fencing and tennis.

Another student in the Chemistry section was Elaine Wilner. Hal liked her, too. Striking red hair and, often, a wearer of tight sweaters, especially the pale blue one, which showed off her assertive breasts to striking advantage. Good rear view as well, with a rather pleasant, unassuming disposition thrown in.Not "stuck-up" just because she looked so appealing—and must have been told so by plenty of boys. Not one of the most stellar students but very competent and she seemed to try conscientiously, even in Chemistry.

There was also Irene Alzani. A very good student, maybe just below the top level, the Hal echelon, but not classically "attractive." Frizzy dirty blonde hair and typical teen—age skin problems, but beyond the average degree. Her features were not really too bad, Hal could even find them pretty—if he stared long and hard enough. Sometimes he did so, secretively. She had been in some other classes with Hal and she would occasionally approach him after class and start talking about something that had occurred during the period. Hal suspected that she wasn't just talking for talking's sake but might like him to ask her out. But he wasn't much motivated and he didn't think that he could ask anyone for a date, ever.

Billy Daniels was a funny case. He was "officially" one of the "toughs" in the junior class, despite very short stature. Black leather jacket, severely tapered, "pegged" pastel pants and ready, indeed eager, to disrupt and create havoc at any time. Barely passed his courses—and sometimes didn't. But he was mesmerized by Mrs. Edmonds. There was virtual adoration on his face as she taught. And, incredibly enough, sometimes after the bell had rung, along with some of the brighter students, (Hal not amongst them,) he would go up to her desk to ask a question about something she had said or taught in class. Hal couldn't believe he really cared about Chemistry.

Along with other students of the highest academic achievement, Hal was asked, during his free period, on Tuesday and Thursdays, to sit on the bench outside the office of Mr. Andrew Rose, the Dean of Boys. His job was to be available to deliver any message that Mr. Rose might immediately need to get to a teacher or other administrator. Usually there were none so, during most of the time Hal spent there, he was able to sit and read a school assignment or, for example, do his math homework.

Hal was reading his Social Studies textbook, one day, when he saw Steven Elsner coming down the hall toward the Dean's office.They were both juniors and knew each other slightly from having been in common classes and such, but, otherwise, they'd never had much contact.They only nodded at each other and, then, Elsner, a little young looking for his age and below average height, went past Hal into Mr. Rose's office. Steve didn't close the door as he entered and neither did Mr. Rose get up to do so.

"Hello, Steve, sit down," Hal heard Mr.Rose say.

The next words, after a pause, were also from the Dean. " Steve, do you have any idea why you're here?"

Another long pause, until Hal, finally, heard Steve say, barely audibly, "No…. no…. I mean not really…."

"Not really?"

" No, I mean … no, I don't know why….any reason…. No."

"Are you thinking as hard as you can?"

"Yes, yes I am…. At least I think so. No, I don't know why."

"O.K., Steve I'll tell you. Let's see if that refreshes your memory. Well, Steve, it seems that three different girls who go to this school have reported that you just went up to them in the corridors, and, against their will and without any indication, whatsoever, of consent by them, started fondling their breasts." Mr. Rose paused. "Do you know what I'm talking about now?"

Hal heard nothing for quite some time.

"Oh…. Oh that…. That's what you mean…."

"Yes, Steve that's what I mean. So you do remember and acknowledge the incidents?"

"Yeah, yes… I guess so….."

"Guess so?"

"Yeah…. I remember."

"Well, Steve, in addition to remembering, do you understand why such behavior resulted in me having to call you down here?"

"Well, yeah, sort of… I guess so."

"You guess so? Again?"

"Well, I guess I know why... what you mean, but I didn't mean anything, or anything like that. They were just so pretty.... I mean, I didn't mean anything bad or...."

"Steve, most boys your age have such impulses, but they control them. You can't just go around giving in to any impulse just because you feel it. Certain impulsive behavior, like what you've done, is just not civilized, not acceptable. The expression of such impulses requires consent from the other party. Do you know what I mean; do I make myself clear?"

"Well, yeah, I guess so... I guess I understand."

"No guessing or supposing, Steve. You must understand! If anything like this happens again, Steve, you'll be in here faster than you can blink and your father will he here as well. And, perhaps, also a police officer. Do you clearly understand what I mean and what you must not do? No guessing or supposing—do you?"

"Yeah, I guess.... I mean I do.... I understand..."

"O.K., Steve, you can go back to your class now. But don't ever forget, not for a moment, what I said."

"O.K."

Hal heard Steve's chair scraping as Steve got up to go. Hal immediately focused his eyes rigidly on his textbook, with his notebook opened beside it, as Steve left the office. Hal didn't dare sneak even the merest glance at Steve as he trudged by Hal and down the corridor.

The first test in Chemistry came about four weeks, about a third of the way, into the semester. You had to know the symbols for most of the elements, some valences and how to do rudimentary chemical equations. Hal studied more than he had to in order to master the assigned material. He found it congenial, playing to one of his great strengths, the ability to memorize. And, in any event, he wasn't taking any chances with failing to impress Mrs. Edmonds. Sure enough, Hal found the test straightforward and pretty easy. He was able to run right through it in about half the period and, so, had the other half to go back and check his work. During the exam Mrs. Edmonds went up and down the aisles of desks, looking at the work of each student and sometimes making a warning comment such as, "I'd be careful on problem three," or "Don't forget the valence of Fluorine." She didn't exactly tell a student the right answer but she certainly alerted an individual who might be on the wrong track or had simply made a common error. When she got to Hal's desk she kept looking at his paper before she ambled demurely on, but she didn't say anything. Hal took that as a further good sign.

It was a very good sign. When Mrs. Edmonds returned the papers, a few periods after that, Hal had received a "96;" two minor, "silly"errors. In fact, when Mrs.Edmonds handed Hal his graded paper she said, "Wonderful job, Hal; just a little sheer carelessness. You can do even better." After she had completed giving back the papers Mrs. Edmonds returned to her usual palce at the front of the room. But, instead of just immediately resuming with that day's work, as most teachers did after returning graded papers, she spoke about the test.

"Now I know that a lot of you must be disappointed with the marks you got. I was certainly disappointed when I graded the tests. I know that some of you have spoken to me about how difficult the test was. I didn't mean it to be so hard and I didn't think it was so hard when I made it up. I still don't think it was so tough. I think some of you need to apply yourselves more diligently, study more. Chemistry is a science. It's exact and precise. It may not be like some of your other subjects where you can be a little vaguer and, what shall I say, 'opinionated.'" Mrs. Edmonds tended to emphasize particular words when she spoke, especially in her teaching mode.

"Your 'opinion' doesn't really count in Chemistry. There's one correct answer and you either work a problem or equation out accurately or you don't. And with sufficient application it can be done. Many of you, more than showed, can do it. Much better, anyway, than you showed here.In point of fact, some of you did quite well on the test. Some very well, indeed. For example Irene got a "98." Well done, Irene."

All eyes in the class turned toward Irene who focused her eyes down toward her desk, as she turned mildly maroon. Hal, already, had his eyes turned downward, too, as he'd anticipated Mrs. Edmonds lauding his paper. But she didn't. She just went on a bit more urging various study techniques she thought would help most students and, then, she did start talking about the text pages which were the subject for that class pe.

Hal was devastated.. Once Mrs. Edmonds had mentioned Irene's "98" he fully expected to be praised for his paper, which, after all, had just one more "careless" error than Irene's. But, apparently, Mrs. Edmonds saw no need to give the class another example of a superior performance, one just a jot away from Irene's almost perfect one. Hal was very disappointed.

When the bell rang the period's end Hal gatherd up his books and notebook extremely quickly, faster, probably, than he ever had before—in any class. Nevertheless, when he exited the room Irene was already standing in the hall, apparently waiting for him. It must have been for him because no one else had left the classroom yet and she started talking to him immediately.

"Hal, I bet you must have done very well on the test, too. I thought Mrs. Edmonds was going to mention your name when she mentioned mine. I can't believe you didn't get a very high grade also."

'Well, yeah.... I did. I mean you got a higher one, but I did pretty well, too."

"I knew you would have, Hal. What did you get?"

"Well, I got a 96... two really stupid mistakes. They shouldn't have happened. "

"Oh, I know. I knew you would know everything on that test."

"How did you know?"

"Oh, I just knew. I mean I've been in other classes with you and I know how smart you are and what a good student you are." She brushed some blonde frizz away from her right eye.

Hal didn't know quite what to say. He just shrugged silently.

"It looks like the course is getting a little bit harder now, with the halogens and all. And figuring out moles and stuff like that," Irene interpolated into the silence.

"Yeah, I guess so," Hal said, almost inaudibly.

He looked down, as he had for most of the conversation, hardly meeting Irene's lively blue eyes. As he did so now, he noticed that Irene's skirt was knee length and showed a good deal of her calves. He couldn't see her ankles because she was wearing sweat socks with her brown and white saddle shoes. But her calves were shapely. Irene had nice legs. He had also noticed that her sweater, while not the tightest, maybe not like Elaine's, was generously filled out. She was not buxom, or anything, but there was no stinginess in her bust line.

When Hal looked up, finally, after another silence, Irene's eyes seemed to be dancing more than they had been and there was something verging on, but not yet there, a smirk on her face. Hal quickly looked down again.

"Well, anyway, I thought we might help each other, with the harder stuff I mean, if, you know, it got really difficult, by studying together. Both my parents work and my sister and brother don't get home from school until later, too, so it would be quiet and we could really concentrate. I mean if you thought you would get something out of it. I know a lot of the course is probably very easy for you...."

"No, no," Hal interjected. "I mean I have to study some of the topics a lot to get the hang…. That might be a good idea. Yeah, maybe we could some time," Hal said as he started shuffling away.

'Well, o.k., just let me know if you would ever want to do that. I could give you my phone number and you could just call...."

"No, No," Hal shot out quickly, almost desperate to avoid such a transaction. "I mean I could just talk to you here in school; you know after class….like this."

"O.K., Hal. Like I say, just let me know any time," Irene mumbled, somewhat flustered now. Then she, too, started walking away, heading in the opposite direction, in the corridor, from the one Hal was taking.

Hal found that he kept on thinking of Irene's vivaciousness and her calves and bust line. And during the Chemistry class sessions he started scrutinizing her with a more and more intense eye. One time she was dressed up, in formal clothes. She must have been going somewhere after school and was wearing high heels. He really liked how her calves stood out in those, firm and trim, but shapely. She really did have nice legs. On most days she wore a sweater or a white blouse. In either case her breasts stood out assertively. The more Hal studied her the more he thought her features, under the acne, became pretty, too. Sometimes she would wait outside the room after class and say something to Hal about Mrs. Edmonds's lesson that day. Hal knew that she was waiting for him to say something about studying together, especially since another big test, the mid—term, was coming up. He was honest enough with himself to know that he really wanted to; but he just couldn't bring himself to actually do it.

But he did spend a lot of time thinking about doing it and about how nice it would be to sit next to her, on a couch in her living room, or maybe right next to her on the bed in her room, with the Chemistry book and their notes spread out before them. Naturally he had no idea of what the living room, in the house in which she lived, or her bedroom looked like, but he constructed them in his imagination. Sometimes he urged himself to make a silent promise that the next time he saw her he would ask her to study together. If he promised himself that he would do it then he would. That was the way he was. But he never actually got to the point of making that pledge to himself. He wondered if Irene ever thought about him the way he thought about her.

But just as Hal continued thinking about Irene, he also looked forward to seeing Elaine Wilner in the Chemistry class each day. Hal's hormones raced eagerly at the sight of her in those brightly colored sweaters which seemed to get tighter and tighter. The skirts, too. Boy, did he wish he could say something funny to her. Something that would make her just break up with her out loud laughter, the kind that pealed silver throughout the room. And Mrs. Edmonds was always just so exquisitely pretty. She was constantly dressed elegantly with a fine, demure looking blouse and a not -too-tight- skirt of rich wool.Hal particularly enjoyed watching how her brow furrowed just so slightly in concentration when she performed one of the experiments she demonstrated to the class as part of her lectures. Sometimes when in bed he would imagine that he were Mr. Edmonds--not that he had the slightest idea of what Mrs. Edmonds's husband looked like. He often started out that way, without any thought of masturbating, but once he really fixed on how Mrs. Edmonds looked… one thing led to another and then another.

As the mid—term test kept creeping up Hal started thinking of Irene even more than he already had been. One day after Chemistry concluded Hal rushed out of the room, as usual, but, then, thought better of it and went back to wait until Irene came out. She was walking briskly but slowed down immediately when she saw Hal seeking to meet her eyes as though he wanted to speak with her.

"Oh, hi, Hal. How are you?"

"I'm o.k., I was just thinking… Well, I mean the mid—term is coming up. So I was thinking about, you know, what you said about maybe we could help each other and studying together and all that."

"Oh, yes" Irene responded ebulliently.

"I mean, do you remember what you said about studying in your house and that stuff?"

"Of course I do. When would you like to come over?"

"I don't know. Any time would be alright, I guess."

"How about tomorrow afternoon, right after last period. I only live a few blocks from the school, so we could walk back together."

"Ok., I guess so. O.K., tomorrow. See ya then."

~

Hal dressed with unusual care the next morning. Absolutely clean shirt, one of his better, untattered, ones, and his best pair of charcoal grey slacks. He noticed, during the Chemistry class, that Irene was wearing a skirt he'd never seen before and a brilliantly lavender sweater which also seemed tighter than any she'd previously worn. When he met Irene after his last period, at the entrance to the school they'd agreed upon, they pretty immediately started talking about the last few lectures Mrs. Edmonds had given. In particular, they enthusiastically spoke about one experiment she had demonstrated which was especially dazzling. Before long they were at Irene's house, still absorbed in discussion about ions, valences, catalysts, atoms and equations.

After asking Hal whether he wanted anything to drink, juice or soda, Irene went to the dining room table and started laying out her chemistry text and note book at one end of the table. She told Hal he could set up his materials at the other end of the eight foot table. Hal was surprised and disappointed at this study arrangement but did as he was told. In that fashion they continued their discussion and went over various topics in the book and challenged each other with quiz type questions and problems. After about an hour they'd reviewed just about every topic that might be tested on the mid—term and Irene said it was just as well,because her family would be coming home soon and she had to do the preliminary dinner preparations which her mom had assigned her. Hal quickly gathered up his book and papers and after he and Irene thanked each other for the mutual studying he rapidly departed. All that night he thought of Irene in her lavender sweater, how he stole glances at her breasts even while working chemistry problems and his desire to fondle her breasts.

Their studying paid off. Each of them got 100% on the test, far outpacing anyone else in the class. (The next highest grade was an "88.") Mrs. Edmonds mentioned both of them for outstanding work when she returned the exam papers. Hal and Irene congratulated each other after class and spoke about how the test results validated what a good idea it had been to study together. Hal tried to give Irene all the credit for the idea but she insisted on stressing how Hal had timed their joint studying just perfectly, so that they would be at peak command for the test.

Nevertheless, Hal and Irene didn't speak, other than for perfunctory greetings, for the next several weeks. But as the next test approached, the last one before the final exam, Hal started fantasizing about studying in Irene's house again. Again and again he became aroused imagining close physical proximity to Irene leading to more intimate contact. Sometimes to the point of undressing her. When his musings went that far Hal felt vaguely ashamed, as well as highly stimulated.

With about a week to go before the test Hal, once again, asked Irene if she wanted to study together. She was again enthusiastic and they quickly established the day they would go over to her house after normal school hours. However, to Hal's monumental disappointment, this session went just as the first one had developed. Irene positioned them, at opposite ends of the dining table, so that they weren't in close contact at all and before Hal knew it the hour and half was up and Irene was seeing him to the door. This session was a little different than the initial one because some of the material they had to review was particularly difficult. It was the hardest of any they'd yet encountered in the class and Hal found that he was basically teaching it to Irene. When they began she really didn't seem to have much grasp of it, but after he'd explained it once or twice she seemed to comprehend it much better.

Hal tried to account to himself why Irene kept him at a distance when they were alone in her house. She had seemed so friendly and inviting in inducing Hal to come to her house. Even he didn't think that she really didn't like him. He thought of various explanations. Perhaps, once they were together in her home it was up to Hal to take the initiative in bringing about physical proximity.Maybe he was to somehow close the gap that existed, over the dining room table, between them. She had laid the groundwork and he was supposed to exploit the opportunity. Or, he thought, maybe Irene believed that since she had worked things out so that they had gotten to know each other somewhat it was Hal's responsibility to ask her out on a conventional date. Maybe she wanted him to show that he wanted to be with her in a true social setting. Or that he wasn't, for some reason, maybe her looks, ashamed to be seen with her in public. Hal thought that he would like to go to the movies with her and, afterwards, for an ice cream soda, or something. Possibly a kiss, with his hands opening the buttons of her coat or jacket, as he walked her home. But he didn't have confidence that he would actually get up the nerve to call and ask her for a date.

Hal cogitated frequently, but time advanced. The test in Chemistry was a tough one. Mrs. Edmonds had put on more of the most difficult type of material than she had on the two preceding tests. Hal saw Irene in the hall after the test and she muttered "I was slaughtered on that" to him as she headed down a different corridor. Sure enough when Mrs. Edmonds returned the papers she told the class that Hal's "95" was "by far" the best grade in the class. She said that she knew that this was the most difficult test she had given but that she had hoped that some of the other students would have done better than they did. She repeated, "No one was close to Hal."

~

Hal thought he'd better wait for Irene after class and commiserate with her about what surely must have been a disappointing grade for her. He loitered in the hall outside the room trying to put an expression on his face which suggested that he had some purpose there. Student after student emerged, some together, some alone, but no Irene. Finally the stream of students stopped but still no Irene. She must be talking to Mrs. Edmonds. Maybe asking a question about the day's lesson or, perhaps, why she didn't get more credit on a certain problem on the test. Another minute or two went by but still no Irene. If she didn't come out right now she'd be late for her next period's class. Finally, Hal stuck his head into the room, angling it to the right around the door frame, toward the front of the room. Mrs. Edmonds and Irene were locked in a tight embrace, their tongues in each others mouths. They continued passionately kissing for the second or two it took the stunned Hal to withdraw and run down the corridor. As he fled, conscious of his heart in his chest, he hoped that he hadn't been seen or heard by them.

~

Later, Hal realized that he didn't know what he would do the next time he saw Irene. Or Mrs. Edmonds.

MUSIC ON FRIDAY

Ed Posner, in his fifty—fourth year, partner at the two hundred lawyer firm of Dingell, Black, Meyer and Dacey, was about to leave his spacious corner office on the 38th floor of a La Salle Street skyscraper at the respectable, if just a trifle early, lunch hour of 12: 15. He would tell his secretary of fifteen years, Adele Youmans , near the same age, with a moderately attractive figure and an open, decent, just short of pretty face, that he'd be back about the middle of the afternoon. He well knew that she knew that he knew that she knew that since it was the last Friday of a winter month, he was headed for Orchestra Hall, a few blocks away, for a Chicago Symphony Friday afternoon Series B subscription concert. Too many times, as few as they might have been, over the years he'd been attending, after returning from a concert, he'd absent—mindedly failed to stuff the program into the attaché case laden with week—end work, and had left it on a corner of his desk, or on a chair in the office. The very competent and highly observant Ms. Youmans would surely have spotted it.

He'd never really figured out why, at some point, he hadn't just started acknowledging to her that after gobbling a quick lunch he was going to a concert and would be back at 3:30—3:45. He supposed it was because of the guilt he felt, no matter how many hours a week he worked, (fifty, sixty, up to seventy even,) at "playing" during normal working hours.And just as the quantity of work didn't give him a pass, neither did its tedium and frequently overwhelming sense of meaninglessness. How many security interests could one lawyer file under the Uniform Commercial Code, how many shopping center leases could he draft, how many acquisitions of one giant conglomerate by another behemoth could a man who'd taken philosophy and literature courses as a Harvard undergraduate and then gone on to the University of Chicago Law School be engulfed by.

"Ms. Youmans I'm going to be headed out for lunch in a bit… I have to take care of something…but I should be back by mid—afternoon or so. If Sanford Lamb calls on the Mylan matter tell him that things are going along pretty well, but that I probably won't have anything definitive until Tuesday afternoon, Wednesday morning, next week. And please call Marty Randsell and say that it looks like he'll have to sweeten his offer to get the other side to be more enthusiastic, or to respond at all for that matter. O.K., that's about it. Anything else I'll handle it when I get back. And, of course, Ms. Youmans, don't forget to go to lunch yourself. If you could just be back by the time….."

"Oh, don't worry Mr. Posner, I'll get some lunch and be sure to be back by the time you come back; probably well before. But what about Radcliffe? What if she calls about that problem with the lessee at the Unicorn Mall—the one who's demanding upgraded cleaning services in the common areas?"

"No, I think she told me she was leaving for Los Angeles, yesterday, to work on some big deal out there. Yeah, she mentioned it when I passed her in the hall Wednesday. Another huge merger. You could check with her secretary to make sure. Otherwise I'll take care of anything you can't handle later…."

" Right Mr. Posner. Enjoy the…. Enjoy your lunch."

He looked directly into her hazel eyes, responding, "You, too, Ms. Youmans. But don't get too cold out there."

When he emerged into the street, after the whoosing express elevator descent for the final thirty floors, the wind whipped frigidity was not as piercing as he'd anticipated after this morning's ordeal in getting to his office from the railroad station. And most of that had been in the "warmth" of the bus. Now things seemed enough this side of fierce discomfort for him to feel invited to walk the few blocks up State Street to Marshall Fields Department Store and its seven different restaurants—cafeterias. By the time he got there it would be only an hour before concert time. But often he was able to get something simple in the cafeteria that featured the health food salads, eat at a small table by himself, perhaps while reading a newspaper left by a previous diner, walk the two blocks to Orchestra Hall and still be in his seat ten minutes before the downbeat.

By the time he went through Fields' revolving doors he'd been so penetrated by vicious slivers of winter that he practically gulped in the temperature increase. He flitted a thought to the possibility that he was cultivating the flu—he hadn't had it yet this winter—while taking the elevator to the fifth floor cafeteria.

Things went according to plan and after another walk in a cold of increasing bitterness and a pre-cautionary trip to the Mens Room—why challenge that irritable prostate—he was , almost grudgingly, removing his wool overcoat and the scant warmth it provided in his first balcony seat at 1:17. (The first balcony was where the cognoscenti sat, the sound was best there.)

Thirteen minutes before Berlioz's "Roman Carnival Overture" was scheduled to provide its sweep to the release, freedom, solace, Edward Michael Posner craved. He remembered that he'd once heard the great English mezzo—soprano, Janet Baker, now Dame Janet, give a pre—concert talk in which she remarked that " music is solace, music is healing, music is peace." Yes, he vividly recalled her beautiful, musical so to speak, enunciation of that final word. Her diction was peace itself. Subsequently he'd read somewhere that she was a religious woman. Her comments must have been influenced by that background. But it didn't matter. What she said was true for anyone who loved , or even just liked, music. In involvement comfort arrived.

After the overture it would be the orchestra's excellent concertmaster, Samuel Magid, as soloist in the powerful First Violin Concerto by the formidable Dimitri Shostakovitch,. It had been composed in the '50os, at the core of the cold war, for the magnificent Soviet virtuoso, David Oistrakh. But speaking of Soviet and that sort of thing, he was also very much looking forward to the second half of the program. Mahler's first symphony, "The Titan," ("A symphony should be the whole world," said Mahler,) was to be conducted by the terrific Klaus Tennstedt who'd initially made his mark in East Germany but had come to prominence in the West in the '70s. Now there were no longer East and West Germanys and Tennstedt's superb interpretations of Mahler and Bruckner symphonies, and other supreme documents of German Romanticism, with almost all the leading orchestras of the world, were among the most cherished experiences of the contemporary musical scene.

Until only a few years ago, perhaps '86 or '87, Ed had been only dimly aware of Tennstedt. Basically as a big name. Maybe he'd heard a few of his recordings on the car radio, snippets mostly. But then he'd caught a Philadelphia Orchestra radio broadcast which had made Tennstedt come alive for him as a man—not merely a great conductor.

The intermission commentator had told a story about the conductor growing up in the Germany of the '30s. Hitler had already imposed all sorts of restrictions on listening to foreign broadcasts. But one evening Tennstedt's father, a violinist, had come come and excitedly reported that that night the short wave would be able to pick up a broadcast of the legendary Leopold Stokowski leading his lush sounding Phiuladelphia Orchestra in Tchaikovsky's famous sixth, and last, symphony, "The Pathetique." He said that he didn't care that listening to such a broadcast was prohibited; he didn't want his family to miss this outstanding opportunity.

After dinner, Klaus and two siblings were gathered, with mother and father, under a huge, thick quilt, in his parents' bedroom. There, with the short wave transmitter at the core of this huddled together family circle, they heard forbidden sounds which they, literally, would never forget: a world famous orchestra pouring out the plaintive themes of Tchaikovsky's cri de coeur, his "Symphonie Pathetique." The announcer went on to mention that when Tennstedt gained international renown he was invited to guest conduct the Philadelphia Orchestra for several concerts. He accepted with great alacrity. A little later, when it came time to determine the programs that he'd be leading the orchestra in, the manager of the orchestra contacted him. When he asked Tennstedt what music he had in mind to perform, the first, totally unhesitating words out of Tennstedt's mouth were "'Symphonie Pathetique' by Peter Ilyich Tchaikovsky."

The only problem these days with a Tennstedt led concert was whether he would actually appear. Posner was surely not in the "know" in such matters, but as a regular concert—goer, who occasionally chatted with aficionados in adjacent seats, and subscribed to several classical music magazines, he was aware of rumors about throat cancer and hip problems. And the unfortunate fact was that the conductor seemed to cancel as many of his engagements as he fulfilled.

But today, thankfully, no insert in the program about a substitute conductor and now, lights dimming, there was the tall, lanky somewhat ungainly German striding out determinedly. Wire rimmed glasses perched on a noble head, with fibrous grey ramparts at the sides.

His purposeful gait might represent self—struggle as well as eager commitment to what he was about to do. For there were other rumors that despite his vast, unquestionable talent he was a man whose intense sense of perfectionism lashed him with insecurities. It was said there were times he couldn't bring himself to take the stage, irrespective of how well prepared he and the orchestra were. On one of those anxiety—ridden occasions the concert master of one of the very top tier orchestras in the world had pleaded with Tennstedt to just mount the podium and go through the motions. The musicians knew the scores intimately; merely having him in front of them would be inspiration enough for a first class performance. He couldn't do it---notwithstanding the additional fervent urging of his wife who tried to push him on the stage.

But there was nothing wrong with him, at least not that he was letting on to, this afternoon. The Berlioz overture was every bit as stirring as Ed had remembered it. All dash, exhilaration and, ultimately, freedom. Then a finely crafted,greatly absorbing performance of the Shostakovitch. Magid superbly executed the perilous technical, virtuosic demands of the violin, (David Oistrakh himself had said he would practice the hardest passages immediately upon arising, even before his eyes were properly open, to achieve utter proficiency,) while Tennstedt guided the Chicago Symphony to robust, yet sensitive, empathetic collaboration.

So, suddenly, as it should be with a superior concert it was intermission. Ed, as he looked around and down at the audience, trickling out for refreshments and the lavatories, usually felt a little self—conscious. He seemed always to be, on these Friday afternoons, one of the relatively few males in the crowd of over fifty—fivish women, many who identified their principal purpose in venturing from affluent suburbs to city streets by the Marshall Field's and Carson, Pirie Scott shopping bags which generously cluttered the aisles. Maybe this sensation was built on guilt at sitting here, at Tensstedt's feet, rather than sitting in his office being about the business of others. "Doing trivial things for trivial people" as a partner of his said.

As he mechanically glanced, from area to area in the seats below, his eyes were captured by an astonishingly attractive young woman in the front section, diagonally off to the left of his central first balcony seat. Because of the angle he couldn't see too much more than her profile, especially since her head was tilted down toward the program she was reading. Yet it was clear that she had the freshness of a singularly perfect—featured, ravishingly beautiful young woman in her mid—twenties.

Actually, she reminded him a lot of Ellen at that age, thrity years ago. In any event, she was certainly not the typical Friday afternoon concertgoer, as proved by just about the entire rest of the audience. Ed was also sure that he'd never seen her in that seat before, on his many visits to the hall for this subscription series. Those long, fully curved legs she had crossed as she read would have previously caught his attention. No, he had the distinct feeling that this was, so to speak, the first time for her.

That, very probably, someone had given her a ticket that otherwise would have gone un—used today. (A mother, an aunt, a boss?) He thought his judgment confirmed by what he sensed as a considerable air of curiosity in her posture and manner as she studied the program. It just seemed all new to her. He enjoyed the few minutes remaining in the intermission simply by watching her, from time to time. He was rewarded with some position shifts which revealed more of her truly remarkable fresh face, framed by rich auburn hair.

Then an hour of rapture from Tennstedt and the band,as orchestra members sometimes called it. From the langorous opening of Mahler's First to the all horns not only blaring, but standing, triumphant conclusion. If not the entire world then, surely, a great deal of life had been stuffed into "The Titan." Mahler had died at fifty—one, so perhaps he knew important things early.

The audience exploded into exultant applause and a profusely sweating Tennstedt turned, although still appearing mesmerized by Mahler, to acknowledge it. Then he tried to deflect it to the orchestra members by urging them, with repeated upward sweeps of his baton, to rise. They were reluctant at first to dilute the adulation being lavished on the great conductor but finally they did so, many breaking into broad smiles. Tennstedt headed off the stage, but sustained, insistent clapping surged on. He was recalled four or five times at least. On each occasion he thrust his arms out, as widely as possible, and made sure to gaze upward, at those sitting, or now standing, in the very last rows of the second balcony, as well as at the high priced ticket holders straight ahead. Ed always got a lot of satisfaction from that gesture of egalitarianism which he'd noticed many of the truly world class artists made. Several times Tennstedt touched his heart to indicate how the response moved him.

Ed had actually met several of his all—time favorites like the legendary violinist, Yehudi Menuhin, and the brilliant mezzo—soprano, Marilyn Horne. He'd found out, a few years ago, that artists were accessible to the public, in the so-called "green room," backstage. Since then he'd girded his courage a few times to go there and tell a musician how much pleasure he or she had given him. He'd realized, somewhere around the middle of the Mahler, that he'd have to do it today. The awareness had made him a bit tense, somewhat dulled the rest of the symphony. The tension didn't come from knowing that this would get him back to the office even later than usual. Rather because approach to heores always risked their diminution. Nevertheless, he had business to transact backstage.

Ed shuffled the several flights of stairs down to the lobby, amidst the viscously departing throngs, as swiftly as possible. Then down the staircase to the left of the lobby area, to wend his way back through the inner caverns and warrens where artists received their public.

When he finally got there Ed was surprised that there were only a few people lined up outside what must have been Tennstedt's dressing room. A distinguished looking young black man, whom Ed recognized as the orchestra's Assistant Conductor, (to Maestro Georg Solti,) was acting as sentinel until the conductor was ready. A few of the waiting devotees held albums of recordings which they obviously wanted autographed. A word or two was exchanged amongst the waiters. Five, then ten minutes dragged. One and another of the autograph hounds, after a wrist watch peek, departed. Ed's eyes met those of the gatekeeper. The Assistant Conductor smiled readily, shrugging his shoulders the merest bit.

" It takes a great deal out of him; but he loves it so."

" Well, it really comes through in the performance," Ed replied.

The Assistant Conductor smiled again, in deep agreement.

In another few minutes Ed had become first on what had dwindled to a very short line.

Suddenly, after the door to the conductor's room had opened and the Assistant Conductor had briefly stuck his head in, he waved Ed forward.

Once he went in Ed was in an anteroom leading to another open door. Through that doorway he could see a mid—fiftyish, non—descript blonde woman, doubtless Mrs. Tennstedt, dabbing at her husband's brow ,with a large white handkerchief, with one hand and straightening his lapel or shirt collar with the other. Some final adjustments to the artist in his civvies. She looked at Ed almost curiously as he tentatively came through that second doorway and then stepped aside---as though to give him a clear shot at her husband. Ed stopped a few feet in front of him and Tennstedt, scattered beads of perspiration still dotting his high brow, peered, also rather quizzically at Ed.He verged on launching a smile and gave two short nods of his head in greeting.

"Maestro, I just wanted to thank you so much for that glorious performance of the Mahler, it was...."

"It is the work that is glorious; I only try to help a little," he smiled.

He spoke fluently, without searching for words, but there were thick knots of a German accent and Ed rapidly got the feeling that the man was far from comfortable in English. He sensed Tennstedt might respond to what was said to him in English but wouldn't be inclined to initiate anything on his own. Ed liked to keep these kinds of encounters short anyway. For several reasons : fairness to others waiting to speak to the artist; he didn't want to overly impose on the performer's time;. he felt stress in trying to not sound obtuse about music to a world class artist. Nevertheless, as Tennstedt began autographing the program booklet that Ed had held out to him, Ed felt himself mentioning the story about the conductor's father making sure that the family heard the broadcast of the Stokowski led "Pathetique."

"... And then the announcer said that when you were invited to guest conduct the Philadelphia Orchestra and were asked what you wanted to do, you answered 'Symphonie Pathetique' immediately."

The German was now handing the program booklet, as well as Ed's pen, back toward him. He looked directly into Ed's eyes, yet his expression was somewhat distant, meditative.

'OH yes, yes. It is so, it is so," he assured, slowly but emphatically, nodding his head decisively, up and down, several times.

Ed accepted the program back. "Thank you, maestro, thank you. I greatly appreciate it."

Tennstedt nodded in understanding as Ed backed away and turned to leave.

Because of the green room stop—off, plus the length of the Mahler symphony, Ed got back to his office later than usual. Ms. Youmans was already gone. Yet he didn't feel impelled , as he often did, to remain there a few hours more. He'd noticed that it was getting even colder out and he resolved to leave between five and five—thirty, as most people who worked in offices did. He called Ellen and told her he'd be home around six—thirty.

He even made the train with more than minutes to spare and settled himself and his bulging attache case into a comfortable window seat. Naturally he hoped that no one would sit beside him in the space remaining on the long seat. It seemed that just about everyone else who took these Chicago and Northwestern Railway trains felt the same way. He'd long noticed that the bench seats didn't start doubling up with two passengers until all possibilities for a solitary seat had evaporated. Of course, if the train got really crowded all the seats would double up. But you could always hope, and for now Ed was safe. He put the attaché case on his lap, but closed his eyes instead of opening it.

He envisioned himself back in his seat in the first balcony. Suddenly, as he slid into sleep, he was gliding toward the front of the balcony and, then, vaulting its railing and hurtling downward, the music soaring to meet him. The railroad conductor, shouting out a station name, woke him just before he hit the floor of Orchestra Hall.

He couldn't ease back into dozing and soon had to pay attentions to the stations, his own destination no longer many away.

Resigned to wakefulness he still defied the contents of the attaché case and permitted his gaze to wander the length of the car. Characteristically, when Ed indulged in this pastime, he searched for faces which surprised him; ones which somehow looked different from the usual ilk speeding to suburbia. He had no success, with only two or three rows to go, when he was sharply surprised by the face of the lovely young woman whose profile, and other aspects, he'd been admiring during intermission. Talk about coincidences or whatever this could be called. He registered that at closer view she was every bit as breathtaking as she'd seemed from his balcony seat.

Then he became conscious that his station was looming and that it was time to gather his things.

The Oldsmobile started right up, although it felt as though the temperature had fallen to zero, or very close to it.

Ed got a transitory jab of satisfaction as the tires crunched the ice and snow in the driveway and he saw the many and bright lights shining within his home. Just as he was about to insert his key in the lock Ellen opened the door and they greeted each other with the customary pecking kisses.

"Do you want to sit in the living room for a few minutes, maybe sip at some sherry, before we sit down for serious eating?" Ellen asked, emphasizing to burlesque the last two words of her question. "That sounds o.k.," Ed answered, as he walked towards the large, bookcase lined, leather chaired room with the cavernous fireplace.

"But maybe you would want to drop your attaché case, your ubiquitous attache case, in the den or something...."

"Oh yeah, that. I can just drop it here until later," Ed responded quickly.

As they moved toward the couch, Ellen remarked, "Maybe you'll even forget to pick it up later. Who knows, maybe you'll forget where it is for the whole week—end."

"Maybe. But somehow I rather doubt it."

Ellen sat at one end of the richly brocaded sofa, shoeless, but shapely nyloned legs drawn up under her. Ed took the other end, hands on his knees.

They exchanged mild smiles before Ed asked, "Heard from either, or both, Marta and Seymour today?"

"A banner day. Both actually. Each got an 'A' on some exam or other. So a Posner excelled on each coast. We should have had another so that the Mid—West could have been covered."

"Do you remember which exams?"

'Nope, I let that slip. I retrained the 'A's though, didn't I?"

"But, for God's sake, I would like to know 'A' in what."

"So call them if it's that important."

"Yeah, maybe later. But it would be more convenient if you just remembered."

"More convenient but not the me you know and so appreciate."

"I guess so," he shrugged, hands still flat on his knees.

"Was the concert as tremendous as you'd anticipated?"

"Just about. I don't know why you don't come once in a while…."

"You do know why. Because I'm a teacher and Friday afternoon is a school day. Just like Monday, Tuesday, Wednesday and Thursday."

"Right, but you could take off a Friday afternoon, once in a great while, for an especially good one, or whatever. You know, the kids wouldn't forget everything you taught them all week, by Monday morning just because you weren't there Friday afternoon." He had put a little bite into his words. "Even I take off the few hours every few weeks to be able to go," he concluded, almost didactically.

"Oh come on," she shot back, her voice starting to rise, "When you've had some big deal, or something, that had to go as fast as possible, you've missed your subscription, given the tickets away, or donated them back to the box office."

She was trying to keep her voice as even as possible and at a normal level but was only partially succeeding."I can think, very clearly, of three or four times that that's happened, just in the past few years. The Bigelow deal, then that Holzem apartment building purchase…."

"But these were things that had to be done at exactly those times. No real options as to timing." He realized he was sounding testy himself, even though he didn't want to. "But if you don't teach the landing at Plymouth Rock Friday afternoon it can wait until Monday morning."

"Oh, now I see, your point is becoming clear. What you do is important. VERY important. What I do isn't. It just isn't." She almost, involuntarily, stamped her right foot.

"Now you come on," he retorted, hoarsely and brusquely. "You know god—damn well that I'm not saying that at all."

"Actually, I'm less interested in the debating points here than why you're in such a foul mood, if the concert was supposedly so great. You came in like you were just waiting to attack, and..." she trailed off, shaking her head disconsolately.

Ed looked up and stared at her lowered head, the still thick and lustrous air.

"You're right; even though the music making was wonderful I'm in a bad mood. A very bad mood actually. Irritable, depressed and all the rest of it. That's right, I am, if you must know."

"And which, or what combination, of my many sins and transgressions...."

"No, no. Stop being so egotistical It's just because the concert was so good. Just because Tennstedt conducted so brilliantly. I even went to tell him afterwards. How many times can he conduct like that again? Did you know that Philip Larkin, when he was Poet Laureate of England, commented that if life is a week long then once you hit your fities it's the final weekend."

Ed shook his head, from side to side, quite deliberately, as he started to get up.

AUNT JEANNE'S LEGACY

THERE AREN'T SO MANY PEOPLE around any more who were rabid rooters for the Brooklyn, (not the Los Angeles,) Dodgers. They left Brooklyn after the '57 season in one of the most notorious betrayals of a community, ever. Similarly, there aren't too many people left in the family who remember my aunt, my dad's sister, Jeanette, Harry's wife, any more. She lasted for quite a few years after the Dodgers left but time, inexorably, makes its claims.

Uncle Harry had the D.D. S. degree but many in the family who'd been his patient would say, "Jeanne is really the dentist." She was his assistant, today's dental hygienist, and while he worked on you she would keep up, in addition to general conversation, a steady step by step stream of instructions to him. "It looks like one more drill will do it, have her rinse, put the cotton a little more to the left," etc., etc. No family member seemed to know whether Harry really needed this prompting. The suspicion, the hope at least, was that he didn't. But no one was sure he didn't.

The theory was floated that he had good hands but little knowledge about the appropriate dental sequences in which to use them and that Jeanne had learned, taught herself, enough about dentistry so that it was best that they worked in tandem. She instructing, he executing. Another theory was that in his younger days Harry was too good with his hands with comely female patients and that this was the main reason that Jeanne had become his omnipresent assistant.

But it's not as though Aunt Jeanne was a shrinking violet otherwise. She was one of a relatively few women of her generation, (she'd actually been born in Russia and brought here, less than a year old, by my dad's folks, at the turn of the twentieth century,) who drove. And she drove even when she didn't. She was an incorrigible, indefatigable back seat driver, from her front seat, when Harry drove. Both in the car as well as the office he always seemed to unflappably follow her dictates. Whether that was because they mirrored his own intentions, anyway, or because he actually often deferred to her judgment, no one ever conclusively determined either.

Aunt Jeanne was assertive and enthusiastic elsewhere too. She belonged to quite a few service organizations and rose high in the local administrative hierarchies of some. It seemed people in the family were always receiving an invitation to a dinner or luncheon at which Jeanne was to be installed as president of this chapter of that group or vice—president of a branch of that organization. Nor did she hang back when men in the family discussed current events.She would join in, often have a decided point of view, and express it gracefully and articulately, as well as forcefully. At family gatherings she often played the piano, in an accomplished fashion. She was one of my earliest introductions to classical music., Chopin her specialty. I still love his music; he's right there in my pantheon with Beethoven and Schubert.

By the time I got to be really aware of Jeanne, to know her a bit, she still had a round, bright eyed, generally attractive face. But she had become a bit, as it was then called, heavy—set. Nevertheless, I well understood when the older extended family members would reminisce about her considerable beauty as a young woman.

When I was nine or ten, I was conscious both of Jeanne as the "dentist" and the great Brooklyn Dodger teams led by Jackie Robinson. I was a passionate fan but a much less forthcoming dental patient. Even though by that time I'd been going to Harry for three years I always dreaded the experience and was ridden by anxiety verging on abject fear. (On one of my first visits, after Jeanne prodded that I probably needed to rinse, Harry proclaimed "Spit" and I did---directly at him instead of into the receptacle attached to the chair's arm. Harry lost his characteristic unflappability) I never knew just how much hurt would be involved in any visit.

One of my appointments came on a September day, in the late forties, when the Dodgers, in the throes of a very tight pennant race, were playing a crucial, very "crooshal," game. I'd been listening to the wonderful Dodger annoiuncer, Red Barber, on the radio until it was time to leave for the dentist. I was very distressed at having to miss the rest of the game. But, naturally, my mother insisted we go as scheduled.

I got lucky. When we got there aunt Jeanne said that Harry was running behind and why didn't we come into the residence part of the apartment and relax until he was ready for me. Another speculation I'd heard, from mom and dad, aunts and uncles, was that when Jeanne told a patient that Harry was behind schedule he was really taking a breather elsewhere in the apartment. Their children were grown and gone, (the son also a dentist, the daughter a registered nurse,) so there was a lot of room in the old—time spacious and gracious apartment where Harry could hide. The origins of these various rumors about Harry and Jeanne no one seemed to ever pinpoint.

Even though I was a shy pre—adolescent I had the nerve to tell aunt Jeanne that I had been torn away from the very exciting and important game which I'd been listening to. She was a Dodger fan herself, also very striking then for a woman of her vintage, and knew all about, and was intensely proud of, the inspiring pilgrimage and courageous adventure of Jack Roosevelt Robinson, No. 42, second baseman extraordinaire.

Immediately she said, "Well, we're sitting here in the living room anyway, why don't we just turn on the game on the radio."

Without my even answering , she instantly tuned the bulky, upright, four foot high, stand-on-the-floor radio to "WGN, 1050 on you AM dial," until Red Barber's voice came through clearly and with its usual mellifluousness. It was a tied ballgame, 2-2 in the top of the eighth, and the opponents, I no longer remember the team, had the bases loaded with two outs. I forgot all about my trepidation of encountering Uncle Harry's fierce drill and quickly became absorbed in my nervousness over this threat to the Dodgers. Barber, in his tinge of a southern accent, calmly described how the carefully hurling pitcher and the cautious hitter worked the count up to 3-2. If the batter walked the Dodgers would be behind with only two innings of at bats remaining. They'd be even further behind if the batter suddenly lashed a hit.If the pitcher could strike him out or otherwise retire him the Dodgers would be out of that peril and given their record that year as a team which often rallied in the late innings would have good prospects for winning the game in the end.

Barber announced:" Here's the pitch, fast ball at the shoulders… it's popped up, in foul territory near the third base line…." I heaved a giant sigh of relief and, also, exultation. Billy Cox, the Dodger third sacker was one of the best defensive players in the league. He had great hands and would frequently turn viciously hit hot smashes, which seemed to have "base hit" written all over them , into brilliant plays in which he threw the batter out at first base. (And all with his "dime store glove," immortalized later on, by Roger Khan in his classic tribute to this classic team, THE BOYS OF SUMMER.) Just as I was slowing down my kinetic pacing and relaxing into hopefulness as to the ultimate fate, this day, of "the Brooklyns" as Barber sometimes called them, he continued: "Cox is under it, pumping his glove, waiting…waiting….whoa he drops it!!! '[Tremendous crowd roar.] Billy Cox, of all people, drops an easy pop—up and the Dodgers aren't out of this yet. Oh, doctor!!"

At first I became absolutely motionless with shocked disappointment and with the deep despair over a triviality which only a ten-year old can afford or dares to display. But, then, seemingly heedless of where I was and who else was there I went into action. I dashed over to the dining room table, started pounding my right fist on it fiercely and then unveiled for my audience whatever "curse" words I then commanded.I definitely took the name of Billy Cox in vain and thoroughly calumniated his ineptness and general lack of abilities and virtue as a human being.

My aunt and mother stoically absorbed this while Barber continued to relate how the pitcher was now taking his time and how the batter had stepped out of the batter's box to repay the pitcher for his dilatoriness. I had to spend my fury rather quickly as I did want to hear what would happen. So I came down from my very high dudgeon just about as rapidly as I'd ascended.But before the next pitch aunt Jeanne very quietly turned to me and said, "Has Billy Cox ever done anything that helped the Dodgers?"

I no longer rememeber if the Dodgers did get out of that eighth inning jam without a run scoring off them, what the final score of the game was, or, even, if it happened in one of the years that the Dodgers won the pennant. But, more than a half—century late,r I do still think about what aunt Jeanne said, although I did not answer her at the time.

TEACHING THE RUBES

HARVEY AND ELLEN SANDERS WERE big city folks in a small town. They had moved from their native Chicago, with their two very young children, to a semi—rural state capital in the Pacific Northwest. All so that Harvey could begin his law teaching career as an Assistant Professor at a small school East of the Cascades. State capital the town of sixty thousand might now be, but it was only a generation, two at the most, removed from its raw farming community origins.

With law students to match. Most were from Oregon, Washington, Idaho, Montana and the Dakotas. But there was an occasional southerner, solid mid—westerner, or, even, but most rarely,an eastern seaboarder strewn amongst the callow bunch. In Harvey's Contracts class there was even an African—American, born in inner—city Detroit. What was the difference Harvey thought. He felt, from his own law student experience, that any class in law school was much like any other—a somewhat diverse orchestra ready to be highly tuned, and, finally, expertly played, by the conductor—professor.

Ellen's third grade students in the Presbyterian school in which she'd landed a job, (she still wondered whether the directrix, who'd enthusiastically hired her, knew she was Jewish,) were much more homogenized, just as, ultimately, was the milk produced on many of the farms, run by their parents, in the surrounding but fading areas. They were truly innocent, sweet, mostly cooperative and certainly hadn't been overly-educated or "sophisticated" until that point.

After about two months of Harvey teaching Contracts to the first year class he felt that, in this instance at least, his analogizing a law school class to an orchestra with different instruments, or, more accurately, different groups of instruments had been validated. Strings, winds, brass in the orchestra, conservatives, liberals, centrists/ pragmatists in the law school classroom. In just that brief period he had learned that when he wanted to put a "left" analysis of a case before the multitudes in the class he could just call on Ken Surtees, who would refer to some aspect of the case that conceivably, howsoever long the "stretch," related to saving the environment or easing the burdens of the poor and homeless. Similarly, if a contrary perspective on the same materials was wanted, Harvey had only to call on Susan Britter to hear why the status quo should be maintained because the law was inherently a conservative institution and should change, if at all, most incrementally and gradually, even glacially. They each had a modest group of cohorts but the majority of the class fit into the "centrist" group which tended to analyze and construe each case as a totally separate entity from anything else .They tried, even if too often inexpertly, to come to a conclusion which followed from given principles of the relevant body of law presumably applicable to all cases of that general type, whoever's ox wound up getting gored as a result.

"So, "Harvey intoned, "we come to the case of Davis vs. Reliable Credit Co. Well, ladies and gentlemen, what do you think of the decision in this case? I'll give you a break here, particularly since there's not all that long to go before the period ends, and recap its essentials for you, instead of the usual script of making one of you reluctant warriors, not that you're very war--like, state the case. Anyway, Davis signed the credit card agreement , four long pages of quite fine print; I think we can all agree on that. One of the sentences in that quagmire, (is that too strong a characterization?) stated that if a regularly due payment were missed, or even late, the original interest rate of 7% would immediately and automatically, no questions asked or entertained, increase to 14%. Davis successfully used the card for three plus years without any incident. That is, he, at least, payed the minimum balance due each and every month on time or before. Some months he paid only partially and, therefore, was charged the 7% interest rate, added to the next balance. However, about five months into the fourth year of this process his payment arrived late and the next month the 14% rate of interest was applied to the entire unpaid balance. Davis objected saying that he had no idea that the interest rate could rise so precipitously, actually double, vrtually instantly, and that he thought he had sent the payment in, as normally, in time for it to reach the company on the due date or before. The company pointed to the clear sentence in the contract, authorizing the doubling of the rate , which Davis had signed. Everyone agrees on that too. Davis asked the company to, at the very least, rescind the increase respecting future balances. The company refused and Davis cancelled the card, paying off whatever outstanding balance there had been except for the small amount, just a few dollars, attributable to the 14% finance charge which had been applied. The company sued for that modest amount and, also, for the "cancellation fee" of $125, likewise clearly provided for in one of the many fine print sentences of the agreement between Reliable and Davis. Since the entire sum the company seeks to collect by its suit is less than $200 and since they are a billion dollar institution, it seems reasonable to assume that suit was brought principally, if not exclusively, to establish the principle that the contract, and the many others like it, could, indeed, be enforced, as per whatever clauses the fine print contained, if actually signed on to by a customer defendant."

"O.K., Ms. Smith, you've had your hand up for a while, so another fair assumption seems to be that you're willing to weigh in here." Ms. Smith, Harvey recalled, from scanning the admission files, was a graduate of one of the better colleges represented in the law school's first year class. Not a spectacularly prestigious one, but solid enough.

"Well, actually, professor I have a question…."

"Fine Ms. Smith; that shows you'r e doing at least SOME thinking, a distinct rarity for a law student, especially a first year one. Maybe your question will provoke further thought—for you or some of your many indolent classmates." Harvey didn't want them to miss the riding that he and his own classmates had been given at the much better law school than this one that Harvey had attended. "What's the question"?

"Well, professor—and I do try to think whenever I can muster the energy" (Harvey loved when they fought back, those would certainly well represent their clients' interests if they did nothing else,) ---"I was wondering if Mr. Davis, in fact, sent in the payment on time. I mean in time for the company to receive it before the late charge applied."

"Excellent suggestion Ms. Smith; perhaps you suspect the company of some skullduggery. Do you have any idea of the answer?"

"I asked the question."

" Touche Ms. Smith, you're practically a lawyer, already. Very good," (praise them when you can Harvey liked to think was his policy,) "attorney—like, evasive, playing for time response. But sometimes we really already know the answers to questions we ask, but just haven't dug deep enough down in our thinking to reach them."

"Well, actually, professor, now that you mention it, I think the case report said that Davis claimed that he had sent the payment in at the time of the month he usually did, about three or four days prior to the due date, the day by which the company had to receive it,but the company said it didn't arrive before the due date. That it had actually come in two days after that."

Nodding, more or less approvingly, but just barely perceptibly, Harvey turned from Ms. Smith to the other side of the classroom.

" I see your hand Mr. Rauch."

"Yeah, it says what she said it says in the second paragraph on page 112."

" You mean Ms. Smith, Mr. Rauch?"

"Yeah, her," Rauch said, pointing to the other side of the large classroom.

"Well, if you're Mr. Rauch then she's Ms. Smith isn't she?"

"O.K., yeah....Miss, I mean miz, Smith."

"And yes, you're right Mr. Rauch, that's where the material Ms. Smith quoted appears, on page 112. Good sticking to the hard core documentation."

"Yeah, but it also says that even though the company's records have a date and time of receipt, in a ledger, you know, of the payment, that when payments are received the envelopes they came in are thrown out, so it's his word against theirs."

"By his and theirs I take it that you mean Davis and the company?"

"Yeah."

"So what if the post mark showed that Davis had deposited the payment in the mail on the date he contended that he had, would that mean that he should win the case?"

"Ms. Ramsey, over there," Harvey said, pointing toward the middle of the masses, "you've been sitting quietly but looking thoughtful and contemplative. Any reflections you 'd like to articulate for the benefit of your classmates and, perhaps, also, for your professor? Should Davis win if the postmark had shown timeliness?"

"Uh, not necessarily, professor, I would think," Ms. Ramsey began in a distinctly south of the Mason—Dixon line accent. Harvey was thinking Alabama, or perhaps Georgia. "Because the agreement says, in effect, that the only thing that counts is when the company actually receives the payment."

"But what if the company is lying!" came an animated, almost agitated, shout from somewhere in the very back rows of the spacious claassroom.

"Ah, a voice from the wilderness," said Harvey. "Can you identify yourself?"

"It was me, over here; Mr. Laskin, Bob Laskin, from New Jersey."

"Ah, well thank you for forthrightly revealing yourself, Mr. Laskin, from JOISEY, [titters] and thank you for your contribution. We'll get to that in a moment---but first, if we're to have a modicum of order and civility in here it's probably best that people seek recognition by raising a hand before shouting out observations. I've tried to establish that by now."

"I'm sorry, sir…."

"Of course that stricture does not apply to me," Harvey interjected, with a wry grin, "who will feel free to interrupt and burst in respecting anything a student is saying—particularly if it's not too relevant or trenchant. In other words most of the time. " (More titters throughout the class.)

"In any event, a toi, as the French say, Mr. Laskin, your turn. No extra fee for the foreign language lesson. What trenchant insight, or ,hopefully, insights,in the plural, do you have for us?"

On the verge of sputtering Laskin expostulated, "This contract, if it is even one, is a TOTAL one way street. Everything's in favor of the company. If the post office doesn't deliver in time, if the company says it came late, even if they don't have any proof, the interest rates are outrageous to begin with….then they can raise them, even more, double it for being one day late….it's ridiculous!"

"So, Mr. Laskin, are you saying, and rather forcefully I might add, that people can't make the contracts they want to make and to which they agree? "

"No, not really, but, Davis couldn't bargain with them at all---and when something is so one—sided and inherently unfair….."

" I see Ms. Ramsey's hand waving rather emphatically. I have a feeling that she is au contraire, to refer once again to the elegant French language. You see, you too get free foreign language instruction in here, too. Ms. Ramsey?"

"Well, yes, professor, merci beaucoup and all that---- at the very, (she emphasized this last word,) least I think you can say I disagree."

"And that would be in exactly what respects, Ms. Ramsey?" Harvey asked.

"Well, I think it takes just a glance at the economic history and history in general of this country to see that a lot of what we are, a lot of what makes us as great as we are, is based on the freedom of individuals to deal with each other and make and execute agreements that they both benefit from."

"Is there another way of looking at this particular agreement, Ms. Ramsey? Oh, I see that both Mr. Laskin and Mr. Rauch, not to mention Mr. Surtees, are waving their hands, and pretty vigorously, I might add. Putting aside Mr. Surtees, who volunteers a great deal in here, for the moment, shall I choose, gentlemen, or does one of you want to yield to the other?"

"Oh go ahead," Rauch waved in Laskin's direction. "He was good before."

"Seems you're on Mr. Laskin," Harvey commented.

"Yeah, that's o.k. I was just thinking , I looked at some of the outside readings the syllabus suggested…." (A patina of boos.)

"I didn't know anyone really took those seriously," Harvey shot in. (Nervous, guilty titters.)

" Yeah, I was rummaging around in…"

"Like it's a piece of furniture?" Harvey, again, interjected, to a somewhat reduced smattering of titters.

"No, I mean I was reading it, you know, 'Liberal Legislation And Freedom of Contract' by T.H. Green, the nineteenth century English guy,but not, maybe, every word from the start, you know one after another. Well, anyway, he was making some good points. First of all he spoke about whether in certain situations there really is 'freedom' for one of the parties in the making of the contract—whether the power of one party is so much more than the other that the weaker one has to agree to just about anything the other one wants. No matter how much one—sided stuff he can cram in there."

"But, then, Mr. Laskin, why would the weaker party agree at all if the contract is so one—sided?" Harvey asked.

" I don't know; I mean maybe he needs something so badly that he has to agree to a lot of conditions that he doesn't want and which become very hard for him."

"But didn't he agree to accept the burdens with the benefits?"

"Well, 'agree 'is, I don't know, funny in that situation."

"So are you saying," Harvey enthused, as he noted that the period's conclusion was drawing very near, "that there really was no choice; that 'choosing' to enter into the contract was illusory, because, given the position of the weaker party there was really no rational choice at all, other than the one that the weak party made by entering into the onerous contract to get the slim benefit that he desperately needed? Putting it another way, are you really saying that the strong party, in effect, took advantage of the weaker one, when the weak one didn't really have any choice,? That, in actuality, the stronger 'exploited' the weaker? In metaphorical terms put a gun to the weaker's head?"

"Yeah, I don't know what the right words are, but something like that. I can't say it like you did...."

"That's alright, Mr. Laskin. That may be to your credit. But I can see from Ms. Ramsey's frantically waving hand that she seems to be of another mind."

"You could damn well say that, professor," Ramsey interjected ,agitatedly, as Harvey looked in her direction.

"Feel free, Ms. Ramsey, to enlighten us. But do it quickly, we only have a few minutes to go. You know how punctual I am. I don't like to make anyone late for his or her next class with a professor from whom you might actually learn something" The laughter was pretty hearty after that one.

"Well, professor, you may not have meant to, but I think you said it all when you said 'agree.' It's not like these people have a right to a credit card. They wanted the card so they agreed to what they had to agree to to get it. For the life of me, in all sincerity, I can't see why we have to go any further than that. A deal is a deal."

"And when you say 'these people," Ms. Ramsey, you mean exactly whom?"

"Well, Davis or anyone who wants a credit card from that company."

"O.K., I see. And you say a deal is a deal. Does that mean any deal is o.k. regardless of how oppressive the terms are to one of the parties? And does the enforceability of onerous terms relate, at all, to how the weaker party might have been enticed, if you will, to enter the deal?"

" Life ain't fair. Not everybody has the same. Maybe one person can get a good deal from somebody. But maybe that somebody can get a good deal from another party. That's what our system of individual iniative is all about. You know it really all comes down to that our system is free enterprise and a deal has to be upheld as a deal."

"As your shuffling of your papers and your books ratifies," Harvey addressed the class," the hour is just about up. So Ms. Ramsey has the last word, more or less. But I do want Ms. Ramsey, as well as the rest of you, to think about, as Mr. Laskin suggested, just how 'free' free enterprise is, and whether, in the contemporary economic system of this country, many people have a real 'choice' as to whether to possess a credit card. Also, specifically, Just what it is, exactly, that they agree to in signing the agreement which allows them to procure one."

The shuffling crescendoed into general student to student conversation and Harvey gathered up his own books and papers.But before he could escape Ms. Ramsey was before him at the podium.

"Professor, I must say, I didn't come here to hear Marxist theory and it just seems that you are trying to tear down, whenever you can, our system and way of life. Now I know that you are very educated, much better than most of us, and that you know a lot, but still…."

"Well, Ms. Ramsey, it seems that you pretty well know what you know and, therefore, don't seem too vulnerable to being "fooled" into disenchantment with our current system. But you never know what you might learn or where. Isn't that what education is about?"

"I suppose so. I guess so, if you put it that way."

"Then we have a deal? You'll keep listening, no matter how critically and combatively?"

"O.K., professor. I get it—a deal is a deal."

"Exactly Ms. Ramsey. See you here on Friday."

~

Only a bit more to go in the law school "year." It was only April, but it would be over in just two weeks. Harvey could bear it until then. By this time the students were ready for summer vacation to begin, (although most of them, of course, had to take jobs to help with tuition,) and Harvey was really ready for the second semester to end. He had played upon and developed the members of the class as much as he could and if they hadn't gotten what he was trying to teach them by now, it wasn't going to come in the last two weeks. For some of them, of course, it never would.

"O.K., class; as you know the case today is probably the leading one on unconscionability, Campbell Soup Co. Wentz. To be brief, no pun intended, the Wentzes agreed to sell their crop of tomatoes to Campbell's Soup. There were all sorts of stipulations in the contract about the responsibilities of the Wentzes regarding the condition and quality of the tomatoes to be delivered to Campbells. When harvest time came the market price of tomatoes was tremendously in excess of the contract price. The Wentzes refused to deliver their tomatoes to Campbell's and, instead, sold them on the market for a much greater sum than they would have received from Campbell's according to the contract price. Campbell's sued for the difference between what they had to pay for tomatoes on the market and the price at which the Wentzes had agreed to deliver under the contract. So, what did the court say and was its decision correct?"

Susan Britter's hand shot up instantly and Harvey quickly acknowledged her.

"We're back to protect the weaker party and people can't agree to what they want to agree to, aren't we?" Harvey yet again marveled at how in not too many months many of them had sharpened up their analytical skills and sense of relevance. Briiter went on. "The court said that it was too much a one way contract, Campbell's had driven too hard a deal against the 'poor ' [she stressed the word,]Wentzes and, therefore, the contract was unconscionable and unenforceable. The Wentzes could get away with not delivering the tomatoes to Campbells and could sell them elsewhere at a much higher price."

"Higher than what Ms. Briiter?" Harvey accepted that even many of the better ones hadn't become overly precise.

"Higher than the contract price for the tomatoes, you know, as per the contract ."

"That's correct Ms. Britter and good work on a concise statement of what the core of the case is about. However, I take it from certain of your phraseology and inflections in your comments that you were not overly delighted with the court's reasoning."

"I don't think there was much reasoning, professor. The court just did its best to rationalize the result it wanted to produce."

"Is that unusual for courts"? Harvey asked. "But I see that there are other hands. Yes, Mr. Surtees."

"A mega—corporation beating on the small hard—working man again. Everything in the contract was for the company. All the risk was on the Wentzes. The company got a low price, but if things didn't go right in some way for them they were off the hook. I think there was something about not having to 'accept'delivery, for various reasons. But they want the Wentzes to stay on the hook even if they can get a much better deal than foisted on them by the exploitative company when things change to their advantage. We shouldn't help companies do that to little hard—working, honest folks."

"But Mr. Surtees," Harvey responded, "how honest were the Wentzes in backing out of a deal into which they entered, as to which they promised performance, as soon as a better deal came along?"

Suddenly a southern—accented voice shouted out: "That's it professor, tell him like it is here in the good old U.S.A." (Some chuckling in the class.)

"Well Ms. Ramsey," Harvey responded, "I see that you have remained true to the faith." (A rather fatigued tittering from about half the class. The other half was just fatigued.)

"I hope so, professor."

"So, Ms. Ramsey, no matter what the company shoves in the contract, howsoever, one—sided, unfair, Draconic, whatever phrase you want to use suggesting extreme pressure, the other party can never deviate, not even an iota's worth, from the written word. In other words no contract, regardless of just how one—sidedly onerous, can be unconscionable to the point of voidability."?

Abruptly Bob Laskin's Jersey tones erupted: "That's it professor; tell it to her like WE know it is!!" (This brought more enthusiastic, robust laughter from the assembled.)

And so it went.

In the bliss of a fresh May early afternoon, with Ellen at work, Harvey was reading, on the outdoor deck, off the kitchen, some material that he thought might be relevant to an article he wanted to write on the concept of "freedom of contact." While in the midst of a thorny passage, which Harvey had already re—read twice, he thought he heard the doorbell ring. Irritably turning down the offending page he traipsed back through the house to answer it. To his monumental surprise the caller was not a neighbor with another zucchini pie, but none other than Maryanne Ramsey, looking, now that final exams were over, a lot fresher and bright—eyed than she had just before they took place.

"Well, professor, aren't you going to ask me to come in?"

Harvey, somewhat flustered, tried to recover, "Well, of course, Ms. Ramsey, come right in"

When he had shut the door behind her Ramsey asked, "Is your wife here?"

"No,...she isn't," Harvey said warily.

"That's too bad, I would have liked to have met her."

"Yes, I'm sure she would have enjoyed meeting you too. Perhaps some other time."

"Well, that's O.K. The reason I'm here, and you must be wondering what it could be professor...."

"Yes, I was and am, Ms. Ramsey."

"Well, it's sort of like discharging a debt."

"Really?"

"Yes, as you know, we've had our disagreements all year. Sometimes pretty vociferously."

"So it was, Ms. Ramsey. And you held your own well."

"Oh, thank you, professor; that's very kind of you. I thought you thought......"

"Not at all. You were a fine student. You are a fine student"

"And so were you professor—I mean you were a great teacher , one of the very best I ever had, anywhere. We may have disagreed a lot, but you definitely taught me something, professor. You taught me something. I got a great deal out of your class. And maybe I even learned how to be a more compassionate, humane person. Who knows."

"Thank you Ms. Ramsey, I very much appreciate what you just said. I had a college professor who once told me that in teaching response is all, as he put it. It's what it's all about. I somehow think that you've always, at the core, been a compassionate and humane person."

"That's all professor, that's all I wanted to say." She was dabbing at her eyes with a handkerchief she had swiftly removed from the pocket of her dress. She opened the door, turned, gave a half—wave and ran to her car. Then she was gone.

BEAUTIFUL GIRLS

WHEN MARTIN WAS FIRST AWARE of Gretta Zenda she really was just barely more than a girl. In any event it was well before the days of political correctness. His first encounter with her was at after school religious instruction when each was about thirteen. Martin was attending as part of being prepared for his Bar Mitzvah and she was just attending. Or at least he wasn't conscious of whether it was in connection with her being confirmed or not.

It turned out that they went to the same high school in Brooklyn---with four thousand other students. Actually, they lived in the same neighborhood. Less than a mile separated the house which she occupied with her mother, who gave piano lessons, from the one bedroom apartment in which he lived with his immigrant parents who worked in Manhattan's garment center.

Martin didn't know much about her. He'd seen her several times a week in Hebrew school but there was little interchange. In high school he rarely saw her, amongst the student hordes, until he would up in the same History class with her in their senior year. What he did know about her, from the first, although the fact became more and more palpable to him, was that she was beautiful.Her hair was unalloyed, freshest blonde and her features simply perfect. But not in an exceedingly sharply etched relentlessly you—must—look—at—me way. They had a soft, inviting quality. She was utterly beautiful, yet intimated compassion, understanding. It might have been her manner that contributed to enhancing this sense. She tended towards tall, slim, willowysome might say. She seemed to move effortlessly and exude calmness. She was subdued, refined.

When he first knew her Martin objectively noted these characteristics but they didn't make much of an impact on him. Even in his over-sexed, early adolescent version. In fact, he started off with some animosity toward her because she was obviously the Hebrew School teacher's pet. Maybe, also, because there seemed something just TOO perfect, maybe too Olympian, about her. An ice princess? Maybe she didn't really reach him because she appeared unreachable. He decided she was a snob, even though she didn't give any concrete evidence of being one. He no longer remembered how his passion for her grew. It must have been after they were in high school for a while. Perhaps not before that History class.

Before Martin fixated on the transcendent Gretta he had other urges. Urgent they may have felt, but he was not adept at converting them into opportunities or experience. Roberta Powell was not classically beautiful but she was pretty and comely. Light brown hair, sparkling hazel eyes, even behind her glasses, possibly even more enticing behind her glasses and an alert, glad—to—see—you affect in an overall trim, but full where desirable for it to be full, figure. She was in his English class early in his junior year. From a forty—five degree angle, across two rows, he spent considerable time staring at her legs, crossed at the ankles, as they emerged from a moderately tight, but not sheath—like, skirt. This perspective also allowed a very good and provocative view of the profile of her right breast as it asserted itself against the light blue or dark grey sweaters and jerseys she often wore. But her appeal for Martin was not essentially prurient. Her face was basically angelic. And its attractiveness was enhanced by her bright, ready for adventure and experience disposition. She was the girl next door who seemed to be waiting for some one to convince her to move out and move on.

It took him many weeks to amass the courage to ask her on a date. And then he botched it, miserably. Perhaps they weren't a good match, but he never got to find that out. Unwittingly, in his characteristic "out—of—it" fashion, he asked her for the Saturday night on which the high school's annual school—wide SING contest was taking place. Each class, freshmen through seniors, fielded a chorus and competed against each other with "original" songs they'd written especially for the contest. The event was held in the large school auditorium and a good part of the student body came to cheer and root. Roberta wanted to go there. But Martin, averse to any "public" display, suggested the Brooklyn premiere of the film version of "Streetcar Named Desire" . As though they would understand what that was all about. Martin won out because he had to—he just couldn't face

SING, much as he wanted to please the pretty Miss Powell. She gracefully adjusted to this fate and they even had a decent discussion about the movie and other things too. But Martin knew that he had disappointed and frustrated her when he wouldn't take her to SING. He should have been flattered that she wanted to be seen with him there. But his anxiety engulfed all. So, he knew that although things had preceded superficially acceptably on the date, they really hadn't. Even though Martin had put a lot of mettle and determined effort into functioning as smoothly as he had, the battle against shyness being ubiquitous, he knew that, fundamentally, he had failed.

He resumed staring longingly at Robeta during English class and they would exchange a quick greeting now and then, but he couldn't find the immediate resolve to ask her on another date. Eventually he did ask. And was refused, fairly forthrightly, as he completely expected he would be. And, not long thereafter, Roberta seemed to start paling around with Roland Horch, a verging on obese and generally undistinguished student in that same English class. They would sometimes walk out of class together, chatting. One time Roland grabbed her hand and started pulling her vigorously and joyfully toward the door. She resisted to the extent of pulling her hand away so that she could better gather her books and things. But then she followed close behind him to the hall. She did not seem nearly as joyous as he, or joyous at all, but she went with him. After that Martin curtailed his longing for her sweetness.

Simultaneously with disappointedly observing Roland's campaign for Roberta, Martin had started noticing another girl in the English class. It so happened that Nancy Morrison was one of the most explicitly popular girls in the entire school. She was very active in various extra—curricular activities like student government and the student newspaper. Nevertheless, everyone seemed to assume that the principal basis for her widely envied popularity was her physical appearance. Long chestnut hair, regular clear features, and a little taller than average body expressing highly alluring curves. She might have been beautiful, probably was, but just about everyone, especially highly hormonal adolescent boys, agreed that she was replete with flagrant sex appeal. Actually there was openness and warmth in her face, but that figure could not possibly have muted her seductiveness. "Statuesque" was the term then. Martin sensed a tinge of disippatedness. Some times her expression was a little too knowing and her dress started becoming more "casual," sloppier. Martin didn't know whether his feelings were accurate or that he began to see her that way because he surmised that given her obvious physical assets and the number of dates she must have already had that she must have begun serious sexual experience.

One day, as Martin filed out the classroom, Nancy was waiting. She just started saying something about what Mrs. Lawrence had taught that day and animatedly went on from there. Martin didn't contribute much to the conversation. She'd taken him completely by surprise, and even if she hadn't he would have been overwhelmed by his customary complete diffidence in the presence of girls. Especially ones as striking as Nancy. It was certainly flattering to have even the slightest attention paid to him by such a stellar girl but he wasn't up to seizing his opportunity—if that's what she was providing. She must have been, because, despite what Martin keenly felt was his very unsatisfactory reaction to her initial approach, only a few days later she repeated the scenario. She waited for him after class and again started gabbing about something Mrs. Lawrence had said during the period. He did a little better this time, before they parted for separate classes, speaking with a little more verve and offering some observations of his own, instead of just mumbling laconic responses to what she said. But it wasn't much better. He wished it had been and thought about her a lot between that incident and the last time she waited at the back of the classroom, a few days later. He even concentrated more on the kindness and softness he saw in her face and not that much on how blissful it would be to touch, caress, kiss her spectacular curves. On her last approach he became even a little more comfortable as the conversation proceeded and began to even enjoy himself.

Then he thought of her even more and hoped that she would give him just one more chance. He fantasized that he might do pretty well , maybe even crack a few jokes, the next time. But she didn't. She must have given him up as hopeless or felt that she'd gone out on a limb enough and that if he were truly interested he should summon enough gumption to ask her out on an official date. However, that was so beyond Martin's capabilities, with someone like her, that when he realized she would not again initiate things he just stopped yearning and gave up. Actually, he never really spoke to her again. He was not in another class with her and didn't seem to even see her passing in the corridors when classes changed. Yet he always wondered what had happened to her. Had she gotten in with the "wrong" crowd, her finer, serious qualities overwhelmed by the glitz of immediate sensation.

In retrospect Martin thought that his deep longing for Gretta must not have crescendoed until they were in that senior year History class.

They had nodded to each other occasionally, an acknowledgment of their joint Hebrew school experience, but there was no extended or sequential conversation.But during those History classes Martin became conscious that he was staring at Gretta a lot more than he looked at anything else in the room, including Mrs. Rudnick, the middle—aged, but still very committed, quite enthusiastic, teacher. He liked the long, flowing very bright, red, blue or green skirts Gretta would wear with severely starched, mostly bright white, blouses. Her shoes were usually basic loafers or those brown and white so—called saddle shoes worn with white socks. Martin couldn't even get much of an idea about where the clothes ended and her body began. Her overall affect was girlish rather than of a fifteen/sixteen year old almost woman.

However, soon after the start of the school year, on some Jewish holiday, probably Rosh Hashonah, Martin was walking on sunlit streets with his parents during a break from temple services. Suddenly he saw Gretta coming down the very long block in the opposite direction. Although he had to look hard to be sure. She too was with some adults, probably family also. She was brilliant looking in a stylish black suit, skirt of moderate tightness and length, nylons and medium high black suede heels. Her hair was swept into a much more tightly concentrated, less flowing configuration than it characteristically was in at school. She had on sunglasses, too, on this crisp, streamlined Fall day. She appeared a very elegant, sophisticated, highly attractive young woman. But no words were exchanged between Martin and Gretta, not even nods. Martin, his heart thumping that there might have to be introductions, pretended not to have seen Gretta. He didn't know what she had seen through the sunglasses.

When they saw each other in class, the next day, neither said anything about this incident and their failure to have any significant exchanges in History persisted. Before long it was mid—term exam time. Martin was a hard studier—very diligent, thorough and conscientious. But he promised himself a reward for the intense preparation that he'd put in studying for five mid—terms. Right after the last of them, which happened to be History, he'd hop on the subway to "The World's Largest record Store" in mid—town Manhattan and make a rare purchase of a classical music recording that he coveted. Something he usually couldn't indulge himself in.. His parents' income was very modest and his allowance was commensurate. The surpassingly great Soviet violinist, David Oistrakh, (some thought he was right there with Heifetz on the top pedastel,) had recorded the recently composed Shostakovitch Violin Concerto under the great conductor, Dimitri Mitropoulos leading the New York Philharmonic. A few weeks previous, Martin had heard the live performance on the Philharmonic broadcast to which he listened every Sunday afternoon. He'd been absolutely swept away. Although a decidedly neophyte and very limited fiddler himself, under the often frustrated tutelage of old Benny Kaflowitz, trained in the Warsaw Conservatory, Martin could, nevertheless, appreciate the astonishing technique and ineffable musicality which Oistrakh brought to the impossibly difficult yet totally absorbing work. At that stage of youth he could not yet hear its cri de coeur. But Martin had become so excited that he could hardly wait to acquire the recording. He wondered if Gretta would like to go to concerts where such music was played. He had noticed that she sometimes brought a flute case with her to class in addition to the typical student paraphernalia of textbooks, notebooks, etc. It turned out that she played in the high school band.

Martin felt that he'd done his customary very solid job on the test and was in fact a little eager for time to be called, (often he had more to say that could be scribbled in the allotted time,) so that he could be on his way to the thrill of the record store. He, very unusually, even left with about five minutes to go. Gretta was handing in her paper at just about the same time.They more or less left the room together.

Once in the hall, outside, Gretta suddenly turned to him and said , "How did you think it was?"

Martin, surprised, offered, "Oh, pretty much as I expected I guess."

"I expected the first two questions, but the third one, on the Civil War, was a bit off—beat, I thought," she continued." We just hadn't spent much time on that aspect of things."

"Well, that's right…" Martin agreed stammeringly. " I just…. I happened to look that stuff over…. I was studying anyway…."

"Well, you did the smart thing. Which doesn't surprise me. I mean that you did a smart thing. I wasn't so smart. So I think I probably didn't do very well on that question. Or on the whole exam for that matter."

Martin was riveted by "Which doesn't surprise me. I mean that you did a smart thing." Especially since it had been delivered with what seemed the full wattage of a deep, sparkling white teeth, eyes merrily dancing smile. She was more enchanting even than he'd fantasized. He was unmistakably, completely enchanted. He was trying to not look too dumbstruck and was struggling to formulate something to mumble which she might find had some sense and charm when Martin's sometimes friend, Bob Gershon, came thundering up. He was a hearty, little too heavy—set type who was an excellent student if too often quick with a supercilious mouth. He burst right in as though Martin and Gretta hadn't been talking. As though, in fact, Gretta wasn't even there.

Looking straight at Martin he blurted, "Wasn't that exam a lot tougher than we thought it would be? That last question was a bitch. I thought the second one had some some 'tricks' too."

Martin wished that Gershon would disappear. But, innately courteous, he felt that he couldn't ignore him, that he had to give him some answer. He did, concisely. But Gershon shot back another remark directed exclusively at Martin. This one was a self—assured, detailed recounting of what the best answer to one of the essay questions should have been. Again Martin felt obligated to respond. And in some detail and length. He again kept his reply as brief as possible, but as he concluded he noticed, fron the corner of his eye, that Gretta was drifting away. She seemed to have spotted a friend of her own down the corridor and had waved toward her and started walking in that direction. Martin's heart sank precipitously, but he didn't know what to do to reclaim her.

He and Gershon chewed over the test for another few minutes, something Martin always basically despised since the more you talked the more you found out what you'd done wrong. By the time they were finished Gretta was nowhere in sight. This ethereal girl had evaporated completely. Martin forever after wondered whether Gershon had even the slightest idea of how rude hed' been, of how he'd destroyed a moment blooming with promise.

After finally extricating himself from Gershon's relentless analytical maw, Martin kept to his plan to head for the subway, Manhattan and the record store. And he did succeed in getting the Oistrakh recording of the Shostakovitch concerto. He was lucky—there were only a few left in stock. (A little more of Gershon's windiness and that project might have been foiled too.) But through the numerous subway stops there and all the way back home, as well, he mused on just how beautiful, pure, unaffected and clean Gretta appeared. Like a magical spirit that effortlessly refreshed and redeemed. And that night, after his mom's pot roast supper, as she and Martin's dad called it, as he listened to the Russian master playing so superbly, he thought again, almost constantly, of Gretta's approving smile.

But, again, when they saw each other the next week, in school, neither made the slightest reference to their post—exam conversation or acted any differently than previously. But form this time on Martin was captivated, almost consumingly by Gretta. His studiousness during History was mostly devoted to scrutinizing every physical and other thing about her. The more he intensively examined her the more his heart was gladdened and sent soaring. He continually proved to himself how lovely, how utterly beautiful—if that word were ever deserved it was here—she was.

When there were only a few classes left in the course Mrs. Rudnick announced that she wouldn't be able to be there one day during the last week. She told the class that they'd have a substitute teacher that day but that since Martin had been such an excellent student all term she wanted him to teach that class. She felt that he'd be more attuned to what she'd been teaching than a one—time substitute and would be able to cover the pertinent material most satisfactorily. Martin, reddening instantly, was immensely flattered but, also, considerably intimidated and very scared. How could he be Mrs. Rudnick, even for forty—five minutes.

However, as was his wont, he prepared and prepared and then prepared some more, so that when the day came he was ready, if still nervous. Maybe less nervous than he'd anticipated.He had decided to go over old state History exams, in areas that Mrs. Rudnick would have covered that day, since they'd all have to take the state exam shortly anyway. He presented the questions one by one, completely ready to recite an extensive answer to each himself if necessary. But he tried to engage his classmates in discussing them and suggesting possible answers. He relied mostly on volunteers but felt comfortable in calling on students when there were no volunteers. He had relaxed that much, once the class was underway, since he felt in command of the material and because the students were cooperating in very good faith. He had worried about that. But they seemed to want to make him and themselves look good in front of the substitute.

Towards the end he asked a question of his own but no one raised his or her hand or seemed near doing so. He called Gretta's name. he didn't know whether it was on impulse or because he wanted to interact with her , even in such an impersonal fashion. She was taken aback. But then she tried. She seemed to be as much at a loss on that question as everyone else in the class but she attempted to string together some coherent comments. But she was unable to continue past a few sentences. Martin's pulse had quickend when he had called "Gretta?" but once she had made a creditable showing he calmed and was able to pick up where she had left the answer dangling and fill in the remaining information. He loved her just as much, maybe more, even though her answer had been less than excellent.

They both graduated that June and Martin didn't see her any more. But he continued to think about her. He thought of her very often. Of how utterly beautiful she was, what a suffusing radiance, whatever her surroundings. Somehow the information came to him, when he was a freshman, that she, too, was attending a college in their home city. He flirted with the idea of calling her. Or, rather, he thought about how wonderful it would be if he could. But he knew he couldn't.

He almost met her adventitiously. He was walking on the active shopping avenue, about midway between where he and she lived, on a chore for his mother. There was a subway entrance and exit on one of the cross streets and while on one side of the avenue Martin happened to turn his head to the other side and saw her emerge from the subway exit. As she came to the top of the stairs she started heading away from Martin, towards the area where she lived. But he'd caught enough of a glimpse, from her angelic blonde profile, and the customary glide, to be sure, indubitably, that it was her. He could have rushed across the avenue, have practically caught up to her in a few determined strides and called her name. That's what he wanted to do. But he couldn't and didn't.

His fantasies about her continued, seemingly more longingly than ever. He even walked past the same subway exit several times, in the months that followed, at about the same time that he'd spotted her, hoping, wildly, that lightning would re—strike. Although if it did he was still not confident that he'd be able to try even an "hello" on her. It didn't and life at college moved into Martin's sophomore year.

During that year Martin met Phillip Schuller in a Philosophy course. Starting with their mutual appreciation of the great John Dewey and an ardent love of James Joyce's imperishable short stoty, "The Dead," they became good friends. They had intense discussions of philosophy, history , literature, whether they would go to law school or graduate school and, eventually, girls. Phillip was somewhat, not very much, more precocious than Martin. At least he'd have occasional dates, even if punctuated by lengthy intervals. And sometimes he even went out a second time with one of the young women. Finally he asked Martin why he, apparently, didn't date at all. Martin took that opening to tell him that he would very much like to go out with Gretta, that he thought of her often, very yearningly. Although Phillip and Martin had not known each other much, back then, they'd gone to the same high school, so Phillip knew who Gretta was.

"Why don't you just call her and ask her out?" Phillip asked. "For all you know she's been waiting by her phone for two years now, waiting for you to call."

"Not very likely, not likely at all," Martin replied, "considering the way she looks."

"Oh, she's certainly a pretty girl, very pretty, but she's no Kathy Messinger, or anything like that, Phillip opined, referring to the indisputably most sexually provocative girl in their high school class.

"No, she's not like that; but she's more beautiful in her way. There's a certain purity…."

"Well, I bet that she's not so pure that she doesn't go out on dates."

"You know, I don't even know her phone number. I once tried to look it up but there are, believe it or not, a few Zendas in the general neighborhood. Probably relatives of one sort and another. I don't know exactly where she lives, so I wouldn't know which number is the correct one."

"You could try the most likely looking ones until you found her."

"I don't think I could do that. It would be a herculean effort to call knowing that I had the right number. I mean knowing that I had to talk to her….What if I called and someone else answered and when I asked for her they said that no one by that name lived there. And so on and so forth."

"What if I got the exact number for you?"

"That would eliminate that excuse, but I still don't know if I could do it."

"Let me see what I can do."

The topic evaporated between them for a month or more. Martin didn't know whether he wanted Phillip to come up with the number or not. Finally, one night Phillip called and told Martin that he had Gretta's number. He'd only had to try two of the listed Zendas. At the first he'd been told, "There's no Gretta here," but on the second crack, when the woman who had answered said, "I'll get her," he'd abruptly hung up. Obviously the right number. Now it was up to Martin.

Martin greatly appreciated, was really touched, by what his friend had done for him. This only accentuated his strong recognition that of course he should make the call. Still, he didn't feel capable of doing it. Yet he kept on thinking of her and felt himself closer and closer to phoning.

Spring sidled into June and for summer employment, necessary to pay some tuition bills, Martin worked at the General Post Office in Manhattan. The 4 P.M. to midnight shift. No normal hours for summer substitute postal clerks. But this afforded most of the day to play tennis with Phillip, late morning, and read and listen to great music in the early afternoon before it was time to head for Ninth Avenue and Thirty- Third street.

Phillip would bring up the subject of Gretta every now and again. Increasing Martin's sense that it was obligatory that he make the phone call—both for Phillip and himself. He was starting to feel guilty. He assured his friend that he would do it soon.

The following week, letter volume was uncharacteristically light and Martin had a day off. He promised himself he'd do it that evening. He listened to all five of Beethoven's piano concerti during the day for inspiration and courage. He had decided to ask Gretta to go to an outdoor concert, at City College's Lewisohn Stadium, at which the brilliant English pianist, Moura Lympany, was to play the last Beethoven piano concerto, Op. 73, E—Flat Major, "The Emperor." Martin somehow recalled opus numbers and key signatures without really trying. They just stuck. The "Stadium Symphony Orchestra," essentially the New York Philharmonic players picking up extra money in the summer months, would be conducted by the redoubtable, now very aged Frenchman, Pierre Monteux. Beethoven's Seventh Symphony and his scintillating "Egmont Overture" would also soar and invigorate. Martin had no doubt that it would be an absolutely thrilling concert. And how much more exhilarating if he could go with Gretta on his arm. Her radiance might exceed even that of the glorious music.

When he called he was predictably very nervous—but somehow also positive and hopeful. Fortified by his full day of Beethoven melodies, harmony, counterpoint and high drama. A mature sounding woman, it had to be her mother, answered but he managed to ask for Gretta without his voice quavering too much. Mom didn't say anything to Martin, but after a few moments of silence Gretta came on with a "Hello?"

He identified himself; she remembered. One hurdle cleared. He skipped virtually all small talk and quickly asked her whether she wanted to go to the concert. Immediately she replied that she couldn't make it and offered no real explanation. Nothing about she had to do this or that, she couldn't get out of.... Martin didn't say much after that either. He sensed that he'd been turned down sharply and basically said good—bye abruptly.

Phillip was almost as disappointed as Martin and urged his pal to wait a week and then try again. He suggested that Martin should have tried to speak with her a little more, that there might have very well been a bona fide reason that she couldn't go the specific night for which Martin had asked her. For instance, maybe she had another date. That didn't mean she didn't want to go out with him. Martin should have spoken to her more, loosened things up a bit, been somewhat nonchalant. But no matter how fervently or cogentlhy, Phillip cheer led and encouraged Martin knew, with absolute certainty, that it was completely out of the question for him to call her again. He wouldn't be able to bear the anticipatory tension , not to mention the distinct possibility that she would turn him down again, and just as unreservedly.

But he didn't really stop longing for her, or the thought and image of her. He kept imagining and yearning. Sometimes particularly when he listened to great music. Especially Beethoven.

On an early evening, the next summer, he was practicing pitching, emulating the Dodgers' Carl Erskine, No. 17, with the rubber "Spaldeen ," (because manufactured by the A.G. Spalding Company,) the urban substitute for a baseball, by throwing at a chalked rectangular strike zone on an armory wall across from the rear of the building in which he still lived with his parents. He didn't play stickball much any more with the boys, no longer boys, with whom he'd grown up on the block, but he wanted some exercise that evening. In between firing pitches he happened to turn his head to the left and, suddenly, well down toward the beginning of the long city block he thought he saw Gretta pedaling towards him on a bicycle. He couldn't be sure from that distance of a hundred yards or more. Maybe he was just hoping that it was Gretta, but the strikingly colored hair was a strong hint. As the figure rode closer he could begin to identify facial features and he became more and more sure that it was her. He didn't stop and stare. He resumed pitching purposefully. It was three and two on this batter and Erskine needed a strike. He got that strike and glanced again. Now he was certain. Another pitch and she would be right there. He'd have to pause in his hurling so that she could pedal through. He did stop, when she was about tenyards away and finally looked right at her. She looked at him too and they pretty much simultaneously nodded at each other as she went by. No words, just minimal geatures or recognition as she glided away. He barely got a good look at her, although in the instant the right ankle, under the long skirt, was slim and shapely and she appeared as beautiful as always. It was the very last time he saw her.

He went on musing about her for a while, but not too much longer. For only a few months afterward he met Phyllis. A deeply auburn brunette, she was, Martin thought, the most spectacularly attractive woman he'd ever seen. She was distinctly sexy, extremely alluring. But unaffectedly so, without in the least trying. She'd been a blind date. But once he met her Martin became highly motivated. Almost immediately he spoke volumes to her. He was amazed at how un—shy he became, on the spot. He only worried that she wouldn't date him again; that there'd be no next time. But she did, again and again as he grew less and less shy and became virtually bold in his confidence. They married about eighteen months later. She remained, simply, the most beautiful girl he'd even encountered, in any way.

Martin never saw Gretta again, yet she infiltrated his life one more time. He and Phillip stayed life—long friends even though, as things went along, they wound up living in different cities. Phillip remained in New York and became a very successful psychologist in Manhattan after realizing that the practice of law just wasn't for him. He'd always been more interested in psyches than procedure. Martin came to recognize the same thing about practice but transmuted it into being a law professor in Chicago where he and Phyllis moved several years after they were married and where they raised two children. They made it a point to return to New York at least once or twice a year to see remaining family and some friends. Most of those times they linked up with Phillip, in some way. Whether for dinner, a Carnegie Hall or Lincoln Center concert, a Broadway show, a film or some combination of such things. Phillip didn't marry until his mid- forties, almost thirty years after high school graduation. About two years before he met Rita the three of them were having brunch, on a glorious spring Sunday morning, near Fifty—Ninth Street and Central Park South.

There, out of the complete blue, a propos of nothing about which they'd been talking, Phillip suddenly asked Martin, "Do you remember Gretta Zenda?"

Martin had told Phyllis about her long ago, so he wasn't made particularly self—conscious by the question. Still, he felt some uneasiness.

"Yeah, sure, of course."

"Well, it just so happens that another of our high school alums, Bob Sandler, he was about two years ahead of us, has a stationery business; his dad and grandfather ran it too. I was down there, the other day, it's still in Brooklyn, ordering my letter head and such, and he suddenly asked me if I recalled Gretta Zenda. Long story short, it seems that when he was in college, at the University of Pennsylvania, when we and Gretta were still in high school, maybe early college, he dated her. He liked her a lot but he said she married someone else. But they got divorced in eight, ten years. Somehow he got back in touch with her, after her divorce. He wasn't explicit, maybe she needed stationery too. He told me that there wasn't any romance left in it. But he still seemed to feel a little paternal about her. He asked if I might want a date with her. I said it sounded mildly interesting. Then he said, 'I could give you her phone number. But I have to tell you, she's put on weight. In fact, she's really pretty beefy, puffy sort of, now.' So I didn't take him up on it. It almost sounded as though he were telling me that I would be very disappointed."

Martin laughed a bit hollowly and nervously. He glanced at Phyllis who was smiling politely. Finally, after some seconds of silence, Martin remarked: "It's hard to imagine how that could be. I mean that she could be so bulky. She didn't have that much meat on her. She was always rather sylph—like."

REUNION

THE PRIEST HAD BEEN ONE of the most prominent of the anti—war protesters. Completely non—violent, of course, but he'd been arrested several times. He was, at the least, obstructive. Also, with others, he'd illegally entered government offices and burned draft records. About such activities he'd written afterwards; "Pardon us good friends for the fracture of good order; burning papers instead of bodies." He was a published, prize--winning poet, too. After that initial activist period, some credited his protests with speeding the conclusion of the war, his efforts had been turned to nuclear facilities. Sitting in, picketing, whatever might get a little publicity for the movement. He was a total nuclear dis—armament man. That goal he had not achieved.

~

It was thirty—five years since Michael had introduced him at the college Michael was teaching at then. The priest had been there to debate a prison warden. He was a prisoners' rights man, too. Michael had worked on the introduction for weeks. He had been especially inspired because a Catholic colleague, who had arranged for the priest to come to the campus, had confided in Michael about a phone conversation he'd had with the priest when they were working out some details of the visit. This fellow historian had told Michael that in the course of the conversation he had mentioned that his father had died only weeks before and that his mother, still back on the other coast, remained disconsolate. The priest had asked for the mother's phone number. And a few days later mother phoned son to say that the priest had called, the very night he had asked for her number, and that they had talked for nearly an hour. And that, in the end, he had comforted her.

Because of the priest's literary background, and since he was Irish, Michael had put allusions, in his remarks, to Joyce, Yeats and also to W.H. Auden's great poem "In Memory of W.B. Yeats."He particularly referred to the transcendent line, in that poem, "The Irish vessel now lies empty of its poetr'y." And he'd closed with the final lines to Joyce's youthful novel A PORTRAIT OF THE ARTIST AS A YOUNG MAN. He had insisted that the priest had gone forth many more than the million times Stephen Dedalus had "to forge the uncreated consciousness of [his] race in the smithy of [his] soul." After the debate was over and someone had introduced Michael's wife to the priest he had said to her, "Your husband gave me the best introduction I've ever had." Michael didn't fool himself that his own laudatory words per se were so satisfying to the priest. It had to have been the various references to the magnificent tradition of Irish literature that had affected him.

During that same visit the priest had spoken at a luncheon. Local political dignataries, as well as academic ones, were invited. W hen he rose to give his talk the priest had started by thanking "the cooks and people in the kitchen who prepared this wonderful meal and the servers who brought it out." This surprised, seemed even to offend, some of the prominent people there to hear him. During the question and answer period a sly student asked , "Do you think that you are a good Christian?" He replied, "Oh come on!!!" He wasn't completely tolerant. Also, in response to a comment about how slow social progress seems to come sometimes, regardless of how arduous efforts are, he observed. "Of course you'll fail. And that gives you not the slightest dispensation to not try." Michael thought of one of the rabbinical injunctions: "You are not required to complete the task. But neither are you permitted not to begin it." The more he heard from Father the more he liked him.

Prior to the debate on prison conditions, the priest had been speaking at yet another site in the university and Michael had also been assigned to conduct him from there to the debate venue. During the stroll over Michael, identifying himself as Jewish, asked about the cleric's outspokenness on the Middle East situation. He had been highly sympathetic to the Palestinian position and considerably critical of Israel's general posture and particularly of its "occupying" activities. He responded with great sympathy to Michael's question. Perhaps more to the need of Michael to ask it. He didn't actually try to convince Michael, in any way, of the correctness of his analysis, or even of his visceral feelings about the situation, but he lamented how his activities on that issue had vexed relations with his jewish friends. He seemed regretful not of what he had done on that specific issue but, rather, about the problems it had caused with such friends and of the urgency he felt to keep doing it. So, in the brief minutes it took them to arrive at the debate site auditorium ,Michael and the priest had not achieved agreement, but they had come to an understanding.

Almost fifteen years later Michael was teaching at another college when he found out that the university's graduate Religion department had invited Father to be "in residence" for a semester. Michael taught a Twentieth Century History seminar for seniors and one of the documents he always assigned the students to read was the priest's anti—war play, 'The Trial of _____", written, many years which he'd before, during his opposition to that war, , risked his freedom to protest. Michael found out the priest's address and wrote him a letter. He tried to recall to the man their previous encounter and asked whether the priest would be willing to come to the seminar meeting during which Michael would lead the students in a discussion of the play. He heard nothing for more than a week. But then a note in the mail. Yes the priest would be happy to participate in the seminar. Just let him know date and time. Michael, with great thanks, did. The seminar session in which the play was discussed would be towards the end of the semester. Michael had given father plenty of notice.

As the date approached Michael grew more and more nervous, highly uneasy about the priest's appearance. For several years Michael had felt that the quality of the students had been declining. Their enthusiasm, willingness to carefully prepare, to engage with controversial subject matter all seemed to be waning, if not, indeed, already in abject decline. This sense could not, of course, be documented in "hard" quantitative terms but by that time Michael was an experienced teacher whose classroom instincts and intuition were practiced and sure. He started envisioning the priest sitting in the seminar room for two hours with most if not all of the students showing hardly any ardor for discussion of the play, if not actually palpable boredom. Michael started sleeping very poorly. He finally accepted the fact that the risk of a fiasco was too great. He had to call off the priest's appearance. He wrote Father another letter excusing the inconvenience he had caused the priest's schedule but indicating that he thought it would not be a good use of the priest's time for him to appear at the seminar. He no longer recalled what "diplomatic" reason he had given for cancelling the appearance. In this letter he included mention of a desire to meet with the priest for coffee, or some such, should Father have any time to do so. He received a polite reply which mentioned that the priest's brother was quite ill and that much time was being consumed by that problem.

Michael had seen adventitiously, in the newspaper, that the priest, now in his late '80s, had just entered an assisted living facility in New York City. Michael was now quite a bit older than the priest had been when Michael first met him. Michael had been thinking of retirement more and more. Were he as old as he is now, when he first met the priest, he would have been already retired. He'd lately been thinking a good deal about how the priest, at the height of his fame and activities, had called the recent widow, whom he knew not at all, and had spoken to her for almost an hour.

Michael was going to be in New York in a few weeks for a professional conference. He wanted to visit the priest. The newspaper story had sufficiently identified the assisted living facilty and Michael wrote the priest care of it. Again, he reviewed for Father their past encounters, in person and through correspondence. It took about ten days but finally a response came. "I would be happy to see you. Please give me some dates and times." Michael did so and another brief note came, this time more quickly. "The first day you mentioned, at noon., would be fine."

The immediate impression Michael had when he entered the building was of the frail man, hands pressing on a walker, waiting expectantly. But then the kindly, yet penetrating eyes and determined set of face and posture registered. This was the priest now. Michael introduced himself and the priest showed recognition that he'd been expecting someone. But hedisplayed hardly any recognition at all of who Michael, a sMichael, was. The priest said that lunch was being served and that he was entitled to bring a guest once every two weeks so he could invite Michael to join him. Michael hesitated, thinking to perhaps follow his original plan and ask the priest to go out to one of the many restaurants in the area. However the walker daunted him, and he, therefore, gratefully accepted the invitation.

The menu was not extensive but not bare bones, either. Before finally giving his definitive order the priest asked many questions of the sympathetic, understanding waiter, who seemed to have served Father many times previously. Were the tomatoes in this dish fresh? Was that dish stir—fried or deeply fried? Approximately how many calories did the waiter think were in the pasta dish? Michael started becoming at least slightly embarrassed for the priest's unrelenting inquisitiveness, but the waiter never flagged in courtesy or responsiveness. When Michael's turn came he ordered unhesitatingly and concisely. The food came rather quickly. Michael, following the priest's lead had ordered only an entrée, foregoing his beloved soup. (Even though he had seen that they had one of his favorites, Black Bean, on the menu.) Conversation started with the weather and sidled casually to one or two "New York Times" headlines of that morning's edition. The priest offered some observations about the situations reported in the "Times" stories but Michael had trouble seeing their pertinancy. Michael tried to hark back to the occasion on which they'd originally met and, then, the correspondence about the priest appearing in his seminar when "The Trial of ____" was to be discussed. But it soon became clear that the priest really didn't remember the episodes to which Michael alluded, although he tended to nod his head, slightly, and say "Yes, yes" at the appropriate times. He was however, very intent on telling Michael that he had written a book commenting on and analyzing The Book of Job. He began regaling Michael with what seemed very finely spun theological points.However, Michael had no capacity to appreciate the arguments the priest seemed to think he was decisively making. Having checked out the priest's particulars, on the internet, only a day or two before this meeting, Michael knew that the book on Job had originally been published more than ten years ago. After the theology finally waned, Michael became conscious of fighting for topics to discuss with the priest and the latter, for his part, seemed content to maintain a great deal of silence. Just about forty—five minutes after they had sat down other diners started rising and leaving the room. The priest, hearing the scraping of chairs, looked around and almost mumbling said,"I guess it's time for my nap." Michael quickly rose, helped the priest up and walked, excruciatingly slowly with him, to the elevators in the lobby. He waited with Father until the elevator came and then the reunion was over.

As he went out into the street an insistent, incisive wind had replaced zephyr like very early Spring breezes and MIchael found himself buttoning his raincoat as protection against the unwelcome, encroaching cold. The grey and sullen sky even foretold the possibility of snow. There flitted across Michael's mind Joyce's magnificent concluding lines in his brilliant story, "The Dead," one of Michael's, (and many others,) all-time favorites. "...snow was general all over Ireland ....the snow faintly falling, like the descent of their last end, upon all the living and the dead." Walking toward the nearest subway stop, moving as briskly as possible, as a further defense against meteorology , he thought of the incident that had been written about by a Nobel Prize winning physicist, who, just like Michael, had been born in Brooklyn. The physicist had grown up revering Einstein and had only become more and more worshipful as he went further along in his own studies and career. He always fantasized about actually meeting with Einstein and talking through with him some of the salient, unsolved problems of contemporary physics. But he never felt worthy enough of approaching the great man, through a letter, or otherwise. But finally the younger man had, himself, won the Nobel Prize in Physics. Through a contact he was able to arrange a meeting with the monumental theorizer of Relativity. But the encounter had not gone satisfyingly. The recent Nobel prize winner realized that the super—annuated Nobel Prize winner did not really appreciate, even comprehend, the problems alluded to by the Nobelist from Brooklyn.. It was, he had written, one of the most disappointing, deflating experiences of his life.

THE CHECK IS IN THE MAIL

WRITING THE CHECK WASN'T REALLY easy, although much easier than it would have been then. It was the easy part now, the hard part was the accompanying letter. Actually the check wasn't very easy at all, it was still a struggle. Phyllis still didn't unreservedly approve of it. But at least now they could arguably afford it , as they clearly could not have then. Their savings could still use it. Especially with the prospect of private schools for the kids coming up. But it wasn't day to day hand to mouth any more. The five hundred dollars were not essential.

In any event, it had to be done, now that it could be. It wouldn't be accurate to say that not a day had gone by that Tim hadn't thought of it, since it happened about five years ago. But he'd certainly thought of it quite often since then. At least four or five times a month. Sometimes it pressed on him with such urgency that he wanted to write the check just to buy release. However, despite all the time he'd devoted to thinking about it, or, rather, how much time had been consumed by the incident unshakably grasping his consciousness he still didn't really know what to say in the letter that had to go along with the check.

As he mused on the appropriate words, trying to formulate meaningful phrases, the episode re—played in his mind yet again. They'd moved from their native New York City to the "greater Pacific Northwest," as the newscasters liked to deem it, so that Tim could take his first teaching job in the English department of a small liberal arts college in Washington.It was east of the Cascade Mountains, a three hour drive to Seattle. Phyllis, with the help of some of the college administrators, had gotten a job also. Teacher in a Methodist church pre—school program. Not quite what she wanted, since she was a high school History teacher, but it was a paycheck.

The children were only four and one when they got there, but, almost immediately, he and Phyllis had looked forward to leaving. English Literature teaching jobs were hard to come by, (even for this one he'd had to compete against fifty-eight other applicants,) but the cultural transition was very difficult for Tim and Phyllis and they weren't at all sure how good, on an overall, long—term basis, the smugly provincial atmosphere, notwithstanding it was a "college town," was for the kids. Tim took his teaching seriously and worked hard at integrating himself as a dedicated, highly responsible member of his department. But, in reality, from the time he got there he started energetically working on journal articles which he hoped would pave his way to a tenure track Assistant Professor job in a location where they all would feel more comfortable. They made it out just about four years after they'd arrived and had been at a large university in the Mid—West, in a city of considerable size, for the last three years.

It was not as though all their experiences in Washington had been negative. They'd made some dear friends with whom they were still in contact. People were generally helpful, not many were aggressive or truculent.But there was flagrant provinciality and they often felt the suffocating miasma generated by Main Street's self—satisfaction—whether real or pretended. Too many denizens were assertive in proclaiming the town just about the finest slice of paradise in all the whole wide world. And they surely didn't want to change anything, not one single thing, about it. There were definitely not many opportunities for the kind of cultural experiences that Tim and Phyllis had grown up with as their New York birthright. It was the effort to infuse just the slightest bit of culture into their increasingly hum-drum lives, about two years after they'd come to town, that had led to the incident which Tim was re—hashing, yet again, now.

From early adolescence Tim had been a devotee of classical music and his small, but select, collection of recordings had made the move west also. He tried to add to it whenever he could. But as the budgeteer in the family, juggling expenses against his instructor's salary and Phyllis's pre—school teacher one, he didn't often find that he thought there were surplus dollars with which to purchase another recording. It didn't really matter that much, because there wasn't any place in town that could come anywhere close to being deemed a classical record store. Temptation from browsing was not a problem. However, there was a musical instrument store, which rented them the one—quarter size violin on which his daughter took her lessons, in which he had noticed a very sparse sprinkling of classical recordings amongst a vastly larger stock of "popular" music which they carried.

One spring day, after finishing writing an article with which he'd struggled, but which he felt had come out as a very good piece of work, building to a flowing, convincing, almost inexorable conclusion, one which he had visons of getting published in an upper rank journal, Tim was feeling expansive and relaxed. He'd worked so hard to complete it trenchantly that he'd skipped lunch for several days and, therefore, was a few dollars in the black for the month. He felt he deserved a little treat and decided to browse the classical offerings, such as they were, in the musical instrument store. Perhaps there would be something there that he and Phyllis would find uplifting to hear, after the kids were in bed, during an otherwise routine evening.

It didn't take him very long to flipthrough everything available but he did come across a worthy. One of his favorite artists, the great English mezzo—soprano, Janet Baker, with the London Philharmonic, under the acclaimed English conductor, Adrian Boult, singing in one of Phyliss's desert island picks, Brahms "Alto Rhapsody." It so happened that one of the cherished moments of their experiences together was the time they were listening to the classical music station in New York and caught a program during which the host played the "Alto Rhapsody." He prefaced it by remarking that a prominent Harvard musicologist had referred to the entrance of the male chorus, toward the work's conclusion, as " One of the ten greatest moments in music." Phyllis practically swooned when that moment came and she also just reveled in the singing of the mezzo. Tim did too. The disc which, so much the better, was in the "budget" category, also had Baker singing "The Four Last Songs" of Richard Strauss and Wagner's paean to a woman he loved, "Wesendock Lieder."

When Tim got to the cash register he saw that the name tag of the fiftyish, frumpy woman who would be ringing up the sale read "Rosalyn Salem." Plain features, glasses, quite short hair, no make—up and no wedding band.The classic "librarian" stereotype flitted across Tim's mind. A silly stereotype no doubt, but, seemingly, too often an accurate one. He remembered an assigned reading in college, by a famous sociologist, claiming that stereotypes got to be such because of their at least fairly high correspondence to reality. He smiled as he pushed the recording towards her and she smiled back. But with obvious shyness. She struck him as someone who'd always needed to fight off being ill-at-ease in order to function.

Then she completely surprised Tim. Looking at the Janet Baker recording, as she punched the appropriate keys on the cash register, she suddenly said, "Isn't she just a marvelous singer!"

"Why yes, yes… She is. She's a great artist. Is she a favorite of yours too?"

"Oh, yes, definitely. I have as many of her recordings as I can get. I particularly love her performances of Schubert lieder. And her Richard Strauss, too. I see she does some of his songs on this recording. Not to mention her Mahler, too, of course."

"You're absolutely right—on all three counts. Actually, about four or five years ago , I heard her do Mahler's "Kindertodtenlieder." ("Songs For Dead Children,") in Carnegie Hall. She was really something. Just tremendous. I think it was with the Boston Symphony Orchestra, Erich Leinsdorf conducting."

Ms. Salem's eyes opened just as wide as would a child's who sees that he has gotten exactly what he had secretly, impossibly, aspired to for Christmas. "You heard her live? In Carnegie Hall? What a thrill!! What a privilege!! A gift from God!! She had drawn out the words "Carnegie Hall" so that they were as long as the rest of the sentence containing them. Her entire affect was that Tim had experienced a miracle totally beyond mere mortals.

"Yes, yes," Tim concurred. It's a great place. I think Isaac Stern, who as you probably know saved it from being razed for a parking lot, once said 'There isn't an artist alive who is not, in some way, touched by the magic of Carnegie Hall.' And, naturally the acoustics…."

"Yes, so many magnificent artsits have performed there. All the names that you see on the recordings in here. Horowitz, Rubinstein, Fischer—Dieskau, Heifetz, Menuhin… Stern himself, naturally. It must be sheer magic, one of the most magical places on God's earth."

She was practically blushing with enthusiasm by the time she'd put the Baker recording in a bag and Tim had picked it up, ready to leave.

'Well, keep on listening," he said. "Music is one of the best balms in the world."

"Oh yes it is," she vociferously agreed. "It surely is."

He had moved a few steps away from the register, towards the door, but he re—traced a bit, an afterthought occurring to him. "You know, I once heard Dame Janet give a little pre—concert talk. And I've never forgotten one of the things she said. 'Music is solace, music is healing, music is peace.'"

"Yes, indeed, it is. It surely is," she emphasized.

Tim unveiled his prize find to Phyllis that evening, to a burst of enthusiasm from her.While they were listening to its glories he told her how sorry he'd felt for Rosalyn Salem because she was such a music lover but couldn't even conceive of the possibility that she could ever hear a concert in Carnegie Hall. He speculated that she'd probably been born some place in Washington, if not in this very town, and had probably not traveled beyond a hundred mile radius in her fifty plus years. Phyllis agreed that the woman's astonishment that someone might actually have been in an audience in the hall was very poignant.

Subsequently, they made it a point to go in to the musical instrument store somewhat regularly. Even when they didn't buy a recording, to be rung up by Roslyn, they would chat with her about music in one way or another. She was very knowledgeable and always fervent about her favorite or preferred works and artists. But Carnegie Hall, as such, never came up again.

Nevertheless, Phyllis and Tim discussed the original incident from time to time. Whenever they did they reiterated amazement at how flabbergasted Roslyn had been about someone actually attending a concert at Carnegie Hall. New York must seem to her not merely a continent away but in another universe. Certainly a universe she would never enter or explore. Somehow, from these discussions it emerged more and more clearly that they felt it their responsibility to get Ms. Salem to have a Carnegie Hall musical experience. They knew that she would never be able to imagine flying to New York much less spending what it took to get there, from her doubtless meager salary. But they couldn't afford to subsidize the adventure for her as, then, they too were just scraping by.

But now they had passed scraping. They'd actually put some savings together and found themselves able to put aside a regular amount each month on their increased Mid—Western salaries. Even after they'd relocated, they kept up their relationship, such as it was, with Roslyn through sporadic correspondence. Al ways an exchange of Christmas cards, plus a few brief notes during the year.

The appropriate language, not too pretentious, or flippantly casual, Tim hoped , finally came to him.

"Dear Roslyn,

"We hope all continues well at your end. Things are fine here and the kids seem to keep on thriving. They like their teachers and they have a million after-school activites so we're in the chauffeuring business big—time, too. (Both now take music lessons.)

"We're apparently still on the Carnegie Hall mailing list and the enclosed brochure of the coming season's concerts and recitals arrived the other day. Looks like, as always, there are quite a few 'not-to-be-missed' performances scheduled. We think you should be at some of them. That's what the check is for. Tell us which ones particularly catch your fancy and we'll meet you there, have dinner, right next door, at the Russian Tea Room, and we'll all stay at our favorite hotel for a short walk to Carnegie, the Rhiga Royal, on Fifty Fourth street, just off Seventh Avenue. (Small map of Manhattan, for 'getting acquainted' purposes, also enclosed.)

"We haven't been back to the city for a few years now, so we're really looking forward to making the trip and having the kind of fun that's a New York specialty. So, look over the brochure and let us know what you want to go to, when.

" Everyone sends regards and we'll really be looking forward to hearing from you.And, soon, seeing you.

"As usual, all best,
Tim and Phyllis"

" P.S. You'll notice that Janet Baker is appearing in a program of Schubert, Strauss and Mahler lieder on October 15th. Fall is a wonderful time of year in NYC!"

A YOUNG TEACHER

JAKE SUPPOSED THAT HE WAS surprised, but not really *surprised,* when he walked into the first meeting of Economics 101 and found that the instructor, and that's all she was, (not even an Assistant Professor,) was a woman. He wasn't shocked because, of course, he'd had women teachers in grade school and high school. But, a sophomore now, this was his first in college.

Indisputably, Charlotte Bell was a woman, if not a conventionally attractive one. She conformed, a little too much for the usual gauges of femininity, to the popular image of the intellectual woman. Short haircut, arranged, if at all, limply, large and thick lensed glasses, a severe, boxy suit which did its best to suppress any curves which might be lurking and skin of some splotchiness. Her features themselves, however, while not pronounced were not entirely without pleasing sharpness.

As the semester wore on she often wore the same suit she'd worn that first day. Sometimes another, and, even, very occasionally, a third. But most of the time it was the one she'd started with. Jake couldn't remember any other outfit but those three suits. He was quite sure there were none. And even in the coldest days of December and early January, she came in the same scuffed, almost peeling, open toed, low heeled light brown shoes. Sometimes the scuffs were roughly polished over.

Just as it was the first time Jake had had a woman instructor in college, it was the maiden voyage for Charlotte Bell in teaching a college course. A freshly minted Ph.D., at the June graduation ceremonies of Columbia, as a new faculty appointee she'd been assigned one of the many sections of Introductory Economics which the veterans of the department fought over not having to teach. Jake and his classmates could see that she knew the material, but whether out of shyness, nervousness, or both, she came across as shaky, uncertain, speaking haltingly sometimes, too rapidly at others, and unclearly and inarticulately all too often. But she was able to impart enough of the relatively simple concepts of basic economics so that by careful study of the textbook along with a good set of classroom notes, a diligent student could master what Charlotte Bell wanted him to comprehend.

Jake was a fine student, in general. Almost an "A" average, driving towards a top—tier law school, someone who probably would have tried his very best in the course in any event. But, sensing the pressure Ms. Bell was under , he devoted particular attention to studying her course, almost as a means of proving to her, by his doing well, that she was a good teacher. He could see, day to day in the class, that she was dissatisfied, insecure, almost defensive, about how things were proceeding. She would glance from student to student sometimes, as she lectured or answered a question, as though desperately searching for verification that there was interest in, alertness about, what she was saying, rather than the manifest listlessness of most, if not almost all, of the students. But try as she might to jolt energy and zest into her explanations, as many times as she would say, "Is that clear? Maybe not. Let me try to say it again. Let me try to clarify it," the bland, bored, uncomprehending expressions of too many of the twenty—five or so students remained unresponsive. Sometimes her shoulders sagged and she would give up, seeming to speak only to Jake and one or two others whom she'd identified as competent and willing to reap what she was sowing.

Jake would get tense over just how badly Ms. Bell was feeling about what could go on in the classroom. He practically literally winced several times when her explanations were especially inarticulate and uncommunicative and the shifting of students in their seats and the fidgeting with their pens and notebooks became unmerciful.

One incident really depressed him.. The text for the course, it so happened, had been written by the Chair of the Economics Department. He was an unabashed, rabid partisan of free—market capitalism, as THE way to allocate scarce resources. But there were a set of twins in the class, the Lane boys, who begged to differ. Both Alan and Baruch always tried to follow what Ms. Bell was saying regardless of how meandering or turgid her presentation. Alan was the more vocal. He volunteered more, asked more questions, (Baruch didn't really say much unless called upon directly by Ms. Bell,) and was certainly the twin with more personality.

One time, after Ms. Bell had spoken of the superiority of capitalism in arranging for optimal use of resources, Alan raised his hand. When recognized by Ms.Bell he said: "But what about a Socialist system as an organizing principle for scarce resources. That's another way to go. The state could control such resources and assign them for use in accordance with the greatest need for them. Or something like that."

"But that would be arbitrary," Ms. Bell quickly responded. "We couldn't be sure that they would go to where they were most valued---as determined by the highest bid for them."

. "But they might really be most valuable and most useful, also, if purposefully directed to where most needed. Regardless of who could afford them most. That might even be a more sensible, better approach. All things considered, so to speak, " Alan argued, rapidly, decisively and with a debater's punch and panache.

Ms. Bell became visibly agitated, flustered. She shook her head in short arcs, emphasizing her "No, No"s, what hair she had flopping against her ears. "No, no, human choice is biased. Capitalism *objectively* selects the most efficient way for resources to be distributed. No, no, capitalism is better; there's no doubt."

Now Alan Lane, in addition to being crisp and very articulate in what he said ,became exercised.

"Whaddya mean? Are you saying that anyone who's a Socialist has absolutely no idea of what he's talking about—is just a rank fool?..."

"No, no… I don't mean that…."

"You know, a lot of really smart, more than smart, brilliant, people have been Socialists. I don't think that they're so stupid that they can't follow the capitalistic argument. They just don't buy it; if you'll pardon the expression." His right hand chopping the air needed a rostrum to pound on. But he didn't have one, so he kept on chopping.

Jake had been moved left in his freshman year, in the mandatory Great Books course, by an extremely dynamic young professor who presented Socialism as a morally preferable economic system. Jake particularly remembered when this inspiring teacher read to the class from Friedrich Engels's "Socialism: Scientific and Utopian." He still heard the ringing words with which Professor Sean Moore had concluded the excerpt. After Engels had outlined his conception of the inevitability of Socialism he insisted that when it finally evolved, "The struggle for individual existence disappears. Then for the first time, man, in a certain sense, is finally marked off from the rest of the animal kingdom and emerges from mere animal conditions of existence into really human ones.... It is the ascent of man from the kingdom of necessity to the kingdom of freedom."

So Jake's emotions were decidedly mixed as Alan Lane and Charlotte Bell tangled on ideology. Intellectually and spiritually he certainly tended toward Alan's corner. But he felt badly, emotionally, for Ms. Bell because of the force of Alan's onslaught, which could well have been taken personally by Ms. Bell, and because of the bumbling, rather pathetic way in which she sought to extricate herself from her plight.

"No, of course Mr. Lane, people can disagree about this sort of thing. It's just that as far as arranging resources optimally productively, for the greatest good.... Capitalism always...."

"For whose greatest good?" Lane interrupted. "Making another widget is not the highest value in life."

'No, no, of course not. No argument there. It's just that capitalism.... Well, anyway, there are differing points of view. Why don't we move on to the chart on page 329?"

Lane, feeling that, by then, he'd made his point, that he had carried his banner with elan and cogency, was also willing to let go. So the class crept on, desultorily as usual, the tedium building through the remaining twenty minutes. Jake kept thinking about the Lane/Bell exchange and, uncharacteristically, approached Ms. Bell's desk, after the class had ended, as she gathered her books, notes and other papers.

He stood there diffidently until she looked up and said, "Yes, Mr. Wolf?"

"Well you know, there are an awful lot of people, major thinkers and all, who do have qualms, considerable ones about capitalism...."

"Oh yes, of course Mr. Wolf. There's no doubt of that. I was just trying to point out that from a strictly analytical viewpoint.... from the perspective of sheer economic analysis, you know, that capitalism delivers the goods better, if you will...."

Suddenly Jake heard himself blurting out, "But what about the *Good*?" He felt himself go red as soon as he'd spoken.

He had already started backing away from her desk as Ms. Bell replied, "Yes, yes, there are other voices, other opinions.... I think we can agree to disagree.... If that's necessary."

Jake, relieved that he wouldn't have to talk further with her, nodded and slowly turned to leave.

In the six weeks remaining Economics 101 proceeded pretty much as it had begun and had persisted. If anything, Jake felt more and more sorry for Ms. Bell and her lackluster efforts, not to mention her failure of pedagogical success. He stepped up his studying so that he could speak more and more intelligently in response to her tries at getting "discussions' going amongst the palpably lethargic students. He also prepared more intensively for the occasional quiz she'd give, "to keep you on your toes," so that just about everyone in the class wouldn't leave doing any studying at all until the reading period prior to final exams. His performance was perfection—he got full credit on every question on every quiz. And Ms. Bell was almost transparently pleased, encouraging, laudatory about his volunteered classroom comments.

Despite his fervid attentiveness throughout the course, Jake spent more time studying for the final in Economics than for any other course's exam . It paid off too. He felt that he had answered just about every question perfectly. He knew he'd get an "A" in the course.

But he didn't. When he received the self--addressed post card that he'd handed in to Ms. Bell, as most students did, in the last week of the course, so that he could get his grade before the official transcript arrived six weeks later, there was marked on it a big red "A+." And under that, in light blue ink, penned in small, neat, yet flowing script, "Excellent job all semester long, and a particularly outstanding final exam. A pleasure to read. Congratulations. C.B."

~

Jake was required to take the second semester of Econ. 101 in order to get credit for the "Economics" part of his Social Science concentration. The other students whom he knew from the first semester of Ms. Bell's course were assiduously avoiding her for the second semester, signing up for sections of other instructors. Jake, on the other hand, felt a strong obligation to show loyalty to her. But he became alarmed when he saw the days and time of meeting of the only section of the course she was teaching. There was a direct conflict with "The Theory of Political Systems" which, as a declared Political Science major, he was unyieldingly required to take in the upcoming semester. No ifs ands or buts if he wanted to major in Poly Sci, (or Government, as it was sometimes less pretentiously called,) which he unequivocally did. There was absolutely no help for it, no way out. The political theory course was the only inflexible component of his schedule. He would just have to take another section of Econ,taught by someone else. But, so it went, thought Jake. He was under no illusion that she couldn't survive without him.

The new semester, beginning near the end of January, started smoothly and stimulatingly. All of Jake's courses appealed to him, especially the political theory one and he felt he had a very sure grasp of it. Jake just reveled in that kind of material. He'd done extremely well in his grades the preceding semester and was confident that he was headed for more success.

The instructor he'd wound up with for the second half of the Economics course,Greg Kaden, was a dynamic and fluent lecturer who made the most abstruse concepts immediately comprehensible to almost every student. And with humorous asides too. Sometimes, seated in that class, jake would muse upon how Ms. Bell would be teaching or trying to teach the same material. He was in no doubt that it would be a lot more strenuous, painful even, to try to master it under her, but he supposed she'd muddle through, with what students she had, somehow. After Kaden's class had met a few times Jake thought of this no more.

Until the third week of the semester when, walking on campus, on his way from a just concluded class to the library, he spotted Ms. Bell coming in the opposite direction. As he planned what to say to her, profusely thanking her for his grade went through his mind, he kept his eyes down. The distance between them narrowed and Jake lifted his eyes to meet hers.

She strode right by him without ever even glancing at him or indicating any sign of recognition. Jake played the encounter in his mind many times. At greater and greater intervals, as time went by. But he never conclusively decided. Had she been so lost in thought that she had never really seen him, for himself, as her former student, Jacob Wolf ,as distinguished from just any student walking towards the library. Or, had she, indeed, noticed exactly who it was and decided to snub him as she must have felt that he had snubbed her.

DEAL?

EDWARD MARSH HAD BEEN CHARACTERIZED as a good student since kindergarten. Too imprecise a description.. He was, in fact, excellent. Intelligent to start with and, on top of that, very studious and diligent. The combination got him very impressive results. "A's" were his common parlance. That was his usual grade on just about every test he'd taken at Adams High School, not to mention his final grade in every course. And he was already in his junior year, heading, in no uncertain terms, toward the Ivy League. Naturally he was very well liked by his teachers and some even thought that he had most unusual and great promise. One was to write, in support of one of his college applications, that she predicted renown for him one day.

Steve Reynolds was a pretty good student, too. But not in Ed's league. (Few were.) But Steve had another league—football. He was the starting fullback on the Adams High School eleven. Adams was much better known for the academic achievements and subsequent brilliant college careers of some of its intellectual super stars, but, still, a starting back on the football team was very celebrated by, and highly popular with, the general student body. And Steve, unlike the great majority of boys on the team, did well in his studies too. He wasn't the sure "A" student that Ed was, but often a solid "B+" one and sometimes in the "A-" range. Since he spent so much time at practices and because he also had such an active social life, most of the most desirable girls craved going out with him, his achieving so fine a record gradewise was hailed as a much more than respectable, indeed as rather a signal, accomplishment.

Ed's social life, to put it in Boolean Algebra terms, (something Ed was confortable with,) verged on the null set. In fact, as for girls—there were none. Period. He had some fairly close male friends, but although he was good looking, in a dark, brooding way, (actually, by conventional standards, quite a bit more handsome than Steve,) he was, simply, too bedrock shy to ask girls out on dates. Bowling with some of the fellows he hung around with at Adams, on Friday or Saturday nights, was about the extent of his extra—curricular activities. No clubs or teams. There was always more studying to do. Sometimes after bowling the guys would also go for ice cream sodas or frappes.

Steve and Ed knew each other by sight, (everybody in Adams knew Steve,) and had been in the same class, once or twice, before their junior year when they found themselves in the same English class. They'd nodded and spoken briefly, now and again,, before, but now they'd occasionally schmooze a little before and after class and had taken to warmly greeting each other when they passed in Adams corridors or the streets around the school. Ed didn't actually attend the football games,because most kids who did went with dates, but he was a big sports fan and closely followed the team. But there wasn't much talk, of any consequence or getting involved in meaty discussions of any sort. They'd just banter a little, sometimes about the team's fortunes or mis—fortunes, or refer to general, superficial school news and gossip.

One of the topics that occupied them the most was Miss Mellen, the more than middle—aged, very plain in appearance, spinster sort, who taught that mutual English class. She was very well meaning, but an inherently bumbling type. She didn't actually stutter, but her speech pattern stuttered, so that she expressed herself haltingly and unclearly. She was definitely not a compelling teacher; not even engaging. Gradually control of the class began slipping away. Her silences, the hemming and hawing, periods of outright confusion were filled by the buzz of students whispering amongst themselves. Sometimes it grew to audible cross-conversations. Then she'd have to virtually plead for, rather than command, quiet so that she could resume in her unfocused, fragmented fashion.

Ed felt sorry for her. Yet he also found that if you listened carefully to what too often seemed her muttering and mumbling it made some solid good sense about the book or story she was teaching. He grew to enjoy her understated, a bit wry, observations and found that when he compared them to his own reactions to assigned readings he almost always found her convincing. The old lady knew what she was talking about, even if she didn't always speak articulately, or, even, sometimes, audibly.

But as Ed gradually developed some respect for her most of the class remained dismissive, sometimes unmistakably derisive. Steve Reynolds was certainly one of these. He would mimic her tics and hesitations and then laugh uproariously at his own imitation. Ed didn't have the courage to not join in when he humiliated her this way. He couldn't even conceive of objecting or saying something like, "Well, if you really listen to her, try to understand what she's trying to get out, she actually knows a lot about the stuff we're reading and she makes good points about it." He already felt himself a far outsider and sensed that attempting to resist in such a way would only push him further and further from acceptability and regular guy status.

Ed had more or less accepted this outsider status, as a "brain,"at best, and hadn't cared much or had much motivation to change it. But about the middle of the term he began focusing on one of the other students in Miss Mellen's class, Roberta Pons. She wasn't generally considered one of that very elite circle of the most popular girls but Ed thought her unflashily pretty with a warm and open smile. She also seemed to always have a pleasant word for everyone. And in this case everyone included Ed.

He found himself trying and succeeding in talking to her more and more before class began and after it was over. She even initiated the chatting sometimes. He could hardly believe this, yet it seemed to happen often enough to validate his ardent hopes. Even the duration of these mini—discussions expanded from when they'd first began. Ed started to feel that he wanted them to be longer and longer and would muse about asking her out on a date. After two weeks of mulling over his chances and trying to boost his courage, by urging himself to believe that they weren't completely dreadful, he determined he would actually call her.

He held himself to his resolve. When he did phone he was so nervous that he couldn't even speak to her as effectively as during their school conversations. Which wasn't all that fluently either. He did manage to blurt out the concept of a date and she, amazingly enough, accepted.

When the appointed Saturday night came he was so nervous that he thought about calling her and saying he was ill. But he liked her, her angelic seeming face and unostentatiously cute figure, a great deal and didn't want to blow his chance.

Meeting her mother and talking with her for the few minutes it took Roberta to appear felt like a monumental trial. Somehow he got through it. They went off to the movies, but once alone with Roberta his nervousness didn't abate. Perhaps it even increased and he didn't chat with her any more smoothly than he had on the phone. Now that they were, officially, on a "date," whatever free and easiness there had been in their school encounters seemed to have desicated.

Roberta was a little more relaxed, more outgoing, than Ed was but the conversation was strained. There didn't even seem to be much to say about the film, although it was a version of Tennessee Williams's "Cat on a Hot Tin Roof," and Ed enjoyed and was stimulated, (maybe mostly by Elizabeth Taylor,) by it. From the little they did say about it it appeared that Roberta had liked it also. But they just couldn't sustain any exchange about it.

After the movie they went for dessert in the leading local ice cream parlor. But the confections didn't sweeten their communication. Ed was actually glad and relieved when he had brought Roberta back to her house. There wasn't even the very slightest gesture toward a good—night peck.

Despite the awkwardness of the first date, Ed wanted to, even fel t he ought to, ask her out again. But he didn't have the fortitude to follow right up.He needed time to solidify his resolve again. He mentally prodded himself for three weeks. He didn't want to risk another clumsily perfunctory phone call , so he asked her after class one day. Roberta quickly said that she had something to do on the evening he'd mentioned. She didn't seem to want to stay around to just casually shoot the breeze with him either.

Ed was almost as relieved as disappointed. He permitted himself to think that she really might have a previous appointment, but, basically, he accepted her swift "no" as a definitive rejection of his ardor. He had fleeting thoughts about whether he'd waited just too long to ask her out again, whether she'd written him off as not caring for her very much. He wanted to tell her that that wasn't true, not true at all. But he didn't know how. And, he also knew that he wouldn't.

Ed absorbed this setback as the term melted to its end. He had much to do in all of his courses. He and Roberta would nod and tentatively smile at each other once in a while,but if they spoke, which was hardly ever, it was only perfunctorily and fleetingly.

Miss Mellen had assigned a ten page paper, due on the Monday of the last week of classes and Ed had worked assiduously on an analysis of Thoreau's magnificent "Walden." A fellow outsider to Ed. He particularly loved Thoreau's stirring assurance that " I learned at least this by my experiment: that if one advances confidently in the direction of his dreams and endeavors to live the life he has imagined he will meet with a success unexpected in common hours. If you have built castles in the air.... that is where they should be. Now put the foundations under them." He memorized it, would repeat it to himself from time to time, and considered it his motto. He was also greatly affected by "Walden"s concluding lines, "The light which puts out our eyes is darkness to us. There is more day to dawn. The sun is but a morning star."

At the end of the Monday class Miss Mellen told the students to hand in their papers by putting them on her desk as they left the classroom. Once outside Ed was heading to his lunch period when he heard Stve Reynolds calling his name. He turned and found Steve smiling broadly and greeting him with half—open arms.

"How's it going Eddie boy? No talk for a while. I've missed 'ya."

"Yeah, I guess that's right. Well, I've been pretty busy lately. You know, writing all the end of the term papers and such. You, too, probably."

"Oh, yeah, you must have put in gobs of work, like always. I'm sure your usual string of "A"s will be the result. The teachers know you so well already that I think they put "A" on the paper as soon as they see your name. Not that you wouldn't get an "A" no matter what."

"No, no, I don't know about that. But I just try to do my best. That's all I can do. Any of us, I guess."

"Your best is plenty good and I mean PLENTY. It's going to make you valedictorian or something damn close."

"No, not a chance.... Maureen...."

'But grades aren't everything, right Eddie boy?" Steve winked.

"No, that's right. There are other things....."

" Like girls, right Eddie buddy?"

'Oh yeah, sure," Ed responded. He tried for camaraderie, but felt uneasy.

"I noticed that you and that cute little Robert P. don't chit—chat as much as you used to."

"No,uh.... Not so much anymore."

"Too bad, she's got quite a nice little chassis there. Some inviting padding, if you catch my drift. I understand that you even went out with her once. Get anywhere?"

"No, no.... not anything like that. We just went out once...." Ed felt himself laboring to not show how flustered and upset Steve's questions were making him feel. "Yes, yeah, she has a nice figure."

"Well. Ya know, I know some of her friends and stuff. Some girls who know her pretty well. I think I could arrange it, Eddie my boy, so that if you asked her she would go out with you again. You wouldn't mind that would you? I bet you'd appreciate it."

"Well, yeah…. but I don't think she would. We didn't…. it didn't go so great. I think, actually, that now she thinks I don't like her that much."

"But you do, right? And you do want to go out with her again." Steve winked again before going on. "Maybe get to rub up against some of that nice curvy padding." He threw in one more wink, for unmistakable emphasis, and continued, "Well, like I say, I think she likes you more than she let on to you and that she'd really like for you to take her out again. Especially after I talk to some girls who would talk to her. Know what I mean? You'll see; it'll work out real smooth and easy."

Ed just shook his head a bit, still disconcerted. " I got to get going, Steve."

"Yeah, yeah, I know what you mean. Me too. But just give me another second. Look, like I said, it's a piece of cake for me to get Roberta to go out with you again. But I need a favor from you, too. Look, you know how busy I am with the team and things. Some extra long practices, lately, a lot of work in other courses, and other stuff, too. Had to do some things for my folks.You know how it is. I just didn't get a chance to get to the term paper in this course.. But Mellen is so mixed up it doesn't matter, What a ding bat, huh!!! Well, listen, when she tells me that she didn't get a paper from me I'm going to adamantly insist that I handed it in. And if someone she likes as much as you backs me up, If you say that you definitely saw me put it on her desk today, then she'll just think that she's dottier than even she thought she was and that she lost it somewhere between here and correcting the papers at her smelly little apartment, or wherever the hell she brings them, maybe a cozy little nook for spinsters at the library, to do that crapola. There's absolutely no way, just not possible, that she'll doubt that I wrote a paper and handed it in if you say that I did. You're totally aces with her. I think she'd go out with you if you were interested in such baggy stuff." A hearty Stdeve laugh." So, that's your part of the deal. A small price to pay, right , for maybe unhooking Roberta's bra, maybe even getting your hand under her skirt." An additional, very braod, conspiratorial wink. "But I know that as boffo as that would be, for a horny guy like you, you're also interested in other stuff, more high falutin', too, right. So I'm going to throw in a ten bucks bookstore gift certificate so that you can get yourself one of those heavy duty, massively thick, intellectual books that I see you carrying around sometimes. Even when they haven't been assigned, or anything, in any course they give around here. I think I'm offering a pretty good deal, don't you? More than generous. The only thing you have to do is vouch for me to Mellen. What's the difference if that old, mixed—up bat thinks I handed in a paper when I didn't. It's got exactly zilch to do with the real world out there. At least the one I'm headed for. The scouts have been sniffing around; I'll probably wind up playing for an Ivy. She'll be forced to base my grade on my exam marks in here. They're not bad. I'll take it. All I've got to do is graduate this joint."

Finally, Steve paused so that Ed could take in his proposal. "So there's the deal. All you have to do is play your very small part. So, I've got your word, right?"

"Well, uh..." Ed mumbled, desperately playing for time. "I'd have to think about that. I mean it wouldn't be right to fool her like that. I mean she'd be trusting me...."

'That's exactly right, guy. That's why it's so neat. There's no problem. No problem for me and, then, no problem for you getting a real shot at Roberta A little nookie never hurts. Even for bookish dudes. Actually she seems pretty fresh and clean. Unhandled. I wouldn't mind getting some myself, except she's a little quiet. Is it 'reserved' you brainiac types call it?"

" Yes, she's pretty quiet. But very nice."

"Sounds to me like you're in love, my friend. So I take it that we have a firm deal."

Ed wasn't really considering Steve's proposition. He was only quickly trying to think how to refuse without incurring too much immediate, explicit vocal wrath. He hemmed and hawed for several seconds more. Then he just shook his head, eyes downcast, lips closed, from side to side.

"No Steve, I couldn't do that, it wouldn't be me."

Reynolds's jaw dropped in genuine surprise. Maybe shock. He started to say something, but stopped after a very few words. The he abruptly turned and strode off. Leaving Ed standing there, alone.

LOVE INTERESTS

"You know," said my friend John, a year older and, at seventeen, virtually a mature man to me., "Once school begins in the fall Barbara will expect you to get a part—time job so you'll have some money to take her out on dates."

"Yeah, I guess so" was all I could muster for an answer. What he said didn't make any real sense to me because I didn't know if I was motivated to take Barbara out on dates. Why should I? Just because she wanted me to? And how did I even know if she did. Just because John said so? It wasn't like I felt she had spoken to him about it.

I didn't even know if I liked Barbara that way. It seemed that a week or two before John made his remark she had decided that she liked me and that I should be her boyfriend. She, too, was about a year older than me and was one of the girls in our group. Six or seven of us hung around with each other, on street benches on our block , during summer evenings. Out of the blue she had started making it clear that she found me attractive, including comments about how good looking I was and how broad my shoulders were. I found her rather plain looking, mousy even, and certainly wasn't physically attracted to her. But I didn't know what to do when started coming on. Passivity was my tendency and it was out of the question for me to be rude and demonstratively act like I didn't like her, or anything like that. Also, at my age I was supposed to be going out with girls, at least once in a while, but I wasn't. This was a low effort, ready—made opportunity.

Not long before the Barbara stuff had started, our group had been walking through the very dimly lit basement of the apartment building in which some of us lived on some nonsensical teen—age escapade. Judith, a redhead with luscious breasts, grabbed my arm in apparent fright. I'd always found her very pretty and would have delighted in holding her tight and feeling those irresistible breasts pressing against my chest. But out of embarrassment about how things might "look," I pushed her arm away with grandstanding abruptness. She never said a word, or showed hurt in any way, but despite my secret, fervent yearning that she'd give me another chance she never made a gesture like that again. No second chances with scorned women as desirable looking as her.

There was an "older" woman who looked even better. More mysterious, and harder to get. She was on the shorter side but wore an enticing tight black skirt which resulted in her buttocks undulating to maximum effect as she walked the same two blocks to the subway that I did. I was headed for my college freshman courses and she must have been on her way to work.

I only spotted her ahead of me a few times, but it seemed like each time she had on that skirt or one very much like it. Usually she also wore a crisp white blouse which her chest assertively filled out beyond expectations suggested by her height. Her hair was dark black and her face sexually appealing, rather than just pretty—although its features were that too. I would think of her, in early morning, awakening from the deep, healthy sleep of youth, and immediately get a fierce erection. Hope also was immediately aroused—that I would see her on the way to the subway. That rarely happened and the few times it did she never even glanced at me, not that I would have known what to do if she had. But I burned for her.

There was a young, adult woman who would pass through our block from time to time, maybe two or three times a week, who was a real favorite of my horny male pals and myself. Almost exclusively she wore tight skirts and tighter sweaters. Whatever her clothing it enhanced and revealed the contours of a voluptuous figure. She just seemed to brim over everywhere, very alluringly. We craved chances to gaze at her as she sinuoulsly passed. We savored for days. We fantasized that perhaps she was a prostitute and that….. I so longed to heft her breasts, even sweater and brassiere encased, from behind.

In senior year in high school there was the beautiful blonde girl who blossomed into a completely striking young woman. Suddenly appeared mature well beyond her age, with gorgeous perfectly shaped legs, and a bust that thrusted prominently regardless of what apparel she covered it with. She was so exquisite that you almost had to look away from the longing induced.

However, it was with Barbara, through her plotting and manipulation, that I found myself on a date, I suppose, in a local park, on a July morning. We strolled lesisurely for a while and then lay down on the grass, like sunbathers, though her chicanery did not include the foresight to bring a blanket or large towel.

She was pleasant enough to converse with and sweet in a passive, non—demanding way. Nevertheless, every once in a while she would make a slightly seductive comment. Nothing really dramatic or resembling a flagrant come- on. Just slightly suggestive throw aways. I was sure she wanted to kiss and, at least, pet. The brutal fact was she inspired no desire in me. But, paragon of courtesy, as we lay on our stomachs, chatting aimlessly, caressed by the sun's perfect warmth, I put my arm around her waist. She didn't protest or shy away, but neither did she further encourage me. She seemed to be waiting. I still felt absolutely nothing and did not want to go on. So I did not, and she did not, and, eventually, we got to our feet and walked back towards our neighborhood, our date apparently over.

As the day drew on, perhaps in mid—afternoon, I started to feel vaguely guilty for holding Barbara's waist, even though I hadn't really wanted to. I became worried that I'd somehow, inexplicably, compromised her even in my innocent fumbling. Also that I'd betrayed myself. I felt obligation but without corresponding joy. That's why I had been upset, disconcerted by John's comment.Whatever he said, whatever he, or Barbara, thought, intent as I was on not directly hurting her feelings, I had started rebuffing Barbara's repeated prompts and encouragement. No I didn't want to go here, and no I didn';t want to go there. Or, less awkwardly and dismissively—I couldn't go because.... And with school starting.... Even she, before too long, had enough pride to back off.

~

The summer after the one of the flirtation with Barbara friends I'd made in my first year of college came over and we all went to dinner in a Chinese restaurant. Afterwards there were a few hours of a bull session of the kind in which guys that age are always indulging. As subjects petered out it was decided that it would be fun to go looking for a street walker. I confirmed that such women could be found in a nearby neighborhood from time to time. I, myself, wasn't wildly enthusiastic about this notion , but, as a member of the group I went along.

One of the guys had a car, so went cruising ten minute or so from where I lived. By the time we got underway it was almost eleven and there was little traffic. Sure enough, as the car proceeded, at about fifteen miles per hour, we saw ahead, on the right, a shapely—figured young African—American woman in high heels, very tight pale blue skirt and a floral, silky blouse. When we drew up beside her we saw that she was pretty too.

The leader of our five man expedition jumped out of the car and spoke to her. He quickly got back in and reported it would be ten dollars a piece, (no pun intended, presumably,) and that she would show us where to drive the car. The whole thing didn't appeal to me as it was nothing like the scenario I'd fantasized for losing my virginity. I wasn't sure whether my friends were virgins too, but I thought they were.

The woman got in the car and directed us to a secluded area, a few minutes away, where the car could be parked so that it wouldn't be visible from the street. Then she stayed in the back seat until four of us got out. When the first client was finished the next man got in the back seat with her. I delayed my turn as long as possible. When it finally came, I, perfunctorily sat down on the back seat.

I turned to her, vaguely put my hands on her blouse, approxiamatelyin the chest area, and gently nuzzled her face, which, in the dim light thrown by the street lamp, did not seem quite as attractive as it had from further away. She quickly ordered, "No kissing." This was surprising and disconcerting. What I believe is called a chilling effect . Apparently I was to get right to business, as she hitched her skirt up and leaned back, away from me. Certainly not the way I'd imagined or fantasized about things. Nothing happened for me. I'm not sure I wanted it to. But having gotten into the situation it was frustrating and humiliating not to have been able to accomplish the mission. Perhaps I could have had I persisted. But I was all too willing to terminate this encounter.

I confessed my failure to the others and couldn't wait to get home. In bed that night, as well as the next morning on arising, I tried to induce erections by fantasizing in all the customary ways. I was somewhat successful but not as unqualifiedly as usual.

Naturally, I mentally, tried to shrug the whole thing off, but even the insouciance of youth couldn't salve my ego that much. The incident had definitely not been a confidence builder. I noticed that my responses to attractive females didn't really change or diminish but, still, I withdrew even more into myself. I started using many of the summer days remaining until classes started up again to walk the four long blocks from where we lived to the main branch of the Brooklyn Public Library. In my freshman year of college my appetite for literature, history, philosophy had been sharply whetted. There were many great books to read, much great music to listen to, sheaves and sheaves of magnificent paintings to study. The possibilities were, literally, endless. And this capacious building was a treasure trove.

The music collection, classical, jazz, popular, on long playing vinyl records, was extensive. And there were recordings of of well known actors and other prominent people reading famous historical speeches and renowned poems, such as Walt Whitman's 'Captain, My Captain," and "The Waste Land" of T.S. Eliot. I started borrowing quite a few of the poetry recordings. There was even one of the great William Butler Yeats reading his own poetry. I can still hear him intoning, with his unmistakable Irish lilt, "The Lake Isle of innisfree." ("I will arise and go now and go to innisfree.….As I stand on the roadways or the pavments grey/ I hear lake water lapping with low sounds by the shore/ I hear it in the deep heart's core.") The duration for which such records were allowed to be borrowed was pretty short--- less than a week, I think. I would borrow a few albums at a time, listen to all eagerly and return them only a few days later, before fines would start running.

Toward the very end of the summer respite, the heat of the midday sun palpable, yet a fresh breeze, hinting the merest tinge of autumn, also stirring, I returned several of these albums. There was one of the poetry of e.e. cummings, the master of lower case. My recollection is that Cummings himself was the reader, enhancing the whole experience. I loved his "Since feeling is first." ("since feeling is first/who pays any attention to the syntax of things/will never wholly kiss you.") Borrowed library items were to be brought back to a "Return" desk where they were logged in by date. That day the clerk was an exceedingly pretty young woman. She must have been just about my own age, a year or so either way. Her soft, plentiful, luxurious brown hair framed verging on perfect features, especially large, limpid brown eyes.

When I put the albums down she looked at them, immediately brightened and said, with verve, "Oh, isn't Cummings wonderful? He's one of my real favorites." I'd hardly recovered from her striking appearance when she offered this comment and, although even I sensed it as an "opening" by which she wanted to initiate a friendly conversation, I went completely blank and tongue—tied. I knew I should answer, I sorely wanted to answer, yet desperately as I mentallyflailed, I could come up with absolutely nothing intelligent .Zero. Empty set. I merely nodded my head tentatively and mumbled a grudging 'Yeah" or something equally curt and off-putting. Then I bee—lined for the main exit of the library as swiftly as possible.

Once outside I could only berate myself for how astonishingly inept I'd been. Both by failing to connect with her on even a very limited basis and because of how badly or hurt she must have felt about my seeming cold unresponsiveness.

But I couldn't wait to go back to the library in a few days and I started thinking what I would say to her if she were again behind the desk. I actually found a reason to go back the next day. I brought back some recordings I hadn't even listened to yet. But she wasn't there. I resolved that I would keep coming back until she were.

LAUGHING----all the way, hopefully

PAST SIXTY IS TOO MUCH, too often, like a joke. So, perhaps best to treat it, "treat" being exactly apposite, that way. Even without any specific afflictions, the whole gestalt, (that's a funny word—German is always good for a laugh, nein?) is like an illness—at least compared. Compared to what? To before. To your thirties, forties, fifties, even-- not to mention twenties.

Sixty plus is arising way too early, too many times, COMPLETELY without enthusiasm. No need to rush, or even watch the clock, because no need to do ANYthing, be ANY where. How will the time be conusmed? Grocery shopping, trip to cleaners? A withdrawl at the bank; the movies later? Well, there's always making breakfast—something, anything you really don't want to eat. Sometimes, once you start eating it you like it better than anticipated. That's supposedly ketones; they accentuate appetite once activated by actual food ingestion. Science knows so much. It also knows that at more than sixty the probabilities are closing in. Life expectancy is no longer boundless.

O.K., you can open the condo door and pick up the paper. Sometimes there's something a little in there which grabs attention. Even the Business section can do that. At least it's about objective factors, numbers, people risking and either succeeding or failing, new products. There could be something about one of those mega-big companies laying off thousands, or even tens of thousands, to get their "earnings" numbers up. Earnings as computed by whom? Accountants who are paid to make this year's profits come out to two cents a share more than last year's? Remember Enron!! Nothing is ever said about the personal impact on the multitudes who've lost their jobs to the scythe of the cost-cutting guru. The reader can supply that; the "human interest." Or, on the front page, some figures on casualties in the current war(s.) Again, so often presented as kill "ratios," (in comparison to what?) rather than in any terms of human suffering, tragedy, despair. A feature about how some "sharp" young rogues have scammed some doddering, (even more than one dodders at sixty plus,) seniors out of a lot of dough. "Arts" may have a review of a concert or recording by a favorite musical performer. Maybe I'd want to clip it out and send it to a friend who is also an admirer- or antagonist—of the artist. That would require underlining stimulating observations by the critic. Time is starting to be consumed. And we haven't even started preparing breakfast yet. The day is off to a rousing, verging on scintillating, start.

Breakfast is big. Lots to do. Have to take out the cereal box from the pantry, extract one paper bowl from the cellophane enclosed pile in the cabinet, (minimizes time loading and unloading the dishwasher—but why do I care—what else have I to do?) pour the cereal, put in the milk. Then it's the massive toast job. First the decision; one or two slices; then, one or two slices of cheese. Which cheese? The muenster, cheddar, or low-fat Swiss? The latter package lasts the longest of the three, eaten the least, because it's a "health" purchase and winds up to be mostly for "show;" i.e. solace to an oldster that he's taking care of his "health." Somewhat of a façade, a little deception. So what, a slice of that stuff is only two or three grams of fat less than most of the other, no declamations of virtue made on the package, cheeses. And as for the sodium content of this one as opposed to that one, 65 mg instead of 80, it all gets tiresome, not to mention flagrantly BORING. Am I supposed to believe that 15mg of Sodium less one morning will prolong my life. 15 mg every morning, even? And one has to boil the water for the no-caffeine, absolutely NONE, cereal type hot drink. The brown sprinkly stuff sans, (a little French, as in French Roast coffee,) any taste. If I have caffeine, even the small amount that's in decaffeinated coffee, I could get heart palpitaitons. They're innocuous, but not likable. You wouldn't invite them to happy moments. Nor, even, to neutral ones. That's about it. Enough calories, scant as they might be, for the approximately five hours between now and lunch on my high octane schedule of reading the paper or rolling that cart up and down the supermarket aisles, after the enormous expenditure of energy entailed in driving the four blocks to the place.

Speaking of health matters, there's the half-hour morning walk, (there's also one in the evening,) to be accomplished. Accomplished is a euphemism. To be gotten over with is more accurate. If one arises especially early, even before five, say, one can get the striding, o.k. maybe more like shuffling, around in before breakfast. One can do it pre- breakfast even if one gets up after five. And, whenever wake-up is, if not before chow then after. Don't get the wrong idea—the walk is an indoor one. The apartment has enough square feet for one person to usefully amble about in it. It's probably a more vigorous, aerobic walk outside. But the big advantage of doing it indoors is that there can NEVER be a meteorological excuse for non-compliance. E.g., it's raining, it's too hot outside, it's too cold outside, I don't feel like getting dressed and going out right now…It must always be done. Except for the emphatically exceptional circumstance: such as sickness unto inability to raise oneself from the bed. Thus the inescapable walk complies with one of the salient health admonitions re: exercise; viz., utter regularity. My son, the epidemiologist, conducted a study demonstrating just how beneficial exercise is to general good health. Also, while pacing along, the diligent exerciser can be listening to great classical music on his walkman CD player. An iPod is too contemporary. Would entail learning more technology. Why do we need things that were unknown fifty, even twenty-five, years ago? So, sidling along for, finally, thirty minutes while listening, for example, to the great Rudolf Serkin, (rather than his son Peter, who's also a magnificent pianist--but he's alive now,) play Beethoven's fifth piano concerto, "The Emperor," opus 73, E—Flat Major, is just not too bad a time of it.

If presentable enough, even if still in pajamas, to open the front door and pick up the paper, on the very good chance that no one else is out in the hall on this floor, yet, this early, one can get the "Times," if it's not so early that it hasn't been delivered yet, by whichever industrious ethnic kid gets it there seven days a week, every day of the year—or most of them, anyway. Then I can start perusal along while slurping bran flakes, (a little skim milk and a few cubes of cantaloupe, low calorie, low sugar, you know, thrown in as well,) and gnawing at whole wheat toast. But sometimes I can get involved in story after story in the paper so that my reading stamina outlasts the food. And then I get guilty that I continue reading the paper when, having finished breakfast, I should "get going." I repeat: To where? For what purpose? Even the supermarket doesn't open until seven. I would love it if it were open twenty-four/seven . Then I would be safe; somewhere to go no matter when I was up. You can always remember something you need. Some days you can even arrange to go twice.

I have a system with the paper. First, any special "extraneous" sections of the day, e.g. "Circuits," which I don't care about, because I don't know and, seemingly, can't learn, anything about contemporary technology, (except how to turn on the computer to read and do e-mail,) are cursorily, totally perfunctorily, glanced at and discarded. In the recyclable paper bin of course. Same with "Styles," largely, and "Dining In" and "Dining Out" when their days come. Then it's "Business" to see, in general, what the markets did the day before, (we upper middle-class seniors have, at least, some investments,) and to check whether there are any individual stories of interest about economic trends or anything else that might grab my attention. If there are I read at least a few paragraphs of each of those. An elementary school teacher taught us that to read the paper you didn't have to read the whole paper—pick out the key stories, she advised, and then read at least the first paragraph of each. Anything that compelled further could be awarded additional paragraphs. After that I check the little index on the front page of the paper to determine where the obituaries are that day. Sometimes they're embedded in the "Business" section, of all places, although on most days they're included in the main news section. Also, most of the time "Sports" are in the "Business" section, too, but not always. Sometimes it's near the final pages of the main section. Sort of the opposite of the obituaries geography.

"Sports" has to be skimmed for anything of particular interest, such as important tennis matches. The big Grand Slam tournaments like Wimbledon, the French Open and the U.S. Open have to be read about for the two weeks each lasts. I've been following world class tennis since junior high school, fifty plus years by now. Also, anything particularly prominent in the sports news, perhaps a hitter in baseball nearing a record, or the tremendous golfer, Tiger Woods, about to win another Masters Tournament. Or, maybe, something about the basketball team of De Paul University, in Chicago, where I taught law, Contracts and Jurisprudence courses, for so many years. After that fun it's on to the first page for a quick skim of the stories there and a check to see if any stories "indexed" on the first page merit riffling the pages, so often stuck together, to get to them inside. After looking at any of these or, if there are none, it's on to the editorial and Op-Ed pages, assuming that the obituaries were, indeed, covered in the "Business" section. If not they must be picked up on the way to the editorial page. I like reading, in capsule form, about the lives of people who have accomplished a great deal or were vitally involved in some project of worldly significance. And it's always fascinating to see whether their family lives were as admirable, as impressive, as their career attainments. The editorial page also has the Letters to the Editor, which I'll read or not according to subject matter. Some seem so marginal (frivolous?) as to anything that I (most people?) care about. Actually, too often the same with the editorials. Do my best to stay up on what I should be informed about. Always feel the burden of good citizen guilt. But hard to be "up" for some of these matters, if you know what I mean. Same judicious selection re: the op-Ed page pieces—correlated to pull of subject matter.

Then it's finally, usually not until later in the day, or even the evening, to my favorite section, "Arts." I usually read every music review, every movie review (except if the film is in the horror, or allied, genre and there is simply no possibility of my going to see it,) and every theater review except, again, if the play's subject matter is something in which I have no interest, whatsoever. There's a certain music critic I'm out to get, also. I just don't like the way he plays favorites amongst artists—some can do no wrong, absolutely none, they're always SUPERlative, while others, however great their general prestige or stature, never get it right enough to please this persnickety demon.So, whenever he acts up particularly egregiously I feel, as a passionate aficionado of great music and world class artistry, to pen some barbs, perhaps even venom, to this miscreant. When I started this expostulatory, epistolary practice he occasionally answered my fulminations. But soon he wrote me a note, after a particularly explosive missive I'd sent him, saying that he could no longer promise to respond to my observations. I retorted that I'd not noticed that he felt compelled to answer each time I wrote previously, but he did not deign to address me again. No matter, it's his hearing me that I want. But I'm not sure that he does. I'm insecure. Does he just throw out the letter, unopened, when he sees my name in the return address corner or does curiosity grasp him, unyieldingly, so that he opens to what he knows will be the odious comments? I must labor on in the belief/hope that he, at least sometimes, reads what I so conscientiously pen.

Actually, any section of the newspaper could present "work" for me. If there's an editorial I disagree with—why not a letter to the editor. Or, even if there's something reported in a news story with which I can take issue.Certainly an Op—Ed page piece with a viewpoint decidedly different from my own can inspire a fervid counter—argument, in letter-to- the- editor form. And I'm not all piss and vinegary malice. I also write complimentary letters to individual columnists. For example, if one of the sportswriters does an effective job on an inspirational athlete role model

I'm only too happy to compliment her or him and indicate that I found the article very winning. The same even with a particularly well-written and stimulating obituary which perfectly apostrophizes an impressive life. Sometimes, if rarely, I get an answer from one of the journalists to whom I 've written. Often a quite brief, almost perfunctory, "Thank you," but sometimes something more expansive and invigorating. Naturally, I reply to any substantive answer.

Who would think it, but it's getting late-r in the morning. I have to get to the bank and supermarket and have lunch, all before it's time to pick up Jason who is a little older even than me. Not much, a year or two. But some consider that a lot, at this point. And, like me, he, too, lives alone since his children also live out of state. Mine are actually closer than his. Not that it matters much as far as frequency of getting together, i.e. visits, with "the kids."

Anyway, Jason had colon cancer surgery not that long ago and goes to the medical center twice a week for follow up radiation treatments. His son and daughter came for the surgery and the immediate after care period but, then, returned to their own out of state lives. I've never been told the prognosis and I don't, unbidden, ask such things.This is not such a funny topic. Jason could go for these outpatient treatments by driving himself, no disability there, but he does get apprehensive on the days he has an appointment and likes company. Going there, even just as his ride and companion in the waiting room, makes me apprehensive too. (How long till I'm the patient?) But what are you going to say to an old-time pal, especially since we supported each other in our nearly simultaneous neophyte widower status, a few years ago No jokes, there, either.

Besides, one of the clerks with whom the patient has to check in and schedule future appointments is this very striking African—American woman. She looks particularly great in pastel colored blouses, like lemon yellow or lime green, and dark, straight skirts and seems like she's in her late forties or, maybe even, early fifties. No rings either. She, I think I've heard the other clerks call her Odana, that's what it sounds like, anyway, also seems very crisply competent and always compassionate with and considerate of the beset, troubled patients. She's a cool-looking, refreshing interlude in the typically dull, soporific, sweltering afternoon.

This check's been lying around for a few days, already, so I'd better get to the bank. I will, after bathroom routine, (thankfully still pretty good regularity in that area,) and the crucial decision of which pair of khaki chinos to put on and which solid, dark colored short sleeved shirt. So one should sweat only extravagantly, rather than profusely, in the mid-day and mid—afternoon sun. God must have made air conditioning because he made the semi—tropical sun. Sometimes the former verges on losing the battle to the latter. It is BLAZING hot between 2:00 and 4:00 when Jason and I usually emerge from the medical center. Cascades of humidity, too. If there's a longer than usual wait for the valet to bring the car we're stifling and pissed. We're all so spoiled aren't we.

There's a single line in the bank, not as long as it used to be—more on-line customers these days, and increasing all the time---- so you get the "next available" teller. My favorite is Miriam. I wonder if she's Jewish as well as Hispanic. I know about the Hispanic because I've heard her speak the language to fellow employees. I love her "accent." Also, her name plate, says "Rodriguez." But she might just be married to a Hispanic man. Nevertheless, there are quite a few "Jubans," or "Jew—bans," in Miami. She's petite, I don't think she can be more than 5'2," but has fine, amply rounded curves for her proportions She sometimes augments the 5'2" with some heels which display very comely ankles. And she chatters very chirpily and brightly. Mucho lively, cheerful. Whatever the transaction she dispatches it, one-two-three, zip-zip-zip, bantering, if you like, all the while. One time one of the vice—presidents was lurking around being officious, as V.P.s are wont to be. When he moved out of hearing range she sighed, resignedly, and said, sotto voce, to me, "I spend more time with him than with my husband." Another time he was again skulking about behind the teller stations and finally announced, "O.K., I'm going to lunch now." Miriam fired back, "So go already, go!" A Jewish locution, no es verdad? But, perhaps, just one that's been shanghaied into the common parlance, like "chutzpah." Miriam, unlike some of the other women tellers, young and older, doesn't give any decolletage but I like the way even a suit jacket tightly fits her upstairs. Or, even, a crisp white blouse on which her medium length jet-black hair lies so contrastingly. Fetchingly, too.

But there's only so much time one can spend, without embarrassment, at Miriam's window completing a trivial transaction like withdrawing a hundred in cash. No ATM's for me. It's on to the supermarket; another monumental drive of about three blocks. (But, because of the one way streets, you have to drive a block past it, make a right turn, make another right turn and come back to its pretty vast parking lot. Vast altogether, but not, certainly, each individual space. On the narrow side. And with so many imposing, sight—blocking, SUVs and Humvees, etc. tough to pull out of without risking impact with a car just meandering down the aisle.

Good opportunity for cursing if you, or the other driver, has to make a short stop.

Looks pretty busy in the super market. You can tell from how many available carts there are. On rare occasions there can even be none, zero, nada—to, again, use what a man from Mars, who suddenly dropped in, would think is the native language. If that's the case probably better to come back a little later. Because that means the aisles are more jammed and congested than usual with oblivious shoppers. By oblivious I mean that they stick their carts right in the middle of the aisle so you can't get around either side and act like they don't know, as they continue their browsing, that you, and maybe others, are standing there waiting to get by. Maybe they really don't know—insentience could be rampant. That's even worse.

I usually start off on the right-hand side, Dairy, and wind up all the way on the left, Produce. This place seems to have eight trillion and forty five thousand different products. Then up and down the appropriate intervening aisles. I do it that way because Dairy is easy—I know where the skim milk, yogurt. low calorie swiss cheese and eggs are. The other stuff is dicier. I can't always quickly pick out the Paul Newman salad dressing from the myriad others which line the "Oils" shelf. Same with the oat bran cereal So many boxes. I end with Produce because that, too, is simple: the broccoli, arugula, romaine lettuce, (greens equal roughage, perhaps the secret of my success,) and cantaloupe chunks are always in the same places.

But, today, there is the added attraction of a mom loading her basket, in which sits a two to three year old kid, with good, organic stuff. I loiter, even after I've gotten the few things I buy, waiting for the inevitable lecture to the kid, the educational spiel. Sure enough, it's soon in progress: "What is mommy looking for now? What is she feeling in order to find a nice ripe one?" The kid is either non-responsive or emits some guttural utterance. So, then, it comes, one of my all—time favorite lines in all the annals of parenting;viz., "Mommy is looking for some ripe TOE—MAY—TOES, isn't she?." This kid is going to learn what a tomato is. No doubt about it—no confusion with a watermelon. The kid doesn't look especially interested, despite mom's raised, enthusiastic, voice. (Everybody in the store has to know what the roundish red things are, too.) Therefore, the lecture must proceed: "Yes,mommy is trying to find some good TOE—MAY—TOES for tonight's dinner." She then moves on to UHN—YUNS. Followed by BA—NAN—UHS. I don't know about the kid, but that's about all I can take, despite having to miss the spectacularly enunciated PO—TAY—TOES.

Time to hit the check—out counter and my friends. I know most of the checkers by this time. Usually young gals, some still going to community college, or what have you, or quite solidly middle-aged ones who are mothers of gals like these younger ones. I also know just about all the bag "boys;" often middle aged plus guys, most with just a bit of a mental delay or some sort of personality "abnormality." I buy my friendship with them, (didn't someone once call psychiatry paid friendship?) because I give the one who wheels my bags out to the car and loads them into the trunk two bucks—however few or many bags I have. Two bucks more than most folks give them, so they love me. Some of them subtly jockey for positon, as they go from checkout station to checkout station on their bagging rounds, so that they can end up where I'm being checked out. This part makes me self-conscious but it's the price I pay for being a big tipper. Rhonda used to take objection to all my over-tipping on those grounds: called attention to oneself—you became conspicuous even if you craved privacy. But I was taught the moral necessity for re-distribution of wealth by one of my favorite college professors.

I get one of the regular checkers, one of the middle-aged, maybe even plus in Marta's case, today. Nothing unusal. A little smiling. A little very fundamental phrase-making en Espanol—how are you, how's your family, etc.---and it's on to Claro, quite unusual name, even for his culture, the bag boy. He's one of the younger ones, about fifty, and carefully places my few bags in the trunk of the Honda and wishes that I pass a good day. As I wish him.

Now, homeward bound for the storing of my just purchased provisions and the preparation of lunch. I've been thinking about and anticipating a t.v. dinner, vegetarian lasagna, I've had in the freezer compartment of the refrigerator for ages. I should probably check the date on it, but who wants to be intimidated and disappointed..

When I drive up to Jason's house, he still rattles around in there, through all the three thousand some odd square feet, by himself, except when his kids and their families visit, he's already standing outside, pacing, impateiently waiting for me to show up. Thus I save a honk. It's Jason's theory that early is always better than later re: a medical appointment—because, that way, you might sneak in before someone who is officially scheduled ahead of you but who shows up on the late side, or not at all. Jason doesn't seem any more nervous today than usually. Well, maybe a little.

Maybe a little more for me, too. Could be because I'm thinking about seeing that attractive African—American clerk again. Could also just be a more than usually nervous day. It seems like a lot of them are more nervous than usual. Maybe the norm for nervousness has increased just like the blood sugar criterion for diabetes has been lowered. A pal of mine, in New York, calls the latter "another instance of grade inflation."

As often, almost always in fact, when we get there, valet the car ,work our way past all the grim reminders that we are really in a hospital,, (e.g. the wheel chairs, attendants and technicians in scrubs purposefully rushing by, the pale, emaciated patients,) and Jason tells the receptionist, not usually Odana, although it can be, that he's arrived for his appointment, the wait begins. They're not TOO bad with that—usually a half-hour, forty minutes is the most. The only really bad aspect is that Jason starts chattering, agitatedly and incessantly,until he gets called into the inner sanctum. Any trivial or banal topic will do. Hard to answer him coherently sometimes. Not that he really seeks or demands response. As long as he can keep jawing.

But there's a reward: the longer we stay there the more I get to see Odana move attractively, dare I think seductively, about. I've got to admit to valetudinarian lechery. I just love to watch her chest challenging the contours of her brightly colored blouses. I can see the brassiere straps, under the backs, but those generous appendages still practically bounce. Speaking of the back, great view from there, too, because of the gently snug, but not immodest, skirts she favors And that effervescence, too. Always trying to be bright and positive.

But I'm worried, today, because even after we've been waiting over twenty minutes I haven't had a single glimpse of her. Finally she appears from one of the inner rooms, where there's a lot of clerical apparatus, behind the reception area. Maybe she was at a late, or long, lunch. A lunch three-hour as we hard-working academics used to call it. Maybe a lunch date with a man her own age—or younger. A lot of that, apparently, if one believes the papers and media. I prefer not to. If true it certainly curtails opportunities with older woman for older guys. Just like Bartleby, Herman Melville's unforgettable, defiant of commercialism, clerk: "I would prefer not to, sir." I'm no longer a clerk, not even a glorified one of academe, but I'm with Bartleby. I prefer not to so envision Odana. I bet she's never read " Bartleby The Scrivener." Maybe she'd like to hear what a deep impression that story made on me as a college freshman. Her close to pretty features are quite alert. I'd bet on a higher than average IQ. And, then again, maybe she couldn't care less.

She seems more dazzling than customary; plus d'ordinaire, as the French might say. The blouse is raspberry, perhaps, cerise, and the skirt a less than authentically navy blue and, just maybe, even a little snugger than d'habitude. She cheerily waves at us. Each of us soberly waives back. I suppose I shouldn't read much, anything, even, into that. After all, we're regulars: she sees us two or three times a week. She's gotten to know us and expect us there. Nevertheless, I'm ignited; I like to think that the wave was mostly for me, even though Jason is the patient. Even if it were for Jason, I don't think he'd be interested. Not that way, I mean. Guys get to know each other. I just don't think he was much interested in how attractive women looked and moved even when he was younger. Just a sense. Anyway, not now. But, of course, Odana's wave might not have been meant "that way." Could have just been a standard "patient" wave Probably was. Who knows. I like to envision her when I'm falling asleep at night The silky movements—not too fast, nor too deliberate. Crisp, yet calm. Re-assuring, but, ultimately stimulating.

Finally, Jason gets called in. At the first syllable in his name he jumps up with alacrity. He's practically through the door leading to the doctors' offices before the nurse has finished his whole name. So, at last, I'm "alone" with Odana. Yeah, so what am I going to do about it? Nothing, just like the previous times. All I would want, at least to start, would be a cup of coffee with her. That shouldn't be so difficult. Eureka!! That's the solution: I could just ask her if she wants to go for a cup of coffee during the half—hour, forty minutes, Jason is in there She must be entitled to at least a twenty minute break. That's it!! I'll definitely do that the next time we come, three days from now. And maybe, in the interim, I'll re-read "Bartleby The Scrivener." For now I'll just read the same two and three months out of date "Newsweek"s and "Time"s they have lying around the waiting room. The ones I haven't read already, that is. By the time I read a few of the stories from beginning to end and flip through some of the others Jason usually reappears. When he comes out he's quite a bit calmer than he was waiting to go in.

So, now, it's time to get the car, drive the much calmer Jason home and then, myself, likewise. Soon after that it's dinner time, followed by calling the kids and, finally, reading the "Times" some more and waiting for bed time.

Tomorrow it starts all over again. Ha, ha.

THE MEETING

Jorge Baron, a South American, Brasileno, actually, had been in London before. He'd even played concerts there. In fact, in his getting to be long career, he'd played the piano publically in many countries. All over South America, of course. But, also, in the United States, most of Western Europe, Japan, Australia. This time he hadn't done it with one of the major London orchestras. It had been a solo recital at the modestly sized Wigmore Hall—and there had still been too many empty seats. Even though the program was predominantly Mozart, Beethoven, Schubert—with just a tad of the contemporary Milton Babbit thrown in. Sic transit Gloria. Although the Gloria had always been limited. Nothing like the super—stars.

Well, he knew his place. He certainly wasn't the GREAT Emil Gilels, born in Odessa, Russia, (before it was the Soviet Union,) world class piano virtuoso extraordinaire. Baron was here, tonight, at Royal Festival Hall, London's biggest concert venue, to see and hear Gilels play a recital. He was the guest of his European agent, Edward Hatcher, who just happened to be Gilels's agent in the UK also. Baron was just looking at the programme booklet, from his way up front orchestra seat, in the brimming hall, virtually every seat taken, when Hatcher, also flipping pages,turned to him.

"It occurs to me; have you ever met Emil?"

"You mean, Gilels? No, never," Baron responded. "Of course I've admired...."

"Well you should, why not? When I go back afterwards, you must come with me, old chap. You two should definitely have a tete a tete."

Baron suddenly felt uncomfortable. "No, oh no, I … I wouldn't want to bother him."

"What you mean 'bother'? No bother. And I must beset him in any event. Assure him how well he sounded, which he will, tell him that the audience was rapt, as they always are with him, the number of tickets sold, basically all. You know, that customary sort of professional rot. You wouldn't be any bother at all. He'll be delighted to have the opportunity to meet you."

"No, he'll have his fans, who'll flood the Green Room, to deal with. They'll want autographs, albums signed, and try to engage him in talk as long as possible. He'll be tired, anxious to call it a night."

" Don't be silly. All part of the business, as you well know."

"I don't get much of that any more."

" More rubbish, you sold very well here. In any event, I wait for all that smoke to clear before I attack him. He's quite accepting. If I didn't show up he'd probably be offended at this point. Been with him a long time."

Baron was about to demur one more time but just as he was opening his mouth the house lights dimmed and Gilels started out. The applause began slowly but by the time the artist had reached the piano it had mounted into a considerable crescendo. He bowed once, quickly, and sat down on the piano bench.The applause petered and he began with the set of Chopin Preludes promised by the program. Baron found the playing searching and even, at times, quirky in its inventiveness, yet also lyrical and melting when it should have been. It put him in mind of something that his childhood piano teacher had once said, when Baron was first studying Chopin, about fifty years ago. After he had rendered the lesser known of the two "Raindrop Preludes," the teacher had simply murmured in apporoval: "Yes, tell me a story. Sometimes it seems all of life is in a single Chopin prelude."

When he'd finished the last of the selected Preludes the applause was even more enthusiastic and boundless than when Gilels had entered. Baron tried to review in his mind the most sustained, wild applause he'd ever received. He thought of Buenos Aires, maybe twenty, twenty—five years ago, Beethoven's "Emperor" Concerto…. However enthusiastic it had been, and probably they'd reacted more to the exhilaration of the concerto than his playing, it had been nothing like this.

After the audience had finally settled back for more, Gilels started on the Beethoven Sonata No. 23, op. 57, F—Minor, "The Appasionata." Scintillating and ravishing as expected. But Baron "pushed" the artist in the final movement, "Allegro ma non troppo." His prostate was intruding, or was it extruding, more and more these days and he required the Men's room soon. Baron's body English was to excise the "ma non troppo," but not too fast, but Gilels remained exquisitely faithful to the composer's marking in the course of singing brilliant interpretive gestures.

Finally, Baron, standing, with many others, joined in the again totally unrestrained applause, but as it finally dwindled and faded he lightly touched Hatcher on the shoulder , pointed to the rear of the hall, meaning the general area of the restrooms, and started stepping over those between him and the aisle. He also spent some time in the hall's foyer after negotiating the restroom line. People were animatedly saying how completely thrilled they were by Gilels's playing. "Never heard anything like it," etc., etc.

Once Baron had returned to his seat, after stepping over the same people, (didn't the men amongst them have prostates he mused ,) Hatcher resumed his campaign.

"I really want you to come with me when I go back, at the end, to chew the fat with Emil. He'll enjoy meeting you and we'll all have a merry chat. About business and pleasure. Maybe even women, too,"Hatcher winked.

"Sounds like an interesting conversation, but,no,, I'd just be a fifth wheel, or a second—rank, but first rate second rank, of course, as you like, pianist, whatever, to him. "

"Stop the nonsense," Hatcher assured, just as Gilels, head down, unsmiling, started out from the wings again.

Baron quickly inserted, "We'll see. Maybe."

The entire second half of the program would be a Gilels specialty, his 19th century compatriot, Moussorgsky's, "Pictures At An Exhibition." Tribute to a visual artist's work. He started with his vaunted delicate touch, a great deal of legato, and built slowly to the magnificent, thundering climax, "The Great Gate of Kiev" section. Baron loved the work, and over the years had played it with considerable success himself. Even in Boston, once. He might once have heard the great Alfred Brendel play it as excitingly as Gilels, but he wouldn't swear to it. As they say in one trade and another, Gilels just played the absolute hell out of it. The house came down as Kiev's gate closed, or opened. The visceral clapping went on and on. Gilels came out six times before he sat down at the piano again, to the sudden hush of the crowd. In broken English he barely muttered to the audience, (Baron, even with his ears, would not have been able to hear it but for being in the fifth row of the orchestra,) "Beethoven, Opus 111, final movement, 'Adagio Molto semplice e cantabile'." Slow, very simply and singing. A collective gasp. An entire movement of a sonata, by Beethoven yet, was by no means a typical encore at a recital. Not to mention the last movement of the last sonata Beethoven ever wrote. His final statement for the solo instrument, his instrument.

Gilels's performance was beyond transcendent. He sang penetratingly, to the core, grasping the soul, from the heart to the heart---as Beethoven had once stated his objective--- keening as a dying swan, where necessary. He summed up all of life, more. About halfway through Baron found himself crying. He could barely stop before the movement concluded. When it did he was amongst the first on his feet, many followed, hardly anyone remained seated, to clap extravagantly. The din just wouldn't subside. Gilels came out, went back, came out, went back, came out, over and over again. They wouldn't stop. The pianist bowed, on different re—appearances, hand over his heart, to each the right, center and left upper balconies, the "cheap" seats, (some said the true music lovers.) Baron counted the tenth return to the stage before Gilels raised his hands in opposition to the continuing roof—shaking applause and the lights dimmed as he walked off. Only then did the fans start diminishing the ovation and begin to file from their seats.

Hatcher turned, visibly exhilarated and bright-eyed, to Baron.

"That was something, indeed," said the pianist.

"Yes, wasn't it," commented the agent, head going side to side in disbelief. "Even for Emil, that was something, extraordinary."

" 'Incomparable' is truly the word. "

"Well, now I certainly hope that you'll accompany me to the Green Room."

"No, I would insist on still demurring on the grounds that I'd just be an unwanted guest at a well deserved party, but that was such a once—in—a—lifetime performance that I would like to pay my respects to a great, great artist. A supreme player, and plyer, of the trade."

" Excellent, delighted to hear it, mon ami. Let's give it a few minutes, time for him to placate the multitiudes and shed the monkey suit for more comfortable civvies, and then head back."

Baron welcomed the additional few minutes of just getting out of the way of the now rushing to depart crowd because it gave him more time to perfect what he wanted to express to Gilels. He had started formulating it as the great Russian had played the encore.Gilels had heard tons and tons of adulation, from professionals, amateurs, and callow groupies, many times. Baron wanted it to be just a little bit different. He was thinking along the lines of "You brought Beethoven, himself, into the hall tonight. Your fingers, his soul, moved the keys." Not good enough. Perhaps, "You were selfless and served the composers as they, ideally, would have wished and cherished." No, too stiif, not quite right....

Hatcher interrupted his musings. "I should think it's a good time now, old chap. Emil will soon be impatiently looking for me over the shoulders of the fans he'll be having forced conversation with."

Actually, by the time they'd wended through the corridors, in the subterranean reaches of the hall, to get to the Green Room, it seemed as though just about all the well-wishers---or maybe there hadn't been that many, Baron's experience had been that not too many in the audience, appreciative as it might have been, took the trouble to come back, afterward and directly tell the performer—had departed. As they entered, Hatcher having been recognized and greeted by the security man, Gilels was talking to another uniformed security man. He waved slightly at Hatcher when he saw him and continued conversing with the hall employee. The pianist's English was again doing serviceable, if limited, duty. Baron was able to decipher, from the almost inaudible mumbling, the words "your son" and "Oxford," the latter with a question mark, from the mangled syntax. "Wife" and "operation" also emerged. It became clear to Baron that Gilels knew the security man from previous appearances at Royal Festival Hall, had become familiar with various aspects and doings of the employee's family, over the years, and was "catching up" now. A few more pleasantries, the security man turned, and walked past Baron and Hatcher while Gilels's eyes raised welcomingly to Hatcher.

"Emil, just an entirely brilliant performance.Stupendous. But before we get down to business, as it were, there's someone I want you to meet."

"Yah Ed?" His eyes turned to Baron.

"Emil, this is your colleague and, I'm proud to say, another distinguished artist I represent, Jorge Baron. Jorge, the master, Emil Gilels."

Suddenly the two sentences Baron had struggled with, and striven to shape, became a jumbled blur.He fumbled for which sentence came first, which the perfect closer. But, as he started stuttering, Gilels broke in.

"Ah!! Wunderbahr—the great Jorge Baron. So happy. Alvays I hev vonted to meet you. Yah. Admire your playing SOOO much. I hev all recordings, no exception, study them much. Many best possible, nothing beats. Thank you so much, Eddie, for this meeting. I so happy now."

Baron was flabbergasted, Hatcher beamed most contentedly.

An hour later, two maintenance men came through and indicated that the hall was being locked up for the night and that the three talkers needed to leave.

They did so, continuing to chat animatedly, anecdotes, memories, vignettes, until they reached the nearest restaurant still open, three blocks away.

IMMIGRATION

Because it was my first time on a plane since 9/11, on the way to New York, to witness what had been done to my home city, I should have been thinking of all that. But I wasn't. I wasn't even thinking that I was going to meet my son—in—law and his dad, both Chicago boys, and was going to give them a whirlwind day and a half tour of the great city where I was born. I should have been thinking about and planning exactly where I'd be taking them and when. Carnegie Hall, the Ellis Island Immigration Museum, the United Nations, the Empire State Building, Broadway theaters, Lincoln Center, could have all been tumbling and jumbling friskily through my mind.

Nevertheless, what I was really thinking of was a telephone conversation, of just the day before, I'd had with my cousin, who lived in southern New Jersey. She was a few years older than I and had also grown up in Brooklyn when Ebbets Field and Jackie Robinson, performing impossible exploits in it, were both still there. I don't know how, in a general, homogenized "How are you? O.k How are you?" conversation how we'd gotten on the topic, but suddenly she was fulminating about all the recent immigrants to this country and their "free—loading." My dad entered this country in the very last year of what is now the seemingly infinitely long ago nineteenth century and, so, any statement like hers is a red flag to my bull—like allegiance to the downtrodden, penurious, often oppressed new arrival to these shores. To this "Goldeneh Medineh" as my mom's parents, born in Poland in the nineteenth century, used to refer to it. So, verging on anger, perhaps with little "formal" logic, I asked here where she'd be living today, (if at all,) instead of her palatial home in Jersey, had not all four of her grandparents been immigrants to America. There were a few more civil, closing sentences, but that was pretty much the end of that conversation.

That's why now, instead of Central Park, I was musing on how my father had travelled here, steerage class, from Kovna, now Kanaus, in pre—Soviet Union Russia. How despite having been here only a few years he'd written a campaign song for Theodore Roosevelt, preceding the 1904 election, and how he'd had the temerity to send it to the White House. He was rewarded with a handwritten response from the President, still today affectionately known as "T.R," and kept and cherished it for his long life. My mom had it for many years after his death, but, finally, it got lost in a move.

A half—century after he'd passed through Ellis Island the son he'd fathered when he was almost sixty won the Theodore Roosevelt medal at John Marshall Junior High School No. 210, in Brooklyn, for an essay I wrote on that Roosevelt's passion for "Conservation." (Today, of course, we'd say environmentalism or ecological awareness.) I was invited to attend an award ceremony, with other medal winners, at the house, in New York's Gramercy Park area, where Theodore Roosevelt had been born. I was completely unsophisticated, even for a raw thirteen-year old, but after intensive training on which subway train to take, where to get off and which way to walk when I did, I found the place at the right time. Kindly received by those in charge of the ceremony I was, nevertheless, duly awed by them, by where I was, and why.

As I slid between these reveries and the present I did make a mental note to try to definitely go to Carnegie Hall with Dan and his father since Dan was a Ph.D. in classical piano performance and his dad an avid barbershop quartet singer.

When I met up with them, Dan's dad, whose own father had come from Ireland through Ellis Island, on his way to his destiny, surprised me by indicating that one of his top sightseeing priorities was touring the aircraft carrier Intrepid, which, he'd read, was tied up at 46th Street and the Hudson River. He'd served in the Navy during World War II and wanted to re—connect with that part of his own biography. So after getting tickets for a Carnegie Hall event that night, promising young singers, sponsored by a foundation established by the great mezzo—soprano, Marilyn Horne—she, herself would be there, too—we fortified ourselves, at the famous Stage Deli, just a block or two from the Sheraton where we were staying. We all had obscenely massive sandwiches and shared "a little" strawberry shortcake for dessert before I hailed a cab and told Deng Uck Kim to make for the Intrepid at the location Tom had mentioned.

While in the Navy Tom had actually done some duty at the then, and for years afterward, thriving, bustling and famous Brooklyn Navy Yard. My son—in—law, who could spin out the slow movement of the Schubert A—Major Sonata, D. 959, so poignantly and achingly, seemed to well understand and appreciate much of what Tom and I, each on his own agenda, were up to.

The cabbie was soon in the general vicinity of the ship, but he couldn't, what with too many "Detour" and "Street Closed" signs, seem to nail the exact location. He did trial and error for a few minutes but the exact street approach to the Intrepid remained elusive. After a few minutes of such random efforts he pulled up besides one of New York's finest, walking his beat, (perhaps the odds of his being Irish weren't as great as they once were,) and asked for instructions. What came back was more complex than might have been anticipated. Presumably that was why the cabbie couldn't find it on his own.

Tom, in the genial, gentle Irish way is a very understanding, compassionate man. I like him immensely. Concerned that the driver might not be able to process all the instructions as to the intricate turns and twists, which the cop was spewing out, he listened intently himself, to the labyrinth being described. Once the policeman had turned away, Tom asked Deng Uck Kim whether he'd quite caught every right and left. With an air of complete focus and purposefulness the man turned and quietly said, "Of course I understood." He spoke in what in pre—politically correct times would have been characterized as "perfect English." He got us there.

We also made it to Ground Zero where we could glimpse the Statue of Liberty as well. We jammed in a ride on the Staten Island Ferry, too.

To further charm my Irishmen with the delights of New York City, after the fine singing we heard at Carnegie Hall that night, I took them to Rosie O'Grady's Restaurant, a few blocks south on Seventh Avenue. (The Stage Deli orgy was wearing off.) I don't recall if I had corned beef and cabbage, but I was thinking of it and one of us must have had it.

We hit a few more high spots the next day, including searching for gifts for the wives. But by mid—afternoon it was time for them to head for the airport and after seeing them off I was on my own.

I ate a take—out sandwich in my room for dinner and went back to Carnegie Hall, perhaps my favorite Big Apple site, to see and hear the great Italian tenor, Carlo Bergonzi, who'd sung at all the world's leading opera houses, the Met, La Scala, Convent Garden, give a farewell recital. He was into his seventies already and had "retired" before, but the voice, while, of course, not the absolutely limpid, clarion bell it had been when he was at the height of his powers, still retained an astonishing amount of beauty and heft. Many of his, themselves "vocal," fans---there were many shouted "Bravo Carlo"s during the evening—found him as irresistible as ever and displayed unalloyed enthusiasm. Much warmth and appreciation, went back and forth, between stage and audience, throughout the recital. After a particularly fervid spell of applause the great musician said, in Italian even I could understand, "Ah, if I were only young again," the word "joven" giving it away. In the end they just wouldn't let him go.I think he did six encores, at least, who was counting by that time, before he held up his hands and pointed to his throat with a resigned shrug, indicating the instrument was out of ammunition, before anyone at all started shuffling toward the exits..

When I left the hall I had a glowing sense of well being. I felt I'd been part of a beautiful musical event. And a stirring extra—musical one, too. The bitter, slicing wind barely reached me during the entire five block walk back to the hotel. The concert had gone on so long that I almost didn't make it back in time to call my wife and tell her about the glory of Bergonzi, as well as the rest of the day. When we'd spoken in the morning she'd imposed an "I'll be sleeping, or trying to, after, 11:00, I have to go to work tomorrow" deadline.

The incandescent, gratified sensation carried over to the next morning, the day I'd fly back. But not before completing my final mission on this jaunt home. I expressed my upbeat mood with a brisk thirty minutes of exercise walking on Fifty—Seventh Street and then devouring a particularly hearty breakfast, taken out from the Rock and Roll Deli.

I took the subway, up to Columbia, 116th Street and Broadway, the way I'd gotten there every day for four years, more than forty years before. I wouldn't be very long. I just wanted to visit the building in which I'd sat in classes on my way to graduating Magna Cum Laude, Phi Beta Kappa.

As soon as I was on College Walk, which effectively ran the length of the campus, I realized, from the paucity of activity, that classes must still be out for Christmas break. So I wasn't surprised when I entered Havemeyer Hall, in whose first floor amphitheater, a very callow freshman had taken General Chemistry, from Larkin Farinholt, (Olympic lacrosse player, as well as Columbia professor, who'd worked on the Manhattan Project, instrumental in producing the Atomic Bomb during World War II,) using the classic text book by the great Linus Pauling, who'd won two Nobel Prizes, Peace, as well as Chemistry, that the building was essentially dark. Only minimally lit.

I opened the door of the large first floor amphiteater, with ascending terraces of hard wooden seats, a small surface for taking notes extending from the right arms, where on many mornings so long ago I watched Professor Farinholt run experiments which proved the words he spoke about the composition and structure of matter. I was content to just stand there peeking in through the shroud of dimness. This was what I'd come for.

Just at that moment a woman wearing a Columbia light blue maintenance uniform suddenly emerged from out of the room 's darkness. A puzzled look crossed her face when she noticed me. But, then, with a knowing smile she said, "I put on light for you." I shook my head vigorously and negatively, mumbling that I'd gone to Columbia many years before and just wanted to take a quick look. But she was much more adamant in her insistence. "No, no, I put on light for you." And so she did.

And, thus, in that illuminating flash, produced by a new immigrant to these shores, specifically to New York, working hard to become part of a new America, many things came together. A great city, a great university, in whose history anti—semitism was not unknown, and the son of a Jewish immigrant from old Russia, who, like that father, had connected with that patrician American, New York born Theodore Rooevelt, and who, in that time present, relived much time past made possible by that magnificent lady, that new colussus, yet bestriding New York Harbor.

It wasn't until I was on the plane, heading back, that I remembered that my dad, Max, until he could no longer get up on his own, would invariably and unfalteringly stand, hand over heart, whenever he would hear the strains, however distant or muted, of "The Star Spangled Banner." I also realized, then, that he would have been deeply ashamed of my cousin and what she had said. Yet, perhaps, he would have understood. After all, it's a diverse melting pot.

ROMAN HOLIDAY; OR, HOW I BECAME A SOCIALIST

WHAT DID WE CARE THAT Al Italia had lost one of our two bags. Hadn't we been told to anticipate such inefficiency from the Italians. And, in any event, after a few hours of traipsing from airport office to airport office, occasionally identifying and justifying ourselves to the soldiers hefting sub—machine guns, we'd been assured by an airline official, who seemed to exercise *some* authority, that the suitcase would be delivered no later than sometime the next day. He did, however, raise an eyebrow at the address of our hotel.

But, most of all, we were a la Roma!! Married only three weeks and with two months of leisure travel ahead of us, before we had to begin our jobs, the first real ones either of us had ever had. I'd be practicing with a medium—sized, but nonetheless appropriate for a Columbia Law School grad, Manhattan firm and the gorgeous Maria, yet angelic looking as a nun, with her long, indelibly black hair, would do her first teaching with sixth graders at a posh private school on the borough's upper East side.

The first time in Europe for either of us. We started in Rome because Maria had dreamed of going there for the past thirteen years. Ever since, at nine, she'd seen on television, on a rainy Saturday afternoon in Connecticut, that wonderful tear—jerker, set in the Eternal City, "Three Coins in The Fountain," starring Clifton Webb, the beautiful Dorothy McGuire and the irresistible Rosanno Brazzi. The hotel, undeniably a bit run down, rugs fraying, paint beginning to peel, was still tolerable to two children of the upper middle—class . We were surely accustomed to comfort and pleasant amenities but we didn't require, or obsess on, luxury. Anyway, when you're fresh off the altar, entirely in love and can hardly wait for your body to demand the next session of protracted sexual activity it doesn't really matter what there is in a hotel room, or any room, besides the bed.

But since we hadn't slept at all the previous night, so excited were we as we flew across the Atlantic, we were actually intent on getting some sleep as soon as we'd been shown to our room. We didn't bother unpacking anything, at all not a stitch, from the bag that had not been lost. And we did get right into the cavernous bed. But we didn't rest until quite a bit later. It was glorious, loving sex, brimming with every yes of life. We enjoyed each other breathtakingly. We breathed *very* hard.

We awoke, several hours later, just before 8:00 P.M . Perfect timing for a truly continental dinner. Walking only a few blocks, we passed two or three small, very inviting looking restaurants. All seemed very active, most tables taken. But no actual waiting in any of them. We savored the keenness of our hunger growing, as we debated and anticipated their prospective and respective delights. The one we fnally decided on had tables on a rear outdoor terrace and we there gorged on an enormous, yet delicately delicious, meal. Although neither of us, usually, ever had more than an occasional half glass of white wine we shared a half—liter of rich burgundy, with our succulent veal. To ever more mood heightening effect.

After settling what seemed like a ridiculously low bill we strolled a bit further and, inevitably, found ourselves at the Fountain of Trevi. As we watched a great many more than three coins being tossed into that unavoidable tourist bastion, which, nevertheless, created a certain serenity, we licked away at some exceedingly creamy gelatos acquired on the way over. Vanilla for me, pistachio for the stunning Maria. Sheer bliss!

By the time we got back to our hotel, which in darkness looked a little better than its verging on seediness daytime appearance, it was nearly midnight. The somnolently benign, late middle—aged desk clerk waved us down to advise that Al Italia had delivered the wayward suitcase and that it had been put in our room.

So it had. Although we both confessed to overwhelming fatigue, the type that insisted on immediate sleep, once in bed the even more compelling urgencies of newlyweds again drove us to passion—with some new variations, even. (Although we were exhausting the possibilities.)

The hotel threw in a complimentary continental breakfast. Coffe or hot chocolate with a very small, very hard roll. The sixtyish man who brought it was dour at best. Irretrievably glum was more like it. Each of us beamed at him opulently, but we couldn't induce any break in his ponderous, relentless grimness. Even when I gave him a robust tip for his limited, not even a hint of a smile, service he would not acknowledge it. Neither with a nod, a "prego," or, god forbid, a "Grazie." The slightest crinkle of a perfunctory smile was beyond possibility. On each of the four mornings we were there this little vignette was repeated. Virtually movement for movement, step for step, gesture for gesture. He never uttered a single word, he never changed his expression.

But our irrepressible buoyancy couldn't be punctured by such minor unpleasantness. The destination of our first walking tour was the Colliseum and even Maria, who tended towards the somewhat reserved, elegantly beautiful type, effervesced with a school girl tourist's excited anticipation. I enjoyed it, things in general and, especially, Maria's shining face. "She lights up the room," people always said.

But I was hoarding my super enthusiasm, could it becalled incorrigible joie de vivre, for London. I'd always craved visitng there. The British Museum, The National Gallery, The Inns of Court, Westminister Abbey, The Thames, London Bridge, the Houses of Parliament....That was cultural achievement, cooly brilliant intellect, institutions of justice—and mercy. The very heights of civilization—with the emphasis on the civil.

On the day we walked up the Via Veneto, on our way to Villa Borghese, Maria's very white teeth drawing streams of juice—which she had to keep on side—stepping—from one of those huge, luscious Italian peaches, so roundly mocking of the brought—to market—before—ripened produce of New York supermarkets, we were disappointed that the world famous street was not teeming with sophisticates of every race, nationality and sexual preference. We finally concluded that late July—early August was not the apex of that area's grandeur. But we so thoroughly enjoyed the Villa Borghese itself—we confidently concluded that it was the most handsomely land—scaped, the most majestic, surely the absolutely most beautiful park we'd ever seen, that, in fact, there could ever be---we promised ourselves that we'd be sure to return to it on our last day in Roma, as we'd started constantly calling the city.

And we did, entering it, this time, by way of the Spanish Steps, after a cup in Babbington's English style tea room at the left after looking at the house, at the right, in which, the guidebook alerted, Keats had died in 1821. The paths bordered by the stately , towering pine sentinels were exalting to walk. Idyllic lanes perfectly carved by acute instruments of the mind. The ear seemed to hear Respighi's sweeping melodies in "The Pines of Rome." The exquisite gardens had been five years in the planning, early in the nineteenth century, and graceful fountains complemented them with cellophane effects.

Since it was a profusely sun—lit Sunday afternoon, yet exhaling a tentative Fall coolness,quite a few Roman families were also enjoying this brilliantly inviting park. At the Lake Garden pre teen—age boys cheerfully raced and wrestled with each other, adolescent girls pouted over just about anything that irritated them and early middle—aged parents seemed reasonably content with each other and life in general. We sat on a bench and enjoyed observing those enjoying. Occasionally we'd punctuate the languidness with a discussion of whether when two women were with one man they were wife and sister or wife and mistress. It was, after all, Italy.

We finished the Villa Borghese expedition by leisurely walking to the other end of the park and then contentedly amblin g through the Casina Borghese, gazing at the incredible documents of Western art, including Bernini's "Rape of Prosperine" and Titian's "Sacred and Profan e," hanging from its walls. Simply staggering.

By the time we became glazed to such splendors, it had been hours and hours since the never smiling little man had delivered "breakfast" and the tea at Babbington's had not inhibited a ferocious hunger from cresting. The first time we'd been at the Villa Borghese on the walk back we'd noticed some small, very appealing looking restaurants and said that we should remember them. We did and went in search.

After roaming two or three blocks we thought we'd spotted one, about another block down, on the other side of the street. It was almost on the corner of the block and holding hands we ran across the street, zig—zagging to safety from Rome's incorrigibly endangering drivers. As we came up to the restaurant there came around that same corner a family of four who also seemed to be aiming for this cozy trattoria.

They were instantaneously recognizable as compatriots from their dress—the best that J.C. Penney's, Lincoln, Nebraska, had to offer. But the children, a rangy yellow-haired boy, just short of adolescence, and a very slender girl, a few years younger, with even yellower hair, weren't acting (out,) in the totally unrestrained, near boisterous manner of most of the other American tourist kids we'd run into. Actually, they were markedly different. Their gait was pretty deliberate, more or less side by side, the boy just slightly aheah, each with head and eyes down. The effect was as though straining at an invisible yoke. The father seemed in his late thirties, medium height and build, nondescript sandy brown hair. His wife was wearing an umbrella type skirt, "sensible" shoes and a pale,orange sleeveless summery blouse. You knew she was about the same age, even though her version of nondescript sandy brown hair had been overwhelmed by patches of gray.

He was helping her to walk. Even so, she gripped a cane in each hand to help drag along legs, encased in gleaming steel braces running their entire length, which, literally, were as thin as broomsticks. Her arms, although without braces, were more or less the same and her husband walking, as a gentleman should, between her and the curb, could only barely touch her at her left elbow, rather than firmly hold her.

Once we'd become aware of them we'd decelerated our pace to the appealing trattoria. However, since we'd raced across the street, by the time we'd slowed to a stroll we weren't more than thirty or forty feet from this family as they came up to the restaurant's entrance. The kids' eyes flickered up, although their heads remained bowed, and both parents, through their colorless framed glasses, hers cartoonishly thick, observed the audaciously beautiful Maria and me. Their eyes registered that we, too, must be Americans , also some expectation, but, mostly, a much practiced amalgam of curiosity and resignation. They continued looking at us, smiling slightly as the man opened the door. But Maria gave the slightest tug at my hand, to which I was only too ready to respond, and we walked past it instead of following them inside.

We looked at each other, shaking our heads sympathetically, making sad, regretful sounds. But neither of us said anything until we'd walked another block and came upon one of the other restaurants we'd had in mind. Almost in unison we each said it looked good and asked "should we try it?" We did, but ordered only some pasta fagioli soup and a green salad apiece. This evoked the rather sharp consternation of our waiter and the proprietor, too. Exchanging broad winks, they intimated, in their fractured yet unmistakably comprehensible English, how a young, obviously just married couple had to "eat heartily to keepa da strent up." And, in any event, where were our appetites?—hadn't we done our share of walking around bella Roma?

Back at the hotel, when we got out of the elevator, before we turned left to head for our room, we noticed, at the other end of the corridor, that someone was mopping the floor. His expression was readily recognizable. It was the same man who had brought us our continental breakfast every morning. We remarked about how this was the first time we'd seen him anywhere else, and at any other time , but our room in the morning.

I urinated and immediately got into bed. For some reason Maria stayed in the bathroom for what seemed a very long time. When she finally came out I was already dropping off. Our last night in Rome was the first on which we didn't make love. I dreamt a hazy travelogue of England: the Buckingham Palace guards in their scarlet jackets and enormously high black cloth helmets, crown jewels in the Tower of London, Henry VIII's lavish palace at Hampton Court… I awoke abruptly, just as the hunchbacked Richard II was about to slay his nephews, and Maria and I held each other for a few seconds before starting to frantically rush to catch our plane.

The customs agent at Heathrow conferred our initial encounter with British grace and civility. He'd asked whether our visit to England was for business or pleasure. When I answered "pleasure," he, off—handedly, commented "I believe it can be arranged."

Soon after I told Maria that the first tourist thing I wanted to do in London was to go to the British Museum. I must have said this insistently, almost peremptorily, because she, somewhat rebukingly, asked why. Especially, she added, since the plan we'd intensively worked out, even before leaving New York, didn't have us going there until our third or fourth day, in the great city-- as Engels had referred to it. First, she said there was the palace, then the National Gallery at Trafalgar Square, then the Victoria and Albert Museum….

'Because," I answered, with a tinge of edginess of my own, "I want to see the chair in the British Museum Reading Room, I think they have it roped off, that Marx sat in when he wrote, 'Until now philosophers have sought to interpret the world; the point, however, is to change it.' That's why.

And that's how.

NEIGHBORS

The six storey apartment house was on a busy block. But we were only on the second floor, a one bedroom apartment which, however, looked right out over the front of the building onto an avenue which surprised urbanites with its width and the many leafy trees lining it. The neighbors in the apartment on one side were the Catholic Kellys, those on the other the Kayes, Jews like mom, dad and myself.

The Kellys were mom, pop, who liked to drink, but who did work regularly, Mrs. Farrell, who was Mrs. Kelly's mother, and two daughters, Lois, still a teen—ager and Marilyn already in her twenties and working. Lois was the beautiful blonde next door, every early adolescent boy's dream, and we pre—adolescent boys loved her dearly. However, we disguised our passion by feigning the opposite. Any time she happened to appear, when we were congregated en masse, whether she was coming or going, we taunted her as our dim lights allowed and shouted after her whatever then passed with us as clever invective . We'd also chase her as she went into the house and ran up the one flight of stairs, her loafers and bobby sox flying, to the second floor. But we made sure we never caught her. For what would we have done if we had? Marilyn was out of our ambit and, although a brunette, was also, I came to realize somewhat later, quite beautiful even if to us, then, less instantly attractive than her sister. As I ultimately perceived, probably mostly in retrospect, she shone with decency. Or, as the Yiddish expression went, "The goodness lay obviously upon her face."

The Kayes consisted of a married couple and their only son, a young adult man already teaching English Literature at the university level. Also living in that apartment was Mrs. Kaye's brother, Jacob, a retired older man with vision problems and her sister, Frances, who, judging from the prim suits she usually wore, had a white collar job. She must have been a secretary.

Who knows why the Catholics took a much greater interest in us than the Jews , but they did. They would always invite us to their annual Christmas party. My mother and father wouldn't go but they sent me. I was sure to be led to some punch and fed some cookies before I was released to return to our apartment next door. I don't know exactly why mom and dad never went, whether it was because Christmas was not really to be recognized by Jews, or because they would have felt "out of place" amongst all the non—Jews, but year after year they didn't go although I was prompted, at the appropriate time, to knock on the Kellys' door.

The Kayes' son was rather aloof and hardly acknowledged any of us. He once was throwing what seemed to be a cocktail party, doubtless for colleagues in his department and other academic types, and he knocked on our door to ask, rather frantically, whether he might borrow ice cubes. He must have run out while energetically mixing drinks.. That was about the extent of our "contact" with him. Mrs. Kaye was genial and always had a smile for me but Mr. Kaye was rather dour carrying his inevitable rolled newspaper home from work, hat brim low on his forehead, blue serge overcoat perhaps a bit too roomy, looking beset by problems and concerns. He would speak to me only very occasionally, usually asking whether Brooklyn's beloved Dodgers, of whom I was a rabid fan, had won that day. His general affect was far from upbeat. Sometimes four of them, all except Jacob, were on a joint vacation and he would ask me to write a letter, which he dictated, because he could not see well enough to do it himself. Other times he would ask me to help him cross an adjoining avenue to get him started on a short trip to the grocery store.

When I still needed to be "baby—sat" I, sometimes, would be left at the Kellys when no one besides Mrs. Farrell was home. One way or another it was always pleasant to be with her, although I certainly do not remember much about how the time went. However, on one of these occasions she taught me "borrowing" so that I could start to become able to subtract two and three digit numbers from each other. Other times we "talked." I experienced her as "old," but not as impaired, as I did Mrs. Kaye's brother Jacob. Once when I was in their apartment the radio carried an advertisement for a new movie which had caused a lot of controversy because of its risqué nature for those times. I think it's title was "Forever Amber." What might, today, be called a bodice ripper. I must have asked Mrs. Kelly whether their family had seen this movie. Maybe I was hoping to get a few more "sexy" details about it than just that it had gained so much notoriety. Byt Mrs. Kelly very sweetly told me that their priest had advised good Catholics not to see it. I nodded acceptance and thought that this confirmed just how audacious it must be.

There came a time when I heard my mother and father speaking about Mrs. Kaye being sick. She was gone from their apartment for a while. Mr. Kaye looked more troubled than usual the times I passed him. I don't think he asked me about the Dodgers when she was away. She came home and pretty much looked her old self. She still greeted me with what seemed a special smile and emphatic cheerfulness.

When I was about eight, I was throwing a pink rubber ball, a "spaldeen" as we called it, because stamped on it was the name of the manufacturer, "A.G. Spalding Company," against a wall in the courtyard of the apartment house. I lunged to try to catch a rebound and fell headlong to the pavement. I abraded my knee badly enough so that considerable skin came off and blood was trickling out. It hurt fiercely, or so my pre—adolescent self deemed the sensation. The combination of the pain and my feeling of humiliation at winding up sprawled face down led to tears. When I was sitting up, but still on the pavement, right arm over my weeping eyes, body heaving, I suddenly felt someone over me, an arm around my shoulders, a face close to mine. I dropped my arm from my face. It was the beauteous Lois. She was kneeling beside me, I could see the loafers, and asked if I was all right. I manged to sniffle an embarrassed yes. With an angelic smile she produced a tissue and gently wiped my nose while she patted my shoulder. She was so pretty, her eyes so kind, her voice so gentle. As I stopped crying and tried to regain my dignity, even while still on the pavement, she rose and asked again if I would be o.k. When I, still sniffling a bit, nodded vigorously a few times, she smiled and continued on her way into the house and up the one flight of stairs. From that point on when I was with my friends and Lois came by I still feigned that I had the same enthusiasm as they did in taunting her and chasing her up the stairs but my heart was no longer in even the phony derision.

Mr. and Mrs. Kaye's son had black horn—rimmed glasses. He was usually dressed in a suit, or, at least a sports jacket and tie and often carried a black brief case. Not a bulging one, but rather a compact one on the neat, flat side. It didn't seem to be holding more than some papers and, perhaps, a slim volume or two. He had a purposeful mien and pretty much looked straight ahead, hardly acknowledging that he was passing another human being, certainly not one as insignificant as myself. As I grew older he would sometimes offer the barest, virtually imperceptible nod at me. It appeared that the older I got the more forthright the nods became. But I don't think that we ever exchanged any words.

As I got older my friends and I also heard, through our parents' conversations I guess, that Lois was going to become a nun. We didn't know exactly what that meant, but we knew that they were different and dressed in those long black gowns and had that stiff white material around their faces We couldn't imagine Lois without her flowing skirts and flying loafers. But not too long after getting this information we started seeing Lois sometimes come home in the company of a young man about her own age. Through our usual various sources we found out that he was the Captain of the football team at Brooklyn Prep, a Catholic high school located just a few blocks away. Lois started coming into and leaving the apartment house more and more with this young man. He would sometimes smile and wave at us. But even when she wasn't with him we stopped taunting and chasing her when she passed. We just didn't say anything and tended to look away as she went by with just a tinge of a beatific smile.

When I was still in the pre-adolescent eight—nine year old range, I was throwing the spaldeen against a low wall which served as one border of a modest sized lawn at the front of the apartment building. Four steps led up to a rather wide walkway which twenty or thirty yards later led into the entrance of the building. There was a lawn area on each side of part of the walkway and I was throwing my ball against the low wall on one side of where the walkway began. The sidewalk was between this wall and the street on which many cars passed and many were parked on both sides. I stood on the curb and hurled the spaldeen, as hard as I could, against the low wall and sought to field it as cleanly as possible before I threw it, as forcefully as possible, against the wall again. On one fielding effort I bobbled the ball, as even a Major Leaguer might from time to time, and the ball went dribbling into the street and out of sight. This was not unusual. When an errant ball did this, for example in a game of punch ball or slapball , often played on the sidewalk in front of the house, the spaldeen was almost always found, by one or another of we kids scavenging, on hands and knees, lodged behind a tire of one of the parked vehicles. It was just a matter of searching diligently enough until the ball's whereabouts were revealed. I immediately employed this methodology under those cars which seemed most likely to be concealing the ball.But to no avail. I looked further down the block, under less likely cars, but with the same result. I checked and re—checked but could espy no ball. I was becoming exasperated but still I checked my work. Nothing.

My exasperation turned into considerable frustration verging on bitter tears. Perhaps I was a "cry—baby," although I never really thought of myself as such. I certainly hesitated before bawling in front of my mom as it generally seemed not to make a very great impression on her. But now I could think of no more to do. I ran up the stairs to the walkway, continued running into the building and then up to the second floor and burst into our apartment in great consternation. I didn't even bother slamming the door shut before beginning my irascible fulminating to my mother about how my constant companion, my spaldeen, was gone.

Responding to this outburst she started uttering some mildly consoling sounds, but the next thing I heard was a voice from the doorway.

"Do I hear someone crying in here"? It was Mr. Kelly from next door. He must have been going out of his apartment and had heard the commotion I was generating.

I tried to stifle the most demonstrative signs of my blubbering but some whimpering continued to leak.

"Why yes," said Mr. Kelly, "It seems that this young man is upset. Maybe you could tell me what the problem is."

"I guess so," I muttered, virtually inaudibly and then tried to explain rapidly, as articulately as possible, how the ball had rolled into the street only to disappear, apparently forever.

"Well, I see. It sounds like you thoroughly checked under all the cars where it might be on this block, so I guess it must have rolled along somewhere else. Balls do that some times. "

Then he held out his hand for me to take and said, " Why don't we go back downstairs and look in other places and see if we can find it."

Hardly aware of what I was doing I gave him my hand and we walked that way to the staircase and then down and out of the building into the street.

"Why don't we walk down toward the end of the block, to the avenue over there. I think the ball might have rolled there. "

I don't think so," I objected. "I looked almost all the way down there."

"Oh I'm sure. But sometimes balls act strangely. Why don't we just try it."

"O.K.... but I don't think so."

He gave my hand a little tug and we proceeded. When we arrived at the avenue, the one I sometimes helped Jacob across, I said to Mr. Kelly, "See the ball's not here either. I just don't know what happened to it. I looked hard every place it could be."

" Oh, I'd warrant you did" he said sympathetically. "But let's cross the avenue and look down the next block. It's a bit hilly there and it could have rolled down that block."

At this point I just shrugged my shoulders and shuffled along beside him. We started walking down the next block and I was surprised because Mr. Kelly kept holding my hand and didn't even suggest that I should look under the cars parked on that block to see if the ball was behind a wheel of one of those. He just kept us striding leisurely along. I didn't understand what he was doing but I just kept holding his hand and walking along with him. When we were about half way down the block he said, "You know, because this block is hilly the ball could have rolled all the way down it to Nostrand avenue. Let's look there to see if we can find it."

To myself I thought that Mr. Kelly was being really unreasonable, almost nuts, in not facing that the ball had just disappeared, to wherever it might have rolled, or been dragged by a passing car, and that we were simply not going to find it. But he was an adult and I couldn't tell him that, so I just kept on going as he wanted.

When we got to the next avenue block, before I could take even so much as a glance for the ball, he guided me to turn right saying, "I have a feeling that it rolled off this way." By now I was truly completely mystified and had no idea why he was still acting like we would find the ball and even less of a glimmer why he kept on following a route which he seemed determined to pursue. A few more steps and we were at the entrance to a popular sporting goods and athletic shop that fronted on Nostrand. I'd gotten my baseball mitt there.

"I have a strong feeling that the ball rolled in here" Mr. Kelly said in his calm and soothing voice.

" I don't think so" I started saying. But I could hardly finish doubting him by the time he had already asked the salesman for a Spaldeen. I stood dumbfounded as he completed the purchase.

I went away to law school and my dad died, but my mother remained in the apartment. But when I got married the year after graduating from law school she moved to another one bedroom apartment about a mile away. Mr. Kaye and his son and Mrs. Kaye's siblings had moved away earlier, not long after Mrs. Kaye died. No one said good—bye. I no longer remember if the Kellys were still there when my mother left. I seem to recall something about Lois getting married. The football captain. Everyone in the building approved. Especially since most of them were not Catholics. The nunnery had not been a popular choice. Hopefully she had many attractive children whom she and Mr. Football guided to be as sparkling, as magical as she was.

Many years later,when I was the father of two children, ten and seven, we were on a family vacation in Italy and found ourselves in a railway station waiting room in Florence. All the way on the other side, of the very spacious, high ceilinged room, I saw the no—longer so young Professor Kaye and Mrs. Kaye's sister, his maiden aunt. They, just the two of them, now, also seemed to be on holiday in Italy. I thought about going over and introducing, it would hardly have been re—introducing, myself, but it would then have entailed multiple introductions. And we were all tired.

That was the last time I ever saw any of the neighbors. Not too many years after that Italian encounter, or lack of encounter, I came across the obituary of Professor Kaye. It was a brief one in "The New York Times" but said he was an expert in Victorian literature and had published a well thought of study of Anthony Trollope. It also said his only survivor was his aunt. He was only 52. Looking back, he must have died of AIDS. I wondered how the aunt would manage.

OUR TEACHER

We were newly pubescent, most of us, and newly arrived at junior high school, grades seven through nine. But we were in the "SP" class,(Special Progress, minimum IQ 130,) and would complete the three years of work in only two years and go in to high school as sophomores.

It was our first experience with changing classrooms, throughout the day, period to period, subject to subject. Also our first brush with a foreign language. French for us in SP 1 and Spanish in SP 2, the only other SP section amongst the fourteen seventh grade classes. Our teacher was Mister, Monsieur he said right off, Fellner. He was tallish, without being "tall," but mostly a bit burly and bear like. As in teddy bear. A fringe of reddish brown hair, sentinel to a bald pate, and with thick, full reddish eyebrows under which his horn-rimmed glasses balanced on an ample, one might say a French, nose.

Most of us had great trepidation of what we would run into en francais, but he started speaking "French" almost instantly. He pointed to familiar items: window was fenetre, door was porte, book was livre, pen, stylo.. Then he would point to the same objects again and encouragingly wave his hand urging us to enunciate the appropriate French word he'd told us.. It was easy for such bright lights and even after just the first class we were highly satisfied with our command if a foreign language.

We did that sort of thing for a few class periods but eventually we got to the text book. Here,of course, there were the usual verbs, grammar and endless exercises. And Mr. Fellner proceeded very slowly. Not because he stayed with any unit or exercise for a particularly long or excessive time but, rather, because almost any topic we worked on set him off on some digression or another. Some very far flung. He loved etymology and was always pointing out relationships between words encountered in the formal lesson and other ones—no part of present pedagogical purpose, but associated in this, that or another way with the regular syllabus work.

One day this proclivity played into the nefarious purposes of some of the less scrupulous class members. Mr. Fellner had given us notice, a few days before, that we were to have a test during this class period. Most of us had prepared for it with the diligence that had made us excellent students all through our brief academic careers. Stephen Shumkin had prepared too—more or less. But he still didn't want a test. Un examen. Or, at the very least, he wanted to see if he could forestall it to another day. It wasn't that he feared the test as such, but he was a boy who exuded a mischievious tinge of humor and enjoyed being a smart—aleck, a wise guy, a kibbitzer, at least some of the time. I don't know how many of our classmates Stephen had taken in to the confidence of his ruse, but once we were in our seats at the beginning of the period and Mr. Fellner had started telling us the ground rules of the exam, Stephen's hand suddenly shot up. Our teacher, always extremely sensitive to student questions, recognized him immediately, suspending his instructions about the test.

"Mr. Fellner, the other day I was just looking through something written in French. It might have been in the book, past where we are in class, but I don't really remember. It could have been in a French newspaper or something which I just picked up. Anyway, I came across the verb "triner." We haven't studied it in class yet and I was just wondering what it meant. I couldn't find it in the dictionary in the back of our text book."

"Well, that's very good Stephen. Either looking ahead or trying to read a French newspaper. Un journal. You say the word was 'triner' Stephen?"

"Yes, Mr. Fellner, I'm pretty positive it was 'triner." It was an infinitive; I'm sure of that."

"Well, Stephen, I can't say that I recognize that particular verb off—hand, but let's see if we can figure it out by looking for associations, cognates and the like, as far as words which I do know."

"Oh, that would be great because I'm really interested in what it could possibly mean. I just couldn"t get any idea or anything from the context."

'Yes, of course, I can stand to learn too. Curiosity is the mother of acquired knowledge."

"Just the way I feel sir."

Our teacher then began writing on the blackboard. He intently scribbled French words, somewhat close in spelling to "triner," with the

English translations next to them. He associated this word with that and related that word to another thing, but he still couldn't seem to come close to penetrating to the meaning of "triner." But every time he flagged and seemed near to resignedly yielding to his "ignorance," Stpehen would ask another leading question which would inspire Fellner to resume the quest. Once more, twice, a third try. By the time he fully petered out and surrendered, saying he would have to consult his unabridged LaRousse Dictionary at home, more than half the period had expired and he wearily acknowledged that it was no longer possible to administer the test he'd constructed.

It was only after the period bell had rung and all of us were on the way to our next class that Stephen revealed, to any and all of us willing to listen, that he'd simply concocted the verb "triner" and that, certainly as far as he knew, it was a complete fabrication which corresponded to no known French word. But he was bursting with pride that he'd saved us from a test that day.

The test got administered the next day but Mr. Fellner made no mention of researching "triner" in his La Rousse. Nor did anyone else say anything about it. I always thought that Mr. Fellner had figured out that Stephen had pulled a complete ruse on him but was never going to recriminate with, or embarrass, Stephen by revealing it to the class. Nor, I suppose, humiliate himself.

When Mr. Fellner did give exams he was very casual about monitoring them. There was a certain amount of students looking at each others papers that tended to go on. Perhaps it was especially prone to occur in our SP class because we were gifted students, all used to getting very good grades. When someone was having trouble with a test he or she could get very frustrated. So there was an effort to alleviate frustration and achieve the usual reward. But Mr. Fellner did not assiduously try to prevent a student's eyes from wandering. Sometimes he would say before a test, "Cheating contaminates your own honor; it's your honor at stake." And if, during the exam, he did, more or less by chance, happen to spot one of us trying to take a peek at another student's paper, he might intone, from the back or side of the room, as he ambled about, "Your honor, monsieur, your honor," or," It's your honor madamoiselle, your own honor."

These admonitions did seem to cast a considerable pall of deterrent guilt on many of us. The cheating that went on in French seemed less than in the other subjects. But not all students were chilled. The Stephen Shumkins of the class had a field day.About the only time they would curtail their eyes from wandering and meandering was when Mr. Fellner happened to be looking directly at them. Something he didn't do very often.

Mr. Fellner wasn't just one of our teachers. He and his family were part of our neighborhood. An extended neighborhood. Three of his children went to our school. In fact, two twin daughters were our SP 1 classmates. It must have been difficult for them. Did they hear uncomplimentary remarks from the likes of Stephen Shumkin about their dad and his teaching style? Did they think he was being foolish in trusting mostly to our honor when too many of us were willing to take advantage of such indulgence and cheat when necessary and possible? Did they think he was being naïve and gullible in tolerating without stricture or chastisement , from others too, the kind of cheap, denigrating stratagem Stephen had pioneered? Their older brother was already in the ninth grade, the final one in that school, and, like each twin, a talented musician. He was the first cellist in the school orchestra and had made the elite and very prestigious All New York City Schools Orchestra. We all knew him as the twins' big brother. They had a younger sister, too, but she wasn't even in elementary school yet.

The only way I found out about little sister was, when playing one of our ubiquitous games of stickball with my pals, just outside the apartment buildings in which we boys lived with our families, I saw Mr. Fellner leading the twins and the little girl home from the borough's main and formidably extensive library, about five blocks away. It was pretty clear that they'd been there because each of them was carrying five or six books, even the little girl as she more or less toddled along. I was still very shy and diffident and became pretty embarrassed at their seeing me in an informal boys- will- be- boys setting instead of the familiar school one. So I pretended I was so absorbed in the game that I didn't even notice them. I'm sure that the Fellners saw me too, but they didn't let on either. Perhaps they valued privacy, whenever possible.

I have a faint image of Mrs. Fellner too. I must have seen her sometime, somewhere, but just don't recall the occasion. While the details are not clear, I remember her as what used to be called heavyset. Today obese might be the term used..

Another time I saw Mr. Fellner, just in passing, in the street, I was walking home from a Hebrew school class. It was late on a radiant autumn afternoon, rich sunlight still sneaking through amply leaved trees. My companion was another twelve year old boy who also went to that school and to the same elementary school I'd attended before I started junior high school. We still played basketball in the elementary schoo yard sometimes. We were headed up the street in one direction and Mr. Fellner was coming down in the opposite one. He must have been coming to pick up the twins who also had after school classes in that Hebrew school. As we passed, Mr. Fellner and I nodded and briefly smiled to each other. He seemed to still value privacy.

As we walked on my acquaintance asked me who it was that I had just greeted. I told him and he waited until the distance between Mr. Fellner and ourselves had lengthened to at least a half block. Then he turned around to Fellner's direction and shouted, as loudly as possible, "Hey, I hear you're a terrible French teacher."

I'm not sure that Mr. Fellner could actually make out what this boor screamed. I fervently hoped he couldn't. But he might have. He didn"t turn or give even any sight indication that he'd heard what, or that anything, had been shouted.Nor in our subsequent encounters, o fwhatever sort, did he ever let on that he had, or had not, heard anythingYet I continue to wonder whether he had, in fact, heard and believed that I'd been complicit in, even the instigator of, that callow, insolent act. When I think he did I still cringe.

About a year after SP 1 graduated from junior highl some of us had a little "re—union" in a neighborhood Chinese restaurant. Marcy, one of the Fellner twins was there, but not Gloria, the other.. Maybe it was just the additional year of puberty, or some other maturation process, but I reacted to her in a way I hadn't when she was my classmate. She didn't register as full—fledged pretty exactly, yet not bad looking at all, and mostly warm, kindly and outgoing. She was friendly to everyone and definitely made me feel that I wanted to be around her more. But nothing came of my impulses. Those kind of urges stayed secret and bottled up for quite some time.

At the time of this mini—reunion Mr. Fellner was still alive. But not for long after. We heard, probably through neighborhood scuttlebutt, that he had suddenly dropped dead in the street. It seemed, most ironically, that he'd had a bad heart.

Fifty years after graduating from junior high we got quite a few of the SP 1 class together for a real re—union. But one of those we couldn't locate was Stephen Shumkin. The same Fellner twin who had come to the first, ersatz, reunion, a half—century before, came again. But not the other. Marcy had become a top flight cellist and taught at a prestigious conservatory. Still pleasant looking, very open face, but she had never married. Just about all of the rest of us there had been married for forty years, give or take. She was still warm and friendly but, apparently, not the marrying kind. Looking back I can see how her sister is probably of the same disposition.

Some things we realize only way after the fact. Perhaps many.

RELOCATION

"No hits by Bevins, eight and two-thirds innings," intoned the mellifluous, still southern tinged voice of Brooklyn Dodger announncer,Red Barber,as, in the ninth inning of Game 4 of the 1947 Brooklyn Dodger---New York Yankees World Series, he broke one of the classical superstitions of baseball broadcasting: never mention that a pitcher was closing in on a no hitter. And surely not in a World Series game. (There had never been a World Series no-hitter.) However, even though Floyd "Bill" Bevins hadn't yielded any hits the Dodgers had a run because he had been wild and had walked nine hitters, including the four in one inning necessary to produce a Brooklyn score. But the Yankees had two runs. But now Bevins had walked two Dodgers in the bottom of the ninth inning, so there were men on first and second as he faced Dodger pinch-hitter, Harry"Cookie" Lavagetto, who stood between him and a feat never before accomplished. Barber's next words validated superstition's dominion: "Lavagetto swings… there's a drive heading out toward right field… Henrich goes back….He can't get it…Here comes the tying run…. And here comes the WINNING run!!."

Brad Lesser had become eight years old only a few days before the day he came in from school just in time to hear Barber's call of the incredible ending to Bevins's almost, but not quite, unique achievement. 1947 had been his first year of really following Major League baseball and, in particular, the beloved team of his home borough, the Dodgers. An uncle, his mom's childless brother, had taken him to his first Major League game and alerted him to the presence of Dodger rookie, the color barrier breakingJackie Robinson, and the enormous lead he would take off first base when he singled or walked.. The Dodgers had another imperishable moment in the sixth game of the '47 Series when a reserve outfielder, the five foot five inch tall Al Gionfriddo, made an immortal catch off a Joe Dimaggio blast, (Red Barber broadcast it as, "Gionfriddo goes back, back, back, back....back.... and makes a one-hand catch at the bullpen.... Oh, Doctor!!) to save victory for the Dodgers and force the Series to a deciding seventh game. The Dodgers led early in that game, the next day, but lost in the end, breaking Brad's heart. His first heartbreak.

In 1949 it only took the Dodgers five games to lose to the Yankees in the World Series. They lost the first game only 1-0, on a ninth inning homer by the same Tommy Henrich who, despite his nick-name of Ol' Reliable, couldn't catch Lavagetto's drive and save Bevins's no-hitter in '47 and then won the next game 1-0 on a brilliant pitching performance by Preacher Roe. Hope sprang. It started eroding in game three and Brad was fully prepared for the inevitable defeat when game 5 concluded the Series in another Yankee triumph.

Red Barber's voice became somewhat of a mentoring experience for Brad. Walter Lanier Barber was a lay preacher in the Episcopal church and and a serious person, just as he was thoroughly professional in his sports broadcasting. As a deeply-bred southerner he had first been appalled at the prospect of having to broadcast about an African-American, (Negro, then,) like Robinson and told his wife that he had determined to quit as Dodger announcer rather than do it.. She urged sleeping on it. He could quit just as well in the morning, she said. He slept, changed his mind and became one of the great boosters in makingNo. 42 every Brooklynite's favorite Dodger. Two of Brad's favorite Ol' Red Head observations: "Mr. Robinson leads the league in batting average, runs batted in, doubles and stolen bases; other than that he's not doing much." And, "The most exciting play in baseball is watching Jackie Robinson run out a triple." Brad never lost these. They stayed in his ear. Barber would occasionally recommend good books to read. Brad took them out of the library and read them. He learned. Barber, perhaps in accordance with his theological bent, was also a moralist. Brad also always recalled him saying, "When a ball-player is in a hot streak, doing superbly, it's easy for him to give you an interview. It's the slumping ball-player, having a hard time, who grants you an interview who shows character." When Brad first heard this apercu he hardly knew what character was. But the remark was the wedge to his eventual understanding of the concept. Ultimately, when complimented on how his broadcasting had eased Robinson's path to the hearts of Brooklyn's citizens, Barber responded, "Jackie Robinson did a lot more for me than I did for him."

However, shortly after the '49 Series Brad developed another interest—females. When he discovered them he discovered them all over. Pin-ups in tabloid newspapers, on the streets, in his classes, on billboards. Even in his building. There was a young, verging on middle-aged, mother in the apartment house in which Brad's family lived. One day he was gazing out the window and saw her, Anita F., coming up the four or five steps that led to the front door of the building. It was Fall, World Series time approximately, as a matter of fact, and she was wearing a very tight, bright orange jersey. He noted generous, luscious, bouncing breasts. She wasn't exactly conventionally pretty, yet her features intimated desirability. Brad realized, suddenly, that he desired her. Interestingly enough, her only child was a pre-adolescent daughter who was just developing breasts. Brad noticed that she started wearing a lot of sweaters and that a chest became discernible beneath them. The breasts were, of course, still a lot smaller than her mother's yet, they, nevertheless, deliciously curved, however slightly, the sweaters. Brad felt desire. He felt desire a lot, then, for a lot of women and girls. Of course Brad's own mother didn't know what was happening exactly when it was happening, perhaps somewhat early. So, during this very period, she was fond of saying to people to whom she was talking, while Brad was within earshot, "Brad hasn't discovered girls, yet." Most of the time Brad permitted the inaccuracy to go by uncorrected. But once or twice he adamantly said, "Yes, I have." This did not really stop his mother's flow of conversation. Nor did it stop her from making the same observation, subsequently.

Brad couldn't talk about such matters with mom, but he certainly could with friends about the same age. Especially Jason, Howie and Larry. In fact, it sometimes seemed like they talked about little else. How do you like that one? Some ass, huh? Look at that pair; they're like headlights. Great legs, but not too much else. Beautiful face, but she's a little flat on top. Very, very pretty, enough to make you not care about the rest. Enough all around and really nice looking and just nice, too.. And the girls in one's junior high school class were collectively rated by the guys. Or by most of them, anyway. There were intense debates over whether this one's tits rated "8" or "9" on the 1–10 scale employed, 10 being best, or whether that one's ass was a "7" or an "8." She certainly had a "9" face, but, unfortunately, not really more than a "6," "7," at the most, pair of jugs. Oh yes, a lot of time and cogitation went into these discussions, verging on debates, about feminine pulchritude. Lists were compiled—and constantly revised. Of course how any one innocent female rated didn't really make a difference in her prospects for a date. The boys were grand theoreticians, but feeble practitioners and actors. Pursuit was scant to nil. Whether these ingénues even sought pursuit was another question. And how did Brad and his friends know what seminars and ranking procedures, ("ranking," interestingly, also meant derogating,) the girls conducted. Perhaps the exact obverse was taking place in the male excluded precincts. In the innocuous end, Brad could only know, if not quite understand, his own horniness.

Soon these assessments and rankings became solitary. In high school, with the mix of constantly changing classes, subject by subject, period by every forty minute period, there wasn't suchconcerted male group think about a given cohort of females. Although, naturally, between and amongst friends, certain girls were often spoken of with, well, naked lust. As Brad's sexual desires intensified his proclivity to share these reactions with others, except if they were extremely close friends, like Howie and Larry, diminished. Especially since he didn't have any actual dating experiences, or just the merest, most perfunctory, few.

But in Brad's mind the desirable females seemed dichotomized into two categories: the sex pots who stimulated pure desire and the just "pure," "nice" girls types whom he wanted to talk to and kiss with feeling. But he always felt unworthy of this second type: the goddesses on pedestals. The first sort could be lustfully fantasized for masturbation. A lot of masturbation was necessary, as there was really no dating whatsoever that produced intimate physical contact. The few times that Brad did energize the nerve to ask out one of the goddesses he anticipated being rebuffed and if, totally unexpectedly, he was not he made sure that the date, itself, was completely chaste. And even if it went well otherwise, he would fear asking that goddess out a second time on the grounds that she couldn't possibly want to be on a date with him again. If a goddess showed interest in Brad, by, for example, striking up a conversation after class, he couldn't believe that she had any romantic, as opposed to intellectual, interest. If he dared hope at all, he sought confirmation of her extra-curricular interest by waiting for her to seek him out again. If she did, he remained dubious and tended to wait for yet one more approach. Almost always he wore out the initially interested goddess with such delaying tactics.

So it was mostly the intellect for Brad in high school. In lieu of anything approaching a real social life he discerned that a little studying would produce big returns on exams and on grades in general. A little more than a little studying, he soon understood, would produce truly excellent academic results. He became an academic star, with one of the highest G.P.A.s. in the school. Yet his triumph was silent. Not too many fellow students, even his bookish peers, seemed to know just how successful he was at the test-taking academic routine. He allowed himself to muse that a goddess or two might be aware. He was sure that the sex-bombs couldn't care less.

When college came, his academic stardom had gotten him to the Ivy league, studiousness was again primary. It didn't matter that the college he went to had a sister institution for women directly adjacent.Just once, in his four years there, rousing his courage to urgent pitch, he attended a "tea," a flagrant euphemism for a mixer, given by the sister institution. Once there, knees quaking, he spotted one of the most beautiful girls he'd ever seen. An absolutely radiant brunette. While most students, male and female, milled about, in groups of same-sex friends, scrupulously avoiding "mingling," she was sitting in an armchair reading a volume which he could, with modest neck-craning, barely see was entitled "Greek Poetry." He longed to talk to her. But in searching his mind, as well as his memory of past courses, for something, anything, about Greek poetry, he came up empty. He walked by her chair several times, but she kept her head down, presumably reading. No one else had approached her despite her great beauty. He didn't either. He left the room looking over his shoulder. Although he hoped he would, he never did see her again.But he always wondered whether she was really interested in Greek poetry or whether she was as truly shy as he was.

Brad went to neither the junior or senior prom of his college and had only a miniscule handful of dates of any sort. Once in a great while, some simpatico friend would "fix him up." A second date with the same young woman was a great rarity. It didn't seem a triumph. But he kept up, perhaps even enhanced, his academic stardom. A grade below "B+" was most unusual for Brad, whatever the course, even the required ones in Science and Math, as well as the Humanities themed ones. He made Phi Beta Kappa with plenty to spare. College, more specifically some professors Brad had found particularly cogent and impressive, had turned his vague Brooklyn liberal political leanings into a more solidly formulated penchant for Democratic Socialism. When he read, in Friedrich Engels's essay, "Socialism: Scientific and Utopian," that the transition from capitalism to Socialism represented "The ascent of man from the animal kingdom to the kingdom of humanity" it made him cry.

Graduate school in History, at the same university, was rather more of the same. Very solid to outstanding academic results; very little social life. There were women, mostly other students, who tried. They struck up conversations after class, they waited for him before class to ask him a question about the course, they warmly greeted him in the student lounge, or the library. But he always failed to capitalize. He treated their purported professional purpose as the authentic one and never sought to expand the opening into a social relationship. But he knew what he was doing, rather not doing and what he was missing. He lamented. And he felt envious of friends with brimming social calendars. He started becoming miffed at himself. He was a twenty-three year old virgin. He wanted to change that. He started agreeing to more of the blind dates that friends had been trying, for years, to arrange. His determination to pursue a normal social life for a male his age coincided with an extremely fortunate piece of luck. After he had been on a few clinical, mechanical seeming dates, a friend he'd met in college offered to double date with him to introduce him to his own date's friend, Valerie, a/k/a Val. She was just about Brad's age and a graduate student in English. It turned out that she was also smashingly beautiful, sweetly intelligent, with values similar to Brad's and that she very much liked Brad as a refreshing change from the slick, smart-aleck, guys who so often had "hit" on her. She was even a virgin, too. But neither one of them was a few months after they met. Neither was sure that pre-marriage coitus was "right," but they found each other irresistible. Anyway, they felt they were going to get married. and, after some standard lovers' quarrels, during the two years it took Brad to finish his doctorate, they did.

Valerie got her degree during their first year of marriage, while Brad, unable to get a professorial job in the metropolitan area, taught high school for income. They were still passionate more than three years after meeting and one night, toward the end of the first year of marriage, they were so totally heedless in their love-making that Valerie conceived.

Brad continued teaching in high school until baby Lois was born but, soon after, added an adjunct position at an area community college to boost income. The adjunct position turned into a full-time one, but Brad still wanted to teach Modern European History at a four year undergraduate college.Val and Brad decided, while Val was pregnant with Dennis, that Brad would try to get such a teaching position wherever he could, however far it might be from their current home in the area where each of had always lived. He started sending his resume to any college, anywhere, which advertised for someone with his kind of credentials. It took two years, lots of postage and flying to interviews, all over the country, but Brad was finally offered a job at an old, but still quite small, undergraduate liberal arts college in the Eastern part of the state of Washington, an almost four hour drive from Seattle. Valerie and Brad prepared to move their young family.

The cross country move entailed much planning and the executing of many trivial but necessary details by Brad and Valerie. Especially stressful while tending two very young children. But when they arrived at their Washington destination they found themselves amidst great natural beauty. The college was located in a small town, of course; a college town, indeed. But the surrounding environs had beautiful wooded areas and imposing, majestic mountains ringed the distance.

They actually settled in fairly smoothly. And a good thing, too, since neighbor after neighbor, tradesperson after tradesperson, colleague after colleague asked whether they had. Specifically, whether they had "settled in." There was no doubt that this was a change for Brad and Val. The words provinces and provincial certainly came quickly to their minds and mouths. Particularly in direct contrast to the throbbing urban areas they'd always known previously. Everyone was friendly and courteous . But if the expression "to a fault" were ever apposite it seemed brutally accurate here. If the blinds had not been raised, by nine A.M., in the house Brad and Val were renting, on the pleasant tree-lined street of similar houses, one of many such streets in Concordia, even on a week-end day, someone would be knocking at the door to determine "… if everything is o.k." In their second week there, when the family drove up, after grocery shopping., they saw someone on the roof of their house. The man, their next door neighbor, was stuffing leaves into a large green garbage bag. As Brad and Val emerged from the car, about to unseatbelt the children, but craning their necks to look upward, George called out brightly, "Didn't want these Fall leaves, pretty as they are, to clog your gutters. " Val and Brad hardly knew what gutters were but they felt compelled to, and did, thank George profusely.

But it was easy to make friends. Almost everyone befriended you. Especially in the college community. It was just a matter of deciding which of the friendlies you wanted to really be friends with. There were dinner invitations galore from colleagues at the college. A new faculty member in Concordia was like a blood transfusion which energized, almost desperately, the veterans. The format was invariable. Three or four couples arrived, practically simultaneously, at the door of the hosts at 6:00 P.M. and no one made a move to leave before 11:30, at the earliest. Dinner wasn't served until almost 8:00 and before, after and during, while there could be a smattering of desultory talk about national politics, at best, there was a great deal of conversing about the weather, seeding and planting and which farmer's market, on which day, had the best tomatoes, onions or rutabagas. In encounter after encounter like this Brad and Val found that they didn't have much to say and that they never really got into the flow of the conversation. But, to "reciprocate," Brad and Val had to host one or two of these at their house. Val nattered about all the cooking she had to do, since anything like having super market or deli prepared food had been unmistakably indicated as verboten, simply "not done." And Brad muttered about all the shopping and cleaning he had to do, especially while he was trying to prepare and teach new courses. They bickered, more than they ever had. The children cried more.

And it rained a lot. Sometimes all day. Or, if the sun finally did come out it was too often at near 6: P.M. when people, Easterners at least, were really expecting and reflexively anticipating the grey of the evening. Grey was, on the other hand, too much the prevailing color during most days. Even when it wasn't raining. But mostly the weather was grey and drizzly, if not grey and full—fledgedly raining. Brad and Val didn't understand how people talked about the seemingly monochromatic meteorology so much. Usually the comments were something like, "We could sure use the water," or "We've had plenty of water, lately." For what? "Crops," doubtless, they intuited.

After an initial "sunshine" period of adjusting to a new, very different, place, finding out they could do it, getting normally functional, Brad and Val started, between themselves, criticizing the town, its inhabitants, its mores, Brad's colleagues. Each of them started feeling depressed. Then they admitted it to each other. But it was worse for Val. Brad had the self-generated, (the students certainly didn't add much, nor did his colleagues, for that matter,) intellectual excitement of learning and teaching material he basically loved. But she was home with two small children, wiping noses, playing with Pat-the-Bunny books, and, often, not getting fully dressed until the afternoon—unless she specifically anticipated the threat of a neighbor knocking at the door.

One of the most depressing things, which occurred early on and too much set the tone, was a "dessert"event, held one chilly Fall evening at the Dean's home. It was for the college's four new faculty members, Brad and three others, and respective spouses, if pertinent. It took place about two or three weeks into the Fall semester and Brad and Val already had a jump start on depression by then. Right off the evening started with one of the social conventions that Brad loathed most: all participants sitting around in a circle on the living room floor with everyone enjoined to"introduce" him or her self and to "tell us about yourself." Brad had actually sworn to himself, and to Valerie, too, that he would never take part in one of these again.But there was little choice, here. The other new faculty members were the baseball coach, the minister and a fresh out of graduate school Ph.D. in French Literature. Or "Litrachoor," as he said. He was yet unmarried and looked unhappier than Brad to be there. So, they went around the circle. Naturally Brad kept his contribution in the mini-range, just the expected major points, barely enough to have complied with the Dean's concept. But Valerie was deft and rather outgoing in these situations. She prided herself on her ability to overcome her inherent shyness and to seem comfortable and eager in such a group. She went into a charm mode which Brad hoped would cover, or compensate for, his own shyness, reticence and mal-contentedness. The minister and his wife, tending to late middle-age, were standard clerical issue. They had bounced around a lot and now they had caromed here to try campus life. They were well meaning Brad perceived, their early ministries had been amongst the very poor in Africa, but just as starchy and platitudinous as novels limned. The baseball coach was more interesting. After college in his home state, Nebraska, he'd actually played Minor League baseball for a Yankee farm team. Class B, but still--- organized baseball. Brad had continued his boyhood interest in the game, if not with quite the same fervor and passion once the Dodgers had moved from Brooklyn to Los Angeles, and he thought that perhaps he and Walt could have a cup of coffee over slugging percentages, runs batted in and earned run averages. Walt's wife , Josie, was even more interesting. But not because of anything she said or her job. In fact she was, at that time, "just a housewife," as she put it with almost studied demureness. It was because of the way she looked. She seemed to be Hispanic in origin, at least in part, and had a dark, robust allure accentuated by a very filled out tight pink sweater. Brad found himself looking at her more than he liked himself for looking.

It was during this inquisitorial session that Brad and Val first heard the phrase "This town is a great place to raise children." The Dean's wife was the utterer on this occasion. But in the ensuing months they were to hear it plentifully, actually inordinately, at these types of faculty get-togethers. It too often sounded as almost an apology for the rest of Concordia life. The frequency tried Valerie's patience and one time someone said it she muttered, "Yeah, I guess so, if you don't want them to ever think about anything." That brought astonished stares and then very nervous laughs and titters. They treated her statement as badinage, from an irreverent Easterner, not true feeling or opinion. Brad told her, when they were driving home, that her remark was probably not helpful to his career and standing at the college. She inquired, "Should we care?" Brad didn't know what to answer and didn't.

Valerie received an invitation to a faculty wives tea. She was even called by the Chairwoman of the Faculty Wives Association and asked to be a "pourer" at this tea. Naturally she agreed with alacrity. A day or so later she was assailed by performance anxiety and called the Chairwoman back to ask what the appropriate dress for such an event should be.

"Oh, it doesn't really matter much dear. We're not overly formal."

"Well, I have a nice pants suit for the afternoon, and I don't really know about my dresses."

"Oh, don't worry about it dear. We wear pants suits, even here in Concordia. We're not THAT far behind the times. Don't give it a thought."

"Oh, thanks very much, Myra, that makes me feel a lot better. Thanks a lot."

"So looking forward to seeing you there, dear. I know you'll make a beautiful pourer."

The afternoon of the tea Valerie was in a buoyant spirit as she went off to pour. Brad stayed home with the children as he had no classes to meet that Wednesday. Mostly he worked on one of his lectures, as the children napped a good deal of the time he was in charge. Only about a half an hour after they had awakened, after he'd changed whatever had to be changed and played with them a bit, he heard Valerie's car roll into the driveway.

He was looking forward to a full report on those wives of his colleagues whom he hadn't met, but as soon as he heard the front door slam he also heard Valerie crying. She had sat down on the first of the three steps that led from the tiny vestibule up to their small living room and had quickly graduated from subdued whimpering mode into pretty much full throated weeping.

"What happened, what's the matter?"

Even more sob-wracked, all-out weeping. Brad put his arm around her shoulders. "C'mon, calm down, calm down, it can't be that bad. What happened? Just tell me what happened."

Valerie started battling the sobs and they became less titanic upheavals and with longer intervals.

Brad, interpolating, repeated, "What's the matter? Just tell me what happened."

Valerie sat up somewhat and her voice became edgy. "You want to know what happened. Good. O.k., I'll tell you what happened."

"O.K., alright, tell me."

Accelerating the sobbing again Valerie blurted: "I was the absolute only totally fucking exclusive one in a pants suit. EVERY single other woman there, including , of course, that bitch Chairwoman, Mrs. fatface Pritchard, was in her just very best dress purchased right here in the most fucking best exclusive shop in all Concordia, Mary Shifton's. I looked like an absolute fool in my deep black Liz Claibrone what the smart New York woman wears in the afternoon two seasons ago pants suit. That's what happened. Are you satisfied that you brought us all here, now!"

"Oh, listen, you wanted to come here, too. What in the hell has that got to do with anything. Just calm down. Take it easy. You were still the most gorgeous one there; I'm sure of that."

"Oh, you're sure of that, are you? Well while you're being so sure of that let me tell you what someone said to me, as I was pouring away so they could have the pretense of balancing a cup of tea while they were stuffing their faces with every imaginable type cookie. Chocolate chip, oatmeal, peanut butter, pure butter, etc., etc."

Her sobbing was ratcheting into high gear again.

"C'mon Val, c'mon, you were calming down, don't start in again Just tell me what happened. What did who say?"

The sobbing decelerated again. "I didn't even catch her name, they were throwing so many of them at me and I was trying to pour without spilling, I bet they were just waiting for me to spill half the pot on the linen table cloth and the four thousand plates of cookies. Maybe her name was Swenson, but I don't know. There was a Swenson there, but I'm not sure that that was the name of the one who said it. I don't know, it could have been Bradford. But, anyway, I'm pretty sure that the one who actually said it, that her husband is in the Biology department, or something. I think Biology. Maybe Physics, or Math. Something in the Sciences. There were just too many of them there to take it all in much beyond the ones I already knew. Anyway, the one I'm thinking of, the scientist's wife ,presented her cup for my pouring skills and as I was doing my stuff she said, 'Dear, your pants suit is so flattering. You must have gotten it in one of those smart

New York shops. But, you know, it doesn't matter what you wear. Almost everyone in town says that you're so pretty for a Jewish woman—especially one from New York.' Believe me, after the astonishment registered, I was tempted to say, 'You mean from Jew York?' but I held my tongue for your benefit."

Then Valerie started sobbing again. She did it, off and on, for the next hour. Brad, mumbling solace, from time to time, didn't feel much better

Life, of course, went on.. They met more and more people, a few even outside the college community. They even adopted some of the town's mores and conventions, like saying "You bet" a lot, while resisting, and deriding to each other, most of them. Soon it was Thanksgiving. The family was invited to a traditional turkey dinner, with MANY people and a VERY groaning table, at the home of the History Department's Chairman. Brad and Valerie and even the kids, ate and ate and ate. Why not two pieces of pie for dessert. Pumpkin and Pecan. A third? Why not? It helped along the weight gain they'd each already experienced since arriving in Concordia.

The Christmas "season" had begun about a week prior to Thanksgiving, but once that holiday was past it swung into the very highest, most pronounced gear. It was almost impossible to enter any store or business establishment without hearing a recording of "Little Drummer Boy," "Frosty the Snowman" or "White Christmas" blaring.

The school threw a faculty and spouses wide Christmas cocktail party, 4-6 P.M., Wednesday, December 20th at the president's mansion- like home. Brad and Val dutifully got a sitter for the children, a teen-age girl who lived on the block, and showed up, with almost everyone else who came, at 4:03 P.M. The holiday cheer and bonhomie were thick enough to asphixyate. A gargantuan amount of hearty laughter. At least ninety percent of it artificial and forced. The alcohol, even Brad and Valerie drank some, was set up in bar fashion in the dining room/living room area, a considerable space. It had to be; at peak there were more than a hundred people there. Many did not drink as modestly as Val and Brad. Most of the hors d'oeuvres, crackers, dips and limp little hot dogs were set up on tables in the main area, too, but some of it was in small rooms leading off the principal room. Not many people stepped out of the large throng, but some adventurers did, in search of additional robust caloric delights.

For the first forty-five minutes, or so, Brad and Val stood together, smiles riveted on their faces, and spoke to other couples who also circulated as grinning units. But, then, a fellow Assistant Professor in the History

Department came up to Brad and, after the obligatory seasonal pleasantries, started asking Brad's opinion on a paper he was thinking of writing.Brad got engrossed and they had a discussion on that and then briefly ranged widely on other professional and scholarly topics. During the course of this tete a tete Brad realized that Valerie had drifted away to speak to others. By the time he and his colleague had reached the natural conclusion of their chat Brad became conscious that the crowd had started to thin considerably. A glance at his watch showed twenty to six. Time to thank President and Mrs. President and depart.

But a look around the big room revealed no Valerie. Couldn't do thanks and farewell without her. Brad started traipsing from one of the small, additional food rooms to the others. After three or four fruitless peerings in he found her. She and a young professorial type were alone in one of the smallest of the rooms, (one without even any food carts set up,) seemingly in deep discussion She had removed her fashionable, chic jacket, which had covered her short—sleeved tight sweater, and was holding it over her arm. It took Valerie some moments to notice Brad although he stood in the doorway to the small room. Finally she did and introduced him to Walt Gerund, an Assistant Professor in the Sociology Department. At first Gerund seemed visibly disappointed that his private talk with Val had been terminated, but he recovered quickly to be cordial enough to Brad. Brad was genial in return.

On the ride home Valerie told Brad something of her discussion with Gerund. It seemed that they had discussed various "sociological" subjects from education to race relations. She appeared more stimulated than she had been in a while.

When they got home Brad remembered having glanced at something about Gerund in the student newspaper only about a week ago Then he hadn't known who he was or been interested in finding out. In fact he thought he might still have that edition of the paper lying around his office. If he remembered, when he got to the office the next day he would read the article.

He did remember and quickly read it. Gerund was about six years older than Brad and this was his second academic job. His specialty he said, as quoted in the article, was American mores. The short profile also mentioned that his most recent paper, published in the "American Sociological Review," perhaps the most prestigious journal in the field, was "The Jew At Christmas." Brad didn't know exactly what that would be about and put it in the back of his mind on the ever lengthening mental to read list. He wondered if Gerund knew that they, specifically Valerie, was Jewish. He also wondered whether Gerund himself might be Jewish. There was something about Gerund that irritated, maybe even provoked Brad, but he couldn't define exactly what it was. He, guiltily, thought that maybe it was just that he had found him in what seemed a little too intense, for a holiday party, discussion with Val-- and with no one else in the room.

At dinner that night, Brad mentioned the "Jew at Christmas" article and Val was as mystified as he was regarding what it might be about. She didn't show any particular interest in pursuing it. However, in the next week, she mentioned Gerund at several different times and referred to things he had told her. This certainly did not mitigate Brad's sense of uneasiness, aversion even,with him.

Charles Garth was in his second year as chair of the four person Sociology Department. An African—American, from Chicago, with an Ivy League educational and training pedigree. Early middle-aged, but still single, he had been brought on to the faculty as chair. Not bad diversity for a small Northwestern liberal arts college in the '70s. Brad had first encountered him on a university committee on "Interdisciplinarianism" and had liked his open, welcoming, warm manner. As might have been expected he seemed liberal in political orientation and inclusive,willing to give anyone a hearing, regardless of how unorthodox an idea might be. Brad experienced Garth's hearty personality at two or three meetings and made a mental note to ask him to lunch, or some such, as a way to get to know him better. But, despite passing Garth on campus several times, when they would smile and nod at each other, he hadn't gotten around to it.

Valerie made some friends or acquaintances, too. One of them was the wife of a History professor, a departmental colleague of Brad's. She had met Lois at a tea/coffee the History department wives had held to welcome Val. Lois also had two children, although they were older than Valerie's toddlers, pre-adolescents, actually. Soon after the welcoming tea Lois had invited Val to a very gracious, almost Edwardian, home and they were off on a mutual support and admiration society. Lois, herself, had a Master's in History. From Radcliffe, as a matter of fact. That's where she had met Tom, in Cambridge, where he had been finishing up his Harvard Ph.D. The couples visited several times, too, although Brad found Tom rather too conservative, a bit calculating and stuffed shirt about academic politics. Other politics, also. Nevertheless, Valerie and Lois seemed to grow closer and closer. They also brought the children together, despite the age gaps.

The older ones seemed to get some satisfaction from "sitting" for, (and ordering around,) Valerie's pair.

On another non-teaching day for Brad, when he could watch the children, Valerie had a lunch date with Lois. It was in the Spring, close to Easter. A buoyant day for lunch. Refreshing, restorative, renewing, Val thought, enjoying the alliteration. It was a long lunch; Valerie left at 11:45, to get there by Noon,(in Concordia a "long" drive was ten minutes,) but she didn't return until just before 3:00

When Valerie came in she was pale and verging on agitated. Brad looked at her and knew things had not gone well at lunch. Before he could ask what had happened Val confirmed it.

"That was a very stressful lunch," she blurted.

"Why, what happened?"

"It isn't what happened. Nothing happened. It was what I was told." She dabbed at beads of perspiration on her brow and tugged at her silk blouse, which clung to her wonderfully shaped breasts, in the underarms area.

Brad was growing a little impatient, but tried to keep his voice level. "O.k., o.k., what did she say to you?"

"You don't have to snap."

"I didn't snap. Or, if I did, I certainly didn't mean to. What stressful thing did she tell you?"

"I don't know exactly what she told me, but I didn't like the sound of it, or, at least, didn't know what to do with it."

"Yes….?"

"I think she might have been telling me that she doesn't love Tom any more."

Brad's mien grew even more serious. "Why, what did she say that leads you to believe that?"

"Well, she didn't say it explicitly, but she told me that she'd gone to a local shrink because she'd been feeling pretty flat, thought she might be officially depressed..."

"Did he say that?"

"No, she didn't say that he did or didn't. She said that it was clear to her, from things like the amount of time she had to wait to see him, when there was no other patient in the office, and just a woman's nose for that sort of thing, that he and his young, blonde, leggy receptionist were having an affair, and during business hours, too. Then she said that she could understand that because the receptionist was young, comely and peppy and because she found the shrink an uncommonly attractive and handsome man. And handsomer and handsomer the more she went to him."

"Well, that may be, but that doesn't mean…."

"No wait; that, by itself, wouldn't mean much, but she went on to say that she found herself dressing for her visits in a way that she thought he'd appreciate, maybe even find provocative."

"Well, that's going a bit farther, but still…."

"But then she started telling me that she told him about certain 'stuffy,' withholding aspects of Tom's personality." She paused before resuming. "Even about various types of unsatisfactoriness in bed. I just felt myself starting to sweat all over and getting more and more upset."

"So what did you do?"

"I just, rather brusquely, I'm very afraid, I just said that I hoped the analysis would help her and that she would feel better soon. Then, sweating pretty profusely by now, I abruptly changed the subject to presidential politics."

"Did that help?"

"Yeah, she reluctantly went with it, but I could tell that she was chafing and had plenty more to say about the handsome analyst and/or Tom."

"I see what you mean about a stressful lunch. Let me make you a cup of tea now."

Valerie accepted the offer.

Several days later, Brad was getting a hair cut in what had become his usual place for that necessary ritual. A one man shop, where the most you waited was a few minutes--until Greg, the old-timer barber, finished up with the customer who might be in the chair when you came in. Most of the time there was no one in the chair. Greg didn't talk much to Brad, but seemed to chat more with other customers. At least that's what Brad had observed. This time there was someone in the chair, another senior citizen in Greg's own age category. So Brad sat down on one of the two straight-back chairs that were there for waiting customers and started flipping the pages of a many months old "man's" magazine. He finally found a short story that didn't seem totally unreadable and started it. About a third of the way into the five page story he registered the voices of Greg and the elderly customer.The man in the chair had asked whether "Bill has been in lately?"

"Yup, still comes in regularly. Think he was here just a week or so ago Yeah that'd be it. Bevins usually comes in every four weeks or so."

That was the end of that conversation, but Brad could hardly believe what he was hearing. Bill Bevins? Bill Bevins who pitched for the Yankees in the '47 Series? Bill Bevins who pitched a no—hitter against Brad's beloved Dodgers for eight and two—thirds innings in the fourth game of that Series? Brad could hardly wait to get in the chair and ask Greg some questions.

Finally he was there, Greg silently clipping away. Brad had learned that you didn't really tell Greg what you wanted, he did what he thought you should have. Brad had also found that most of the time the two coincided fairly closely.

"Greg?"

"Yup?"

"Greg, I hope you don't think I'm being nosy or intrusive…."

"We'll see."

"I heard you and the previous customer talking about a Bill Bevins…"

"Yup."

"Could that possibly be Bill Bevins who was a Major League pitcher with the Yankees….."

There were a few seconds of silence before Greg spoke. "Sure thing; that's the guy alright."

Brad was elated. "Really, no kidding!"

"Why shouldn't it be? Came back home when his playing days were over. Was born here, even before they had the hospital. Coached at the high school for a while, before he retired. Still shows the kids a thing, now and again. Doesn't like to sit home that much. Wife died on him. Like I said to Roy there, before, comes in here about once a month for a trim."

"Tremendous; just tremendous!"

"Nothin' that tree-mendous about it. He's just a regular guy who had his kicks in the big city but knew enough to come back home once the lights faded."

'Yeah, right. I suppose that's the way to do it. I remember listening on the radio, as a kid, when he was pitching a no-hitter against…."

"You mean fourth game of the '47 Series, right?"

"Yeah, that's the one. You don't suppose…."

"You want his autograph; you want to meet him?"

"Both—but meeting him would be unbelievable!"

"Nothin' unbelievable about it.Like I said he's just a regular fella. Usually calls a day or two before to tell me when he's coming in.Next time

I could call you and let you know when he'd be here. You could come in a little after. Know what I mean?"

"Oh yeah!! That would be just fabulous!!! Very exciting!!"

"O.K., give me your number and I'll call you in about three weeks."

After his haircut was complete Brad dutifully wrote out his telephone number and gave it to Greg. He knew, however, that that would be the end of that.

On the Friday afternoon, before Easter Sunday, Brad saw Garth coming from the opposite direction, as Brad was heading to the library. Brad thought of making an appointment with him, for lunch the following week, but decided, before they drew abreast of each other, that he just didn't want to tie himself down with unneccesary commitments for that week. A lot of writing to do. So, as they approached, they merely smiled and nodded at each other and Brad gave a little wave of his right hand as they actually passed each other. As usual, no words were spoken.

On Monday morning the campus buzzed with the news that Garth had been found dead over the week—end. Nothing was said definitively, but the word "suicide," kept being repeated. Brad felt even more distressed than he ordinarily would have at hearing such news. If he had only reached out to Garth, shown that he valued his friendship, although they weren't really close friends.... Brad knew that that really shouldn't have made a difference. If someone has determined to kill himself.... But would Garth have come to such a decision if, for example, Brad had proposed doing something during the week—end. Invited him over for dinner, or some such. Maybe Garth felt completely isolated, with no connections. Or insufficiently solid ones. Brad knew, intellectually, that Garth's taking of his own life wasn't anything for which Brad, himself, was responsible, but he couldn't shake the guilt for not having followed his impulse to have made some appointment with Garth. Despite the obvious rationalizations Brad went on feeling terrible.

On Wednesday night, after the kids had been put to bed, Val was doing some ironing, in the kitchen and Brad was just sitting in the small living room thinking of Garth and how he'd failed him. The phone rang and Brad hauled himself up to answer, knowing it would be more disruptive for Valerie to have to come out from behind the ironing board to handle it.

"Hello," Brad said evenly.

"Is this Brad?"

"Yes, that's right."

"It's Greg. You know, the barber."

" Greg....Oh, right, Greg, the barber. How're you doing Greg."

"Not too bad. Fair to middlin'—or even better. That's pretty good, right? For someone my age,right? Or anyone, maybe, wouldn't you opine?."

"Oh yeah, Greg,that's it. Fair to middling is pretty darn good, I'd say. No complaints allowed for that."

"Yup, that's the way I look at it. Just that way."

"Right."

"Well, he's comin' in.

"He's coming in?"

"Yeah, like I said; Bill."

"Bill?.... Oh! You mean Bill Bevins? Brad's voice took off with a noticeable increment in both dynamism and dynamics.

"Yeah, Bevins. Like I said, he comes in pretty regular, about every three weeks."

"Yes, yes, you did say that."

" I told you I'd let ya know."

"Yes you did; you're a man of your word."

"Like to think so.Other folks seem to too."

'Oh, I'm sure they do."

"He'll be in Friday at 3:00. Usually takes me about twenty minutes, half-hour to do him. Why don't you come in at 3:15, just to be safe."

"Oh, terrific!! You mean it Greg.?"

"Yeah sure,I told you, didn't I."

"Yeah, you did. You can count on my being there."

In fact,Brad got there at 3:10. Bevins was already in the chair, but Brad tried to be as casual as possible.

"Hi Greg, how's it going?"

"O.K, no worse than usual. I been telling Bill here, what a big ball fan you are."

"Yeah, right. Well, at least I was."

"Well, anyway, Brad, this here as you know is Bill Bevins, Yankee pitcher. I already told him how, as a kid, you listened to the ninth inning of the fourth game of the '47 Series."

"Yeah, I got in from school, just in time...."

"Hi, Brad, it's nice to meet you."

Although Brad had, of course, prepared, he was still rather awe struck.

"Well,it's a real privilege to meet you. I was a Dodger fan, but that was such a great effort by you."

"Yup, but not good enough. We lost the game didn't we?"

"Yeah, but, still…."

Bevins cut Brad off, "Anyway that was then this is now." Then he turned from Brad and resumed talking to Greg about something else.

Brad sat down in one of the chairs set against the wall, for those waiting until Greg got to them, and reached for a magazine.

WALTER

Walter Bernson, like myself an only child, was a few, maybe three, four, probably not five, years older than me. So, for most of the time we lived in the same apartment house, we were irrelevant to each other. When he entered high school I was still in the middle of grade school. When he was finishing high school I was still in junior high. But there did come a time, about when he was a junior at Brooklyn College, that we played in the same stick ball games, on the block behind the apartment house.

Until then Walter had come and gone without seeming to notice me or ever saying much of anything . It wasn't that he was unpleasant, or anything; but it was maybe a clinical nod here and an odd "Hi" there, and that was it. After all, he was one of the "older" boys.

His parents, Sam and Gertie, were two short Jewish first generation Americans with whom I had almost more of a relationship than I did with Walter. Not much more, but somewhat. Sometimes one or the other of them would stop with me for a moment and ask how I was doing in school, or how I'd be spending the upcoming summer. I think that was more interchange than my immigrant father and first—generation mom accorded Walter. Sam didn't project too much ebullience, but Gertie usually smiled at me, whether or not she said anything, and her demeanor was basically cheerful.

So, to me, Walter was always in a different realm. One defined by his seniority. He was ahead of me, functioning in areas I would evolve to only eventually. But there were some guys even older, really older, who played stick ball also. They were in their twenties, one or two perhaps even early thirties. I'd get to play with them very occasionally. For example, if they needed an extra man to make the sides "even." Even if I wasn't invited to play, and no one my own age was around, I'd sometimes throw a ball against the wall, but not obstrusively, in the very general vicinity of where they were intensely competing.That way I could at least watch them exercise their considerable skills and hear the repartee, not all in the King's English, which they shot at each other. I think money may have been on the line too.

Because of their advanced age they had jobs during the week and tended to play these high—skilled games on Saturday and Sunday mornings and early afternoons. Sometimes an attractive woman would walk by and they would issue complimentary appraisals. This was another attraction of them for me. I was aware of girls by that time but still afraid of them.

I must have looked sufficiently competent, from the way I threw, and caught the rebound of, the pink rubber ball, the Spaldeen," used in these games, for them to ask me, one day, to join them. It was a "Hey kid, you wanna play?" invitation, but to me it was as if a great honor had been bestowed. I used a beat—up baseball mitt to increase my sure—handedness in the field, (the Spaldeen couldn't "hurt,") but they all played bare—handed. One of them questioned using the glove but another, more dominant guy, pooh—poohed his "complaint" and said, "He always uses it. You've seen it. Let him play the way he always plays."

The first time I played with them, a batter hit a sizzlingly sharp drive which seemed destined to become an extra base hit. A double for sure, maybe a triple. However, with a very quick start, a leap and then the outstretched glove, I was able to snare it, back—handed, before it fell in safely. The two guys on our team were ecstatic. I got a "Whoa!! Way to go!!" and, from the other, an "O.K.!! Alright!!"

The next day I was asked to play again. Once more I made a difficult, very good catch. One of the opponents, who hadn't been there the day before, respectfully said, "Hey, the kid can play." But one of his teammates remarked, "He made one yesterday that makes that look like crap."

Nevertheless, my participation was confined to when these titans showed up with an odd number. That hardly ever happened. But I would still stick around while they were playing , throwing my own Spaldeen against the wall, in the hopes that, somehow, I might get the nod.It was almost like a Minor League player at a very high level, triple A, who had been in the Majors once, but then sent down, waiting to be summoned, once again. Up to the big—time, "the show."

Walter became one of their "regulars." He wasn't there each time the core group played, but he was played a good deal. It seemed that if they knew they wouldn't have their usual cohort of four or six Walter was phoned and asked to meet them and fill in. In that company he was an adequate player, more or less held his own. He'd drill a solid hit now and then, usually no more than a single or a double, and was competent enough, pretty reliable, in the field. But he wasn't outstanding or anything. Not at the level of the best two or three guys in that group. Not that I really followed his performances that closely.

But I did take in, the first time was on a sunny, crisp Fall Saturday, there wasn't much to go before the World Series, that some of the other players had started criticizing, chiding Walter. It seemed to get to outright derision pretty quickly. If he swung and missed they might let loose with a chorus of mock weeping sounds. If he made an error in the field or was slow to getting to a bouncing ball one of them might call out, "Oh. Little Walter messed up again. It's hard for him to move."

At first, almost good—naturedly, Walter tried some mild, conventional retorts to these taunts. Like, "Oh, sure, speak for yourself," or "It takes one to know one." But as the barbs increased, from episode to episode, as they intensified, he ultimately retreated into a resignation of weak empty smiles and determined shakes of his head, one fist pounding the other hand in self- exhortation to do better.

I didn't know what, exactly, had prompted the campaign against Walter. He seemed to be playing pretty much the way he always had. During the games, there was usually conversation and banter amongst the participants, but I couldn't hear anything but fragments. Maybe Walter was saying things which angered the others. But why would he have started to do that? The animus towards Walter finally degenerated, the last time I saw him with them, into some of them flinging the ball repeatedly at him as he tried to dodge, and dance out of the way of, the hard pegs.

Finally, with anxious glances over his shoulder, the smile confused, he just part walked, part jogged, away. Back to the apartment house, to Gertie, I imagined. The catcalls followed him. I sympathized, but had no idea what to do.

Gertie's previous spiritedness started eroding. When we passed, instead of the quasi cheerful smile I'd grown accustomed to, there was a pre—occupied nod, perhaps a monosyllabic acknowledgment. The buoyant step, component of what had been a more or less purposeful bustle, decelerated to just short of a trudge. Not that she was a clothes horse, yet the colors she wore grew duller. Sam, not abundantly lively to begin with, became more deflated. An expression of concern and remove replaced the moderate glumness. He even walked noticeably more deliberately. Someone could have wondered how the couple had slowed down to so subdued a state so relatively early in life.

Walter himself, the few times I ran into him, was less communicative than usual. I was just mystified by him. Not that I gave it a lot of thought—but I didn't know what was going on. Only that something had changed.

Eventually I realized that I was seeing Walter even much less frequently than usual. It seemed that he almost never was around. Long intervals between sightings. My parents weren't friends of his folks, so nothing came back by that route. Maybe they knew something, perhaps it was neighborhood scuttlebutt for adults, but they certainly didn't fill me in.

On summer nights, the kids in the neighborhood, those more or less my own age, would congregate outside the building in which a few of us lived. One night, after we'd been gabbing and bantering, as usual, for a while, Walter ambled out of the entrance. Gertie was with him, but then she turned and went back in while he came toward us with a determined wave of greeting.

My first thought was of how much weight he'd put on, how his gut hung over his belt a good deal. But there was more bounce and pizzazz to his affect than before he'd virtually vanished. He smiled broadly and, trying for bonhomie, asked, " So what have you boys and girls been up to. Anything interesting here that Uncle Walter should know about?"

At first we were too stunned for anyone to say much beyond a mumble. At his age he'd never really been part of our adolescent group. But finally someone piped a "Hey, how's it going?" and another kid emitted a "Some time no see—what's going on with you?" I, myself, remained too surprised to say anything to him.

After these minimal verbal sorties we, gradually, somewhat self—consciously,resumed our customary persiflage and horsing around. At first Walter just stood there, without making any comments or remarks. He just smiled, at the appropriate moments, at some of our nonsense. But then he became verbally active. However, almost every sentence and phrase had what we still called "dirty" or "curse" words. He didn't deprecate anyone or anything. They were mostly adjectives. This was "shitty" and that was "fuckin'." And it wasn't that we didn't know the words or use them occasionally. But the sheer shower and profusion of them was disconcerting. It was as if anything he said was merely an excuse to perfunctorily spray four—letter words. When this phenomenon petered out there came assertions of sexual prowess. With no transition he started describing, in extravagant detail, romantic adventures he'd allegedly experienced. They grew more and more lurid and graphic. The girls in our small group started blushing and squirming. The boys, too, actually.

One of the girls was very pretty. The belle of our particular ball. Unpretentious about it—but a knockout. As our hero, Holden Caulfield, would have said, "She just killed you." Walter started making suggestive remarks to her. Nothing too flagrant, but double entendres, at least. She was getting upset. Suddenly I felt her tightly clutching on to my arm. Her fingers started digging in between my elbow and wrist. One of the boys said, "Hey, Walter, take it easy. Samantha's only fourteen and a half, you know."

At first Walter shot back, "So what?" belligerently. But, then, it was as if the admonition had punctured a carbuncle. He softened in intensity and agitation. His speech slowed and he backed away from Samantha. He let a few more curse words go, and another sexual innuendo or two, but not specific to Samantha, and gradually lapsed back into near silence. We resumed out usual riff and only a few minutes after that Walter interjected," I got to go now," and headed back toward the entrance to the building. I noticed that he had gotten so heavy set that he almost waddled.

This type of episode, half anhour to forty five minutes, with the foul language and the come—ons to Samantha, was repeated on a subsequent night, a few days later, and, also, three nights after that. That third time Walter got especially scatological and wouldn't really back off until one of our kids actually went and got Gertie. She came out and waved Walter to her. When he saw her he began quieting down and a within a few minutes, with her still standing there, waving, he muttered "I got to go."

He didn't bother our group again. A few more weeks of the summer went by and I realized that I hadn't seen Walter since that last night, in front of the building, with my friends. And once school started I had a lot to do, all the time it seemed. I was very busy, not only with my courses but with various extra—curricular activities. I just didn't give many thoughts to Walter. But I was conscious that he seemed to be away again. The hiatus grew longer and longer and I got more and more involved with college application matters, of one sort and another.

But I never completely lost the sense that Walter was missing. I still have it. I never saw him again, although I would pass Gertie or Sam from very infrequent time to infrequent time.